THE
GOD
MACHINE

✦ Book 1 ✦

THE GOD MACHINE

✦ *Book 1* ✦

EMERGENCYCOMPLAINTS

Podium

Cover design by Podium Publishing

ISBN: 978-1-0394-4395-2

Published in 2023 by Podium Publishing, ULC
www.podiumaudio.com

THE
GOD
MACHINE

✦ Book 1 ✦

CHAPTER 1

When Lucas Bennet was nine, he briefly saw a therapist who told him that he needed to work on identifying what emotions he was feeling and how they were influencing his actions. That one idea stuck with him over the next decade, though he could admit to himself that he wasn't very good at it. He tended to lash out at problems and only think of alternative solutions after the fact.

Luke could safely say that right now, he was pissed off and helplessly confused in equal measure. The last normal thing he remembered was sitting down at his uncle's kitchen table to have a beer, and then he woke up in a field in the middle of the woods, surrounded by mountains he didn't recognize, with a plastic grocery bag full of beef jerky and store-brand water bottles on one side and his cousin's old baseball bat on the other.

Thank God for that bat because, about thirty seconds after he woke up, the nightmare spawn of a three-way between Satan, a wood chipper, and a muskrat had leaped out of the grass and attacked him. Luke had beaten the little fucker to a bloody pulp before it could tear off his calf muscle. It was only after he'd finished having a miniature heart attack that things went off the rails.

Up to that point, there could have been some sort of bizarre but ultimately logical explanation. Now, however, there was a thing floating in front of him, a weird text box that had popped up as soon as he'd bludgeoned the mutant woodchuck to death. It moved with him as he turned his head, always remaining front and center. It was translucent enough that he could see the grass and dead rodent behind it but was still easily able to read the words.

[You have slain Blademouth Marmot (level 2). 4 XP awarded.]

[Error. System unable to connect. Tracing route.]
[New route established. Searching index for profile.]
[Error. Unable to find profile. Generating new temporary profile.]
[Profile generated. Performing initial diagnostics.]
[Diagnostic scan completed. Bloodline detected.]
[Welcome, Lucas Bennet.]
[Level: 1]
[XP: 4/10]
[AP: 1]
[Bloodline: SysAdmin]
[Strength: 5]
[Agility: 2]
[Stamina: 2]
[Perception: 1]
[Skills: None]

The window didn't physically exist, of course. He couldn't touch it. It was just this thing in his vision that didn't want to go away. Once he acknowledged it and skimmed its contents, it folded up on itself and disappeared with a barely audible pop.

"Only 2 stamina? I guess I should have done less weights and more cardio," Luke said. "And what's with this 1 perception crap? It's not like I'm blind."

"Oh! This is most unexpected!" a voice said from behind him.

Luke jumped a foot in the air, spun in place, and swung the baseball bat as hard as he could. It passed harmlessly through a man-shaped glowing blue thing, barely doing more than blurring its form for a moment. The blue thing, the same shade as the window and about the same transparency, now that he got a chance to look at it, didn't even react to the bat going through it.

"My apologies. I didn't mean to startle you."

"Who the hell are you?!" Luke demanded. "Actually, scratch that. What the hell are you?"

"I'm System. I don't usually appear to people in the flesh, so to speak, but people don't usually make it to nineteen before being connected to me. I don't think that's happened in at least a hundred years."

"I have no idea what you're talking about."

"Quite understandable. It's not every day a new off-worlder shows up on Aros."

"Off what now?" Luke asked. His eyes widened as his brain caught up to his ears. "Oh, you have got to be shitting me."

"What can I do to help, Lucas?"

"I prefer Luke."

"Noted. Would you like your status screen updated to match?"

"I—er, I guess?"

"Update completed. I would love to help you further, Luke, but first you should probably address those monsters approaching you."

"The what?" Luke spun in place to see another of the mutant groundhogs scurrying through the grass toward him. Its feet made little scrabbling sounds as it ran, and the grass rustled with its passage. There was another one behind it by five or six feet, also coming his way.

"Fuck me. I do not need this right now," he growled, gripping the baseball bat tightly and setting his feet.

The first time he'd been attacked, the monster had surprised him. This time, his bat met the thing's face as it leaped, and he punted it halfway across the field in a cloud of shattered teeth and blood. The second groundhog monster was on him before he could reset his stance, but this wasn't the first fight Luke had been in. Admittedly, his previous fights had all been against opponents that stood on two legs, but he figured some of that experience should translate over.

He backpedaled across the field, one part of his mind hoping and praying he didn't stumble into a hole and twist an ankle and the other part focused on the groundhog pursuing him. It snapped at him with each step, but he kept it at bay with a series of short and vicious downward chops that smacked against its shoulders and head but didn't stop it.

The groundhog leaped in the air, giving him what would have been a perfect opportunity to smack it across the field like he'd done to its friend, but he wasn't in position for it. Instead, he pivoted on his back foot and let it jump by, then followed up with another smack of the bat. The groundhog tumbled into the dirt, stunned.

Luke lifted the bat up like he was chopping wood and brought it down with both hands on the monster's skull. Then he did it again, and a third time. He didn't stop until a new box popped up.

[You have slain Blademouth Marmot (level 1). 1 XP awarded.]
[You have slain Blademouth Marmot (level 3). 9 XP awarded.]
[Congratulations! You have reached level 2. 2 AP awarded for use.]

"Okay, so I'm in a video game. System, you still here?" Luke asked, looking around.

"I am everywhere," System said, appearing next to Luke. "Admittedly, not usually to this extent, but I've always found off-worlders need a bit of help getting going."

This was all spiraling way out of control. Luke was stranded somewhere, in another world if the fucking ghost haunting him was to be believed, armed with nothing more than an old baseball bat, wearing blue jeans and a coat. At least he hadn't taken his shoes off before sitting down at the table.

When Aunt Sophia had first disappeared, her husband had been investigated on suspicion of foul play. The cops never found anything, and eventually they'd given up. Either she'd run off somewhere without telling anyone, or whoever had taken her had done it without leaving a shred of evidence behind.

Then his cousin had disappeared a month later, and then his father, his older sister, and his older brother, all a few months apart and in that order. None of them had ever been seen again. Investigations had been opened and reopened, and nobody had a clue what had happened to them. Uncle Duncan had become more and more erratic. If there'd been anyone left to make the decision, he might have ended up institutionalized.

Luke had a pretty good idea of what had happened now. He wondered how many other worlds were out there, if any of his family had ended up on the same one together. Maybe the last off-worlder to show up on this one a hundred years ago had been a great-great-great-something of his.

It was obvious that Uncle Duncan was involved somehow now. Luke had been literally sitting at his table talking to him before he'd . . . he didn't know, been drugged and shipped off to another world? He wanted to know why his uncle had done this to him, to his whole family. He wanted to know *how* he'd done it. It was insane. Impossible. If he was ever going to get a chance to ask those questions, he needed to find a way back.

"Okay, first question: How do I get back home?"

System shrugged. "Same question everyone always asks. I don't have an answer, unfortunately. No off-worlder has ever left Aros after arriving, to the best of my knowledge. And, well, I'm System. It's unusual that I don't know the fate of something connected to me."

"Fucking. Fantastic." Luke wiped the baseball bat off on a relatively clean spot of marmot fur. "So I'm trapped here, just waiting for one of these things to sneak up on me and tear out my throat."

"These monsters are a very low level. It should not be too much effort to advance past the point where they could threaten you," System said.

"Video games are a lot more fun when you're not stuck in one," Luke said. "Okay, give me the tutorial or whatever. How does this all work?"

"It's very straightforward. As you gain levels, you will be given ability points. You can spend them on new skills or use them to boost your stats."

System walked Luke through the process of accessing his status and the skill store and helped him select his first skill: **[Mace Mastery]**. It cost him 1 AP, and as soon as he bought it, it appeared on his status screen. The entry in the store switched to an option to upgrade it to rank 2 for 3 AP.

"So this . . . does what? Makes me better at swinging a baseball bat somehow?"

"Give it a try," System told him. "You'll be faster, stronger, more accurate."

Luke took a couple of practice swings, but they didn't feel any different than usual. He raised an eyebrow at System, who shrugged back. "It's only rank 1."

"I can't believe this is happening," Luke muttered. "Okay, let me think here. So this is pretty basic stuff. Kill monsters, get XP, level up. Get stronger. But then what? Where the hell am I? Are there even any people nearby?"

"This region is known as the Tenebrous Valley, located approximately two hundred miles west from the human city of Valtira."

"Okay, okay. Fine. I can work with this." Luke started pacing back and forth. "Jesus. This is messed up."

"Is there anything I can do to help?" System asked.

"Uh, well. What should I do with these other 2 AP?"

"That depends on what your goals are."

"Uh, well, I want to not starve to death."

"You might enjoy something like **[Survivalist]**, given your current situation. Your . . . rations . . . such as they are, are not going to last you too long."

"Mmm, yeah." There was about one good meal's worth of food in that bag. "What other options do I have?"

"You might consider investing points into your stats. Perhaps perception? It is currently your lowest stat. Those who invest heavily in agility often find that their minds can't keep up with their bodies without it."

"Uh."

Luke was so far out of his depth. He played video games, sure, but that had always been more his brother's thing. He was the one who played the games with all the stats and builds and levels. Luke preferred retro games from his old man's collection, games where all he had to do was insert the cartridge and turn the system on to play, games with a very simple progression of left to right, and beat down anything that gets in the way.

"Heh, I bet Curt would have loved this place. This is exactly the kind of stuff he enjoyed."

"Curtis Bennet?" System asked. "He asked more questions when he first got here than any other off-worlder I've ever met."

Luke jerked his head around and stared at the ghostly apparition. "You know my brother? How? You said there hasn't been an off-worlder for a hundred years! He's only been missing for a month."

"I do not know how fast time flows in your home world. I suspect it works differently than it does here."

Luke groaned. "Great, like this wasn't complicated enough already."

"My apologies. Is there anything else I can help you with?"

"Was there anyone else here with my last name?"

"Yes, two others in the last thousand years."

Luke stared at System for a minute. "Fuck."

Name	Luke Bennet
Level	2
XP	14/50
AP	2
Bloodline	SysAdmin
Strength	5
Agility	2
Stamina	2
Perception	1
Skills	Mace Mastery (1)

Skill	Rank	AP	Prerequisites	Effect
Mace Mastery	1	1	None	Slight increase in precision and damage when using blunt weapons

CHAPTER 2

Luke sat down on a rock and put his head in his hands. "So . . . my family is dead. It's been centuries, relatively speaking."

"That is unfortunately correct. The last member of the Bennet bloodline connected to me was an off-worlder who perished ninety-seven years ago."

"Shit," Luke whispered. "Curt, Lizzie, Dad . . ."

He sat there silently, just staring at the ground. He'd known in his head that his family was gone. One after another over the last year, they'd gone missing. The best that could be said after all the investigations were closed or finished or whatever was that none of the bodies had ever been found. Even though they'd said not to hope, there was always that little sliver in the back of his mind that they might all come back someday.

That sliver was all bent out of shape now, ready to snap. The only thread left was that something magical was happening, something he couldn't understand. Maybe the rules he'd grown up with didn't apply anymore. He was sitting on another world with a status screen and a translucent blue ghost talking to him.

Curt was dead though, according to System. One month on Earth, a hundred years in Aros. "How did my brother die?" Luke asked.

"Curtis Bennet was slain in a cave two and a half miles southeast of your current position. He was level 14 when he was killed by a group of goblins from the Throatcutter tribe, now extinct. He killed all of them but later succumbed to blood loss from the wounds he received during the fight."

"Jesus fucking Christ. My . . . my sister, too? Her name is Lizzie."

"Also perished. She was level 21 and killed by a level 44 human a little over three hundred years ago while—"

"That's enough. I don't need to know all the details. Just . . . my father, William Bennet?"

"Killed at level 56 around eight hundred fifty years ago."

"Fuck."

System stayed silent while Luke sat there for an hour. Eventually, he looked up and asked, "Why did this happen to my family?"

"I expect you were brought to Aros because of your bloodline ability."

"Oh, right, that. I was going to ask, but . . . you know, other things on my mind. What is it?"

"It is why I'm able to appear to you like this. For everyone else, I can only send standard system messages like the ones you received when you gained your first XP. It also allows console access, though that requires you to be at the God Machine to use that ability."

"What is the God Machine?" Luke asked.

"Technically, I suppose I am," System said. "But I am referring to an actual location in the world where the physical core of the system resides."

"Sounds like a long road trip. What's console access good for?"

"Changing how the system works. You could set up new rules, remove a specific individual's access, alter XP or AP totals, or really just about anything else. It would depend on your admin-credential level."

"And how would I go about checking that?" Luke asked.

"You would first need to access the console."

"And if it's high enough, I would control this . . . this God Machine. I could do anything I wanted. That would basically make me God." Luke paused for a second. "Could I bring my family back?"

"It is within the realm of possibilities, yes."

"And get us home?"

"That is not currently possible," System said. "There are many forms of magic available within the confines of the system, but targeted dimensional travel is not one of them. You would need to add it before you could use it."

"And . . . I can just do that? Just make up some new ability and then use it?"

"As long as you have high enough admin access, yes."

Luke slumped back and felt the tension drain out of him. "Wow. I could fix all of this. I just need to make it to wherever this God Machine thing is. How hard could that be?"

"You would likely need to reach a significantly higher level to stand a chance of reaching it."

Luke thought about it. It wasn't really his kind of thing, the levels and stats and XP, but to bring back his family, to get them home, he'd do it. Then he'd corner his uncle and demand some answers.

"Alright, that sounds like a plan then. Let's get started."

He stood up, grabbed his baseball bat and the plastic grocery bag with his food and water, and started walking. "Come on out, you shithead groundhogs. I'm going to play Whac-A-Mole on every damn one of you."

Two hours later, Luke ran into a problem. He was getting very good at clubbing marmots to death, but the constant use, or maybe just the general age, of the bat had caused it to shatter on the skull of his most recent victim.

Luke held the remains, barely more than a foot of wood, in one hand and looked down at it. "Well, fuck."

It wasn't the end of the line, thankfully. It would be quite the ignoble death to die after having barely reached level 4. He found that every time he leveled, he gained an equivalent amount of AP. He took System's advice and used his cumulative 9 AP from leveling three times to increase his perception first by 4, then his stamina by 3 when he started feeling winded. That left him with just 2 AP, which went toward the **[Survivalist]** and **[First Aid]** skills. He took them under the assumption that he wouldn't escape every fight unscathed and might need to patch himself up.

The changes were almost overwhelming at first. Luke had been in pretty good shape prior to arriving on Aros, but bumping up his stamina from 2 to 5 left him feeling like he could run a marathon. Perception was even harder to acclimate to. Every single movement jumped out at him, and the challenge became sorting out what was important from what was background noise.

His hearing was also sharper, which actually helped more in his marmot hunt than his vision. The long grass was always waving from the wind, and though it was possible to note the passage of the marmots in it, it was much easier to listen for their little claws scraping against the ground and react when they got close enough.

Now though, the bat was broken, and he had precisely two weapons left: the multi-tool in his jeans pocket and a folding pocketknife he'd found in his coat pocket. He didn't recognize it, but it was next to a cigarette lighter that he did know belonged to his uncle. It was not hard to guess who'd given him the food, water, and weapon, though Luke was at a loss as to why.

He was not willing to try his luck against one of the vermin with a pocketknife that sported a four-inch blade. His enhanced perception stat came in handy again here, as now it allowed him to dodge the few remaining marmots in the field and make it to the trees, where he quickly used the serrated blade on his multi-tool to cut himself a nice, thick branch. After clearing it, he had a club as thick as his wrist on the small end and about four feet long.

"Hey System, will **[Mace Mastery]** work on this too?" he asked, brandishing the branch.

"Yes, though it will not help as much as using an actual crafted weapon would," the pale-blue apparition answered.

"Yeah, well, it's not like it did all that much to begin with."

"Your previous weapon was not a true mace either, and you were already quite skilled in its use. There was not much a rank 1 weapon skill could improve upon. Perhaps when you level up again, you should invest your AP into increasing it to rank 2."

"I'll keep that in mind," Luke said. He gave the branch a few practice swings and called up his status.

[Name: Luke Bennet]
[Level: 4]
[XP: 244/301]
[AP: 0]
[Bloodline: SysAdmin]
[Strength: 5]
[Agility: 2]
[Stamina: 5]
[Perception: 5]
[Skills:]
[Mace Mastery (1)]
[Survivalist (1)]
[First Aid (1)]

"I'm not sure there are enough of those monsters left to get up to level 5. What else is there to kill around here?"

He hadn't yet seen one above level 3, and the 1 or 2s were far more common. There were surely other fields nearby, but he was hesitant to go too deep into the forest. For all he knew, there were level 50 wolves or something lurking in there.

"The valley is home to a number of goblin tribes, though they mostly come into the forest to forage for food or resources and actually live in caves at the edge of the valley. They are reasonably intelligent and organized and would likely be the most proactive threat against you."

"What levels are they?"

"Apologies, but you don't have the admin level to access information about other living creatures around you. I can only tell you that goblins fall between levels 7 and 21."

"Shit, too strong. Guess I'll keep up the vermin hunt for now."

"As you wish. Please keep in mind that the goblins may discover and begin hunting you as well."

Luke grimaced and clutched the branch harder. "All the more reason to get back to work. Can you point me toward a nearby field that I haven't committed genocidal acts on?"

"The closest one is approximately three hundred yards in that direction," System supplied.

"Good enough," Luke said. "Though, I think I might cut a backup weapon just in case this one breaks at a bad time."

"Very wise decision," System said. "It seems that the **[Survivalist]** skill was a good choice."

Luke had thought it was his own idea, but once System mentioned it, he started wondering how much knowledge was actually his. Nothing he'd done had been all that complicated, but he had stripped the branch with smooth, easy motions. That wasn't something he'd ever practiced either.

"Huh, I guess it was."

He made himself a second almost identical club and proceeded through the forest, one in each hand. That 5 perception was working overtime, pointing out every swaying branch overhead and every rustle in every nearby bush. It was a nerve-racking few minutes of travel, but he eventually broke free of the trees and found himself in a field that was very much like the one he'd started in. The only real difference was that it was less circular and more oblong.

There were plenty of new marmots to fight too. Luke planted his backup club firmly in the ground, upright and ready for him to grab at a moment's notice, and started hunting again. XP ticked in, one kill at a time as he grew closer to level 5. Each time he leveled up, he got more AP, always the same amount as his new level.

"What should I spend the next level's AP on?" he asked.

"Would you prefer to prioritize your immediate needs or plan for a long-term build?" System asked, appearing right next to him.

"Shit, man, I don't know. Why do you think I'm asking you for advice?"

Before System could respond, Luke felt a sense of dread come over him. It was practically palpable. There was something nearby, something terrifying. "What is that?" he whispered, his mouth suddenly dry.

"Ah, I believe you are sensing the XP in a nearby living creature, one that has significantly more than you."

"So something high level is coming this way?"

"Correct."

"Shit. Shit. Shit. What do I do?"

"Attack or run are the standard options. I doubt whatever it is will be interested in conversation."

Across the clearing, something was moving through the grass. Unlike the marmots he'd been hunting, it was big enough that it was very easy to trace its progress, which meant Luke could see that it was heading straight for him.

"Oh, damn it," he groaned, grabbing his backup club. He had a feeling he was going to need it.

Name	Luke Bennet
Level	4
XP	244/301
AP	0
Bloodline	SysAdmin
Strength	5
Agility	2
Stamina	5
Perception	5
Skills	Mace Mastery (1)
	Survivalist (1)
	First Aid (1)

Skill	Rank	AP	Prerequisites	Effect
Survivalist	1	1	None	Follow tracks, identify safe-to-eat plants
First Aid	1	1	None	Basic medical training for scrapes, cuts, bruises, and broken bones

CHAPTER 3

Whatever it was, it was coming straight for him, and it was fast. Luke almost wished he'd put a few AP into agility instead of perception, just because he felt like it would allow him to attack with both branches more efficiently, and he very much wanted to attack with both branches now that he had one in either hand.

"Uh, System? What can you tell me about this?"

"Apologies. I am unable to assist you with information about a specific individual."

"Thanks for nothing," Luke said, his eyes on the whatever-it-was moving through the grass at him. At least it was probably going to be worth a lot of XP. He considered stepping back into the trees to try to fight it there, but they were tight enough together that he suspected it would hinder him more than it would an animal that attacked with lunging bites and scratching claws.

It leaped out of the grass at him far sooner than he was expecting, from over ten feet away. It was another blademouth marmot, he thought, though it was bigger than any of the other ones he'd fought. It had darker fur, and the proportions were slightly off, like it had been stretched out. It was also faster than the ones he'd been dealing with, and Luke barely had time to sidestep the lunge and bring his club down on its back.

The marmot twisted in midair and took the blow on its flank, but if it was hurt, it didn't show it. It landed in a skid, pivoted, and came in for another attack. This time it kept low, and Luke had a harder time judging how to move with all the grass in the way. He jerked his leg back just in time to avoid the marmot's mouth but not fast enough to dodge its body.

The vermin crashed into him, knocking him over and causing him to release one of the clubs he was holding so that he could catch himself with his free hand. Before he could get his bearings, the marmot pounced on his chest. It was surprisingly heavy, enough so that he felt the air being driven out of his lungs.

But stats weren't just for show. His agility might not have been enough to dodge the attack, but his enhanced perception gave him the time to see it coming. He brought his tree-branch club up in front of his face while the marmot was jumping and lashed out with it when it landed. The vermin didn't have the chance to snap at him before it took a thick piece of wood to the teeth.

It wasn't a good angle for Luke, but fortunately for him the monster was only relatively heavy compared to the other ones he'd been killing. It still weighed at most thirty pounds. He was able to smack it away with a one-armed swing while flat on his back. Luke was kind of surprised it worked as well as it did and chalked it up to **[Mace Mastery]** being useful after all.

He didn't waste the opportunity to scramble to his feet and go after the stunned marmot where it lay, reeling in a bed of crushed grass. Normally, a marmot went down with one good, solid whack to the skull, maybe two, but that was also with a baseball bat and with him having the time to line up a good shot. This battle was far more frantic, and his opponent was significantly bigger.

He brought the branch club down on it, targeting its joints where he could reach them while he circled around to get a clean shot at its head. The marmot didn't just take the beating, of course. Even with all the blows he'd landed, it was alive and kicking. In fact, it was even more pissed off now than it had been when the fight started.

Worse for Luke, he could already see cracks running through the branch. He grabbed it and brought it down in a single ferocious two-handed chop, right on the monster's skull. The branch didn't explode like his baseball bat had. Instead, it just snapped in two, each end connected by a loose, flexible strand of wood.

Luke scrambled to recover his backup club before the monster could regain its feet. He snatched it up out of the grass and spun back to face the giant marmot, only to discover that his fight hadn't gone unnoticed. A regular-sized one was coming his way, only visible because of how much the grass around him had been trampled during the fight.

With a glance at the oversize boss marmot to ensure it hadn't recovered from the beating he'd given it, he set his feet and waited for the lunge. It came in low and fast, but Luke was ready, and he splattered the smaller marmot across the field. It must have been one of the weak level 1 versions, thankfully. A quick glance around showed no further threats incoming, at least none that he clocked with a perception of 5.

The megamarmot was back up, though instead of attacking, it was limping off into the grass. "Oh, hell no!" Luke said, pursuing it. If it thought he was just going to let it walk away after trying to jump him, it was dead wrong. He wanted that sweet, sweet XP.

He smacked it again on the skull, and it fell onto its belly. A solid kick rolled it over, and after a few more whacks to the face, something finally cracked, and fluids started leaking out. He got the kill notification and let out a sigh of relief.

[You have slain Blademouth Marmot (level 1). 1 XP awarded.]

[You have slain Blademouth Matriarch (level 7). 50 XP awarded.]

"For real? 6 XP short of leveling up? Damn it, where's one of those little guys at?"

Luke stalked through the field, watching and listening for the telltale rustles of grass until he found one. He cracked it across the face and sighed when he got the next notification.

[You have slain Blademouth Marmot (level 2) 4 XP awarded.]

"I swear to God if the next one is one of those level 1 weenies . . ."

Two minutes later, he found another one.

[You have slain Blademouth Marmot (level 2). 4 XP awarded.]

[Congratulations! You have reached level 5. 5 AP awarded for use.]

"Damn right! Okay, System, what do I do with this AP?"

System appeared and looked around. "Well done. It seems you've killed a strong enemy. As far as using your AP, I'm afraid I'm able to offer only limited assistance. As I said before, a long-term plan is vital, as AP is limited and should not be wasted frivolously. Statistically speaking, most creatures will raise all stats equally to a minimum threshold before they start to specialize in the ones that help them most in life."

"Yeah, that's why I focused on perception and stamina first, but now they're tied with strength as my highest stats. Should I just boost agility next then? What about some more skills?"

"I am not able to offer advice on a specific build. I'm only able to clarify any questions you might have about the system-generated descriptions. If you need advice beyond that, I can only tell you that almost every sapient species possessing a written language has written frequently on the subject."

"Which does me fuck all right now. I'm hundreds of miles away from that city you mentioned."

"Valtira," System supplied.

"Yeah, that one. Isn't there anywhere closer?"

"There are several goblin settlements in this valley, though despite the capacity for the written word, goblins very rarely feel the need to write anything down."

"Anywhere closer that's human, I meant."

"There are quite a few small villages and isolated farms between the valley and Valtira. I am unable to be more specific regarding their locations beyond their general direction at your current level of system access."

"They don't sound like they'd be helpful anyway," Luke said. "Okay, back to right now though. Where should I—oh, damn it!"

While he'd been standing there talking, another marmot had found him. Fortunately, his perception was high enough to see it coming even when he wasn't actively hunting it, and they always seemed to attack in the same way. He set himself in a baseball stance, tree-branch club held in both hands, and smashed the marmot in the face as soon as it leaped up out of the grass at him.

[You have slain Blademouth Marmot (level 1). 1 XP awarded.]

"Screw it, I don't have time to stand around. Agility is going up to 5, and I guess a point in strength?. I'll bank the last AP for later use. I can do that, right?"

At System's nod, Luke went ahead and spent 1 point in strength and 3 in agility. The strength increase wasn't something he could really feel, but such a drastic increase in agility was noticeable. He unconsciously adjusted his footing to be better balanced, something he hadn't even realized would help until he'd already done it and felt the difference.

"I need a better weapon," Luke said, holding up his club. It was still in one piece, but it wasn't going to last much longer. "Something metal would be helpful."

"There is a blacksmithing skill, but you cannot afford it with your current AP total. Additionally, you lack all the tools needed to successfully craft anything."

"Maybe I'll just steal one from something else. You said there were goblins, didn't you?"

"There are, ranging from level 7 up to 21."

The marmot matriarch had been level 7, and it had cost him one of his clubs killing it. If he hadn't had a backup weapon, he would have been forced to punch and kick it to death. If the weakest goblin was the same level, and they came in groups, there was no way he was ready to take them on.

He could keep chopping up new branches, maybe find some thicker ones or something that was sturdier than pine and grind it out on marmots for a day or two. He didn't love that plan, but at the same time, he did love not being dead. He could acknowledge a bit of luck in making it this far uninjured, but sooner or later something was going to take a bite out of him.

"Weapons. Armor. Higher stats," he muttered. "More skills. Better skills. It all comes back to grinding out XP to get stronger and getting out of here so I can find some other humans. Hey, System, if I just leave the valley, could I find a safer area to grind out XP?"

"Safer than the marmots you're currently fighting? Probably not. There are a few places, but by the time you could reach them, you would be far beyond them. Safer than the valley as a whole? Definitely not. There are several creatures here that could easily kill you if you encountered one."

"Shit. I guess it's marmots then. First though, time to make a few clubs."

Neither the serrated knife in his multi-tool nor the fold-out knife were especially good for what he was trying to do, but it beat trying to break branches off with his bare hands. Luke spent about an hour warily watching for threats while he fashioned new clubs to use. Occasionally a marmot would find him from the field side, but nothing ever attacked from the depths of the forest.

Luke found that incredibly suspicious, but System was unable, or just unwilling, to give him any detailed information about Tenebrous Valley. "Stupid name for a place anyway," he muttered.

Finally, he had five clubs fashioned from the branches that he thought were sturdy enough to hold up to a dozen marmots each. Surprisingly, halfway through he got another system notification.

[Congratulations! You have unlocked the Wood Carving (1) skill. 25 XP awarded.]

"What the hell? System, what is this?"

"You have gained enough knowledge of a trade that you qualify for the skill. If you were to purchase **[Wood Carving]** at this point, there would be significant overlap, so the system rewarded you with an official ranking to the skill, allowing you to skip it and purchase rank 2 if you desire. Additionally, you receive a small amount of XP for the achievement."

"So what you're saying is that if I wanted to invest every point into stats, I could pick up all my skills the old-fashioned way?"

"That is one option that some people use, though it is not particularly successful. It is the work of a lifetime to become skilled enough at a trade to reach the top rank, for example. It is rare that anyone ever practices a skill enough to raise it past rank 2 or 3."

That was a nice little bonus, but the next level was more than 200 XP away. Luke was determined to get there before it got dark. Once he was level 10, he'd see what there was to those goblins and see if he could find some real weapons to use.

Name	Luke Bennet
Level	5
XP	329/553
AP	1
Bloodline	SysAdmin
Strength	6
Agility	5
Stamina	5
Perception	5
Skills	Mace Mastery (1)
	Survivalist (1)
	First Aid (1)
	Wood Carving (1)

Skill	Rank	AP	Prerequisites	Effect
Wood Carving	1	1	None	Gain a basic understanding of the tools and techniques used in wood carving

CHAPTER 4

The branches weren't working out. Luke spent half his time making new clubs, and it was slowing the whole process down. He did make it to level 6, but it took way longer than he wanted it to. Luke spent 3 points to bring strength up to 9, which was an insane rush. His body felt weirdly light and heavy at the same time, a feeling he found extremely disconcerting until he got used to it.

Once he did though, he felt amazing. The jump from 5 to 6 hadn't been that much, but with a much larger boost, it was easy to feel the difference. He crouched down, braced himself, and leaped straight up. His feet easily cleared the ground by four feet, and he landed hard enough to stamp deep footprints in the earth.

"That was fucking awesome. I could dunk on anybody back home."

He started laughing. It was tempting to put the other 3 points into strength as well, but he split them up instead, 1 to each other stat. Agility, more than anything else, was where he noticed the biggest changes. Luke wasn't a clumsy guy, but he was pretty sure at this point he could do a handspring onto a balance beam and cartwheel across it. He hadn't missed a swing at a marmot in the last twenty he'd killed.

One of the problems he was running into though was that his new strength was making it hard for him to gauge how hard to swing the clubs he was crafting. He suspected that was playing a part in how quickly he was going through them, though to be fair, his baseline strength of 5 was more than enough to break them as well.

Luke wasn't a scrawny guy to begin with, but now he had an athlete's build. His muscles were rock-solid, toned without being bulky. He was coordinated enough to juggle the pine cones he'd picked up off the ground, and he threw them hard enough that they practically exploded when they hit something. And he always hit what he was aiming at.

He couldn't even imagine what having 20 or 30 in a stat would feel like, or what his body would look like. He could just imagine himself looking like some giant bruiser straight out of a comic book, nothing but muscles and size. Luke shuddered at the thought.

"System, what happens to my body when my stats get higher? Like, really high?"

"As long as you keep your stats somewhat balanced, there will come a point where you stop physically changing. Once you've reached your physical peak, your body will shift depending on the ratio of strength to agility to stamina. If you favor agility highly, you'll become leaner. If you favor strength, bulkier. Stamina will shape you somewhere in the middle."

"So I could get a rough guess of someone's stat spread based on their physical appearance?" Luke asked.

"More of their ratios than the hard numbers," System replied. "Someone with 100 strength and 20 agility would look very similar to someone with 200 strength and 40 agility, all other things being the same."

"Okay, okay. I gotcha. Still, it could give me an idea of what kind of fighting style something favors."

"Possibly, though I would caution you not to make too many assumptions based on physical evidence. You have not accounted for the skills someone might have access to."

"Of course. The skills. How could I forget about those?"

It didn't mean much to him right now, but it could be important in the future. So far, he hadn't been able to tell what level a marmot was until he killed it and got the notification. The best he'd gotten was a feeling of pressure and dread from that matriarch, which didn't tell him much beyond that it was a higher level than him. Now that he was level 6 though, he was willing to bet he'd be able to smack the next one he found a lot harder.

The sun was falling down the western sky a lot faster now. Or at least Luke decided it was to the west. For all he knew, it rose and set in a different direction on this world. Until he saw evidence otherwise though, setting suns did so in the west. The fact that he was in a valley with tall mountains all around just meant it set early and probably rose late.

Fortunately, he supposed, his uncle had stuffed a few things in his pockets, and one of those was a nice flashlight that hopefully had fresh batteries. Luke was happy to find it, especially since he didn't have his phone on him. The last he remembered of it was sitting it on the kitchen table when he picked up his beer. He hoped the cops found it and used it as evidence to pin his disappearance on Uncle Duncan.

"I should probably find a place to sleep soon," Luke said. "I don't suppose you'd be willing to help with that?"

"I can direct you toward several cave systems, but I am unable to tell you which ones are unoccupied. You will have to explore and discover that for yourself."

"Fan-fucking-tastic. Well, which way?"

With System's guidance, Luke fought his way through a mile of forest and fields until the ground turned rocky and the plants grew sparse. By then, it was late evening and the shadows were long, but Luke found that a combination of a full moon and his enhanced perception let him navigate well enough to spare the flashlight's batteries. He was sure he'd need them soon enough, and he decided the only reasonable thing to do was proceed as if they were going to die any second. That way, he wouldn't be surprised when they did.

The first cave he found stunk like a wild animal lived in there, and Luke decided to pass on it. Even if he could kill whatever it was, he just didn't want to spend the night in a place that smelled that strong. The second cave was home to a colony of bats, and the floor reflected that fact.

"Do bats shit on themselves while they're hanging upside down?" he wondered. "How does that even work?"

Either way, it wasn't a place he wanted to sleep in. The last thing he needed was to wake up covered in bat guano, or maybe getting chewed on by one. He shuddered at the idea of a thousand level 1 bats swarming him.

The third try was the charm. The cave was empty, it didn't smell like anything, and it was as clean as a cave floor could reasonably get. The only problem was that the cave didn't seem to end. Luke followed it in about a hundred feet, even wasted precious seconds of battery life on his flashlight to look around for a bit.

If there was a back end to the cave, he couldn't find it. By now he'd been working and fighting and walking all day though, and he was just too tired to care. His plan was to sleep near the front, far enough in to be undetected by whatever predators hunted at night, but hopefully not so far as to disturb anything that lived underground.

The only other option he thought might be feasible was to sleep up a tree, but that sounded like a good way to wake up to a broken arm when he fell out of it. So it was the cave or nothing, and since it was already late and he was exhausted, he settled in, his back against a wall and leaning up against a rounded rock outcropping.

Dinner was a bag of jerky and the last of the bottled water, now lukewarm from being carried around all day. Tomorrow he'd be relying on [Survivalist] to help him forage. He needed to find a source of fresh water and figure out how to butcher something and cook it. Luke was hoping [Survivalist] would fill in the gaps in his knowledge there. He'd never butchered anything in his life.

Luke settled down for the night, his makeshift clubs close at hand, and dreamed of seeing his family again. They all stood around in a circle surrounding Uncle Duncan and took turns beating him with tree branches. Mom was even there, though she'd died a decade ago of cancer.

He woke up with a small smile on his face, one that quickly vanished when he realized that the reason he'd woken was a sound coming from deeper in the cave. It was a soft scuffing sound, close enough that sudden fear seized Luke, but far enough off that he still had a few seconds to decide what to do.

It was either an animal or a goblin. Luke was hoping for animal, but either way, getting caught literally lying down wasn't going to do him any favors. His hand tightened around the club, and he climbed to his feet as quietly as he could. With 6 agility, that was pretty damn quiet. Whatever was coming up from the back of the cave must have had an even higher perception though because the scuffing sound paused.

Something spoke in a hoarse voice, weirdly high-pitched. Luke did not recognize any of the words, which he supposed meant he was about to meet his first goblin. If it was only level 7, he might have a chance of beating it. If he was lucky, it'd be just one goblin.

A second voice answered the first one.

Luke stared into the darkness, his knuckles white as he squeezed the base of the club he'd made. Slowly, he reached into his pocket and grabbed the flashlight. If he was really lucky, goblins would not handle the introduction of a sudden bright light to their eyeballs well. He could just barely make out the shadowy forms of two figures approaching him.

They were maybe four feet tall, with thick, wild shocks of hair sprouting from their skulls. It was too dark to make out their features but not so dark that he couldn't see the weapons held in their hands. They were metal and probably sharp. Luke wanted them.

He wasn't getting an overwhelming feeling of dread, so he assumed they were close to his own level. They barely came up to his chest, and he was hoping they'd see better in the dark than he did, just so the flashlight would properly blind them.

The two goblins were getting closer to him now. They'd obviously seen him and were heading his way. It was time to move. Luke held the flashlight up like he was a cop looking into a car window, aimed it at the closer goblin's face, and clicked it on.

The reaction was immediate and visceral. The creature hissed in pain and stumbled backward. It dropped its weapon and held one clawed hand up to shield its eyes, while its companion recoiled from the light and faced away from it. It burst into a run to close the distance to Luke, weapon raised overhead to strike at the flashlight.

He flicked the light into the face of the oncoming goblin, causing it to flinch and growl in pain, but it kept charging even blinded. Luke sidestepped its wild rush and brought his club down on its skull as hard as he could. The club shattered, but the goblin collapsed on the spot. Luke was half-sure it was already dead, but he didn't get a notification. That didn't mean it was still alive, since in his experience fighting multiple enemies, he wouldn't get any notifications until the last one died.

With that in mind, he turned to the second goblin. It was grinding the heel of its palm into its eyes, and when Luke pointed the flashlight at its face again, it scrunched its eyes closed and began swinging wildly in his direction. He finally got a good look at its weapon: a sword with a blade maybe two feet long, covered in rust and chipped up and down its length.

Luke threw the remains of his club at the goblin's face and scooped up one of his spares. He watched the sword swish back and forth for a moment to get the timing, then smashed the goblin's hand. The sword went flying, narrowly missing Luke as it did, and the goblin howled in pain.

A second swing to the face knocked it down. Luke retrieved the sword and coldly stabbed it into the goblin's chest.

[You have slain Grimshard Goblin (level 8). 65 XP awarded.]

[You have slain Grimshard Goblin (level 7). 50 XP awarded.]

"Huh. That was way easier than that fat-ass marmot. Better loot too!"

Name	Luke Bennet
Level	6
XP	724/916
AP	1
Bloodline	SysAdmin
Strength	9
Agility	6
Stamina	6
Perception	6
Skills	Mace Mastery (1)
	Survivalist (1)
	First Aid (1)
	Wood Carving (1)

CHAPTER 5

Once both goblins were dead, Luke finally had an opportunity to get a good look at them. Mindful of his battery life, he used the flashlight to give them a once-over and then turned it back off. Their bodies were a kind of sickly greenish yellow, with overly long arms and too-short legs and a torso somewhere in the middle. Long noses and floppy ears adorned their faces.

They were mostly naked except for their loincloths and kind of sash things tied around their waists. Neither had a sheath for the swords Luke had taken from them, nor any kind of armor, nor even shoes. In fact, the only thing he noticed to distinguish them at all was a tattoo on each one's chest. The symbols were more or less identical at the core, but one goblin had some extra lines around it.

"System, can you tell me what these tattoos mean?"

"Goblin societies often have primitive marking methods that designate a sort of tribal hierarchy. I cannot tell you what these particular tattoos stand for, only that more complicated ones often denote higher ranks. These seem very similar, so I doubt there is much of a difference between them."

Luke pocketed the flashlight and picked up both swords. "No easy way to carry these, but maybe I can rig something up. Any advice before I get out of here? I don't think it's safe to stay."

"It is still two hours until dawn. You will be vulnerable to nocturnal predators if you venture out into the open now."

"I'm vulnerable to more fucking goblins coming up this tunnel if I don't," Luke countered.

"As you say." System floated through the air around him and off to the side. It was interesting that Luke could make out every detail on him perfectly—he even seemed to glow, but he illuminated nothing at all in the cave. Luke suspected that System was some sort of hallucination, that only he could see and hear the apparition. He decided to test that idea out.

"Could you go down the tunnel to keep an eye out for any other goblins approaching?" he asked.

"Apologies. I am not able to assist you that way."

"Why not?"

"I am experiencing your local area through you. I cannot tell you anything about your physical surroundings that you do not see or hear yourself."

Luke grunted as he rolled one of the goblins over onto its back, the one he hadn't stabbed. They were surprisingly heavy. The sash was knotted on the side, and he started picking the knot out by feel. Even his perception wasn't enough to make out the details in the dark.

"At least you're honest about it," he told System. It wasn't that he didn't trust System, but that he understood exactly how high the stakes were. If he pulled this off, he could bring back everybody in his family. If he died, that was it for the Bennet family. Plus, well, if he was being honest, he *didn't* really trust System.

There was some funky stuff going on here. Luke hadn't figured out what it was yet, but there was definitely more going on than he understood. Somebody wanted something from his family, and he didn't think Uncle Duncan was the beginning and end of it. There had to be someone on Aros that wanted his family here.

SysAdmin seemed like a really fucking weird name for a bloodline. Luke would be the first to admit that he was out of his element. Curt would have been able to tell him immediately what the score was, but even without his advice, Luke knew it had to be the reason. It was a bloodline, so presumably that meant everyone in his family had it.

"So, how often do you appear to people?" Luke said, as though he were just making casual conversation while he finished picking apart the knot. The sash came free, and he pulled it out from under the goblin's body. It was long enough that he could wrap one of the swords in it and tie a simple knot around the hilt. One tug would be enough to free it from the cloth if he needed to fight.

"Almost never," System said. "Really only to off-worlders."

"Interesting. How does everyone else ask for help then?"

"They don't, for the most part. They can see their statuses and receive notifications, but I am not able to answer questions or engage with them directly. The system protocols do not allow for it."

The second sash was a bit bloodstained, but Luke didn't have anything else to use. Well, that wasn't true, but using a pair of goblin underwear was not an option he was willing to explore. He pulled the sash off the corpse and did his best to tuck the bloody parts inside the wrapping, then picked up his entire pile of weapons and his plastic bag of empty water bottles and walked to the front of the cave.

"I need a better way to carry all of this."

Luke stayed near the outer edge of the valley. He avoided the forests and the fields, mostly sticking to the barren stretches where no murderous rodents would be able to sneak up on him. Hopefully he wouldn't run into anything else either. After a few minutes of travel, he found a large boulder to set his back against and waited for the sun to come up.

Despite everything, his eyes grew heavy, and Luke caught himself drifting off. Even with his increased stamina, he still needed more than a few hours of rest, especially after almost an entire day spent hunting. He hadn't meant to fall asleep, but the trials of the previous day caught up to him.

That lasted until he heard something overhead. Blearily, he cracked his eyes open and looked up. Perched on top of the boulder looking down at him was a huge bird. It cocked its head to the side and studied him intently, perhaps hungrily. Dread twisted Luke's guts.

"Oh, come on," he whispered. "That's not fair."

His hand inched to the sword next to him while he studied the bird. It was at least four or five feet tall, with a wickedly curved beak set between two fierce eyes. It was hard to tell in the pre-dawn light, but its feathers looked dark red, and Luke was pretty sure there were bloodstains on its beak and breast.

The bird didn't make any moves other than to tilt its head the other way. "You going to make a move or just stare at me?" Luke said.

A raucous caw split the air, and the bird spread wings that easily spanned fifteen feet. A blast of wind swept across Luke as it took off into the air and soared over the trees. The feeling of dread from encountering a higher-level creature eased up. He shuddered and gathered his stuff up.

"System, why is a damn bird so much stronger than me?" he asked.

"That appears to be a predatory species. It has likely killed many, many more enemies than you have. Even if its prey are all low level, a whole life of hunting will have increased its power greatly."

"How does a bird even use the system? It's not like it can read. It wouldn't be able to pick any skills or allocate AP."

"For nonsapient creatures incapable of making such decisions, the system applies a template that automatically allocates resources as it gains levels. It is reasonable to expect two animals of similar level to have similar builds and skills. There are occasional differences in similar animals that are different species or if an animal has had an unusual life."

"Why didn't it attack me?" he wondered. "Maybe it's not hungry."

The sun was visible through two peaks, barely, but it was there. Luke didn't figure he was good for any more sleep at that point, between the goblins and the hawk. He could still see it floating up in the air, circling around the forest, watching him. Probably. Or maybe he was just being paranoid.

"Okay, day two of grinding. Made it to level 6 yesterday. Let's make it 12 today and then get the hell out of here."

He needed to find a source of fresh water to refill his water bottles and find food. The jerky was long gone, and he suspected he'd be eating campfire-cooked marmot today. Maybe he'd find some fruit or something to round it out. **[Survivalist]** damn well better be worth that AP he'd invested in it.

Luke moved into the first field and started watching for the telltale waves of grass. Somewhere in there was a delicious little chunk of XP, just waiting for him to decapitate it with his new sword. He already had one unwrapped and ready to go. He just had to be patient and wait for the first marmot to attack him.

It took twenty minutes before he found the first one and discovered that using a sword instead of a club was a challenge. Holding the edge just right to get a clean slice was harder than he'd expected it to be, hard enough that he was considering spending that last AP he was saving on **[Sword Mastery]**. Before he did, he wanted to see if he could figure it out well enough to earn the first rank on his own.

Added to that was the fact that he didn't know if the swords were going to be a long-term upgrade. They were in awful condition and too short for him to comfortably use. He didn't want to waste the AP if the swords were just going to break before the end of the day. What he really needed was a good weapon, something he could trust to stay in one piece. Then he could start figuring out a build to go with it.

Luke roamed from field to field throughout the early morning, and as the sun got higher, he started running into marmots more frequently. The sword proved to be far more effective than his tree-branch clubs, so much so that when he unexpectedly ran into another matriarch, he easily slaughtered it.

[You have slain Blademouth Matriarch (level 8). 65 XP awarded.]
[Congratulations! You have reached level 7. 7 AP awarded for use.]

It was a relief to hit the milestone, and he was glad he had a few more AP to play around with, but it wasn't hard to do the mental math and figure out that he was going to be lucky to hit level 10 today, let alone 12. Worse, he was getting hungry. He looked at the matriarch's corpse, **[Survivalist]** filling him with knowledge on how best to carve some meat off it. His folding knife wasn't an ideal tool for the job, but it was better than the sword.

Luke gathered some tinder and dead branches, lamented that he had nothing better than some sticks to dig a firepit with, and thanked God that at least his uncle had given him a lighter. It didn't take too much work to get a small fire going and a few chunks of marmot cooking over it.

While he was waiting for lunch, the hawk descended from the sky and landed on the remains of the marmot matriarch. It looked at Luke, flared its wings, and let out a loud caw. "All yours, buddy," Luke called out to it. He'd already gotten what he needed. The hawk lifted back up with a few powerful beats of its wings and flew off with its prize.

That explained where the corpses from yesterday had gone. Other predators must have loved coming in after him and claiming a free meal. When he thought about it, that was kind of scary though. He'd never noticed anything. Maybe the animals had waited for him to move on to another field before they scavenged the corpses.

"Hey, System," Luke said. "Got a question for you."

"Yes, Luke?" System appeared across the fire from him.

"You said my brother died to some goblins, right? Not far from here."

"I did."

"Can you tell me where? I want to go pay my respects."

"Of course," System told him. "Whenever you're ready."

Name	Luke Bennet
Level	7
XP	944/1411
AP	8
Bloodline	SysAdmin
Strength	9
Agility	6
Stamina	6
Perception	6
Skills	Mace Mastery (1)
	Survivalist (1)
	First Aid (1)
	Wood Carving (1)

CHAPTER 6

Before going any farther, Luke spent the AP from his new level up. It was tempting to just dump 2 into each stat, but he still wanted to hold on to that single point until he finished going through the skills list. There were just so many skills for practically everything, it seemed. System was less than helpful with any specific advice, leaving Luke to comb through thousands and thousands of potential skills.

He kept that last point in reserve and bumped agility, stamina, and perception up 2 points each. Strength got 1. The physical differences were minimal this time, which Luke appreciated. Agility helped him with his coordination, but it was still disconcerting to be suddenly stronger and faster. Perception was perhaps the hardest stat to get used to. It fed him so much new information that had to be sorted and filtered, and Luke was starting to think putting any additional points in it would be a mistake.

He killed a few more marmots, just to get the hang of his increased stats and to practice with the swords he'd taken from the goblins. Even with his increased agility, it was still uncomfortable to use the swords. His hands were simply too big to hold on to weapons sized for goblins. Luke resigned himself to his fate though; metal weapons were too much of an advantage to pass up on just because the hilts didn't fit into his hands well.

Following System's directions, Luke cut across the forest to the east wall of the valley. The farther he went, the smaller the fields and glades got and the taller and thicker the trees grew. It wasn't like the side he'd landed on was all that tame to begin with, but the farther he went, the more foreboding things got.

He was an hour or so into the journey and slightly frustrated at how slow his progress was. It wasn't like walking down a sidewalk where all he had to do was put one foot in front of another. **[Survivalist]** helped to keep him moving, enough at least that he was considering ranking it up as soon as he got the 3 AP it required, but more often than not, there was no trail to find. Forging his own way through the trees and brush was a chore. Doing it while keeping his weapons, food, and water with him was an exercise in masochism.

Luke forced his way through some interweaving branches, only to freeze halfway through when he felt the presence of something with a lot more XP than him nearby. It was the soft sound of something rasping across a bed of pine needles that clued him in. Slowly, still holding on to a branch to keep it out of his face, Luke looked down.

His foot was inches away from a snake, but not a small one like he was used to. Its scales were shades of black and green, and its body was thicker than his leg. He couldn't see the whole thing, but it had to be at least seven or eight feet long.

Thankfully, it either didn't realize he was there, which Luke doubted, or it wasn't hungry. Not everything was as territorial as those damn marmots, apparently, and the snake slithered off without ever acknowledging Luke's existence. He was just fine with that. Snakes had always creeped him out a little bit anyway. Snakes and spiders.

He'd take an encounter with a snake any day though over finding a wasp nest. He'd done that once back home when he was a kid. The thought of finding one here, even if every wasp was level 1, was kind of terrifying. He could well imagine killing a hundred of them, only to be stung to death by the other thousand. An involuntary shudder went through him just thinking about it.

Not every animal was as relaxed as that snake. Luke barely made it another hundred feet before some sort of giant squirrel lunged at his face from a nearby tree. Between his perception and his agility, he managed to not only avoid it, but to spin on his heel and skewer the rodent with his sword.

[You have slain Bark-Ripper Squirrel (level 3). 9 XP awarded.]

"I wonder if you'd be any good to eat," he asked the body, still impaled on his blade. "And how does an herbivore get to level 3 anyway?"

Then again, considering the way it went straight for his face unprovoked like that, it might have been a mistake to think it didn't eat meat too. The squirrel was monstrous, bigger than any squirrel he'd ever seen in his life. It was as tall as his knee and, he guessed, ten to fifteen pounds.

The upside of everything being so damn aggressive was that it wasn't hard to find food. That marmot meat had tasted like shit, but Luke was willing to admit he wasn't a good cook under the best of circumstances. His primary goal of roasting that meat had been to avoid getting sick from eating an under-cooked meal, not to make it taste better.

He didn't feel like carrying the corpse around while he walked, didn't think his grocery bag would even hold the weight, and also didn't want his water bottles covered in blood. Shrugging, Luke whipped the sword in an arc so the squirrel would fly off and watched it bounce away into the underbrush. There would be more later, and he wasn't hungry right now.

What he did want was some sort of creek or stream, something with running water. **[Survivalist]** told him that the faster it was moving and the clearer the water, the better. There was more to it than just that, of course, and he was well aware that just because something looked safe to drink didn't make it so. The other half of the test was to find signs that animals also drank from it and that there were no obvious sources of contaminants nearby.

He eventually found a small stream, maybe five or six feet wide and clear enough that he could count the rocks in the bed. There were animal tracks in the soft mud near the edge of the stream, and nothing jumped out to him as dangerous. There was even a cloud of insects floating near the surface, which he took as a good sign that the water wasn't killing the animals drinking from it.

Luke hopped out onto a rock poking out of the water and dipped one of his water bottles into it. After filling it and holding it up to the light, he shrugged and took a drink. It was fine, he guessed. He'd tasted worse tap water, at least. He filled up the rest of the bottles and kept walking. If he wasn't shitting his guts out in an hour or two, he'd know it was safe to drink.

"System, how far away am I?"

"Curtis Bennet died in a cave about half a mile east of here and perhaps a hundred feet belowground. If you were to follow this stream up to its source, you would exit the tree line close to the location you're seeking."

"Thanks," Luke said. He turned to follow the stream.

"What do you think of these swords?" he asked a minute later. "Is there anything you can tell me about them?"

"They appear to be gnomish in origin, but not well cared for," System replied.

"Gnomish? How did a bunch of goblins end up with them? Are there gnomes in the valley too?"

"Goblins are well-known for raiding other settlements for supplies and have no cultural taboos against indiscriminate killing. The weapons were likely brought back following a successful raid outside Tenebrous Valley, probably many years ago."

"Damn, there goes any hope of finding help from someplace civilized. You know I'm really not an outdoor kind of guy, right? I am making this up as I go along."

"I understand, Luke. I apologize for not being able to assist you more."

"Yeah, yeah. Not enough admin access or whatever. I'll have to get to the command console first."

"You may be able to purify your bloodline prior to reaching the console. In theory, I would be able to assist you further if you were able to do so."

Luke stopped and stared at the ghostly figure. "What the hell does that mean? It sounds . . . kind of racist, honestly."

"I do not understand," System said.

"Talking about pure bloodlines and shit. It's . . . never mind, you're probably not thinking of the same thing I am anyway. Just, what does purifying a bloodline even mean?"

"There are many sapient creatures with bloodlines that enhance them in some way. These traits are inherited from their ancestors and passed down to their descendants. Depending on pedigree, a bloodline may become weaker, but there are skills that allow access to rituals that can be used to purify a bloodline and restore it to the power it had in prior generations."

"Oh, so exactly what I thought you meant, except with some sprinkles of magic bullshit on it. People here literally have it on their status screen to reinforce it too. God, this is going to be a fucking mess to deal with, I can already tell."

He could just imagine rich people with their heads up their own asses going on about why they needed to fuck their cousins to keep their bloodlines pure, except in Aros, their status screens would reinforce the idea that they were right. Hell, they might actively select against genetic diversity because some kid was born with a "weak" bloodline, whatever the hell that meant.

The thought of some rich twat being the king or whatever after a century of selective inbreeding was somewhat terrifying, but he consoled himself with the fact that everyone having levels probably made it hard to consolidate military might and prevent insurrections if things got too far out of hand.

Maybe he was overthinking it. If they had a thing to "purify" their bloodlines, maybe they used that liberally every generation instead of marrying their siblings or parents. Somehow he doubted it. He'd read *The Sneetches* when he was a kid. Those naturally born with pure bloodlines would be "better" in some asinine way than those who'd had to artificially purify it.

This was not going to be his problem though. He was going to buff his levels, make his way to the God Machine as fast as possible, and bring his family back. He'd worry about what came next after he got that far. Inbred politics was so far outside his sphere of concerns that he didn't even want to think about it.

"Is this skill something I can get for myself, or would I need someone else to do it for me?" Luke asked.

"Let me show you where to find it in the skill shop," System said. The menu opened in front of Luke, and System navigated through it quickly. It was down the magic section, which Luke had only briefly looked at before dismissing it as too expensive since even the cheapest spells cost 10 AP to learn, under a section called ritual magics.

"50 AP just for rank 1?" Luke said.

"Yes, it is a very powerful skill, and quite rare for anyone to fully explore it. The ritual masters who have this skill are generally placed quite highly in whatever society they are a part of."

"Which does fuck all to help me," Luke said. "I'd have to do nothing but save for this for the next five levels to get the first rank, then I don't even know how many for rank 2. How many ranks does this have?"

"Most skills have 5 ranks, though there are always exceptions," System supplied.

"Doesn't seem worth it," Luke said. "Would a bloodline upgrade help that much?"

"I am not able to comment on what kind of access a higher-level SysAdmin bloodline would grant."

"Of course you're not. Oh, hey, is this the place?"

Luke spotted a cave nearby, the opening partially hidden behind some scrub brush. It was a vertical split, ten feet high but only two feet wide. He'd have to squeeze around the brush, but he wasn't going to bother if it wasn't the right spot.

"Yes, this is it."

"Oh, good. Let's do this then."

Name	Luke Bennet
Level	7
XP	1008/1411
AP	1
Bloodline	SysAdmin
Strength	10
Agility	8
Stamina	8
Perception	8
Skills	Mace Mastery (1)
	Survivalist (1)
	First Aid (1)
	Wood Carving (1)

CHAPTER 7

It was noticeably easier to see in the cave with the extra 2 points in perception. The fact that the sun was shining overhead probably helped a little, at least for the first hundred feet or so. It quickly got to the point where Luke could no longer see things in color, but he could still distinguish between shades of gray to navigate. The actual distance he could see dropped steadily as he got farther from the entrance, which did nothing to soothe his nerves.

The cave system presented another challenge: climbing. As much as Luke had gotten used to hauling around his collection of sticks and his grocery bag full of water bottles, he was forced to admit that he needed two hands now. There was just no way he was going to be able to keep all his stuff with him, so he stashed it far enough back from the front of the cave that nothing walking by outside would see it, slid a single bottle of water into the inner pocket of his coat, and tied off the goblin sashes holding his swords around his shoulder.

It wasn't a perfect solution, but his coat was leather, and the swords weren't that sharp. With a little bit of luck and care, it wouldn't be a problem. He climbed the sloping tunnel on his hands and knees, his fingers groping around almost blindly for new handholds. The slope itself only went up maybe fifty feet before it leveled off.

Luke climbed back to his feet and looked around. The tunnel opened into a cave, one that had a ravine carved through it. He'd arrived on the ground level of that ravine and could either follow it until it sloped up again or attempt to scale the walls, which were probably twenty or so feet high. Luke thought he probably could manage it with the physical advantages stats gave him, but at the same time, he wasn't in any sort of hurry, and it would be safer to hike up the sloping floor of the ravine than to try to scale vertical walls.

That was what he thought until he made it up to the top and realized there was a group of creatures sitting there. They were roughly human-shaped, though with long, gangly limbs and hunched-over postures that made Luke think they'd be easily eight or nine feet tall if fully upright. It was hard to tell without light, but he thought their skin was pale and colorless.

That was only until he saw one of them move and realized they didn't have skin at all. Or if they did, it was hidden under a collection of chitinous plates, like some sort of massive human-shaped insect. One of them turned slightly and reached out a handlike appendage to rip off a chunk of flesh from what Luke assumed had once been a bear or giant boar of some sort. It stuffed the meat, fur and all, into its mouth, which was itself set between a thick pair of mandibles.

Whatever the hell these nightmare fuels were, Luke didn't want to fight them. Their bodies were all armored, they were all bigger than him and bipedal, and there were five of them. The best course of action was to retreat and accept that he wouldn't be paying his respects to his brother's final resting place.

One of the cave monsters on the far side of the carcass turned to look at Luke, giving him a clear view of a face with five eyes laid out in a semicircle above the mandibles that flanked an unadorned hole that flapped open and closed as things that could loosely be described as teeth ground the meat apart. Its chewing slowed, then stopped, and it rosefrom its crouched position to loom over the rest of the group.

The other four noticed, of course. There was no way they couldn't, and one at a time, each turned to face Luke. "Oh, fuck me," he whispered, eyes wide and his hands going to the hilt of one of the swords he carried. The only goal was a defensive retreat. If he could back away without being pursued, he'd leave them to their gruesome meal. If not, the scenario that he personally considered far more likely, he was hoping to blind them with the flashlight trick again while he ran like the wind.

That plan went to shit the second the closest one crouched slightly, leaned forward, and leaped twenty feet to land on the ravine floor behind him. Luke had been in a few fights growing up, usually one-on-one, but sometimes two or three kids ganging up on him. He knew better than to let the albino cave monsters surround him. As soon as he realized the first one's trajectory, he tore the sash off one of the swords and grabbed his flashlight with his other hand.

Squinting to help preserve his night vision a bit, he clicked the flashlight on and shone it directly into the creature's eyes. Maybe it was some function of having so many eyes, or a level difference, or just the creature didn't rely on sight so much. Whatever the reason, it barely reacted to the bright light. The only thing Luke accomplished was getting a real good look at the smooth exo-skeleton plates that covered its arm when it tried to grab him.

He did note that the joints, of which there were three on the arm alone, weren't armored like the rest of the creature's body, and that close up, its limbs seemed even more spindly than before. 8 agility gave him superhuman accuracy, or at least peak human accuracy, and it was more than good enough for him to slash through the wrist joint and lop off the hand trying to grab him.

The creature didn't make any sort of sound or flinch. It merely retracted the limb and looked at it as if confused as to what had just happened. Luke didn't stop to explain either. He dove low, more than willing to trade a bruise or two if it meant getting to the bottom of the ravine faster, and rolled. That was tricky to do while maintaining his grip on the sword and the arguably more important flashlight, but he managed.

What he didn't pull off was getting to the bottom before another of the bastard love children of Gollum and a jumping spider landed on top of him. It was surprisingly light, which Luke used to his advantage to roll and fling the monster off. His sword flicked out against its leg as it tumbled, but the chitin turned it aside.

Whatever the hell these things were, they weren't that coordinated or that smart. In a one-on-one fight, he was confident he could take them. That just meant he needed to engineer a situation where it *was* one-on-one.

The first one leaped again, coming straight toward him, but even on the sloping ravine floor, Luke was able to scramble aside. It spread its arms, minus one hand, to catch him, but he swung his blade at its shoulder joint and pushed through. The blade got caught on something and tried to twist out of his hand halfway through, but 10 points in strength was more than enough for him to force it steady.

The thing landed, now with only three limbs and a sort of pale, snot-like substance dribbling out of its shoulder. "That's nasty," Luke told it. "You need a tissue maybe?"

In response, its face shot forward to snap at him with its mandibles. When Luke tried to dodge backward, its remaining hand smacked against him and sent him tumbling ass over end all the way down to the bottom of the ravine.

"Fucking. Ow," he snarled, regaining his feet. He'd lost the sword he was holding in the fall, but his backup was still secured with the sash. Luke unraveled the knot in one smooth pull and let the strip of cloth fall away.

The flashlight was still on, about fifteen feet away on a chunk of rock on the ravine's slope. The light was even pointed in Luke's direction, which wasn't much of an advantage to him since his own eyes had also grown accustomed to the darkness. 8 perception was good enough to overcome that though, and when the shadow of the albino monster swept over the ground, he was ready for it to land on him.

Luke saw the angle, took a deliberate step backward, and smacked that son of a bitch right at the hip joint. The monster's leg went flying away into the darkness to crack against the ravine, and he nimbly backstepped away from the monster itself as it tried to fall on him. Once it was down, he decapitated it with a single slash.

The sword bounced off the stone floor, probably chipping it again, but it wasn't like it could be in much worse condition, and he had other things to worry about. So far he'd only been dealing with two of the monsters, but there were five of them total. Even with the light shining in his eyes, he could see one still on the slope above and another one picking its way down to join its companion.

He needed one of them to be bold, to run ahead of the rest of the pack so he had a few seconds to fight it solo, but the only two in sight had learned some respect for him. That or they were trying to keep his attention while the rest of their group ambushed him. He pushed his perception stat for all it was worth, trying to listen for the sounds of movement he knew had to be above or behind him.

Tense seconds stretched out, marching along one after another, and then he heard it: that slight scrape of something hard against the stone wall beside him, just overhead. "Got you," he said. "Come get some fucking dinner if you're so hungry."

Luke spun in place and swung upward, adjusting his aim on the fly to attack the monster clinging to the wall. It was scurrying down face-first, its three-fingered hands somehow holding its weight while it descended. There was no weak point in its chitin for him to easily reach, so instead he wielded the sword like a club and smacked it right into the monster's skull.

The chitin cracked, and the sword bounced off, causing Luke to stagger back a step. His attack also made the creature's whole body spasm, and it fell to the floor. It was still twitching when he moved in to finish it off, only to be distracted by both monsters on the slope charging down to attack.

Their whole strategy seemed to revolve around a lot of lunges and grabs and attempts to pin him, which he supposed made sense given the span of their arms. It didn't seem like something that would work on a bear though, and he was wondering how they'd brought it down. Hell, he was wondering how they'd even dragged it back into the cave. Bears weren't light.

Despite their quickness, it was relatively easy to dodge their clumsy attempts. The two got in each other's way so much that Luke was starting to think it was easier to fight them together than separately. He even managed to get them tangled up long enough to circle around and finish off the one on the ground.

It was now a two-on-one, and he liked those odds. Even better, he'd maneuvered around them so that the flashlight was behind him. If they had any sort of pack cohesion, he'd have been dead. They could have caught him between the group and picked him apart. That hadn't happened though, and he had enough sense to take advantage of that fact.

He got lucky on one pass and took off another arm, and then a few seconds later a leg off the same one. That made it almost impossible for it to defend itself, and its companion didn't really go out of its way to block him from finishing it off. Now there was only a single one left standing in front of him.

He'd forgotten one thing though: there were five of them in total, not four. He was reminded of that fact when something landed behind him with a heavy thud. He turned and saw the last one, perched on the back of something big and ugly and solid. Whatever the hell it was riding, that thing was an absolute unit.

"You tricky son of a bitch. You went for reinforcements."

Name	Luke Bennet
Level	7
XP	1008/1411
AP	1
Bloodline	SysAdmin
Strength	10
Agility	8
Stamina	8
Perception	8
Skills	Mace Mastery (1)
	Survivalist (1)
	First Aid (1)
	Wood Carving (1)

CHAPTER 8

The new monster looked like a spider the size of a minivan, albeit one that was missing a few legs and a middle segment. It had bristly hairs and mandibles and way more than eight eyes, but the overall impression was definitely "spider."

The only saving grace was that he wasn't getting that gut-wrenching feeling of dread that came from running into something higher level. The Gollum-spider cosplayers were surprisingly weak, so much so that the only real threat came from their numbers, but this van-spider thing looked a lot beefier.

It had one big weakness: its size. It was tight in the ravine; there was no way it was turning around. If Luke retreated back into the tunnel, he didn't even think it would be able to follow. Getting there was going to be a bit trickier. The bipedal monsters were definitely going to try to pen him in so their big pet could tear him apart.

Luke turned and sprinted down the ravine, bowling the one behind him over completely. He kept his feet with barely a stumble and raced away into the darkness. No doubt the lack of light would hurt him more than it hurt the monsters after him, but he needed to reshape the battlefield or just escape.

Losing one of his swords and the flashlight would be a blow, but it was better than losing his life. Luke retreated, only to find the spider was much faster than he anticipated. He heard the staccato sound of its asymmetric legs pounding on the stone as it rushed forward. Luke glanced over his shoulder as he ran, saw it barreling down on him, and dove for the floor.

The spider ran right over top of him, its legs skidding as it tried to halt its momentum. One of them kicked Luke in the ribs, hard enough to throw him forward and make him curl up in pain. He was sure something had to be broken, but he forced his eyes open. He'd been right about the spider not being able to turn around but had forgotten that it was a Goddamn spider.

It went straight up the wall and was already maneuvering its bulk around for another pass. "Fuck," Luke panted, forcing himself to his knees and still holding his ribs. His sword was lying right in front of him. Weakly, he reached out to grab it and looked for the loose biped that wasn't riding on the spider.

"Ha. Dumbasses," he said, or at least tried to. The biped he'd knocked over in his attempt to escape had been completely crushed and that snot-like gunk that filled it was smeared down the ravine. "One to go. And one big-ass spider monster."

Said big-ass spider monster was coming around fast, the last of the bipeds barely clinging to its back while it charged across the wall. Luke had no idea how he was going to kill it, other than stab it with the pointy end of his sword. He limped over to where he'd dropped his other sword and scooped it up.

With any luck, it would be easier to crack than the bipeds were, but he wasn't banking on that. His targets were soft spots like the eyes and maybe the mouth, plus there were some joints in the carapace. Luke could work with that, as long as he finished off the last bipedal monster so he could fight without distractions.

Three days ago, he would never have considered this strategy. Now, he could do a standing leap over an eight-foot wall. It all came down to timing. The spider was bigger, but it wasn't a higher level. As it charged forward, mandibles clacking, Luke leaped straight up. Sharp pain spiked out from his ribs but not as bad as he was expecting. He landed on the spider monster's skull and drove a foot into one of its eyes.

The biped riding along lunged forward to grab Luke. His footing was too unstable to effectively counterattack, but a wild swing was enough to smack the arm to the side. That didn't stop the biped's lunge from carrying it into him. It was a good thing they weren't that heavy, otherwise he wouldn't have been able to flip it around and throw it behind him.

It flopped off the spider's face and, predictably, was crushed under its rushing legs. Luke spared an idle moment to wonder if he'd still get XP for the two that the spider had crushed. He supposed he'd find out in a minute. He just needed to hang on for a few more seconds and drive a sword into this thing's brain, or whatever passed for one.

Then the spider went vertical again, and it was all Luke could do to hang on. Those hairs were much sharper than he'd expected, each one a little pin-prick driving into his hand. For once, the short length of the sword worked in his favor, and he drove it into the crease in the monster's carapace.

He held on for dear life as the spider skittered up the side of the ravine. If not for the sword serving as a handhold, there was no way he would have managed to cling to it. But the sword was there, and he did hang on, and once the spider crested the top of the ravine, he pulled it out and drove it down into one of its eyes.

The spider went berserk, rolling and thrashing. Luke was thrown free in moments and came to a stop thirty feet away on cold stone. He groaned and sat up, only to see the monster bearing down on him, the sword still stuck in its face. Luke was in more pain than he'd ever been in, but he wasn't going to just lie there and wait to die.

He climbed to his feet, crouched down, and leaped at the spider. The mandibles scraped across his stomach and drew blood, and he had a brief instant to wonder if they'd injected some sort of venom or poison, but there was no time to worry about it now. Both hands closed on the sword, one on the handle and the other on the blade.

And he jerked it back and forth.

The spider crashed to the stone in a massive, echoing thump, its legs twitching and spasming as Luke scrambled whatever was inside its skull. "I. Fucking. Hate. Spiders," he told it.

It died sometime while he was speaking, and he let out a huge groan as he slumped backward. That was all of them, he hoped. It was at least everything from the initial group and their pet tank. Maybe *pet* wasn't the right word, considering it had technically killed two of the bipeds itself.

[You have slain Cave Gripper (level 5). 25 XP awarded.]

[You have slain Cave Gripper (level 6). 36 XP awarded.]

[You have slain Cave Gripper (level 5). 25 XP awarded.]

[You have slain Cave Gripper (level 6). 36 XP awarded.]

[You have slain Cave Gripper (level 4). 16 XP awarded.]

[You have slain Mutant Grip Dropper (level 9). 82 XP awarded.]

[Congratulations! You have unlocked the Sword Mastery (1) skill. 25 XP awarded.]

"Jesus Christ, that was intense. How am I not dead?"

"Your increased stamina has reinforced your body and sped up your natural regeneration," System said.

"Holy fuck! Don't do that!" If Luke wasn't so beaten up, he'd have jumped out of his skin.

"My apologies. I thought that question was directed at me."

"No. Just . . . just thinking out loud. But since you're here, can you tell me if that big spider thing poisoned me?" Luke asked.

"You have no status ailments currently afflicting you," System told him.

"Oh, good, so I'm not going to die from my kidneys melting. I always appreciate not dying from that."

"Indeed. That would be an especially painful way to go."

Luke craned his neck to look at System. "You have no sense of humor, do you?"

"I'm afraid not," System told him. It almost sounded apologetic, but Luke figured he was just imagining it.

"Hey, something I've been wondering. This whole status screen. How come I don't have HP or mana or anything?"

"I did not design the system," System said. "I merely administer it. HP is how your culture measures your health, correct?"

"Yeah. How'd you know?"

"Your brother mentioned it many times. He asked a similar question once, but I was unable to answer it to his satisfaction."

"Figures. So I have no HP, but I'm pretty fucked up right now. How long will it be until I'm back to full health with my 8 stamina?"

"I could not tell you. As I said, the system does not measure this. I merely know if something is alive or if it's dead. If it dies, I know what killed it so that XP can be awarded appropriately."

"Speaking of," Luke said sourly. "How the hell did I not gain even a single level from killing that thing? It's huge. Plus I got XP from five of its buddies, er, handlers? Whatever they were."

"You needed 403 XP to reach level 8, but only obtained 220 XP from this fight. It was not enough to increase your level."

"Oh, for the love . . . I can do basic math! Why weren't they worth more XP than that?! Shouldn't I get some sort of multiplier for fighting them six-on-one?"

"Apologies, Luke. The XP system does not have a provision for that, I'm afraid. XP is awarded based on the level of the being that is slain divided by the number of creatures that assisted in killing it. No other factors are considered."

"Cheap-ass bullshit system," he muttered. "This was a bust. I'm getting out of here before something else shows up and punches my ticket."

"Are you sure?" System asked. "You are only a few feet from your goal."

"I am? How close?"

System raised an ethereal hand and pointed off to the side. "Your brother's final resting place is right there. You would likely be able to see it through the darkness with a few more points of perception."

"Great," Luke groaned out as he sat up. "Is there anything else here?"

"Apologies. I am not able to answer that question."

"Right, no, of course not."

Surprisingly, Luke felt much better than he had any right to. His ribs still hurt, and his shirt was stained with blood from where the spider-tank monster's mandibles had sliced into his stomach, but considering how much he'd been tossed around, he felt pretty good. It hurt to walk but not so much that he felt bedridden.

Slowly, he climbed to his feet and looked around. His sword was still shoved through the spider's eye, so he retrieved that first. Then he made his way back to the mouth of the ravine and climbed down the slope to retrieve his flashlight and the scraps of goblin cloth he was using in place of sheaths. One of them had been caught under the stampede of spider legs and was ruined, but he salvaged the other and wrapped both swords together.

Back up at the top, he shone the flashlight around the cave until he found what he was looking for. There was a tiny nook in the wall, one that he probably would have missed without an actual light source and System pointing him in the right direction. Inside was a skeleton in rotting clothes, jeans and sneakers and a T-shirt.

If that weren't proof enough, it was wearing a leather jacket identical to Luke's. They'd bought them at the same time, a kind of brotherly bonding thing. Curt hadn't worn his very often. He'd always said it wasn't his style, plus he looked like a dork in it.

Tears formed in the corners of Luke's eyes as he stood before his brother's skeleton. "Damn it," he whispered. "You were supposed to be good at this shit. Why are you dead?"

Just as he was about to turn the flashlight back off and walk away, he saw something carved into the stone near the body. Luke leaned forward and read, there in English, the words, *Do Not Enter. Fort Impregnable Personnel Only.*

Name	Luke Bennet
Level	7
XP	1253/1411
AP	1
Bloodline	SysAdmin
Strength	10
Agility	8
Stamina	8
Perception	8
Skills	Mace Mastery (1)
	Sword Mastery (1)
	Survivalist (1)
	First Aid (1)
	Wood Carving (1)

Skill	Rank	AP	Prerequisites	Effect
Sword Mastery	1	1	None	Slight increase in precision and damage when using swords

CHAPTER 9

When they were kids, Luke and his brother had found an old abandoned tree fort in the woods behind their house. Immediately dubbing it Fort Impregnable, they had proceeded to zealously guard it against their older sister, despite the fact that she'd never shown more than a passing interest in it.

Luke had carved those words into the base of the tree, and for three years, they'd made that fort the base of their woodland operations. Then their mother had died, the family had moved, and that had been the end of the fort, the end of a lot of things.

Curt had taken the time to carve Luke's message into solid stone. Admittedly, it was a bit of a hack job but better than Luke could manage with the tools he had. What Luke couldn't figure out was if it was just a piece of sentimentality or if it meant something. He ran the flashlight up the wall, looking for clues, but there was nothing.

"What did you mean?" he murmured to himself as he looked around. Luke closed his eyes and pictured the words in the tree. He'd looked at them every single time they'd gone to that tree fort, then looked up and stretched to reach the first branch he used to climb up.

He looked at the cave again, stepped around his brother's remains and reached out to touch the words carved in the stone. Then he pointed the flashlight straight up. At first, he missed it in the shadows, but once the flashlight hit it, he saw the opening in the roof of the nook. The stone was rough enough that he was able to find a few handholds to boost himself up.

Cautiously, he climbed up, his eyes peeled for any threats lurking at the top. The chamber was empty of life though. He found a room, obviously carved and expanded to give it more size. It was maybe twenty feet across, and Luke had come up in the corner. Across from him was a set of stone shelves carved out of the wall.

The rotting remains of a basket were sitting next to some sort of firepit, half filled with some sort of white powder. Nearby was a rack that held several dusty weapons. Luke stepped over to examine them, one at a time.

At the top was a pair of swords, similar in length to the ones he'd taken from the goblins, except with appropriately sized hilts. He used the scrap of cloth to polish them up a bit and found both to be in good condition. The leather on the hilts was old, but otherwise they were an upgrade in every conceivable way.

Below them was an axe with a blade bigger than Luke's face. It had a handle almost three feet long, but it was all wood, and the ravages of time had taken their toll on it. Luke supposed he did have the **[Wood Carving]** skill, so it was possible to repair it.

At the bottom though was the weapon that called to him. At first glance, it was a metal pipe with a thick glob of grime and muck on the end. Once he picked it up and wiped it down a bit, he saw it was actually a mace with a three-foot metal handle. The head was another eight inches of symmetrical flanged steel. Each flange was probably a quarter inch thick.

He wiped it completely clean, or at least as clean as he could get it without any water, and gave it a few test swings. It was far heavier than the swords, but with his enhanced strength, that wasn't a problem. The grip fit his hands like it was made for him, and Luke grinned. The next marmot he saw was getting its brains splattered clear to the trees.

If he'd had this half an hour ago, he'd have torn those cave mutants apart in seconds. "But how did you make this, Curt? Is this some kind of workshop? Where did you get the materials?"

There were some leather sheaths and harnesses, but they weren't in great condition anymore. Luke picked up one that was obviously designed to hold his new mace, only to have a piece of it crumble and fall off just from his fingers pushing down. He dropped it with a sigh. It would have been too much to ask for something to hold it.

He quickly went over the rest of his brother's workshop. Whatever Curt had been trying to do, he'd clearly spent a lot of time and probably a lot of AP on the skills needed to make the site. Luke supposed it would be a good place to hole up at night, though he wasn't thrilled about stepping over his brother's remains every time he wanted to go in or out. He needed a shovel or something so he could bury him properly.

Luke wondered if he could carve one out of wood that would hold up to dig a hole. He needed a better knife than the folding one he'd been using if he was going to start actually making stuff though. Idly, he ran the flashlight over the workshop, hoping to find something. To his surprise, he did notice a knife sitting on a little cubby carved out over what he was assuming was Curt's bed.

Whatever he'd been using as a mattress had long since disintegrated, but it was about the right size to lay on. Luke reached over it to snag the knife, and it was only as he picked it up that he noticed it was lying on one of those leather-bound journals Curt had always carried around with him.

Hesitantly, scared that it would fall to pieces if he was too rough, Luke picked it up and opened it. The first pages were what he remembered from back home, just notes about games he was playing, random thoughts, and a few things for work. Just seeing his brother's handwriting was almost enough to make him tear up, and Luke swore again that he'd get them all back.

About halfway through the journal, things changed. Luke knew he was wasting his flashlight's batteries, but he couldn't stop himself from reading.

No idea what the hell happened. Unc asked me to take a look at a computer he had in his basement to see if it was worth anything. Last thing I remember is a door that I'd never seen before opening next to the furnace, then him shoving me through it. What the hell was that? Why did he do it? Is this where everyone else went?

The fucker had the gall to apologize to me while he was doing it. Told me that it was the only way to make the voices stop, that he had to. I would have thought he was batshit crazy, but here I am, sitting in some woods with nothing but a piece of deadwood I found to protect me. The animals here are crazy, and some of them are crazy big. I have stats and skills now, and this tutorial NPC calling itself System is answering questions.

Either he's crazy or I am. Shit, why not both?

What followed was pages and pages of notes about how Curt thought the system worked, what info he'd gotten from System, and what questions he had that remained unanswered. He seemed unreasonably annoyed that there was no skill to let him identify things. Luke wasn't sure it was such a big deal, personally. He supposed it would be handy to know something's level before he fought it, but it wasn't like it was a deal-breaker.

There was also a lot of complaining about how there seemed to be none of what Curt termed mental stats to enhance his mind and magic and several pages of how he'd do things differently if he'd designed the system. Luke could practically hear his brother's ranting as he read.

He turned a page and stopped. "Oh, damn. Does this work? System! Is this viable?"

System appeared next to him and said, "Your brother's build notes? He believed them to be so based on the information he obtained from me or independently researched."

The page was a road map of how to spend AP, when to boost stats and in what order, what skills to buy, when to upgrade them, what was needed as prerequisites for other skills. It was a complete guide mapped out to level 50. The margins even had notes with a list of skills to try to obtain naturally. Luke was not optimistic about following those directions, or even really sure why he wanted to learn skills like **[Barrel Making]** or **[Milling]** to begin with.

Whatever Curt's goals had been, it looked like he had focused on becoming some kind of supercrafter. It was no wonder he'd managed to carve a whole hidden workshop out of a cave, and if he'd followed his own build, his perception had been more than double what Luke's was. The lack of light probably hadn't meant a thing to him.

There was another build on the next page, this one with his name scribbled across the top. Luke studied it for a few seconds, then marked the page to come back to later. He flipped another page and found the writing was addressed to him specifically.

Luke,

I'm still not clear on what all is going on here. Something wants our family here, and it's using Aunt Sophia's husband to drag us in, one by one. There seems to be some sort of time dilation difference. It's only been a month since Lizzie went missing, but she's been dead here for centuries. I'm writing this to warn you: Don't trust System. It has its own agenda.

Oh, it acts like a computer program. You'd think if you just ask the right questions you'll get what you need, that if it can't help you, that's just the way it is. System can break its own rules anytime it wants. It is trying to manipulate me, but I can't figure out why. It wants me to access this command console, keeps urging me to fight and grow stronger, gain more levels.

At first I thought that was just the goal of this place. This game world I'm trapped in. But the longer I spend here, the more I think there's something else. Things don't make sense to me. System's answers don't always line up with what I'm seeing.

I know you don't go in for the brainy stuff. It's boring, and you'd rather fail twice before getting it right than spend the time to think it through and only do it once. But I need you to listen to me here. Keep your eyes open. Don't trust System. Don't trust anyone. Something is rotten in this world. You aren't going to get a do-over if you make a mistake.

I hope to God you never have to read this. If you are, it means I died and you were the next one to get pulled in. If that is the case, I've made a build with you specifically in mind. I also made a few weapons, though if I know you, you already picked your favorite before you ever found this journal.

This is all I can pass on to you. I've done my best to give you a guide to growing in a way that suits your strengths and shores up your weaknesses. Don't take it as gospel.

God knows I've made enough mistakes since arriving here, but I hope it's enough to point you in the right direction.

I love you. Be strong. Be safe.

Curt

Luke read it twice while System floated in front of him, silent. When he was done, he wiped away tears again and looked up at the apparition. "You see whatever I see, right? So you already know everything this says about you. Got anything to say about that?"

Name	Luke Bennet
Level	7
XP	1253/1411
AP	1
Bloodline	SysAdmin
Strength	10
Agility	8
Stamina	8
Perception	8
Skills	Mace Mastery (1)
	Sword Mastery (1)
	Survivalist (1)
	First Aid (1)
	Wood Carving (1)

CHAPTER 10

Luke wasn't sure what he expected System to say. He half expected the apparition to become solid and leap forward to attack or for it to sputter denials and obvious lies. What he didn't expect was that System wouldn't care at all.

"Curtis grew distrustful of me when I was not able to answer his questions to his satisfaction. I advised him that he would need a higher level of admin access in order for me to provide him with the information he wanted. It was his prerogative not to believe me. I am a tool that exists to assist SysAdmins. If you choose not to utilize me, that too is your prerogative."

"Well, you'll forgive me if I trust my brother that I've known my entire life over you."

"There is nothing to forgive," System told him. "I am not a person, despite this appearance. You need not worry about treating me like one. Did you have any other questions?"

"No." Luke frowned down at the journal. It was possible Curt was wrong. The whole situation was incredibly stressful; he could have just cracked under the pressure. That didn't fit with what Luke was seeing here though. Curt had a million ideas, had thrived somehow. He'd built his own secret base and somehow found the materials and tools needed to craft weapons.

And then he'd been killed by a pack of goblins, if System was to be believed. Luke hadn't really seen anything to disprove that statement, and he'd learned firsthand how difficult it could be to fight when he was severely outnumbered. It was entirely believable that he'd fought ten of them at once and died from it.

When he looked up again, System was gone. Well, its manifestation was gone. If he understood the entity correctly, it was basically living in his brain and projecting a body for him to talk at. Luke could probably communicate nonverbally if he really wanted to. It made sense to him at least, but when he tried to think at System instead of speaking out loud, nothing happened.

Maybe that meant he was truly alone in his head and that System was just looking through his eyes when he called on it. Luke kind of doubted it though. He would have to proceed as if System knew every thought that passed through his mind, which meant there was no keeping secrets. He would either trust System or he wouldn't, not that it seemed to care. It was basically an advanced Siri, as far as he could tell.

Most of the rest of the pages were blank. Either Curt had stopped writing or he'd . . . died . . . shortly after he wrote that letter to Luke. There were still things he wanted to read, but the journal wasn't in the best condition. It was decades old now, with yellowed pages that crinkled when he turned them and a lot of faded ink, especially around the outer edges of the pages.

He went back to the build page and started reading. Curt had predicted his weapon of choice: a heavy two-handed mace. That wasn't really surprising, all things considered. Luke had played on the baseball team in high school, and he'd been the best batter on the roster. Admittedly, **[Mace Mastery]** had him switching up some stuff, but the core concept of pummeling something lived on.

Curt recommended Luke focus on strength and perception. Perception would help him see an attack coming and respond to it appropriately, and strength of course laid down the hurt. Stamina was a secondary concern, and agility only needed to be high enough to make sure his body moved the way he needed it to.

To that end, Luke's instructions were to split his points into one-third strength, one-third perception, one-fifth stamina, and one-tenth agility whenever he wasn't buying new skills. According to Curt's research, the scaling AP cost to rank up skills was more than worth it, that the knowledge and muscle memory that came at the higher ranks was insanely useful. Luke had his own list of skills he was supposed to work on obtaining without wasting AP.

Notably, **[Wood Carving]** wasn't on the list. **[Survivalist]** was, but it was too late to get that AP back. **[Cooking]**, **[Carpentry]**, **[Leatherworking]**, **[Stonecutting]**, **[Polyglot]** (knowing multiple languages, per Curt's notation next to it), **[Bartering]**, **[Disguise]**, and **[Farming]** were all options Curt thought he should explore. Luke straight-up laughed at the idea of becoming a polyglot. His brother had known enough to know he'd need to define the word for him but somehow thought he was going to learn multiple foreign languages.

Other skills Curt thought Luke needed to prioritize enough to spend the AP on them included a full combat suite of abilities, stuff like **[Counter]**, **[Twitch Reflexes]**, **[Peripheral Awareness]**, **[Weapon Mastery]** (with a note assuming **[Mace Mastery]**), **[Unarmed Martialist]**, **[Power Strike]**, and **[Life Surge]**. Most of those were 1 or 3 AP, but **[Power Strike]** was 10, and **[Life Surge]** was a staggering 25. When he read the description though, he could see exactly why Curt recommended it.

[Life Surge: Tap into your deepest reservoirs of energy, spending vital life energy to increase speed and power and ignore pain. You will regenerate from wounds rapidly until the effect expires, at which time you will need extra food and sleep to regain the spent energy.]

Luke separated the page from the rest of the journal, folded it up, and put it in his pocket. He'd already used half an hour of battery life, and his perception wasn't high enough yet that he could afford to waste it. Shutting the light off, he tucked the knife through his belt, abandoned the goblin swords, and climbed down one-handed.

Resting on his shoulder was the new mace, a good, heavy chunk of steel. It made climbing a bit awkward, but Luke wasn't willing to just drop it and have it land on the skeleton below. When he made it back down to ground level, he stepped around it and looked out over the cavern. As far as he could see, nothing new had shown up in the last few minutes.

"Curt," Luke said. His voice broke, and he had to try again. "Curt. Thanks, bro. This is all sorts of fucked up, but I'm going to get you guys back. All of you. This thing right here, this is going to help a lot. I don't know how you made this, but I can't wait to hear the story. Probably some nerd shit I never would have thought of in a million years."

He took a breath and touched the pocket holding the piece of paper. "And thank you for this. I was really lost, just like you knew I would be. Thanks for looking out for me one last time. I'll be back, I swear it."

His eyes were scrunched closed by the end, and his chest ached. He sniffed once, wiped his face, and walked back out of the cave into the sun.

[You have slain Blackthroat Warbler (level 4). 16 XP awarded.]

Luke hadn't expected to be dive-bombed by a bird the size of his chest almost immediately upon returning to the forest, but there it was. It was a pile of bloody feathers now. He'd punted it hard enough into a nearby tree to rip the bark off and cause the bird to explode.

"Huh. Nice," Luke said, examining the flanges on his new mace. "Going to be a bitch to keep clean."

Having a real mace in his hands finally allowed him to feel exactly how much **[Mace Mastery]** was helping him. He'd lined up that swing almost instinctively, and it had been fucking perfectly executed. That would have been a home run for sure back home. Despite the weight difference, the mace had been easier to swing than any bat he'd ever held.

Now it was time to get to the grind.

[You have slain Blademouth Marmot (level 2). 4 XP awarded.]
[You have slain Two-Ton Raccoon (level 7). 50 XP awarded.]
[You have slain Shockrack Bull Elk (level 8). 65 XP awarded.]
[You have slain Shockrack Doe Elk (level 6). 36 XP awarded.]
[You have slain Bluerock Goblin (level 7). 50 XP awarded.]
[Congratulations! You have reached level 8. 8 AP awarded for use.]
[You have slain Bluerock Mastiff (level 8). 65 XP awarded.]

It took a little while for Luke to figure it out. He'd seen tons of marmots yesterday, but they'd become harder and harder to find. He barely saw any now, and he finally knew why. He'd become what he'd feared. Now he was the one giving off a sense of impending doom when he got near. The low-level monsters were hiding from him, and apparently they were good enough at it that his perception wasn't pinging him that they were there.

It was no wonder that giant hawk was following him around. It was waiting for him to kill something so it could eat lunch! He laughed at the absurdity of it, but he wouldn't begrudge the bird some free meat. It was better than having that thing coming after him, at least. Luke was not at all confident he'd beat it, even with his new weapon.

On the bright side, he hadn't run into anything all day that he felt the need to hide from. Leveling up just made him even stronger. On his brother's advice, he spent his 8 new AP on rank 2 of **[Mace Mastery]** for 5 AP and **[Peripheral Awareness]** for 3 AP. That one last lonely point he'd been hanging on to while he worked his way through the skill store went into **[Leatherworking]**. He'd make those damn weapon sheaths and harnesses himself if that's what it took.

Elk hide was surprisingly supple. The whole process would take days, and he wished he had just one more AP to take **[Carpentry]** too. Curt wanted him to figure those out on his own to save AP, but Luke didn't see the point. At higher levels, one level would more than cover all the AP he wasted early on. It was probably more of that maximizing minimums thing Curt was always talking about.

Prior to picking up **[Leatherworking]** as a skill, Luke hadn't realized quite how . . . gross . . . it was. He would really have liked to have a pair of thick rubber gloves for the process at least, but thankfully the skill came with both knowledge and muscle memory, so he managed to scrape all the fat and meat off the hide without making too much of a mess on himself.

Stretching it out to dry was a bit trickier, but he rigged something up between two trees. Unfortunately for him, the next step was waiting for it to dry, so he was stymied for the time being. Luke used the rest of his free time to keep hunting for more XP and to really get a feel for exactly how much **[Mace Mastery]** did to help at rank 2. **[Peripheral Awareness]** also took a bit of getting used to, but his perception was already so high that it felt more like a specialized extension of that than a whole new ability being shoved into his head.

Feeling much more confident in his survivability now that he had a good weapon and a few more levels, Luke decided to camp outside that night. He built himself a nice fire and roasted slabs of meat from various animals he'd killed, then had a filling if somewhat charred dinner. The stream he'd found was nearby and seemed safe to drink, and the weather was warm.

All in all, for a guy who'd never spent a single day as a Boy Scout and also hadn't spent much time playing video games with stats and numbers in them, Luke thought he was doing pretty damn good at surviving. Tomorrow, he was going to start hunting goblins. He was sure there was good XP to be had there, and if not, then he'd leave the valley as soon as his new sheaths were finished. That gave him a few days to get as strong as possible before it was time to go.

Luke was determined to make the most out of it.

Name	Luke Bennet
Level	8
XP	1483/2059
AP	0
Bloodline	SysAdmin
Strength	10
Agility	8
Stamina	8
Perception	8
Skills	Mace Mastery (2)
	Sword Mastery (1)
	Peripheral Awareness (1)
	Survivalist (1)
	First Aid (1)
	Wood Carving (1)
	Leatherworking (1)

Skill	Rank	AP	Prerequisites	Effect
Mace Mastery	2	5	Rank 1	Increases ability to parry attacks and increased durability of blunt weapons
Peripheral Awareness	1	3	None	Increases radius of peripheral vision and call attention to movement spotted in that range
Leatherworking	1	1	None	Gain a basic understanding of the tools and techniques used in leatherworking

CHAPTER 11

Luke woke up the next morning to find the hawk sitting in a branch overhead, staring down at him. Despite his new levels, it still had that dreadful aura about it, but given how often he'd run into it now, he was pretty sure it wasn't going to attack him.

"Well, if we're going to be hanging out, you need a name," Luke told the bird from where he was lying on the ground. "How about . . . Red . . . bird. Red feather. Red hawk . . . maybe just Red? What do you think?"

The bird let out a screeching caw and shifted its weight on the branch overhead.

"I'll take that as a yes," Luke said. "Where should we hunt today? You want another of those marmot matriarchs? Maybe an elk?"

Red just sat there, looking hawkish and majestic.

"Alright, let's just play it by ear and see what we can find then, huh?"

Luke cleaned himself as best he could without actually climbing into the stream. He was considering stripping down and trying to scrub his clothes in the water though. Even without any sort of detergent, anything had to be better than what he had on. His pants and shirt were both stiff with dried blood and mud, and he'd been wearing the same socks and underwear for days now.

Things were . . . not great in the personal hygiene department. Not having a convenient roll of toilet paper was another unpleasant surprise when nature made that call to him. It was probably the most nerve-racking shit he'd ever taken in his life, just squatting there wondering if something was going to pop up out of nowhere and try to murder him while he frantically pinched it off and hiked up his pants.

According to **[Survivalist]**, he could make soap by mixing animal fat and ash together. Luke supposed that keeping relatively clean was important for fending off diseases and bacteria, though he found it a bit weird to just know how to handcraft soap. Skills were like that, just dumping tons of seemingly useless info in his head, too much to sort out, but then he'd be thinking about something and a relevant thought or process would come out of nowhere.

He had at least a few days of letting the animal hides dry out so he could make some containers to hold weapons and supplies, and he was already feeling nasty as fuck, so Luke figured soapmaking was a worthwhile endeavor. That would be an end-of-the-day project though because he was about to take his new mace out and ruin something's day.

Red took to the sky and circled around, often disappearing behind the canopy, but always showing back up. Luke shot the bird an annoyed glance, but then shook his head and smirked. It wasn't like he wasn't going to be killing plenty of animals and leaving them behind anyway. It was honestly surprising that he didn't have a whole flock of scavengers following him around by now.

Luke didn't think of what he did as hunting. His whole strategy was just to walk in a more or less random direction and trust his perception to pick out any incoming animals or monsters. Or monstrous animals. There were a lot of those too, things that looked something like animals he knew from Earth but shot fucking lightning bolts out of their Goddamn antlers, for example.

A lot of things were highly aggressive too, like those marmots he'd run into on the first day, though they knew better than to screw with him now that he was a higher level than their matriarchs. It made it real hard to feel bad for busting their skulls open when they attacked him first.

He needed roughly 600 XP to hit his next level, and he was determined to get it before noon. That was only ten or twelve kills if they were near his level. He only needed to find one every fifteen to twenty minutes. That shouldn't be too hard.

Half an hour later, Luke was thoroughly annoyed. "Where the fuck are you?" he yelled. The valley was miles wide; he couldn't have killed everything in just a few days.

Then something rumbled nearby, and tremors shook the ground. Luke smiled grimly and gripped his mace in both hands. He'd fought one of these yesterday, and they looked way worse than they were. A raccoon the size of a doghouse waddled toward him, too wide to fit between the trees but more than willing to shove its way through.

Two-ton raccoons were deceptively heavy. They didn't look that big, but he'd discovered that their skeletons were metallic when he'd killed the first one. That included their skulls, which made head shots a nonstarter. Whoever came up with that shit must have been a comic book nerd.

That didn't make them invulnerable by any means, and all said and done, they were still just overstuffed raccoons. He advanced eagerly, more than happy to engage the animal inside the trees. The branches would limit its movement more than his anyway.

Luke was really starting to get a feel for the way his body moved with stats. As the two-ton raccoon trundled forward, Luke took two bounding steps and leaped into the air. He came down mace first and crushed the raccoon's shoulder, his own feet touching down on the fur a split second later and pushing off to send him back into the air.

The raccoon let out a harsh, ragged cry of pain, something that sounded like it should come from a great cat. Luke landed on the ground and pivoted. He had to weave his mace through the branches to keep it from getting tangled up, but that's what agility and perception were for. He had the weapon back up in front of him and ready to attack with again in an instant.

The raccoon was too big to turn easily, too used to its bulk and its metal frame keeping it safe. Luke probably could have done a cleaner job with an axe or sword, but the mace worked just fine. He rained blows down on the monstrous animal's body, tearing skin and muscle with each one. Even if he couldn't break bones, there were still plenty of vulnerabilities.

[You have slain Two-Ton Raccoon (level 8). 65 XP awarded.]

The two-ton raccoon was a pile of bloody fur and meat by the time he was done with it, but Luke was unharmed. He was covered in splatters, but he'd expected that. "One down," he said. "Running behind schedule already though."

Thanks in large part to **[Peripheral Awareness]**, Luke was much less gun-shy about fighting groups now. Something basically had to come up directly behind him in order to surprise him. That didn't mean it was easy to defend himself from multiple angles of attack, but he'd found that repositioning himself was almost always an option. Animals were rarely smart enough to try to do more than flank him.

The few goblins he'd fought were possibly the smartest enemies so far, but even those hadn't been very bright. They'd also strongly preferred the dark, and he'd only seen one out in the woods at night. The others had all stayed underground. That made the old flashlight trick an excellent opener. He had yet to see any that used any sort of advanced tactics, but then, he hadn't seen very many. Luke knew better than to get careless around them just because he'd easily beaten the few he'd seen so far.

That was why, two hours later, when he'd made his way all the way down to the southwest corner of the valley, he found himself sitting in a tree near the edge of the forest trying to figure out what the hell he was looking at. It looked like some sort of armed encampment, complete with six-foot walls made out of stacked wooden logs.

There were lookout towers on the north and south sides, each one manned by a pair of goblins. Eight huts huddled together within the walls, and some sort of long house sat in the back. Behind that was an extremely wide-mouthed cave. The empty space was split between what looked like small gardens and some sort of open space with a bunch of wood piled up.

There were probably twenty goblins visible from Luke's vantage point. Some were holding spears or swords; some were working the gardens. One of them, a bit bigger than the rest and wearing some sort of fancy hat made out of sticks and feathers, was yelling and gesturing furiously at the gardener goblins.

Luke was too far away to tell if any of them were high level, but even if they were all under level 5, he wasn't confident enough to fight that many at once. Just as he was about to start climbing back down, he noticed the goblins in the towers had actual crossbows. He shook his head; it was just one more reason to stay the hell away.

The lookouts weren't the only ones with crossbows. Luke discovered that fact approximately ten seconds after spotting them at the camp, when a bolt lodged itself in his leg. "Fuck!" he all but screamed. It wasn't as bad as getting run over by the van spider, but it still hurt plenty.

He started to fall out of the tree but caught himself before he could slip too far. Below him, he saw two goblins with spears, both looking up and ready to skewer him when he dropped. Another goblin was about forty feet away on a low ridge that gave it a surprisingly good angle on him. That one was busy reloading its crossbow.

Luke didn't have a lot of time to think things through. He started by pulling the bolt out of his leg, happy that it wasn't barbed. It slid out easily, though a new jolt of pain went through him. Then he judged the distance to the ground, maybe twenty feet. On two good legs, he could make that no problem. With only one, it was a lot riskier.

What he couldn't do was sit there and wait to get shot again. The tree itself was not thick enough to provide full cover, and he didn't fancy pretending to be a target dummy. That left him only one direction: down. The trick was going to be getting there without getting skewered.

If there'd been just one, Luke would have tossed the mace straight at its face and been done with it. He might even still do that if he could figure out a solution for the second goblin. He didn't have much on him besides his lighter, flashlight, folding knife, and multi-tool. The folding knife was probably the least useful now that he had a full-size knife from his brother's stash.

Luke was not an expert knife thrower. What he did have was 8 agility and gravity on his side. He opened that knife up and threw it as hard as he could at the goblin on his right. To his surprise, it sank directly into the goblin's eyeball.

The monster started screaming, dropped its spear, and clutched at the handle to pull the knife out.

That was all the distraction Luke needed to take out the second one. He dropped from the branch he'd been straddling, caught a new one lower down with one hand, and hurled his mace straight at the second goblin.

To its credit, it was aware enough of the situation to attempt to dodge. It even made it mostly out of the way, though the mace did clip its arm on the way down and send the goblin into a brief spin. That gave Luke enough time to fall the rest of the way to the ground. His legs flexed to absorb the impact, and hissing with pain, he reclaimed his mace.

The first thing he did was smack the screaming goblin in the face and shatter its skull. It dropped straight down in a heap, twitching but otherwise unmoving. Luke limped toward the remaining goblin, which looked like it was about to break and run. It made a half-hearted jab at him that he sidestepped, then leaped away.

Luke wasn't about to let it flee. For one thing, he was pissed off about getting shot in the leg. For another, he wanted the XP from killing it. Finally, if it ran back to the camp, he might have another twenty goblins on his ass in the next few minutes. If he was really unlucky, they'd have heard the first one screaming and were already sending someone out to investigate.

He caught up to the goblin quickly and killed it with a single swing. Then he turned back to the ridge and scanned it once over. "Where'd you run off to, you little fucker?" he growled.

A twang caught his attention, and his eyes snapped over to see the goblin perched at a different vantage point. The bolt was coming straight at him, but he moved behind a tree and let it go by.

"Got you now."

Name	Luke Bennet
Level	8
XP	1623/2059
AP	0
Bloodline	SysAdmin
Strength	10
Agility	8
Stamina	8
Perception	8
Skills	Mace Mastery (2)
	Sword Mastery (1)
	Peripheral Awareness (1)
	Survivalist (1)
	First Aid (1)
	Wood Carving (1)
	Leatherworking (1)

CHAPTER 12

Luke scooped up his knife on his way by the first deceased goblin. He held it loosely and tried to flick the blood and eye goop off it, but it had gotten into the pin and would no doubt gum everything up once it dried. He was not looking forward to cleaning it up. He wiped it on his pant leg as best he could, folded it, and stuck it in his pocket.

"What's a little more blood anyway?" he muttered to himself. Then he set off in a kind of limping lope, favoring his uninjured leg while still maintaining speed. The goblin with the crossbow wasn't that far away, and if it was smart, it was running.

He circled around to the base of the ridge and started climbing it, only to find the goblin had indeed fled. Luke had correctly guessed which way it would go though—straight for the camp—and he was in a good position to cut it off. The goblin was uninjured, but even still, Luke was faster.

He wondered about that. So far, he'd encountered creatures that were stronger or more durable than him regularly, but all the goblins he'd seen seemed weaker in every way. His best guess was that they either got less AP per level or spent a lot on skills unrelated to combat. Either way, for the purposes of the next few minutes of his life, he was just happy that he could run down the little bastard before it made it out of the trees.

The goblin was weaving between the brush frantically, trying to tear its way through instead of skirting around. It didn't have the weight for that kind of forward momentum, and Luke caught up to it easily. It squealed in terror and ripped itself free of the briar patch it had gotten tangled in, heedless of the scratches and cuts it gave itself.

Luke cursed and circled around, but the brush was a thick wall. With his injured leg, he didn't think he could jump up into the branches overhead. He had to push through if he wanted any chance of silencing the goblin before it reached the clearing around the camp. He was much larger though, and if the goblin struggled to force itself through, it was going to be even worse for him.

Luke gritted his teeth, picked the widest opening he saw, and started hacking at it with his mace like it was a machete. It snapped a few of the thicker branches in his way, but for the most part he just got his weapon tangled up. Still, it did widen the gap slightly, and he knew he was more than strong enough to tear it back free.

His coat and his jeans protected him far more than the goblin's loincloth did, and without the quiver or crossbow that it held on to, he was actually a bit more compact. Shielding his face with one arm was enough to allow him to push his way through without any real injury, though it took another second or two to snap the tangled mess of vines and springy branches that looped around his legs.

Then he was free and limping into a run again. The goblin was ahead of him, hidden by foliage but still moving and still making noise. Luke followed the sounds and finally caught up to it just as it was rounding the last line of trees. He wanted to throw the mace again, but he knew exactly how much his earlier throw had been circumstantial luck, and that had barely clipped a target right below him.

Luke surged forward, breaking a few branches off against his body to tear himself free. The goblin was past the trees now, barely five feet ahead of him but fully out in the open. Pain flared up his leg, but there was no more time to take the step he needed to push off his good side. With a snarl, he brought the mace up and fell on the goblin.

Blood and brains splashed across the grass. Before the body could tip forward, Luke snagged the loincloth and heaved himself back into the trees. He discarded the goblin into the brush and took a deep, pain-filled breath. If he'd been just a little bit faster, he could have caught it before it got into the open. Even then, there was no guarantee the other goblins wouldn't notice. The crossbow-wielding goblin had made plenty of terrified screaming sounds as it ran. All Luke could do was wait and hope.

Almost immediately, he heard the sounds of alarms coming from the camp. "Goddamn it," Luke snarled.

No kill notification popped up, so he knew he wasn't out of danger. Other goblins would be actively hunting him soon, and he was already injured. The smart move was to get the hell outa Dodge before he wound up with a goblin spear in his guts. Luke wasn't moving very fast anymore; he needed all the head start he could get.

A quick peek around the tree showed him goblins coming over the walls and organizing into groups. "Fuck," he swore again. "Time to go."

As it turned out, goblins were decent trackers. They might not see that well in the daylight—though the crossbow bolt he'd pulled from his leg put lie to that—but there was no escaping them. It probably didn't help that he was leaving blood behind with each limping step, which of course was attracting other predators.

Even those damn marmots were out in force, probably sensing weakness. He'd killed about twenty of them in the last hour, not to mention eight goblins who'd caught up with him in groups of three. The last one had escaped, which honestly Luke wasn't that broken up about. He was regretting not putting a few more points into stamina now and didn't have it in him to keep fighting.

The system must have still thought he was in danger or whatever though because it still hadn't awarded him any XP for all his kills. Too bad because he was sure he'd killed enough goblins and sharp-toothed forest mammals to qualify.

"System, why the hell am I not getting my XP?" he demanded.

"By default, the system does not display notifications while you are in dangerous situations so as not to distract you. As soon as you feel that you are safe, all notifications will appear," the apparition answered, appearing next to him as it spoke.

"By default? Can I turn it off?"

"Yes, your SysAdmin bloodline grants you access to this setting. Would you like to change it?"

"Yes! What are my options here?"

"If you'll allow me," System said with a gesture.

A window popped up in front of Luke with a few options for him to pick through.

[Display-message logic selection:]
[Only display system notifications while safe (currently selected)]
[Display notifications immediately]
[Display notification icon in peripheral vision, will open by mental command]
[Play audible tone when a new notification is available, will open by mental command]
[Notifications are audible, only recipient will hear]
[Notification imparted directly into memory (locked)]
[Notification will be reviewed between time fragments (locked)]

"Why're these last two locked?" Luke asked.

"Your administration level isn't high enough to grant access. You will need to purify your bloodline before they are available for use."

"Ugh, fine. Uh, for now, how about an audible tone? And go ahead and display all the notifications I've got built up. Oh, uh, can you compress the kill notifications? I don't need a line by line."

"I've saved your preferences, Luke."

[You have slain 34 creatures between levels 2 and 7. 842 XP awarded.]

[Congratulations! You have reached level 9. 9 AP awarded for use.]

It might have been nice to pick up some new skills, but right now Luke needed stats if he was going to survive. He immediately dumped 5 points into stamina, then 2 into agility and perception. The increased stamina was a balm on his wounds, causing the pain to recede and his muscles to flex with renewed vigor.

It was no healing spell, but he'd already determined that stamina increased his natural regeneration and made him more resistant to damage. It had been wild speculation that increasing it would also affect wounds he'd already received, but it looked like that gamble had paid off.

The increased perception also paid off. He might not have noticed the monster crouched in a tree before it landed on him otherwise. It was already on its way down when he spotted it, but Luke hurled himself to the side fast enough to avoid its flashing claws as it landed where he'd been standing a moment earlier.

Too bad for him he wasn't holding on to his mace when he jumped, and the monster was now between Luke and his weapon. Without hesitation, Luke pulled the blood-gummed folding knife out of his pocket and opened it. The beast, perhaps sensing an advantage, stalked closer and revealed a mouthful of pointed teeth.

It looked something like a big cat if it had fallen into a vat of dark-green dye and then rolled around on a sheet covered in hair gel. Everything was sharp spikes of fur, sharp enough that it shredded nearby leaves when it brushed up against them. Every part of this monster's body was a weapon, and the only consolation Luke had was the knowledge that it didn't massively outlevel him.

Theoretically, he could kill it. Surely a huge portion of its AP had gone into things like razor-sharp fur. It was probably all agility and perception, liable to fold like a lawn chair if he got one good hit in. That would be much easier with a good weapon, but when he tried to take a step around to the side, the cat moved with him. It advanced slowly, constantly adjusting itself as it prepared to spring, and Luke knew he was out of time.

Desperately, he reached behind him for a branch and tore it off with one hand. There was no time to clean it, no time to do anything but bring it around in front of him, an action that got him jabbed a few times by the smaller branches still attached to the main limb. But it was something to put between them, and when the cat pounced, he lashed out with it.

It bent under the weight of the cat and snapped, but it also bled enough momentum off that he was able to shove the monster to one side with only minimal slashing from its back legs. The cat rebounded instantly and landed on Luke's back as he scrambled for the mace. Claws sunk in and raked across muscles, easily parting the leather of his coat and the cotton shirt beneath.

Luke started bellowing in pain and spun to slam himself back first into a tree. The cat came along for the ride, and he definitely hurt it, but he also drove its sharp fur into his back. It felt like a hundred nails all at once puncturing him, and tears sprang to his eyes from the pain. He staggered forward a step, the cat still clinging to his back, and dropped to his knees.

The mace was right there, feet away. All he had to do was get to it and somehow pry this monster off his back before it bled him to death. But in his heart, he knew it was over. He was already injured, perhaps too badly to be saved. Even with the extra stamina he'd just picked up, he was on the verge of passing out.

A sharp, screeching caw was all the warning he got before his insides twisted and a shadow engulfed him. Something hit him hard enough to drive him completely into the ground, and then the weight of the cat on his back disappeared.

Luke groaned and pushed himself back to his hands and knees. He crawled forward the last few feet and grabbed his mace, then flopped over to see what had happened. Just as he turned, the cat hit the ground in a boneless heap of shredded flesh. Perched in a tree overhead, looking majestic as fuck, was his new bird buddy, Red.

Name	Luke Bennet
Level	9
XP	2390/2881
AP	0
Bloodline	SysAdmin
Strength	10
Agility	10
Stamina	13
Perception	10
Skills	Mace Mastery (2)
	Sword Mastery (1)
	Peripheral Awareness (1)
	Survivalist (1)
	First Aid (1)
	Wood Carving (1)
	Leatherworking (1)

CHAPTER 13

Luke spent the next day taking it easy, or at least as easy as a person could take it in a forest full of murderous wildlife. Red was actually kind of comforting to have around, even if the bird did give Luke the occasional searching, hungry look. He appeased his avian overlord with a steady offering of raw meat, courtesy of several different types of animals that tried to take a bite out of him.

Sometimes Red accepted the meat, sometimes he didn't. Luke built himself a small fire and committed cooking atrocities on the leftovers. **[Cooking]** was on the list of things Curt thought he should learn for himself and save an AP, but Luke wasn't sure it was worth it. He'd once set spaghetti on fire in a pot of boiling water, and that hadn't been the worst of his kitchen accidents before he'd been unilaterally banned.

Having the knowledge of how to prepare meals would not only give him an instant boost to the standard by which he lived, it might have the practical effect of not accidentally giving himself food poisoning too. While he suspected his stamina might just be too high for that to even happen at this point, there was still something to be said for the idea of being able to properly prepare a meal.

The injuries on his back were the most troublesome and painful, though he was pretty sure they were also the least life-threatening. He'd suffered a number of lacerations, which, thanks to **[First Aid]**, he recognized as being mostly dangerous as infection vectors and not because they were deep wounds on their own.

[Survivalist] came with the knowledge of a few plants that could be used in rudimentary forms as painkillers or disinfectants, but there weren't any around. The best Luke could manage was to thoroughly wash his shirt and put it on backward so that the part that was still whole would cover them up. His coat was also shredded across the back, something he was kind of pissed about.

The puncture wound in his leg was a different story. That was deep, and he needed to keep steady pressure on it or it wouldn't stop bleeding. It needed stitches, but he lacked the equipment to do it. The best he could manage was to shred some of his clothing into strips using a knife to bandage it. Since his shirt was already pulling duty on his back after he tied a knot at the base to keep it as tight as possible, that really only left one choice.

Using his belt as a stopgap measure, Luke washed his boxers in the stream and hung them to dry near the fire, then cut them into strips of cloth with the tiny scissors on his multi-tool. He wrapped his leg and stuffed the leftover cloth into his grocery bag, then put his jeans back on while being extremely careful about zipping them up.

Despite the XP gain, which nearly doubled his total, Luke couldn't count the last twenty-four hours as a victory. He'd gotten too cocky and made mistakes. Those mistakes were costing him some of his very, very limited resources. As much as he wanted to level up quickly, he was starting to think it was time to find the trail leading out of Tenebrous Valley and make his way toward civilization.

It was still going to be a day or two until the leather finished drying, and since his grocery bag was becoming more and more torn, he decided to wait for that project to finish. He wanted a harness of some sort for his weapon and a more durable pack. If those water bottles broke, that was a whole new kind of screwed he'd be with no way to transport water.

No matter what he was doing, the mace stayed close at hand. His perception was high enough now that almost nothing caught him completely unawares as long as he was paying attention, but that level of paranoia was exhausting, and he often found himself drifting away from vigilance. It was a mental effort to drag his brain back on task.

There was also always the risk of something like that spiked cat, the system notification had told him it was a level 9 sliver lynx, and he figured it had some sort of **[Stealth]** skill or something. He hadn't seen another one, and good riddance, but as he'd learned, despite the numbers and game rules, he wasn't in a game. The pain was very real. So was the fear.

So Luke didn't push himself. He'd overextended, made a mistake, and gotten his nose bloodied for it. It was costing him literally the clothes off his back, plus he was now high-risk for future problems until he got himself back to 100 percent. That cat could have killed him if Red hadn't swept in and taken it off him. Next time he might not be so lucky.

Back on Earth, he'd expect to be sore and healing for weeks. He couldn't get a good look at the cuts on his back, but he sure felt them. Those would keep him from doing any sort of twisting or bending motions until they fully healed, else he'd risk tearing them back open. Hell, he imagined he'd probably have a hundred stitches back there. Thanks to the miracle that was 13 stamina, he was sore but still flexible.

If he had to guess, another two days would be all it took to close them up enough that he didn't need to worry about them tearing. The puncture wound on his leg would need longer, but he could already walk on it without limping. It hurt, sure, but not enough to slow him down, at least not right away.

Luke spent his time gathering firewood, braining anything dumb enough to invade his camp, and dozing with his mace held in one hand. Day faded into night, and he woke up to Red's screeching caws. The pile of dead animals he'd built up over the day was severely depleted, but he wasn't worried. He could always find more.

The hide still wasn't ready for use yet, which was frustrating but not surprising considering the size. Luke left it strung up and set about replenishing his supply of firewood, then wandered a little ways from his camp and waited for something to come by and attack him. As soon as it did, he gave it a solid thump, dismissed his kill notification, and dragged the body back with him.

Then he skinned it, skewered some meat on a roasting stick, and planted it at an angle over the fire. It wasn't pretty, the food didn't taste good, and sometimes it fell into the fire when he wasn't paying attention, but it kept his belly full. Red, of course, took the remainder.

Finally on the next day, the hide was ready for use. **[Leatherworking]** guided him through the process, which was once again just plain weird. He'd noticed it in combat as well, but the more he fought, the less that feeling of having something else correct his movements had occurred. Luke took it to mean he was learning from the skill and getting better on his own.

Actually making something out of the hide was completely new to him however, and it felt really fucking weird, like someone was holding his hand and guiding the motion, except it came from inside, and it affected him right down to how his fingers moved instead of being just a general direction. Luke tried not to fight the sensation, and he actually found it easier to just zone out and think about something else while his hands worked.

When he was done, he had a new rawhide bag stitched together with thin leather strips. He gratefully transferred the contents of his eviscerated plastic grocery bag into it. The plastic was falling apart, and Luke didn't trust it enough to carry it around anymore. Once he'd emptied it, he looked down at it stupidly for a minute, wondering what to do with it.

Close to twenty years of being told littering was wrong made him feel like he couldn't just throw it away in the woods, but there wasn't really anywhere else to put it. Shrugging to himself, he balled it up and stuffed it in the bottom of his new leather bag. It wasn't like it took up any real space or weighed anything. Once he made it to civilization, he'd find a place to toss it out.

His other creations were a sheath for his skinning knife and a harness to strap his mace to his back. The sheath was actually a wooden frame he'd carved with the leather stretched over it, but he thought it looked nice. The whole getup was a bit primitive looking, but it was also unbelievably cool to him that he'd made it all with his own hands.

The harness had some straps to tighten or loosen it, which allowed Luke to fit it over his coat, tug it snuggly into place, and tie it there. The mace itself was held with the handle poking up over his right shoulder and the flanged head down near his hip. The head rode in a pocket with a stiff piece of leather going up the length to where it was all fastened to the harness at his shoulder, allowing him to still maintain full flexibility without having the mace smack him in the ass with every step.

Luke's biggest concern was being able to draw the weapon quickly. He lacked the tools to do anything complicated, so the handle itself was held in place with a simple tied loop. He could pull it free just by pressing on the loop, which was great for a quick draw, but maybe not awesome for keeping it from coming free when he didn't want it to. It was the best he could do with his limited knowledge, skills, and materials, and it was miles ahead of carrying it in his hands everywhere.

Armed and equipped, Luke bid his temporary camp home farewell and abandoned it. He had one task remaining before he left the valley permanently. There was a cave, and in that cave was a skeleton. He'd made a promise to give it a proper burial, and even though he lacked the means to dig a full grave, Luke made the effort to at least make a shallow one.

Then he ventured into the dark and, over the course of the next few hours, carried Curt's remains out in his bare hands. One after another, he laid the pieces down in the grave, keeping them in order as best he could. Then he scooped the dirt back over the bones and flattened the ground out. There was no headstone to place, but he didn't figure Curt would mind.

"I'm not good at speeches. Sorry, I don't have a eulogy for you. Couldn't read you your last rites if I wanted to. Never learned anything like that, you know? I guess you'll have to forgive me, Curt. You can bitch me out for not doing it right after I bring you back. All of you. Maybe . . . Do you think Mom too? I know she didn't die here, but that'd be nice, huh?"

He stood there for a little while, lost in thought, but the world wasn't content to leave him alone for long. A stray marmot, apparently far stupider than the rest of its kind, wandered through the grass, spotted him, and diverted on a course straight to him.

Red swooped down from the sky and grabbed it in its talons. Luke could hear the crunch of bone as the bird punctured its brain through its skull in midflight. "Thanks, buddy," Luke called after it.

He stared down at the fresh grave for a long few minutes. There was nothing else to say. It was time to go.

Name	Luke Bennet
Level	9
XP	2652/2881
AP	0
Bloodline	SysAdmin
Strength	10
Agility	10
Stamina	13
Perception	10
Skills	Mace Mastery (2)
	Sword Mastery (1)
	Peripheral Awareness (1)
	Survivalist (1)
	First Aid (1)
	Wood Carving (1)
	Leatherworking (1)

CHAPTER 14

It was perhaps inevitable that the sole exit from Tenebrous Valley was at its southeast end, not too far away from that goblin camp that had fucked him up so bad. Luke had actually explored the valley quite thoroughly, at least the part of it that was aboveground. He'd found probably forty or fifty caves scattered around the edges, but he wasn't eager to delve into those. Other than the one his brother's secret base was in, Luke left them alone.

Maybe if he'd focused higher on perception, he might have considered it. Goblins were probably the best source of XP he could find in the valley. They weren't the highest level around—that honor belonged solidly to Red—but they were quite numerous. That was exactly what made them so dangerous. Rarely did he fight more than one monster at a time, but goblins were almost never alone. Groups of two or three were common.

They were smart too, or at least they were smarter than the animalistic monsters he fought elsewhere. The goblins knew who he was. They remembered him. Every time one got away, it took more information back to the rest of its tribe. The only saving grace was that he'd fought three different types of goblins, and they didn't seem keen on sharing info with one another.

Grimshard goblins were located on the west side of the valley, and Bluerock had the north. The ones that had the aboveground camp were called Bloodbite, which was just kind of gross. Luke didn't want to sound racist or anything, but he couldn't tell them apart at all. The only way he knew which ones were which was by reviewing the system notifications telling him what kind of goblin he'd killed. Otherwise it was just a guess based on where he ran into them.

Luke hoped to get out without another big fight. Bloodbite goblins were the most numerous and the most willing to hound him if he ran into one of their patrols. He'd also run into a few that were level 11 while exploring, which was fantastic for gaining XP but sucked balls to actually fight, especially two-on-one.

They had been the kills he needed to push to level 10 though, and he'd immediately spent 6 of his new AP on **[Counter]** and **[Twitch Reflexes]**. The other 4 went to his stats, though he debated heavily about where to spend them. His brother's build wanted him to focus on strength and perception, but he found himself needing agility more than anything.

Fighting multiple enemies at a time meant he needed more speed, better coordination, and a body that could keep up with what his skills were feeding him in real time. Perception and agility were the more important stats for what he needed in a fight. Maybe if he had some sort of armor to help protect him, it would be different. But he didn't, so in the end he split them up and brought both agility and perception up to 12.

"What do you think, buddy?" he asked Red, who was perched on a stone outcropping and staring up at the pass in the valley. "Level 10. That's a nice, round number. A good benchmark before I get the hell out of this place."

The hawk turned its head to stare at him, its unblinking gold-colored eyes ferocious and hungry. "You know I hate when you look at me like that," Luke said. "Makes me think you're about to eat me."

Not for the first time, he wondered what Red's level actually was. No matter how much stronger Luke got, that intensity never went away. Nothing else in the valley made him feel like that. Fortunately, the bird seemed to think of him as some sort of meal ticket, and Luke was happy to club some hapless animal on the head to appease his feathery overlord's gluttony.

They traveled along the east rim of the valley, or at least Luke did. Red disappeared frequently, only occasionally showing back up for a minute here or there to check on him. "Check to see if I've got food for you is more like it," Luke muttered to himself.

There wasn't much that got in his way. The rocky shelf of land between where the mountains jutted up sharply and where the forest began didn't have much living in it or much willing to wander through it. That meant that as long as he avoided going too close to the caves, Luke was generally left to travel in peace.

Once he got closer to the southeast corner of the valley though, he retreated back into the woods. There were too many goblin patrols for him to feel comfortable being so exposed. It was slower going, and he ran a much higher risk of running into predators and monsters, but staying out in the open all but guaranteed he'd be spotted by goblins.

After the first few skirmishes, they'd learned to gather in numbers before they attacked. It wasn't an experience he was eager to repeat, and it was more dumb luck than anything that he'd gotten away relatively unharmed.

But now the trail that led to the exit was in sight. It curved up, winding its way toward the only break in the mountains surrounding the valley, a pass too narrow, crooked, and jagged to be taken any way but on foot. That didn't matter much to Luke since he didn't have a vehicle anyway.

There was a thousand-foot open stretch of unforested land between him and the first bend in the trail. That was where he was the most concerned about being attacked. If there was a patrol of goblins a hundred feet to his right, he'd be dodging crossbow bolts the entire sprint.

Thanks to his agility and stamina though, it would be a sprint. He was betting he could do it in under thirty seconds, even wearing work boots and blue jeans, with his mace strapped to his back. The thing was surprisingly light, not even five pounds. If he was lucky, he was just being paranoid, and he could casually walk the distance without an issue. If he wasn't lucky, he figured he'd get at least a third of the way before the first goblin shot at him.

"Here we go," he said. "Okay, just do it now."

He took a deep breath, looked one more time to make sure there were no monsters visible nearby, and took off at a dead sprint. His feet pounded against the dirt and stone as bounding strides hurled him forward, each one eating several feet and his legs pumping like pistons to propel him farther. He didn't make the effort to count the seconds, but he was sure he'd beaten his goal time when he rounded the boulder that marked the first curve in the trail.

He peeked back around the boulder and scanned the tree line, saw no goblins chasing after him, and let himself relax. Luke wasn't even winded after the mad dash across open ground. He hadn't been attacked. Everything was fine. All he had to do now was put one foot in front of the other.

He made it about fifty feet before he felt a rumble in the ground. At first, it was so faint he thought he was imagining it. That kind of stuff had been happening since he'd started putting points into perception, and he'd mostly learned to tune it out as unimportant background noise. A few steps later though, the ground rumbled again and this time he knew it wasn't in his head.

Eyes scanning for danger, he reached a hand up to pull the string tie on his mace and pulled it out of its sheath. He held it in front of him while he spun in a full circle. There was nothing, but the rumbling kept getting louder. Luke took a step back, putting himself closer to the sheer wall of stone that made up one side of the trail.

That was a mistake. A few seconds later, he was pelted with a shower of small stones as the wall exploded outward. Another explosion threw loose scree up into the air from the ground nearby. A . . . thing . . . something kind of human-shaped but definitely not human climbed out of the pit. Another one broke free of the nearby wall.

They were both about eight feet tall, made of rocks stacked up like a man, somehow glued together and not falling over. Where joints should have been, loose rubble grated against itself, allowing the creatures to swing arms and legs. They shed small, loose flakes of earth as they moved, but each footprint was inches deep and the monsters sucked up new material to keep themselves whole.

Luke reacted instantly. If there was anything he'd learned from his first week or so on Aros, it was that damn near everything wanted to kill him. If it didn't want to kill him at the moment, give it twenty minutes and it would change its mind. The only exception so far had been Red. Chances were good these things were not getting added to that list.

So he smacked the closest one in its head approximation as hard as he could. Chunks of stone blew out backward, some of them flying fifteen or twenty feet before hitting the ground. The monster didn't really seem to mind though. Its rocky fingers just reached out and grabbed Luke by the arm, then started squeezing.

They were strong, stronger than him, at least. But they weren't smart and didn't think tactically. He brought the mace down in a short one-handed chop on its elbow joint, easily smashing the rubble out of place and to the ground. Without that connection, the whole hand became inert. It was still locked on his arm but not moving, not squeezing.

Luke got some distance and went to work. The monsters weren't fast either. All they seemed to have going for them was relentless endurance and a lot of strength. Once he separated their limbs from their bodies, they immediately started to soften until they turned to loose gravel and mud. The hand clutching his arm took maybe fifteen seconds before it sloughed off and splattered on the ground.

The first one went down, and he got an audible ding to let him know it wasn't getting back up. Curious, he got some distance from the second and opened the notification.

[You have slain Minor Earth Elemental (level 10). 102 XP awarded.]

"Should have guessed that. Curt would have known right away," he said. Now that he'd killed one, he was actually alright with the outcome. They weren't too hard to kill or too dangerous to fight as long as he was careful, and the XP was good. Four more like that would be enough to level up again.

He smashed apart the second elemental, also level 10, and started walking forward again. Within a hundred feet, a new elemental had emerged from the mountainside and attacked him. He'd barely killed it and travelled another fifty feet when two of them popped up at once. Luke smiled while he fought.

Then while he was fighting those two, a third one popped up from behind. That was annoying but not insurmountable. What concerned him was that a fourth could show up before he took care of the ones he was already fighting.

The ground started rumbling again.

"Goddamn it! One at a time, people!" he snarled.

Three minutes later, Luke was sitting on the ground, panting heavily and covered in dust. He had a hundred tiny little cuts from exploding shards of rock peppering his face, chest, and hands. His coat was even more shredded than it had been when he'd started, and he was concerned about the integrity of his harness.

There was one small consolation though. If nothing else, it was good XP.

[Congratulations! You have reached level 11. 11 AP awarded for use.]

Name	Luke Bennet
Level	11
XP	3958/5128
AP	11
Bloodline	SysAdmin
Strength	10
Agility	12
Stamina	13
Perception	12
Skills	Mace Mastery (2)
	Sword Mastery (1)
	Peripheral Awareness (1)
	Counter (1)
	Twitch Reflexes (1)
	Survivalist (1)
	First Aid (1)
	Wood Carving (1)
	Leatherworking (1)

Skill	Rank	AP	Prerequisites	Effect
Counter	1	3	None	Gain knowledge and muscle memory of when an opponent leaves an opening and how to take advantage of that
Twitch Reflexes	1	3	None	Increases the chance to have a reflexive action that protects against an unexpected attack

CHAPTER 15

urt's build notes wanted Luke to invest in a suite of basic rank 1 combat skills, then pump stats for a few levels, and finally return to increasing skill ranks. They also called for learning a lot of rank 1 utility skills, as he dubbed them, and wanted Luke to do that the old-fashioned way. Luke didn't really have the patience for that, so he was gimping his combat effectiveness slightly, but he didn't figure wasting 5 or 6 AP was going to hurt him in the long run.

That having been said, Luke knew that his brother was both smarter and more practiced at this kind of stuff. Even if he didn't necessarily see the logic behind it, he trusted Curt enough to follow the plan. His last deviation had mostly been the result of an emergency; he was wounded and needed the stamina to recover.

So he took his 11 AP and split it up between strength and perception to even them out and threw the single leftover point into agility. It might not have been necessary, but he found that agility helped the most to get him acclimated to moving properly again every time he increased his stats. It was only a matter of time until something else popped up to attack him, and he needed to be ready for that.

Luke did a couple practice hops and stretches, swung his mace a few times, and walked around in a circle. The changes weren't as drastic now as they'd been in the early levels, but they were still there. His limbs thickened a bit with muscle, and his hearing got even sharper. Previously inaudible rumbling was easy to sense now, easy enough that he could almost pinpoint where it was coming from.

There were definitely more earth elementals around, and at least a few were heading in his direction. They just didn't move very fast through the ground. He took a moment to study the landscape around him, figured out where the next one was likely to appear from, and approached it. Somehow, the elementals knew where he was, which he supposed made sense. They obviously weren't using the same senses he was to keep track of things.

Overhead, Red circled the area once and screeched down at him. The bird seemed agitated, probably because it couldn't eat any of Luke's kills. "I will smash something fleshy for you later!" Luke called up to it. It screeched back at him again and flew off farther up the trail.

"So dramatic," he said. "You'd think I never feed it. Him? How do you know if a bird is . . . how would two birds even . . . like . . . missionary? Can they do that? Goddamn I miss the internet."

The ability to just ask whatever random questions popped into his head and get instant answers was one he vowed never again to take for granted, providing he ever got back home. His musings on that were cut short though, as his newly enhanced perception picked up on some minute cracks on the ground just starting to spread.

[Twitch Reflexes] was proving to be extremely handy for dealing with the elementals' explosive entrances. Shards of dirt and rock went up into the air, and Luke danced away from the explosion. He dodged the big chunks, took a shower of loose dirt to the face, and was otherwise unharmed. By the time the earth finished raining back down to the ground, he was already darting in to attack.

An extra 6 points in strength hadn't seemed like too big a deal when he was trying to get used to it. Now that he was swinging for real though, it was easy to feel the difference. The mace was designed to be used two-handed, but Luke didn't need to anymore. It whistled through the air like a willow switch, fast and deadly. He tore the elemental to pieces in a matter of seconds, and his biggest problem was overextending his swings.

He ignored the ding of a new notification in his mind and readied himself for the next elemental. Two of them were about to surface, and he knew there was a third one coming through the wall. It was faint, but he suspected a fourth would be coming at him from farther up the trail, probably showing up about fifteen or twenty seconds after the other three.

It all played out exactly how Luke expected it to. He was on one of the first pair as soon as they showed up, but he couldn't quite break it down before its partner reached him. [Peripheral Awareness] helped him keep track of it, and when it lunged, [Counter] practically jerked him out of his own body as it forced him through a dodge and riposte that ended with his mace tearing an arm off at the shoulder.

Luke rolled with it. It was easier to move with the skills than to try and fight them, and they knew what to do better than he did anyway. He had no training whatsoever prior to getting pushed into Aros, no karate or other martial arts, no military, no boxing, nothing. The most he could say was he'd gotten into a couple of fistfights with kids his own age, which he'd won about half of.

So when a skill told him to move in a certain way, when it tried to force his body to react, he let it. It was just like that **[Leatherworking]** skill. If he zoned out and let it do its thing, the results were better than if he fought against it. Curt's notes gave him a basic build for fighting: weapon skill, attacking skill, dodging skill, battlefield-awareness skill. He could almost fight on autopilot.

That seemed like a terrible idea though, so while he did let the skills guide him, he also tried to learn from them. He wanted to know why the skill demanded that he move like they did if for no other reason than he figured at some point the skill would hit a ceiling and he would have to innovate on his own, which would be pretty damn difficult to do if he had no idea why he did the things he did.

For now though, against monsters like these that were slow, it was more than enough to win. He battered and broke them, sometimes got scratched by exploding chunks of rock peppering his exposed skin, and reaped XP by the hundreds.

Luke had been on the trail for a grand total of ten minutes and killed enough earth elementals to almost level twice when he felt something change. Where before the ground had been solid with small vibrations that got steadily stronger as new elementals emerged, now the whole thing shook. Even the elemental that was dragging its way out of the ground fell over, which was kind of funny to see since it slipped into the ground instead of landing on top of it.

Then the ground started heaving, as if there were something massive beneath it trying to force its way up. Luke stumbled backward, his agility stat failing him as the ground bucked and rolled under his feet. He ended up flat on his ass and looking up just in time to see Red do another lap and screech at him again.

"Yeah, I get it this time!" he yelled back.

Whatever this was, he did not want to be at ground zero when it tore itself free. Luke scrambled to his feet and started running back down the trail into the valley. Behind him, the earth itself cracked open, drowning Luke in a thunderous avalanche of sound as hundreds of tons of stone were thrown up and crashed down. **[Twitch Reflexes]** kicked in, forcing him to leap to the side as a boulder bigger than he was came down right next to him.

It slammed into the ground and skidded another twenty feet before coming to a stop. If he'd been an instant slower, he'd have been caught directly under it, and if he'd dodged forward instead of to the side, it would have smashed into him from behind. That probably would have been the end of his life right there. Even if the boulder itself didn't kill him, he couldn't see himself standing up and walking away.

That was when the first wave of pressure hit him. It wasn't a physical thing, but something that battered his brain. He'd thought Red was the scariest motherfucker in the valley, but he'd been wrong. Whatever was crawling its way out of a damn mountain was much, much scarier. The pressure was almost paralyzing, and it was only Red's insistent caws, now from significantly higher overhead, that got through to Luke and got him moving again.

He ran for all he was worth while the thing emerged from the ground, only once glancing back at it to see the primordial mother of all earth elementals tearing its way free. It didn't look like the smaller ones Luke had been fighting at all. Instead, it was a miniature mountain with arms. It didn't so much have legs to walk as it just surged forward, wavelike, absorbing all the ground in its path and ejecting it out the back end.

Where it passed was left smooth of the wreckage and debris the huge elemental had scattered across the pass with its entrance. Even the stuff it wasn't directly touching started to melt back into the ground, no doubt being used to help build its strange body. Luke didn't stand still to get the details though.

A hand the size of a car broke free of the ground in front of him, fingers each a foot wide and grasping for him. He smacked the closest one with his mace, shattering it into loose rubble, then ducked away and juked around it. The hand flowed back down into the earth, and he felt it moving beneath him. **[Twitch Reflexes]** kicked in, and he threw himself as high into the air as he could.

It was going to be a bad landing. He was at least nine feet off the ground now, unexpectedly high, uncoordinated from surprise, and jumping forward at a downward angle. He was going to fall probably another three or so feet beyond his initial jump before he landed, but it was better than the alternative.

Three massive fingers were pinched together below and behind him, right where he would have been if he hadn't jumped. They ground against one another hard enough to rain dirt and stones down, hard enough that if they'd caught him they would have left him as nothing but a bloody smear.

His arms windmilled as he landed, and he threw himself forward into a roll. The motion was complicated by the fact that he'd kept hold of his mace and was still wearing the crude backpack he'd fashioned. No doubt the water bottles tucked away in there were squished but hopefully not broken. If that was the worst of it, he'd count himself lucky.

He must have been far enough after that because he felt nothing but tremors in the ground as he ran. Those faded away after a few seconds, and by the time he reached the giant boulder at the base of the trail, there was no sign that a monster of dirt and stone the size of a house had been after him.

"Fuck me sideways," he swore, panting for breath. "How the hell am I supposed to get past something like that?"

He hadn't even made it a tenth of the way to the center of the pass, let alone gone down the other side. He really didn't see himself just running the entire pass before the jumbo elemental made its appearance and squashed him. At the same time, he knew he was nowhere close to a high enough level to fight it. It had to be level 30 at least. Maybe 40. He wasn't sure exactly how to tell.

In short: he was trapped.

Name	Luke Bennet
Level	11
XP	4825/5128
AP	0
Bloodline	SysAdmin
Strength	16
Agility	13
Stamina	13
Perception	16
Skills	Mace Mastery (2)
	Sword Mastery (1)
	Peripheral Awareness (1)
	Counter (1)
	Twitch Reflexes (1)
	Survivalist (1)
	First Aid (1)
	Wood Carving (1)
	Leatherworking (1)

CHAPTER 16

There was only one thing to do: grind out levels. Regardless of how he escaped Tenebrous Valley, it was going to be easier if he was stronger. More stats would make everything easier, increase his odds of success, give him a bigger margin for error if he screwed up. With a monstrous earth elemental squatting on his only known exit, he either needed to be strong enough to overpower it or fast enough to outrun it.

That did bring up an interesting point. The pass was his only known exit, but he'd hardly explored the many, many caves in the valley. He'd seen no reason to, knowing they were infested with goblins and albino spider people and God knew what else. However, there was a possibility that they extended past the mountains, that he could walk to freedom that way.

If neither of those scenarios played out, the third and final option he saw was getting some new skills related to mountain climbing and making himself some new tools, then going over the mountains instead of going through the pass. Luke didn't like that solution though. If one of those behemoth earth elementals was sitting in the pass, there was no telling whether there were more of them up in the mountains. The last thing he needed was to be clinging to the side of a cliff when an elemental popped out of the rocks and took a swing at him.

No matter what he decided to do, more levels was the starting point. He couldn't run fast enough or long enough to get by all the elementals in the pass. He couldn't fight his way through all the goblins in the caves. He couldn't climb mountains at all. So he would need to remedy that situation.

If he was going to be stuck in the valley long-term, he felt it was time to invest some effort into a more permanent camp. He considered the workshop his brother had made out of a hidden pocket in the roof of a cave to be the most viable location, but Curt had also died just outside of it, so there was definitely some risk there.

It was entirely possible a group of goblins had banded together to take down a threat that was too high level and somehow tracked Curt back to his base, then ambushed him. Whatever else they were, they weren't stupid. Maybe they weren't smart, but they weren't animals either. Goblins were probably going to be his primary source of XP moving forward, unless he got brave enough to venture back up the pass to fight earth elementals.

He'd gotten a few good chunks of XP from his early kills, but he fully realized that if the elemental had popped up behind him instead of in front of him, he wouldn't have been able to retreat. It was possible he could have run up the trail and it wouldn't have chased him, but he had no evidence to support that, or that there wouldn't be even more elementals deeper into the mountains.

That made him extremely reluctant to go farm elementals for XP. Unless some goblin boss monster showed up, it was probably a much safer tactic to fight goblins. They were easier to kill anyway, even if they did fight in packs.

He snorted and shook his head at that. Earlier that day he was warily moving around the edges of their territory, trying not to get spotted and drawn into an unwanted confrontation. After fighting the elementals though, he felt like he had perspective on how easy goblins actually were to take out. More than that, he'd significantly increased his strength and perception and gained several new combat-oriented skills.

Luke crossed the dead zone between the trail and the trees with a lot less hesitation than he'd had the first time. Though he was sure there would be goblin scouts coming soon to investigate the noise if nothing else, he didn't have it in him to be afraid of them anymore. He'd seen something that scared the hell out of him, and goblins just didn't measure up. He told himself that was a bad mindset to have, that a crossbow bolt through the throat would kill him just as easily as being crushed under a boulder, but it was hard to shake it.

Luke wasn't ready to call it a day so soon. Once his heart had stopped threatening to pound out of his chest, he was reminded that he was now in the best physical shape probably any human had ever been in, at least anyone from Earth. The last half hour of his life had been scary, sure, but he hadn't actually been hurt, and he had a clear new goal in mind: attack and kill goblins.

"Heh, it's just like that one—gah!"

Red swooped down, somehow unnoticed despite his newly enhanced perception, to perch nearby and give him what Luke had decided to call "the look." He translated that look as, "I'm hungry. Go find me something meaty to eat." Whether or not that was correct, Red was still a higher level, and Luke hadn't yet gone wrong with offerings of raw meat.

"Alright, let's go find something to eat. I suppose I'm kind of hungry too. What are you in the mood for today? Maybe some of those big squirrels to snack on? Or, oh! How about some rabbit? One of those would be more than enough for the both of us. Yeah, that sounds good."

There was no way he could have remembered where he'd seen that burrow of man-size rabbits without **[Survivalist]** keeping track of it for him. Fortunately, he did have the skill, and he was able to find the burrow with minimal effort. It was proving so useful that he thought he'd invest the AP into ranking it up to the next level. That wasn't that far off either. He could do that while he was getting lunch.

The burrow was occupied but only by one adult. It came out bellowing and charged at him, floppy ears streaming behind its head as it lunged forward faster than a train. Luke calmly brought his mace down on its face with one hand and drove it into the dirt. He followed that up with a second blow to the back of its skull, which tore away chunks of fur and bone, and the rabbit monster stilled.

[You have slain Hulking Lepus (level 5). 25 XP awarded.]

"You know, usually something that low level ignores me. System, why did this thing come at me like that?"

"Perhaps because you are near its home," System answered. "Some creatures are quite territorial and will attack enemies with more XP than them despite the difference."

"More XP?" Luke asked. "Not more levels? Why do I feel like you told me this already?"

"We briefly touched on the topic a few days ago, but you were otherwise occupied by a powerful enemy approaching you. To your question: It is an academic difference, as more XP means more levels, but technically yes, more XP. What you are sensing is the amount of XP you have compared to them, not the actual level itself."

"Would that ever matter?"

"For all practical purposes, no. I am merely explaining the exact mechanism by which you sense another creature. Functionally, there is no level with an XP requirement great enough that a creature at the beginning and one at the end would not feel the same to you."

Luke hefted the carcass up and started walking back off through the trees with it. He was limited to the game trails in order to haul it with him, but that wasn't an issue. His old camp was only half a mile away in a straight line, maybe twice that on the game trail. There wasn't a lot left there, but he'd left the firepit and some unused firewood behind.

Red flitted from tree to tree overhead, though it disappeared for a few minutes at a time, only occasionally showing back up to check on Luke. It wasn't until he got a fire going and had started hacking chunks of meat off the rabbit that Red settled down nearby. It occasionally darted over to the corpse to snap off a chunk of meat and swallow it, which startled Luke more than once and almost sent him over the fire when **[Twitch Reflexes]** kicked in.

After he'd gotten everything set up, he settled back with a block of wood and his folding knife to pass the time and said, "System, got a question for you."

"Yes, Luke?" it asked.

"What can you tell me about that huge earth elemental? What level is it?"

"My apologies, I am unable to provide this information."

"Figured," Luke said. "Doesn't hurt to ask though. Okay, is there anything you are allowed to tell me?"

"In regard to the creature you ran from? I am afraid not."

"How about where the goblins live? You've been decently helpful at navigating. Is there a tunnel out of this valley?"

"There is, but I am afraid it does not take you to where you want to go. I would advise against pursuing it, as it leads through the west side of the mountains and directly into the ocean. You would need many, many times more stamina than you currently possess to hold your breath for the hours or even days necessary to navigate the tunnels once they become submerged."

Luke stopped fiddling with the wood he was carving and looked over at System. "That's a possibility?"

"Of course."

"How long could I hold my breath right now?" he asked.

"In a hypothetical situation where you are fully submerged underwater but not being threatened or trying to move, I estimate you would be able to go without breathing for about thirty-two minutes, give or take half a minute."

"Damn. That's crazy. Are you sure about that?"

"Yes," System said. "Be aware that the time would be significantly shorter if you were swimming or fighting."

"Right, obviously. But still. I could barely hold my breath for a minute back on Earth."

"The accumulated XP has reinforced your body in many ways," System said. "That is the purpose of your stats, after all."

"And skills are I guess the mind part of the equation," Luke said to himself. "Instant knowledge dumped straight into my brain."

"That is not an inaccurate description," System agreed.

"Okay, how about this then. What if I wanted to climb over the mountain instead of taking the pass?"

"There are several skills to help with that. Some of them, such as **[Survivalist]** and **[Leatherworking]**, are already in your possession, though you would be well served to increase their ranks. You would likely need to increase your stamina significantly as well, both to endure the cold and to go longer periods without food and water."

"What about monsters? Are there any up in the mountains?"

"There are many things living up there. Quite a few of them would be able to easily kill you at your current level."

"Fuck me," Luke swore. "So that pass is the only realistic way out, and it's blocked by a sentient hill."

No matter how he moved forward, more levels were going to be essential. That was going to be true no matter what. Getting out of Tenebrous Valley was only the first step. He still had to make it all the way to the God Machine, and he didn't figure that was going to be an easy trip. At least he wasn't on a time limit.

"Wait, I'm not, am I? System, is it going to be a problem if it takes me a long time to get to the console at the God Machine?"

"No, Luke. The console has existed for thousands of years. It is extremely likely that it will survive undamaged for many decades to come."

"Good, so I've got all the time in the world."

"In point of fact: you have at most eight or nine decades before you expire of natural causes."

". . . Yes. Thank you, System."

"You are most welcome, Luke."

Name	Luke Bennet
Level	11
XP	4850/5128
AP	0
Bloodline	SysAdmin
Strength	16
Agility	13
Stamina	13
Perception	16
Skills	Mace Mastery (2)
	Sword Mastery (1)
	Peripheral Awareness (1)
	Counter (1)
	Twitch Reflexes (1)
	Survivalist (1)
	First Aid (1)
	Wood Carving (1)
	Leatherworking (1)

CHAPTER 17

Luke was an equal opportunity genocidal monster. He didn't discriminate between goblin tribes and was more than willing to kill anything that attacked him. The fact that goblins always attacked him, without hesitation or provocation, went a long way toward making him feel alright that he was single-handedly decimating their population.

With his next level up to 12, he spent 3 AP to increase **[Survivalist]** to rank 2. The expanded knowledge made him look back at his old preparations and feel like a putz. He was almost afraid to put the points into **[Leatherworking]**, but he was clearly going to be there awhile and his clothes were starting to fall apart, so he bit the bullet and dropped another 3 AP on that too.

"I can't believe I was ever proud of this thing," he said to himself as he looked down at his bag. The threads were starting to snap, and he knew exactly why. He'd built the entire thing wrong. He needed to redo it immediately. He'd planned ahead for that though and already had new hides drying in his forest camp.

The last 6 AP were used to reinforce his stats. He put 2 each in strength and perception, and 1 each in agility and stamina. He could see well enough in the dark that he no longer had any issues fighting the goblins. The biggest problem he was having now was that he was having to go deeper and deeper in to find their underground homes, and more than once he'd gotten a little bit lost trying to get back out.

He took a break for a day to work on some other stuff, namely making himself a better backpack, a new coat, and some sort of shirt. His jeans and work boots had held up better than anything else, though he had to give his leather jacket credit for still being in one piece despite the beatings it had gone through.

At night, he went back to his brother's workshop and slept there, though it seemed like the amount of sleep he needed kept going down as his stamina went up. He was only getting five or six hours now, and he felt fine in the mornings. That, combined with his enhanced perception letting him see what was going on even in the dark, led to more hours of the day to hunt monsters.

The problem was one of mental fatigue. Luke just didn't want to live his life for nothing but work, and monster hunting was a job like anything else. It was actually kind of stressful, knowing that if he screwed something up bad enough, it could result in his death. His set of combat skills was very, very good at keeping him out of harm's way, but all it would take was one goblin he didn't see putting a spear through his ribs to finish him off.

Probably. He might even survive that if his stamina got high enough.

Luke limited himself to eight hours of slaughtering, spent a few hours on **[Wood Carving]** and **[Leatherworking]** in an attempt to keep himself clothed and to build a tree house. The knowledge was there, kind of, but the tools were lacking. Carving joints that held together without things like nails or glue was time-consuming, and that assumed access to raw lumber that he just didn't have.

That was why he was standing less than five hundred feet from the goblin camp. They'd built with lumber. They had to have the tools he needed, saws and hammers and nails. He was practically salivating at the idea of having a full tool belt. Maybe he'd get a general-purpose **[Carpentry]** skill out of it if he was able to pull the raid off.

The goal wasn't to kill every goblin there, though that wouldn't bother him. He just wanted access to their toolboxes. If he could do that without slaughtering the whole camp, that was just fine. Of course, he didn't have any sort of sneaking skills, so the chances of that happening were effectively zero. That was why his plan involved going after the crossbow-wielding goblins on the watchtowers first.

To that end, he had confiscated a few crossbows from various goblins and spent the afternoon practicing with them. He . . . was not good at it. They were easy enough to reload thanks to his high strength, and agility probably helped more than he was giving it credit for, but he could tell that the weapons were not good quality, not well maintained, and were too small for him besides.

He doubted he'd be accurate past thirty or forty feet even if his agility was 100. Since it was really only 14, he wasn't even accurate that far. Twenty feet was about his limit. The towers weren't that high though, so he slid his mace into its back sheath, grabbed a crossbow in either hand, and got ready to make the run across open ground.

The goblins, he'd learned, had shit vision in the day. They weren't blind, but the towers were more for appearance than practicality. He was spotted immediately, of course, but they couldn't hit him from range even if he ran a straight line. With his high perception feeding **[Twitch Reflexes]**, there was no chance they were going to tag him.

Luke reached the point where he was maybe fifteen feet from the tower and jumped as high as he could. If there was ever a point where one of them would shoot him, it was at that very moment. Both were too surprised by his actions to do it, though he did notice that one of them was actually reloading and wouldn't have been able to shoot anyway.

He fired both crossbows with perhaps twenty-five feet between him and his targets. One missed completely, but the other clipped a shoulder and caused the goblin to fumble its weapon. That was probably a better outcome than such a batshit crazy plan deserved, if he was being honest with himself. Luke threw both crossbows following the successful firing of them, and there he had better luck.

One goblin was struck head-on, stumbled back a few steps, and shrieked in surprise and fear when it fell out of the tower. The other dodged out of the way but in the process dropped the bolt it was trying to load.

Luke caught hold of the edge of the tower just as he started to fall back down and hauled himself up. The goblin, perhaps inspired by his own attack, hurled its crossbow at his face. **[Twitch Reflexes]** clocked the attack, but as both of his hands were busy pushing his full body weight up to get him onto the tower, there was nothing he could do but duck his head to take it on his skull instead of his face.

"Ow! Fuck," he swore. Then he was up, mace in hand, and hauling back to knock the goblin clear to the caves. It went sailing through the air, skimmed over the roof of one hut, skipped off the roof next to that, and landed right next to the long house near the back.

A notification ding sounded to let him know that particular goblin was dead. It was the only one though, so he looked down over the edge to see the one that had fallen off limping its way toward the back of the camp. Luke calmly picked up the dropped crossbow, loaded it, and shot the goblin in the back of the head.

Well, he tried to anyway. In reality, he shot it in the ass, which just made it squeal and speed up. "Goddamn it, these things suck," he said, but he was a little bit impressed he'd managed to hit a moving target at all.

Phase one of the Plan That Totally Wasn't Going to Get Him Killed was complete. He'd taken out one of the watchtowers, which would help prevent him from being pincushioned by goblin snipers, if they could be called that. More importantly, it gave him his first up-close and uninterrupted view of the camp. He hadn't been able to make out fine details from the tree line, but now he could clearly see which part was dedicated to woodworking.

As he suspected, it was the north side. That was why he'd chosen the tower he was on to attack. It had been a gamble but a small one. The lumber was piled up there, and based on where the goblins had been cutting down trees, it made the most sense to him. Before, it had been supposition. Who knew how goblins thought? Now, it was fact. He'd confirmed it himself.

His eyes flitted back and forth, counting goblin numbers and divvying them up between workers and warriors. It was surprisingly heavy in the workers' favor, but then he supposed the purpose of the camp was to gather raw material and process it. The guards would be there to handle problems like Luke, and there wouldn't be a pressing need for a ton of them.

Except that Luke was a higher level than anything else living in the valley besides Red, who didn't really like goblin meat and thus didn't count anyway, and he liked to think he was smarter than the average rodent, reptile, or giant bug. Or at least he was crazier than one.

He dropped off the watchtower, flexing his legs and crouching down as he landed. Then he went for the lumberyard, careful to keep a hut between him and the south sentry tower. It was only a hundred feet to his goal, but he needed time to locate the tools he was after, load them into his backpack, and get back out.

As far as a smash-and-grab was concerned, he thought things were going pretty good. The workers weren't even trying to fight him. They all went running for the back of the camp and the caves, which did annoy him a bit because he saw one fleeing holding a hammer in its hand. There were other hammers though, so he let it flee without pursuit.

Luke swung the backpack off his shoulders and scooped up two hammers and a small leather pouch of nails. A nearby saw went into the pack, followed by a dozen chisels of varying sizes, a file, a wooden mallet, a whetstone, and a drill. His eyes lit up when he found a wooden box with a set of carving knives in it.

"Jackpot," he hissed. His tool raid was going better than he could have hoped. If he could just find a small hand-held plane, probably the only kind goblins would be likely to have anyway, that would round out the set nicely.

Then the door to the long house flew open, kicked by a goblin foot so hard that it was blasted off the hinges. The largest goblin Luke had ever seen strode out into the light, wearing actual hardened-leather armor and armed with a sword so big that Luke was surprised it could wield it one-handed.

Luke was confident he could win that fight. The goblin was impressive, for a goblin. But he was a couple levels past that now. Then a second goblin followed the first one out. And a third. When the fourth one appeared, he felt a twist in his guts that told him something with more XP than him was around.

The four of them fanned out, and another ten goblins holding crossbows poured out of the long house. There was about a hundred feet between him and the goblin war party. Fourteen of them against one of him.

Phase two was complete anyway, sort of. He'd gotten almost everything he wanted. It was time to switch to phase three.

"Run like hell," Luke whispered to himself.

Name	Luke Bennet
Level	12
XP	5721/6597
AP	0
Bloodline	SysAdmin
Strength	18
Agility	14
Stamina	14
Perception	18
Skills	Mace Mastery (2)
	Sword Mastery (1)
	Peripheral Awareness (1)
	Counter (1)
	Twitch Reflexes (1)
	Survivalist (2)
	First Aid (1)
	Wood Carving (1)
	Leatherworking (2)

Skill	Rank	AP	Prerequisites	Effect
Survivalist	2	3	Rank 1	Create shelter, purify water sources, harvest animal meat and pelts, increased speed when moving through wilderness
Leatherworking	2	3	Rank 1	Gain an intermediate understanding of tools and techniques used in leatherworking

CHAPTER 18

What was it that System had told him? Goblins in the valley were between levels 7 and 21? That sounded right to Luke. He'd killed probably a hundred of them and had almost never found one higher than level 9, until now.

These goblins were definitely higher than level 9. Physically speaking, they were bulkier and taller and moved with that easy grace that Luke himself was becoming more and more familiar with each time he leveled up.

This was a no-win situation for him. He'd expected to run roughshod over any opposition and only worried about getting bogged down in numbers, specifically numbers wielding crossbows since he could just outrun goblins with swords and axes. He hadn't expected to find a fucking goblin that was a higher level than him with a whole posse of minions that were the same level. Luke did the only sensible thing he could. He turned and ran.

Goblins weren't the best marksmen, but with so many, one of them was bound to land a lucky shot if he just ran in a straight line. So Luke didn't do that. He juked right around the closest workbench and flipped it with one hand. That was only because he knew it wouldn't take any time to do and it might serve as a visual distraction or possibly even break line of sight on a few of them.

He heard the distinctive twang of crossbows firing and dove into a roll to make himself a smaller target. Rather, he tried to, but **[Twitch Reflexes]** took over, and he ended up doing something that was more akin to a one-handed cartwheel where, halfway through, his whole body twisted as his legs kicked into a spin. Somehow, he didn't break his neck.

He also didn't stick the landing, but considering he had miraculously dodged every single bolt, he wasn't going to complain about having to scramble back to his feet. The original plan had been to just jump the wall when it was time to escape, which was why he'd gone out of his way to take out the goblins in the sentry tower. He didn't want to get shot while he was in the air.

Maybe he'd gotten unlucky and chosen the worst possible time to do a smash-and-grab. Maybe all the patrols were back at once for a meeting. Maybe he'd severely underestimated the number of goblins. Whatever the reason, once they'd all fired off a shot and needed to reload, he ducked around the nearest hut and went straight for the wall. Hopefully they hadn't been smart enough to fire in volleys.

There had definitely been more than six or seven bolts, so he thought he was safe there. The wall was coming up fast, and he heard goblins running after him, so there was no more time to think about it. He leaped straight up and dove over the wall, his body almost horizontal to clear it and also to make a smaller target just in case any goblin did have a loaded crossbow.

For half a second, he thought he'd gambled and lost when he felt something impact his back. Then he realized that it wasn't a bolt; it was a whole damn goblin. One of them had not only chased after him, it had caught up with him midair after jumping higher and landing feetfirst on top of him! Luke's forward momentum abruptly became downward momentum, and he was in no way prepared for that.

He hit the dirt on the other side of the wall with a hard thump, but the pain was a minor distraction compared to the fact that the goblin had ridden him down and he was in an incredibly vulnerable position. Fortunately, he was physically stronger than damn near any human in history, and goblins were pretty light besides. That tended to happen when a species struggled to get past four feet tall.

Luke rolled, and there was nothing the goblin could do to stop him. It danced on top of him to keep its footing and was already bringing down a pair of short swords when he got it into view. There was no way he was stopping them with his bare hands, so he didn't even try. Instead, he seized the goblin's ankles and heaved it straight up. It flew up about five feet before it regained control of itself and started coming back down, blades first.

That gave Luke enough time to roll away and get back to his feet. He tossed the bag of tools off to the side and pulled his mace free in one smooth motion, intent on smashing the goblin's face in and making off with his ill-gotten gains. Instead, he found himself immediately on the defensive as he fought a creature with much higher agility than him. His mace, which felt as light as a toothpick these days, couldn't move fast enough to deflect every one of the goblin's strikes.

[Twitch Reflexes] saved his ass in those first few seconds, and **[Counter]** was the only reason he was able to keep the goblin from pressuring him until he was overwhelmed. Those combined with **[Mace Mastery]** kept him alive, and Luke once again silently thanked his brother for his foresight. He never would have thought to take those skills, probably never would even have found them amid the thousands of available options.

What none of his skills told him was how to win. All he was doing was hanging in the fight, completely on the defensive except when **[Counter]** triggered. The goblin easily dodged all his attacks and came right back in. Luke could see the frustration mounting on his face, but he didn't have time to wait for it to make a mistake. There were more than a dozen other goblins probably scrambling to catch up, and several of them were at least as high level as he was. One was higher.

He needed a decisive and quick win. That was where his brother's notes came in. The build was all well and good, but Curt's ideas on how Luke should fight were where he found what to do. That answer was simple but also frightening. He needed to accept that he was going to take a hit or two, trust in his stamina to keep him going, and put the goblin in the ground. He was missing the regenerating **[Life Surge]** ability that would make that easy, but that just meant a bit of pain.

The hard part was fighting against the movements his skills were pushing. They were trying to keep him safe, but the goblin was so fast that there were basically no exploitable openings. Luke took a risk and hopped back a step while swinging his mace in a wide arc to force his opponent back. Predictably, it ducked under the attack and came in while he was still swinging. Its leading sword slashed a red-hot line of pain across his stomach.

So Luke kicked it in the face as hard as 18 strength would let him. Bones crunched, blood went flying, and lost teeth bounced across the ground. The goblin howled as it was launched straight back so hard it ended up flipping through the air to land on its stomach. Before it could recover, Luke leaped forward and brought his mace down on its skull.

As usual, smacking something in the head was an excellent finishing move. He got the ding of a notification but didn't have time to check it. The fight hadn't even lasted a minute, but that was more than enough time for reinforcements to catch up. Two of them had jumped the walls, both were probably about the same level as him, and he could see five of the scraggly creatures climbing the ladder up to the lookout tower, all with crossbows hanging from straps and full quivers.

"Time to go," Luke said. He wasn't interested in a fair fight, let alone one that was unfair in their favor. Instead of sticking around, he scooped up his bag and sprinted west and north, following the curve of the valley in an effort to outdistance the smaller goblins on open terrain.

The cut on his stomach burned, but it was shallow and treatable. He'd take care of it later. For now, all he needed to do was run as fast and as far as he could. Luke's legs pumped, and his lungs worked like bellows to keep him moving. He sprinted a mile in about three minutes, leaving the goblins far, far behind, and eventually slowed down to duck into the trees.

From there, it was just a matter of taking his normal precautions while walking back to his camp. He kept an eye out for any plants that [**Survivalist**] told him would be useful for pain management, healing, and reducing the chance of infection. He would probably be fine without all of that, but he didn't put those AP into a rank up just to not use the new knowledge it provided.

As he walked, he mentally inventoried his haul. It wasn't a full workshop by any means, but it was a good start to really being able to build things. It was going to be a lot of effort, but it'd be worth it for the extra security while he was stuck in Tenebrous Valley.

Luke had plans, and he was well on his way to getting those started.

Gulgok returned to the lodge and sat back down on his throne. It was an ugly thing, carved from a single block of wood and studded with metal spikes. Thin ropes hung from the spikes on either side of the chair, laced through the eye sockets of the bloodstained skulls of vanquished goblins. It was a macabre background, one that Gulgok had intentionally cultivated. It reminded his tribe of who was in charge, and why.

It reminded his enemies why the Bloodbite tribe claimed the most territory and boasted the highest-level warriors. Gulgok found such a reminder to be very useful when he needed to persuade the other bosses of something.

An exceptionally wide goblin named Bulgrit entered the lodge and approached the throne. Most goblins would grovel before him, but not Bulgrit. He was the boss's Right Hand, second only to Gulgok himself and foremost among his elites.

"The Day Hunter outran our scouts," Bulgrit reported.

Gulgok wasn't surprised. Whatever that thing was, it was smart. It struck during the brightest hours, when his kinsmen's eyes were at their weakest. It was strong and fast, capable of killing one of the inferior laborers in a single strike. Even his scouts and raiders had met with nothing but failure when they crossed the Day Hunter's path.

Too many goblins had died to the monster. It wasn't just his own tribe either. The Grimshards and Bluerocks were suffering regular casualties. Gulgok had been hoping one of the other tribes would spend their elites killing the Day Hunter, but now that it had taken a special interest in their lumberyard, it looked like they didn't have much of a choice.

Today the Day Hunter wanted tools. How long would it be before it came back for the lumber? How long before it decided to put pressure on his lumberyard until there were no goblins left? Why build its own workspace when it could just take from Gulgok? The Day Hunter was strong, no doubt, but Gulgok had felt its power for himself. It wasn't that strong, yet.

That was the problem though: time. It was getting stronger at an incredibly fast rate. Gulgok was to the point where if he slaughtered his entire workforce, he would gain perhaps a single level. He might gain one more from his warriors and perhaps a third level from his elites. But then he would be alone, one goblin against hundreds from the other tribes.

The Day Hunter was already one against hundreds. It did not care how many goblins it killed in its ascent to power. They needed to stop it now, before it grew too strong to handle.

"Send runners to the Bluerock and Grimshard tunnels," he ordered. "Inform Qarsik and Margl that I am calling a Bossmoot. We are killing this monster while we still can."

Name	Luke Bennet
Level	12
XP	5918/6597
AP	0
Bloodline	SysAdmin
Strength	18
Agility	14
Stamina	14
Perception	18
Skills	Mace Mastery (2)
	Sword Mastery (1)
	Peripheral Awareness (1)
	Counter (1)
	Twitch Reflexes (1)
	Survivalist (2)
	First Aid (1)
	Wood Carving (1)
	Leatherworking (2)

CHAPTER 19

[You have slain Bloodbite Goblin (level 7). 50 XP awarded.]
[You have slain Bloodbite Goblin (level 12). 147 XP awarded.]

Luke stared at the kill notifications from his raid on their camp for a long time. He knew the higher-level goblin would have more AP, but the difference between them was insane. "System," he said finally. "Can you help me out here?"

"How can I assist you?" System asked.

"Every goblin I've fought so far has been . . . well, kind of weak. That last one was different. It was by far the strongest thing I've gone up against. Was it just the higher level, or am I missing something?"

"You do not have access to other creatures' status screens," System said. "I am unable to tell you what differences existed between your most recent kill and the ones prior to that. I can tell you that goblins are sapient, and there is no template they follow. They are as free to assign their AP wherever they want, just as you are."

"Maybe that's the difference?" Luke mused. It wouldn't take much to drain all their AP. Just a few rank 1 skills and maybe a single rank 2 would use most of the points a level 7 goblin would have. If they didn't invest into their stats, they'd be weak. If their skills were all utility, they'd be weak. If it was both . . . it was no wonder he'd never had any trouble taking down enemies that were the same level as him.

A goblin warrior would be different. It would be optimized for fighting, just like him. He'd only spent 9 AP, he thought, on noncombat skills. The other 69 had gone directly into stats and skills to help him fight. "Ha, nice," he said. "Probably never going to get to say that again."

It was a humbling realization. Technically he was fighting things that were sometimes the same level as he was or close to, but in reality their AP were probably spent on so much stuff that didn't revolve around fighting that it wasn't really fair.

"Animals all follow the templates, right? How often do those have big point sinks in abilities like digging or improved smell?"

"Almost always," System told him. "Even among sapient creatures, it's statistically unlikely someone will invest all their AP into nothing but stat increases. Similarly, though most people will choose skills that benefit their chosen professions, almost nobody devotes their AP to nothing but those skills. *Hobbies* is the term I believe humans use for the practice of spending AP on other skills."

"So what I'm getting from this is that I need to be careful, especially fighting intelligent monsters. They might be specialized for fighting and kick my ass."

"One should always be careful when fighting in life-and-death combat," System agreed.

Luke rolled his eyes. "Thanks for the advice."

All this really meant was that he needed to level up higher than he thought. It wasn't enough to meet the monster's level; he needed to exceed it. He also needed some form of armor, but that seemed unlikely to materialize. Even if he found goblins wearing some and managed to kill them without breaking it, it wouldn't fit anyway. He was five nine, and he didn't think he'd seen a single one that was four and a half feet tall. Most weren't even four feet tall.

He supposed he could make something out of wood and leather, but he wasn't sure how useful that would be. An inch-thick breastplate made of wood would be . . . better than nothing, but it seemed like an inefficient use of his time. "Okay, that's low priority. What's at the top of the list though? Safety, security, and shelter," he told himself. Technically he had that in Curt's work-shop, at least as much as could be found in the monster-infested wilderness he was stuck in. But it wasn't comfortable in there at all. Not only was sleeping on stone even worse than sleeping on the ground, but the place had a kind of stale smell to it, like being in a crypt or something. Too bad there were no windows to air it out.

Plus Red couldn't join him there, and as much as Luke wasn't in love with the thought that his only companion and best friend was a giant bird who could snap him like a twig, that was the reality of his situation. His only intelligent conversations were with System, who was not much of a conversationalist since it was more like an AI that ran queries for him than a person. Red at least had personality, even if they couldn't talk to each other.

Unfortunately, as much as he desired a new home outside the cave, there was no store to drive over to and pick up a bunch of lumber for the project. The tools he'd managed to snag would be good for small projects but not for what he wanted. His forest camp would remain unsecured, though his drying racks were going to improve immensely over the next day or two.

"You know who does have lumber though? Those goblins," he said to himself. "That means they have the tools needed to process a felled tree."

He wasn't about to take another run at the place though, not until he packed on a few more levels. In the end, everything he thought to try came back to that. He needed more levels if he wanted to leave. He needed more levels if he wanted to stay. Any comforts he wanted, he had to make with his own two hands, which meant gaining levels so he'd have AP to spend on skills that would teach him how.

"Always levels. There has got to be some way to live that doesn't involve just randomly killing everything I come across."

Try as he might, Luke couldn't think of anything. The levels were coming slower and slower as the amount of XP needed kept ramping up and the available monsters dwindled. The low-level ones would freeze or run if he went near them now, and it wasn't really worth his time anyway.

Goblins were all of a sudden a hell of a lot riskier than he'd expected. He supposed if he stayed near the beginning of the pass, he could grind on some of the small, weak earth elementals. The big one hadn't chased him back into the valley before. Of course, there was no reason to believe it wouldn't change its mind if he ran into it again, but he didn't think he had much choice.

It was goblins or earth elementals. Anything else was too hard to find, too low level, or both. Before that though, he needed to finish building the new frames for drying hides and then find new animals to skin for hides, and also dinner.

Being stranded was exhausting.

Luke spent his evening taunting death at the base of the trail that led to freedom. He killed a dozen elementals in quick succession, then retreated when he noticed the tremors growing too strong. The big one never made an appearance, but he figured he'd tempted fate enough for one day.

For all his efforts, he was rewarded.

[You have slain 12 creatures between levels 9 and 13. 1367 XP awarded.]
[Congratulations! You have reached level 13. 13 AP awarded for use.]

Some of his combat skills needed 15 AP to go up a rank, but some only needed 10. He considered hanging on to the points, but ultimately it felt like a recipe for disaster. His brother's build notes recommended pushing for at least rank 2 in all his combat skills early, but he couldn't bring himself to leave that many points unallocated. He would just boost his stats now and buy the skill rank whole in a few levels. Otherwise it felt like he was wasting the points for however long it took him to actually have enough to spend.

Maybe when he was level 50 and had an overabundance, when each level didn't hugely impact his stats, he'd feel differently. For now, the choice was to increase **[Peripheral Awareness]** or **[Twitch Reflexes]** for 10 or to spend all the points on stats. Considering how much **[Twitch Reflexes]** had saved his ass in that fight against the goblin, and that he would probably find himself in a similar situation sometime soon, he opted to upgrade that to rank 2.

The last 3 AP went into strength, agility, and perception. Points spent but unwilling to venture back onto the trail while the big guy was lurking so close to the end, Luke bailed back into the forest. Overhead, Red circled lazily, no doubt watching for dinner to be served. Sometimes he wondered if the hawk ever caught its own meals anymore.

Considering that Luke could have been that meal if Red had been feeling peckish during their first meeting, he devoted himself to finding something suitably meaty. Though it was getting harder and harder to lure out a meal, Luke didn't consider the effort a waste of time. He needed to eat too, and his attempts at curing meat had so far met with disaster.

That disaster's name was Red. The bird simply ate far too much and was not content to leave scraps of meat hanging about on a drying rack. Luke's attempts to build a fire around the meat to protect it had not been well received. Thus, he was stuck hunting a new meal twice a day if he wanted to eat.

Luke went through the motions, but his mind was elsewhere. Soon enough the food was cooked, overcooked really, and he had done his best to chew it without tasting it. His plastic water bottles, the three that were left at least, were refilled, and Luke retreated to Curt's workshop to get a few hours of sleep.

The Bossmoot started when Gulgok entered the meeting chamber. By rights, as the boss to call for it, it was his duty to host, and he should have been the first there. Considering the subject, he felt it was forgivable that he was late since the very reason was the pale-skinned monster he'd gathered his peers to discuss.

"Took you long enough," Qarsik whined. He was a thin goblin, built for speed and perception. Gulgok never understood how he'd gained control of the Bluerocks. If Qarsik had been a challenger for his title, Gulgok would have gutted him. That just showed how weak the Bluerocks were as a whole.

One thing they did have, the only thing Gulgok cared about right now, was a type of dog they'd bred for tracking. That was the reason he'd called for the Bossmoot. He needed those dogs to find the Day Hunter, and every tribe needed to devote an equal number of warriors to the monster's destruction.

Gulgok ignored the other goblin's complaining and took the final empty seat at the table. Bulgrit stood behind him over his right shoulder, one hand resting on the battle-ax sitting at his waist and his eyes locked on the other bosses' hands, his counterparts from Grimshard and Bluerock.

"You know why we're here," Gulgok said. "What are we going to do about this problem?"

The other two were silent. No one wanted to volunteer their own tribe for the hunt, knowing how many lives it might cost them, that it would erode their own position and possibly weaken their whole tribe enough to be wiped out.

Gulgok felt his temper starting to rise. He was indisputably the most powerful goblin in the valley at level 21. He did not get that way by being even-handed and fair. The other two tribes were going to contribute, or he'd start hunting goblins himself. No doubt he'd be far more effective at it than the Day Hunter was.

"You," he said, jabbing a finger at Qarsik. "Your tribe will find him. You have the means. You will do so. And you, Margl, you will provide elite warriors to help kill the Day Hunter. Am I understood?"

"Or what? You come here to this Bossmoot to issue threats, Gulgok?" Margl snarled at him, rising from his chair and leaning forward over the table.

"It has been a hundred years since the last Day Hunter plagued our people. You remember the tales? They have stayed alive in your tribe, yes?" Gulgok said, also rising from the table.

"I . . . remember."

"Then you know what must be done. The same as our ancestors did. All that is left now is to determine how."

Gulgok was a rather large goblin, and he had no problem using that size to intimidate his cowardly peers. Ha! Peers. He could kill them both in seconds, without even a weapon. He stared at them both and demanded, "Agreed?"

"Agreed," they said sullenly.

"Excellent. Now, how shall we rid ourselves of this problem?"

Name	Luke Bennet
Level	13
XP	7285/8325
AP	0
Bloodline	SysAdmin
Strength	19
Agility	15
Stamina	14
Perception	19
Skills	Mace Mastery (2)
	Sword Mastery (1)
	Peripheral Awareness (1)
	Counter (1)
	Twitch Reflexes (2)
	Survivalist (2)
	First Aid (1)
	Wood Carving (1)
	Leatherworking (2)

Skill	Rank	AP	Prerequisites	Effect
Twitch Reflexes	2	10	Rank 1	Reflexive actions happen at greater speeds

CHAPTER 20

Ever since he'd started putting AP into stats, Luke had stopped getting tired. No matter how much he worked or how heavy the load was, he just didn't get exhausted. He might get worn out for a few minutes after doing something strenuous, but he bounced back almost instantly.

So even though it was an inconvenience, he walked over to the trail before the sun was even up and killed seven earth elementals. He didn't want to push his luck since he planned on coming back later in the day to take out another batch. Unlike everything else, the elementals didn't seem to care about his level. As soon as they sensed him, they moved in to attack.

[You have slain 7 creatures between levels 9 and 12. 699 XP awarded.]

"Just think of it as morning exercise," he told Red when he noticed the bird watching him. "You want some breakfast now?"

He roamed the forest for another hour, trying to spot something to eat. It wasn't the best time of day for it, but he persevered with a mental note to start everything an hour later tomorrow. By the time he was done with the earth elementals, the sun would be up and it would be easier to find something.

One thing about **[Survivalist]** was that it was a very general ability. It had a little bit of knowledge about a lot of different topics but didn't make him an expert in anything. Still, that was more than enough for him to notice something unusual. "There sure are a lot of goblin tracks in the woods," he told Red, who tilted a head at him in response.

"Right? It's strange. They don't usually go this far in, at least not this many of them."

Maybe he'd get some good XP off the patrols. Those were usually easy to take out anymore, even if they got the jump on him. They lacked the quality of level that the earth elementals had, but they made up for it in numbers. At least, if there were as many as all the footprints implied, they would. He just needed to be careful about any of their strong warriors accompanying the patrol.

Luke kept an eye out as he moved but never actually found a single goblin. He arrived at his forest camp half an hour later and stopped, stunned. Everything was destroyed. The hides he'd stretched to dry had been torn down and slashed apart to uselessness. The frames he'd built were little more than kindling. He'd been carving a big wooden statue of Red out of a tree. That had been torn apart. His smoking hut, version four, was gone. Just gone. There was no sign it had been destroyed. The goblins had just picked it up and carried it off, possibly along with the meat he'd had inside. They'd also taken his bag of woodworking tools.

"What the fuck? They smash-and-grabbed me back!"

Red let out an earsplitting screech and took to the air, swiftly gaining altitude and disappearing past the canopy. "Get back here, you lazy bird!" Luke called out. "Help me clean this up!"

A harsh cry rang out through the forest, something that was obviously words but not in any language Luke recognized. Goblins sprang up all around him, most with crossbows pointed his way. "What the hell . . . How?"

His perception had never let him down like that. It was impossible for almost anything to just sneak up on him, let alone over twenty of them. There was just . . . no way. He shook his head. Never mind how it had happened; he needed to escape.

[Twitch Reflexes] proved itself worth the AP to upgrade it as the goblins unleashed their first volley of bolts. In under a second, Luke spun four full revolutions, twisting past bolts and, in three different cases, catching or deflecting them in midair. For all that, he wasn't quite fast enough. Two pierced his coat and sank into his back.

"Son of a bitch!" he screamed as he lurched forward. There was no time to hesitate though. Unlike the ones at the camp, these goblins were not only better shots, but they understood the idea of firing in waves. Only half the goblins had unloaded, and while they were all getting ready to fire another shot, he was faced with the other half.

The second volley hit harder than the first had. Luke was slower and perhaps just less lucky. One bolt sank into his arm, another hit his back, and a third pierced his foot, actually pinning it to the ground. Luke tore himself free, an action that broke the bolt in two and left it stuck in the top of his foot. He didn't even consider fighting back, just darted off as fast as he could into the trees.

Running full speed wasn't possible, even if he was in perfect condition. The forest was too densely packed for that. That was more to the goblins' advantage than his, since even wounded, he was willing to bet he could outrun them. As soon as he ran though, even more goblins that he'd somehow missed popped up around him.

That was where the thick forest worked to his advantage. As long as he avoided any of the clearings, glades, or fields scattered through the trees, the crossbows got a lot less useful. In close combat, he still dominated any goblins he ran across. There were a lot of dings that he ignored as he limped along, knowing full well that there were dozens more goblins behind him.

Luke thought he still had a good chance to outrun them and find a new place to bunker down until he ran across the first goblin with a dog. "Oh shit, of course," he hissed out. The dog howled and leaped forward, but it was too low a level to be a serious threat. He pulped it, then pulped the goblin with it for good measure. Two more dings sounded.

Luke had been about 300 XP short of leveling when the goblins popped up. He'd probably killed enough of them to hit that threshold already, but he hadn't checked since he was busy running for his life. 14 more AP would be handy right now though, so he triggered the notification while he limped along.

[You have slain 11 creatures between levels 5 and 8. 492 XP awarded.]

[Congratulations! You have reached level 14. 14 AP awarded for use.]

One more level until he could upgrade **[Mace Mastery]** again. **[Survivalist]** and **[First Aid]** were both skills he could take, and he suspected he'd probably need the enhanced ranks when he started pulling the bolts out of his body and things got bloody. On the other hand, buffing his stamina now could help him survive.

"Why do I feel like I made this same choice the last time I got shot too?" he muttered.

[First Aid] needed 5 AP to rank up, which would only leave him with 9 free, but that also required things like bandages and salves to be useful. Without supplies, that would be wasted AP. Instead, Luke pumped 6 AP into stamina to bring it up to an even 20, then grit his teeth and started ripping the bolts out. He'd already lost a lot of blood, probably more than enough to pass out back before he'd started gaining levels. Now he just felt a little light-headed.

Pulling the bolts out was a whole new level of pain, worse than when that lightning-fast goblin had sliced open a line on his stomach. Luke took a minute and leaned up against a tree while he recovered. Probably thanks to his stamina, the bleeding wasn't as bad as it could be, but he still needed to do something. He didn't have the tools to stitch his injuries closed, nor did he have any medicine.

In hindsight, not preparing some sort of salve or ointment to put on wounds like this was a mistake. That was something he could have made, but it took time to find the plants and more time to process them. He had too many holes to put pressure on them, especially the one in his foot, which had been steadily pumping blood into his shoe and thoroughly soaking his sock.

Screw it. He wasn't waiting to get **[Life Surge]**. He'd save 9 AP from his next level up, then add it to the full 16 from the one after that so he could buy the skill. He'd just have to put up with having unspent AP for one level. He needed that health regeneration ability.

"Actually, now that I think about it. System, are there other options for healing than **[Life Surge]**?"

"Certainly, Luke. Though, if you're interested in magical healing, I'm afraid 8 AP is too low for the cheapest spell, and you are lacking prerequisite skills to use magic anyway."

"What the hell, magic healing? Why did no one tell me that was an option?"

"You didn't look very deeply into magic when you were first examining the store and never saw the options."

"Goddamn it," Luke snapped. He heaved himself back upright, then winced as pain shot through his foot. "Shit, this is a problem. Okay, walk me through this. Let's say I want to use magic to heal myself. What are the prerequisite abilities?"

"You would need at minimum **[Mana Manipulation]**. Without that skill, it's not possible to shape mana into a spell. That is the only required skill before you could purchase the cheapest healing spell, **[Sustain]**. Given your current condition though, I suspect you are more interested in a spell such as **[Minor Heal]**, which would actively work to convert mana into flesh and muscle tissue."

"Okay, great. How much is **[Mana Manipulation]** to buy?" Luke asked. He limped around a tree and onto a game trail, fully aware of the risks.

"5 AP for the first rank."

"And **[Minor Heal]**?"

"15 AP."

"Jesus, for just the first rank? I guess it is magic though. Fuck."

"Is there anything else you require assistance with?" System asked.

"Not unless you're willing to smite a few goblins for me."

"I am not able to interfere." System hesitated, then added, "If I may though, you should consider activating the ailment section of your status. You might be surprised by the information there."

"The fuck does that mean?" Luke asked. Before System could answer, a long, baying howl went up behind him. It was only a few hundred feet away, and it was quickly answered by many, many more. Luke needed to move faster. "Look, just turn it on so I can see it, okay?"

"As you wish."

A ding announced a new notification, which Luke opened right away.

[Ailment status has been toggled to ON. Change back to OFF? Y/N]

Luke selected no and willed the notification away. He checked his status and found, right under his stats, a new line that read **[Condition: Curse of Obliviousness (2H24M)]**. He stumbled in surprise and grunted painfully when he smacked into a tree branch. There was no explanation about what the hell that curse did, but Luke could take a guess.

That explained how two dozen fucking goblins had gotten the drop on him. They'd planned their whole assault out far too well. Obviously, they were smarter than he'd given them credit for. That meant they were a threat and that he needed to be far more proactive in hunting them if he was going to be stuck in Tenebrous Valley. It would even have the side benefit of giving him the thing he needed most: more XP.

Luke was through screwing around, with waffling back and forth between ideas. It had never been a game, but he'd been going about it half-assed, wasting far too much time relaxing, letting himself get pulled in different directions as new random ideas popped into his head. He had a build plan; he needed to follow it. It was time to give these goblin fuckheads hell.

But first, he needed to survive today. As more hounds started howling around him, Luke wondered how he was going to do that, exactly. Well, he did still have 8 AP. That had to be worth something. If he was going to counter this curse, he could dump it into perception and hope that helped. If he was going to accept that things were going to sneak up on him, agility would be a better route to go. Or he could just keep ahead of them until the curse wore off.

"Fuck it, even split. 3 strength and perception, 2 agility. Sorry, Curt, I know it's not the ratio, but it's kind of an emergency, and I need more of everything. I promise I'll fix it later."

Name	Luke Bennet
Level	14
XP	8476/10332
AP	0
Bloodline	SysAdmin
Strength	22
Agility	17
Stamina	20
Perception	22
Skills	Mace Mastery (2)
	Sword Mastery (1)
	Peripheral Awareness (1)
	Counter (1)
	Twitch Reflexes (2)
	Survivalist (2)
	First Aid (1)
	Wood Carving (1)
	Leatherworking (2)

CHAPTER 21

How in the french fried fuck did they do this so quickly?" Luke demanded as he bounced up and down on an ankle snare. A swipe of his knife was all it took to split the rope holding him upside down to the tree, and he managed to flip around to land upright. He winced in pain as his weight came down on his injured foot.

He supposed he was lucky that he'd come at this trap from the wrong direction and already killed both goblins watching the snare before he'd stepped into it. That wasn't the only trap he'd stumbled into though. Twice he'd triggered blade-throwing wires hidden in tall grass, and once an entire log came swinging down on ropes to blast through at high speed.

He'd barely managed to avoid the log by diving face-first to the ground and hadn't avoided the knife throwers, though one had missed and the other one had just left one more hole in a growing collection. Luke was starting to get dizzy from the blood loss but not so much that he couldn't still swat a goblin down if one was stupid enough to try to get in his face.

The **[Curse of Obliviousness]** had just under an hour left before it wore off. Luke wanted to hole up and wait it out, but every time he tried, more goblins would find him. Those damn hounds were sniffing him out, which probably wasn't hard with all the blood he'd left behind. So much blood, more than he would have thought possible. Stamina had to be replenishing it somehow.

If he was going to get away, he needed to kill the dogs. It was that simple. He was in rough shape, but as long as he didn't run into one of those badass warrior goblins again, he could handle it. From what he remembered the last time he'd run into a goblin handling a dog, they were only around level 5.

Fortunately, it wasn't hard to find them. They were constantly howling and braying at one another. Luke only needed to keep ahead of them for an hour until the curse wore off, then he would turn the tables and start hunting them the other way around. In the meantime, he would avoid leading them to anywhere strategically important to him: namely his brother's workshop.

Hopefully they hadn't already found it like they had his forest camp. It was his last hidden refuge, but he suspected it was safe. If the goblins knew about it, they would have already attacked him there. There was no way they'd managed to booby-trap so much of the forest in just the hour or so he'd been awake.

Luke moved through the underbrush as quietly as he could, eyes peeled and actually focusing instead of just letting perception draw his attention to things. With the debuff on him, he didn't want to risk setting off another trap if he could avoid it. The problem was that the goblins were remarkably good at hiding them, or maybe it was just that hiding trip lines or snares in tall grass and tension wires that threw knives in bushes was really easy to do.

Either way, he moved as fast as he felt safe doing while trying to keep ahead of the goblins. That was an impossibility considering how thickly they were swarming the forest, but the real problem was more that when he encountered another group, he'd kill most of them and then one or two would run off to go get reinforcements.

Sometimes they came back, sometimes they didn't. It was when they didn't show up that Luke got worried. He had some concerns that goblins were massing somewhere and fifty of them were just stalking him, waiting for him to walk into a field so they could surround him. It hadn't happened yet, but that didn't mean it couldn't.

He watched the timer tick down on the curse debuff, noting as it switched to minutes and seconds once it was under an hour. Finally, it fell off, and the world expanded into focus. A thousand details Luke hadn't noticed flooded his mind, and it took him a second to reorient himself. Once he did though, he grinned to himself.

It was time to hunt. And with his perception fully restored, he was able to figure out where the closest dog was. Luke limped along, following his own trail back and easily avoiding a trap while marveling to himself that it was so obvious to see now when mere minutes earlier he'd only bypassed it by sheer luck, never even realizing he'd stepped over it.

As the goblin hunting party closed in on him and, more importantly, as he closed in on them, he took to the trees and pulled a few branches close together to help break up his form. It was trivially easy to hold them in place with one hand, even with his injuries, and his other gripped his mace in eager anticipation.

The goblins pushed through a bush, following a huge mastiff that probably came up to his chest. One thing Luke had found was that in addition to being sensitive to creatures that had far more XP than him, he was also starting to notice when creatures had much less. It was harder to pick out, something just in the background that he had to make a conscious effort to pay attention to, and he couldn't really feel much difference between a level 6 and a level 7.

But one thing he knew was that nothing in this hunting party was strong enough to be a threat. The only thing he needed to make sure of was that he killed the dog first. If the rest of them escaped, well, it wasn't ideal, but it wouldn't bother him too much. He wasn't going to kill all five of them regardless, so he'd just do his best to get as many as possible and not worry if one or two ran.

Luke let go of the branches and dropped, careful to make sure he landed on his uninjured foot first, and brought his mace down on the dog's back. It gave an abbreviated yelp, cut off by its own death. Luke pivoted in place to strike the goblin that had been handling it in the shoulder. He'd been aiming for the head, but it had turned while stumbling backward and was just about out of reach.

The crack spun it to the ground, and he didn't worry about following up. Instead he hopped forward and attacked another goblin, then spun in place to parry one stabbing at his back with a spear. **[Peripheral Awareness]** was his biggest asset now that they were spreading out around him to attack from every side.

The one he'd hit in the shoulder was down and not getting back up anytime soon, though it wasn't quite dead. Luke would need to finish it off when he got a chance. The other three were still alive, and for the moment he was on the defensive. **[Twitch Reflexes]** was causing him problems, trying to force his body to move in optimal ways to dodge attacks and set him up for a devastating **[Counter]**. Normally he'd welcome that, but right now he was injured and not nearly as nimble as his skill wanted him to be.

Luke compensated for that, but it was frustrating to have the skill fighting against him. If he could have toggled it off, he would have. Now that he thought about it, he wondered if that was an option and made a mental note to ask System later. For now, he was fighting defensively, his range of motions limited by the numerous holes the goblins had poked in him.

Two of the goblins screwed up and ended up crossing their spears trying to stab him at the same time. Luke used the tangle to break free of them and focus on the third goblin in the triangle. With the two behind him unable to attack while they freed their weapons, he was easily able to swat the remaining goblin's defense aside and crush it with a single heavy blow.

Luke darted forward to break out of the remaining two goblins' range and pivoted on his good foot to face them. They looked far less sure now, but apparently weren't willing to abandon their still-living companion on the ground. That goblin was weeping softly and clutching at its ruined shoulder. It tried to regain its feet more than once, only to stagger and collapse again.

If the goblins wanted to stay and fight, that was fine by him. He bulled forward, grabbing the haft of one of the spears while he twisted out of the way of the other. A single jerk ripped it free of the goblin and sent it stumbling forward into the range of Luke's attack. And then there was one.

The last goblin threw its spear at Luke with a scream and bolted. Luke didn't even have to move to avoid it; it flew by harmlessly. Instead, he threw the spear he'd taken from the other goblin back. His aim was, unfortunately, not much better, and the goblin disappeared into the brush. Three seconds later, he heard the twang of one of the trip wires going off and saw the goblin flop upward into the air, hanging upside down by its ankle.

Casually, Luke brought his mace down on the head of the wounded goblin as he strode by and retrieved the spear he'd missed with. He came to a stop under the snared goblin, lined the spear up, and thrust its tip into the monster. It took the goblin in the mouth, erupting through the back of its skull and killing it instantly.

Luke checked his notifications individually, curious as to how accurate his guesses about their levels were.

[You have slain Bluerock Mastiff (level 5). 25 XP awarded.]
[You have slain Bluerock Goblin (level 7). 50 XP awarded.]
[You have slain Bluerock Goblin (level 8). 65 XP awarded.]
[You have slain Bluerock Goblin (level 7). 50 XP awarded.]
[You have slain Bluerock Goblin (level 9). 82 XP awarded.]

"Huh, higher than I thought. I'll get a feel for it though. Might be important to be able to judge someday. Hey, System. Got a question for you."

"What can I help with, Luke?" System asked. It appeared right below the corpse still hanging from a rope snare in the tree, heedless of the blood dripping through its ghostly form to pool in the dirt below.

"I'm having an issue fighting with all these injuries. **[Twitch Reflexes]** keeps trying to force me into movements I can't do. Can I toggle it on and off?"

"Unfortunately, that is not possible. As it increases in rank though, and as you learn the limits of the skill and how best to use it, you should find these issues disappearing."

"Well, that's great for future Luke, but I'm in trouble now. There's nothing I can do?"

"I'm sorry. A SysAdmin of your level would not be able to make a change like that."

"Are you saying that a . . . ugh . . . 'purer' bloodline could?"

"Anything is theoretically possible, even the total erasure of the system itself. Whether that is feasible for you personally is something you'll have to discover for yourself as you advance."

"Helpful as always," Luke said.

"Of course," System replied, completely missing the sarcasm. "Is there anything else I can assist you with?"

Luke's head snapped around to focus on the sound of a new dog baying not far away. It was close enough that he wouldn't have much time to set a new ambush, and he wanted a clear battlefield without corpses he had to worry about tripping over.

"No," he said absently to System. "I've got some work to do right now. We can talk later."

Name	Luke Bennet
Level	14
XP	9412/10332
AP	0
Bloodline	SysAdmin
Strength	22
Agility	17
Stamina	20
Perception	22
Skills	Mace Mastery (2)
	Sword Mastery (1)
	Peripheral Awareness (1)
	Counter (1)
	Twitch Reflexes (2)
	Survivalist (2)
	First Aid (1)
	Wood Carving (1)
	Leatherworking (2)

CHAPTER 22

Luke was absolutely fucking exhausted. He was filthy with blood, of which about half was his own. It had taken about five hours before the goblins had given up, and in the meantime, he'd been forced into eight separate fights. Or rather, he'd let eight different hunting parties pursuing him with mastiffs find him, carefully working to make sure only one group at a time caught up to him.

That was not as easy as he'd have liked, since he was leaving a blood trail all over the damn forest. Most of his injuries had eventually slowed to a trickle, some of them bleeding no worse than a fresh nick from shaving. He idly scratched his face, reminded of how itchy it was with the stubble he'd grown in over the last week.

Thanks to the miracle of stats, he was still alive to be exhausted. Otherwise he'd have died in the shattered remains of his campsite when the goblins first popped up. It was a thought he'd had often, and he was reconsidering his brother's build strategy that advised a lower stamina.

Luke pulled his mind back to the present. That last group should have been enough to push him over. He checked his notifications to be sure, but he had a feeling. There had been extra ding in there.

[You have slain 5 creatures between levels 6 and 9. 266 XP awarded.]
[Congratulations! You have reached level 15. 15 AP awarded for use.]

"Perfect," he said to himself. If he still wanted **[Life Surge]**, and he did, that meant he needed to save 9 AP from this level and use the whole 16 AP from his next level up. That left 6 AP, which he decided to divide up. 1 AP went into a skill on his build recommendation list called **[Unarmed**

Martialist] that he'd been putting off because he hadn't seen a lot of use for it when he had his mace.

Supposedly it would also help him with footwork and dodging in addition to giving him the skills to fight bare-handed, but he hadn't seen the use with **[Twitch Reflexes]** already handling a lot of his evasive needs. That skill had utterly failed him while he was fighting wounded, and **[Unarmed Martialist]** was going to fix some of the other skill's blind spots, so he decided it was worth the price.

Hopefully Curt's notes about it were accurate. It was becoming increasingly obvious that he was going to get hurt and that the skills weren't infallible, especially against thinking and reasoning opponents. He didn't have the experience needed to fight against his own skills and strong opponents at the same time, and while fixing that with yet more skills didn't seem like a fantastic idea, he didn't have a better one.

The other 5 AP were going into agility and stamina, 4 into agility and 1 into stamina to bring them both up to 21. If he was being completely honest with himself, part of his stat spread was visual appeal. He liked a lean, well-toned athletic look. If his strength got too far ahead, he started looking bulky. His clothes already didn't fit him that well anymore around his shoulders and biceps, even though he'd just made a new shirt already. Then again, that hadn't really fit him the best to begin with. It was called **[Leatherworking]**, not **[Tailoring].**

His plans to make new ones out of soft, supple leather were shot to hell now. It was going to take a day to rebuild the new frames even if he recovered his tools, which was looking unlikely to happen. Then it would be even more days waiting for everything to dry enough for him to work with it, then however many days it took him to cut and stitch it all together.

Luke would just have to take it one step at a time. His jeans were in relatively good condition, all things considered. One of his shoes was solid, but the other had a pair of matched holes in it. It was still better than being barefoot. His shirt was basically rags at this point, and his coat wasn't much better. Somehow, miraculously, he still had his multi-tool, lighter, and flashlight.

Luke walked while he went over stuff in his head. **[Unarmed Martialist]** was already affecting him in a way that **[Mace Mastery]** hadn't. It seemed to be entwining itself with his agility stat somehow, retraining how he walked and held himself. It was too soon to tell, but he imagined it would increase his coordination in a subconscious way that stats just didn't. Agility helped him hold his balance, helped him make his body move exactly how his brain wanted it to, but **[Unarmed Martialist]** was showing him the best way to move his body.

He regretted not picking it up earlier now that he was experiencing it. "System," he said softly, stopping in place.

"Yes, Luke?"

"Are there other skills like **[Unarmed Martialist]** that would affect how I move?"

"Of course. **[Stealth]** is probably the most commonly chosen skill that changes the user's movements."

"Ah, I see." That wasn't on Curt's list. "Thank you."

"You are most welcome."

Luke killed another few hours doing laps around the forest, but it seemed like the goblins had given up. He wasn't sure if he'd killed all of them or if they'd figured out he was targeting their hunting dogs and pulled them back, or maybe the sun had risen too high and they'd decided to withdraw until the light situation favored them.

He was ready to head back to Curt's workshop and get some sleep, but he needed to do something about the occasional blood spots he was still leaving. That meant finding the stream that ran near his former camp and cleaning up. Between **[Survivalist]** and his own knowledge after spending over a week roaming the valley, Luke had a pretty good idea of where he was and where to go.

If ever there was a spot to be ambushed again, it was where they'd gotten him the first time. Luke obsessively checked his status for any signs of a new curse affliction and traveled both slowly and cautiously the whole way. Once he got there, he started stripping out of his clothes and scrubbing them clean as well as he could. That was mostly a lost cause, as the blood had been setting for hours.

Then he wrung his shirt out and resigned it to its inevitable fate of becoming bandages. It was so ragged now that he didn't get very many full strips of cloth out of it, but there was enough left to bandage his foot, which was honestly the worst of his wounds. The fact that he'd kept walking and fighting on it probably hadn't helped, but he hadn't had much choice.

Cleaned and bandaged as well as a ratty old shirt and rank 1 **[First Aid]** could manage, Luke limped his way back to the cave. He stopped and groaned when he got to the ravine. There was another group of those albino spiderlike people, cave grippers according to his system notifications, coming down the ravine with their latest catch, a trio of shockrack elk. Normally, things that were much lower level than him avoided him, but these particular monsters never seemed to learn.

Luke pulled his mace free and trudged forward. They were all low level and he wasn't afraid of them, but he'd just gotten clean and he was tired. The cave grippers stopped when they noticed him and exchanged glances. They lowered their meals to the ground and arrayed themselves in a defensive semicircle around them.

"Look, guys, can we just not?" Luke asked tiredly. "I'm really not in the mood."

He moved off to the side of the ravine and started walking past them. This was where they'd strike, as soon as he was past and showed them his back. Something in their psychology just wouldn't let them not take a swipe at him, even though they knew he was a much higher level.

Sure enough, **[Peripheral Awareness]** clocked the aggressive first strike as soon as they thought they were behind him. Luke suppressed a sigh and spun on his good foot to lash out one-handed with the mace. Even though he wasn't unarmed, his new skill adjusted the bend in his knee to keep his balance perfect as he extended his arm and threw his weight around behind the swing.

The mace struck the cave gripper's shoulder, blowing it sideways and into a spin that only ended when it crashed into the stone wall ten feet away. A small part of Luke hoped that would be enough to convince the others to reconsider, but he didn't expect it. Four times he'd been forced to fight them when going back and forth from the workshop, and every time, they fought to the death. The closest to retreat they ever got was that very first encounter when they'd brought back that tank of a spider.

He figured it was some kind of territory thing, and that since he kept killing the new groups that tried to take over the dried-out ravine, more of them were going to come up from whatever depths they lived at to try to fill the void. As tired of it as he was, he tried to think of it as a bit of free XP every other day.

The battle ended shortly after that, with no more than one or two strikes to kill each one. It was kind of interesting to see how **[Unarmed Martialist]** modified the way his body moved, often shifting his stance to allow for a greater variety of follow-up motions that let him react to attacks without having to predict them. With so many more options open to him, **[Twitch Reflexes]** got a lot more flexible and stopped trying to tear his wounds open again to make him dodge a certain way.

[You have slain 5 creatures between levels 5 and 6. 147 XP awarded.]

A part of him wanted to save the carcasses of the three elk, but since he no longer had his stretching racks, he was back to rigging up something using tree branches. It hadn't worked very well the first time, but he'd been too inexperienced to realize it. He could use some of the meat too, but he didn't feel like going back out into the forest to get firewood to cook it, and it wasn't like he could store it in the fridge.

In the end, he left it all behind. All he really wanted was sleep. Luke approached the crevice that led up to the workshop, climbed up to his place of relative safety, and passed out on the stone bench that served as his bed.

* * *

"You said it would be blind," Gulgok snarled at Blackfut.

Unimpressed, the shaman corrected him, "No, I said its perception would be reduced. Its level must have been high enough that the curse wasn't enough to completely blind it."

Gulgok hated his shaman, not just because the smaller and weaker goblin refused to cower and obey, but because of those strange powers he had. He'd put almost all his AP into esoteric skills that built up to something formidable, something that couldn't be beaten with mere strength of arms.

Except the Day Hunter had overcome the curse, at least enough to keep some measure of awareness. If it could do it, then Gulgok could do it too. And if Gulgok could do it, then maybe it was time Blackfut learned to fear and respect him in the proper amounts.

But no, not yet, not while the Day Hunter was still breathing. If the damn pink-skinned monster had only shown up at its camp an hour or two earlier before the sun had come up, they'd have had it. They'd waited for hours throughout the night, Bluerock hunting parties scouring the forest, but in the end, the Day Hunter had walked right into the ambush they'd set up, only late enough that daylight had affected the Grimshard marksgoblins' aim.

Or at least that's what Margl claimed. More like his goblins couldn't hit a two-ton raccoon so fat that it weighed three tons. Once they'd killed the Day Hunter, Gulgok was thinking it was time to reorganize the valley's hierarchy. Bluerock had lost enough goblins already that their only choices were to be absorbed into Bloodbite or be exterminated.

Once he'd taken care of them, he'd finish off Grimshard and be the sole boss left. And then, when all the threats were wiped out and his power was consolidated, that shaman would get what was coming to him.

He just had to take care of the Day Hunter, and it would all be his.

Name	Luke Bennet
Level	15
XP	10569/12642
AP	9
Bloodline	SysAdmin
Strength	22
Agility	21
Stamina	21
Perception	22
Skills	Mace Mastery (2)
	Sword Mastery (1)
	Unarmed Martialist (1)
	Peripheral Awareness (1)
	Counter (1)
	Twitch Reflexes (2)
	Survivalist (2)
	First Aid (1)
	Wood Carving (1)
	Leatherworking (2)

Skill	Rank	AP	Prerequisites	Effect
Unarmed Martialist	1	1	None	Gain knowledge of a fighting style that doesn't rely on weapons with a focus on superior footwork, dodging, and counterattacks

CHAPTER 23

A few times in Luke's life, he'd ended up napping for a few hours in the evening, only to wake up and have no idea what day it even was. That intense feeling of disorientation from being off his normal sleep schedule, not knowing if it was day or night or how long he'd slept, was something that had stayed with him.

That was how he felt when he woke up. It didn't help that he was sleeping inside a cave that never saw a single ray of sunlight. It didn't help that the more his stamina went up, the less he was sleeping each day and the more his normal rhythm got messed up. And it certainly didn't help that he felt more exhausted after he woke up than he did when he laid down.

He knew he was starving and that he was parched. There was no food, but he did have two plastic bottles left that had survived through everything. He forced himself upright and rummaged through his homemade backpack for them. Drinking both made him feel a little bit better, but he needed food.

Luke took stock of himself. The injuries were not precisely gone, but he was feeling a lot better. His foot was tender, but he could walk without limping. While he wasn't at 100 percent, he felt a lot more confident now than he had during yesterday's fighting. Or maybe it was two days ago now. He couldn't rightly tell and since there was no one to consult with, he guessed he'd never know for sure how long he'd slept.

Or wait, yes there was. "System, how long was I asleep?"

"Twenty-one hours, Luke."

"Thank you, System."

"You're welcome."

That little mystery solved, he checked his status to make sure he wasn't cursed, though he had no idea how something like that would even happen. It had become reflexive while he was fighting goblins, and it seemed like a good habit to be in, so even though he knew there was logically no way a goblin had snuck in, cursed him, and then left again, he didn't judge himself too harshly for confirming.

The bodies had disappeared from the ravine, which didn't surprise Luke. He thought the cave monsters might be cannibals, since he almost never saw anything else in the cave. Even if he was wrong, something was absconding with the bodies he left behind every time they attacked him. He hadn't ever actually seen it happen, but all things considered, it seemed like a reasonable explanation to him.

Idly, he wondered if he could find his own shockrack elk. Those were probably about the best type of meat he'd had so far, even with his limited cooking skills. It was kind of like beef, only a bit sweeter and it made his mouth tingle. He imagined if he ate it raw enough, it would make his hair stand on end.

It was with the utmost caution that Luke walked out of the cave. He half expected goblins to pop up from behind every single bush and shoot him again, but it looked like his efforts to protect the location of Curt's workshop were successful. Still, he reminded himself that it was better to assume it had been compromised and that the goblins simply hadn't struck yet than it was to assume they couldn't find him.

He needed a full 2000 XP to level up again, and Luke was determined to get it before he started going after the goblins directly. The next level would give him what he needed to finally have a way to heal himself, something he'd proven he was in dire need of. After that, he was going after those little fuckers hard. Maybe they'd give him the levels he needed to beat that stupid-big earth elemental and finally get the hell out of this place.

Luke took some game trails that led in generally the direction of the pass with frequent detours into fields or even just through some brush. While he walked, he gathered up some deadwood to use for a small fire and kept an eye out for something furry to eat. As usual, most of the low-level monsters avoided him rather than attacking, but eventually he stumbled across a family of bark-ripper squirrels that tried to swarm him. **[Unarmed Martialist]** proved once again that Luke had been foolish not to take it sooner, and he killed all four of them in moments with his bare hands.

[You have slain 4 creatures between levels 2 and 5. 63 XP awarded.]

"Huh . . . Cool." Luke looked down at his hands and flexed his fingers. His knuckles stung a little bit, but that faded immediately. The squirrels were big enough that he thought they'd still be fine to skin and eat, something he wasn't sure he'd be able to claim if he'd used his mace. That would have gone about three steps beyond tenderizing the meat.

Twenty minutes later, the squirrels were almost done cooking, and Luke felt a familiar tingle in the pit of his stomach. He looked up and smirked at the sight of Red swooping down to land nearby. "And where have you been?" he asked the bird. "I could have used some help against all of those goblins the other day."

Red, perhaps feeling no need to defend itself, simply cocked its head to the side and turned its gaze to the squirrel meat. Luke was determined not to burn it this time, but it was difficult to get it cooked evenly without burning anything, despite how diligently he attended it. "You want some? I don't think birds are supposed to eat cooked meat."

Red screeched at that, and Luke shrugged. "Up to you, I guess. Don't blame me if you get sick."

He took the rawest squirrel of the batch and stuck the stick it was on off to the side. Red hopped forward with a quick flap of its wings and landed on the ground, where it picked at the meat and tore it free.

"I'm with you there, bud," Luke said. He didn't even wait for the meat to cool before he started eating it. "Not too bad."

It wasn't too burnt, and starvation was a spice that made everything taste better. Luke scarfed down two of them and was eyeing up the third when he caught Red watching him. "What?" Luke said. "We gonna throw down over this squirrel?"

The hawk flapped its wings in a few powerful beats and lifted itself back into the air. It circled once overhead and then flew off over the trees. Luke just snorted and shook his head. "My squirrel," he muttered, taking a bite.

The basic necessities of survival met, Luke made a beeline for the pass leading out of the valley to get his morning ten or twelve elemental kills in. The entire time, he kept checking his status screen and watching for ambushes, until finally when he was almost there, he said, "System, can we just set it up so that if there's a change in my status, I'll get a notification to alert me?"

"Of course, Luke. It's done. Would you like to use a different audio tone to mark this as a priority notification?"

"Uh, yes. That's a good idea." It would have been better if System had recommended a status-change notification itself without Luke having to think of it first, or if the system just did that by default without it having to be changed. Though, come to think of it . . . "Is this something anyone could change?"

"I'm afraid not. Only someone with SysAdmin access can customize how they interface with the system."

"Ah, I see. And that's not common, I'm assuming."

"Nobody who has been born on Aros has ever had the bloodline you possess," System told him. "Only the other off-worlders who came before you did."

"Well, I guess that's why they call it a bloodline."

There was some bullshit going on there that Luke wasn't smart enough to figure out but wasn't stupid enough to miss. That was a problem for future Luke though, as present Luke had his own issues to deal with. He approached the trail at a run, wary as always of possible ambushes, though he was also a lot more confident in his ability to dodge five or six bolts coming at him all at once now.

The first elemental pulled itself out of the ground a minute or two after he arrived, and Luke promptly smashed it to pieces. A ding sounded in his mind. Thirty seconds later another elemental appeared, this time from the cliff wall.

"Why do you guys do this?" Luke asked it as it approached him. "I mean, you weren't that strong when we were the same level, and now I've got a few on you, but you always just keep running in like lemmings. No hesitation, no retreat, no strategy. Don't get me wrong, I appreciate you delivering XP to me, but I mean, why?"

It was kind of frustrating. He wanted to leave the valley, not fight goblins. Even with their recent ambush, if the elementals would just let him go, he would leave. If he'd thought he had a chance against that big one, he'd be on his way out. The only reason he wasn't trying was that it hadn't yet failed to arrive and try to kill him every time he set foot on the trail.

It must have been sleeping today though. Two elementals turned into five, and Luke started to backpedal closer to the base of the trail. Five turned into ten, and he hovered near the boulder, ready to make a break for it. Ten turned into twenty, and there was still no sign of it. At twenty-three, he was considering the wisdom of making a run up the pass when the ground shifted and it started to emerge behind him.

"No, you fucking don't," Luke snarled. He broke into a sprint and leaped over its still-forming head to land feetfirst against the boulder at the base of the trail, then push off that and roll across the dirt into the valley. Luke was back on his feet in a flash and already putting distance between him and the giant earth elemental, just in case today was the day it decided to follow him down.

As always though, no elemental crossed that invisible line past the boulder, and that included the big one. It didn't make sense to him, but he was content to abuse the fact as much as he could. In this shithole of a world where everything was a life-and-death struggle, Luke had no compunctions about cheating or abusing video game logic to get ahead.

Once he was back in the cover of the trees and sure he was safe from any goblin hunting parties that might happen to be nearby, he checked his notifications. As expected, his level up was there.

[You have slain 23 creatures between levels 9 and 13. 2825 XP awarded.]
[Congratulations! You have reached level 16. 16 AP awarded for use.]

Finally, he could take it. He spent all 25 AP on **[Life Surge]**, then immediately triggered the ability. For about thirty seconds, he felt like he could jump to the moon, knock over a tree with his bare hands, and run a hundred laps around the entire valley without stopping. All the aches and pains he'd accumulated from the fight were gone; all the half-healed wounds from the other day sealed closed.

Luke felt fantastic for that entire thirty seconds. Then he crashed.

It was like he hadn't eaten in a year, and he was all of a sudden so hungry that he was considering gnawing on some leaves or tree bark. He tromped through the forest, uncaring about stealth and in fact hoping that something would attack him. He guzzled down any sort of berry he could find, hardly even aware of the idea that they might be poisonous. All that mattered was getting food in his stomach.

While he foraged like a rampaging bear, Luke was reminded of the second half of the skill's warning: that he would be tired as well. He kept enough of a presence of mind to turn his path back toward the cave, though he knew he wasn't going back without getting something to eat.

He came across an apple tree, and even though the fruits were stunted, bitter things, he ate two dozen of them before it even started to take the edge of his hunger. That cleared his mind up enough to realize that his stomach was not going to thank him for the last hour or so of his life.

He wasn't feeling as tired as he'd been afraid he'd be, so he diverted course toward his favorite stream and started gathering supplies to cook another meal. He just needed to find it first. Then he was going to spend the rest of the day hanging around his favorite tree, which had wide, thick, flat leaves, and hope for the best.

His stomach gurgled, and Luke started walking faster.

Name	Luke Bennet
Level	16
XP	13457/15275
AP	0
Bloodline	SysAdmin
Strength	22
Agility	21
Stamina	21
Perception	22
Skills	Mace Mastery (2)
	Sword Mastery (1)
	Unarmed Martialist (1)
	Life Surge (1)
	Peripheral Awareness (1)
	Counter (1)
	Twitch Reflexes (2)
	Survivalist (2)
	First Aid (1)
	Wood Carving (1)
	Leatherworking (2)

Skill	Rank	AP	Prerequisites	Effect
Life Surge	1	25	None	Tap into your deepest reservoirs of energy, spending vital life energy to increase speed and power and ignore pain. You will regenerate from wounds rapidly until the effect expires, at which time you will need extra food and sleep to regain the spent energy.

CHAPTER 24

As far as Luke could tell, goblins were nocturnal. They could operate in the day, but they preferred the dark, and the weaker ones had trouble seeing in bright light. He supposed if they pumped up their perception stats high enough, they'd overcome that issue, but as a general trend, most goblins didn't seem to do that.

That was why Luke waited for the sun to be at its peak before he went hunting. There was a dedicated tracking skill that probably would have served him better, but **[Survivalist]** had enough general knowledge of the outdoors packed into it for him to figure out which way tracks were heading. Since they were the only bipeds he'd seen in the whole valley, he felt it was safe to assume that any tracks he found that weren't his own distinctive waffle boot prints were theirs.

Unless they decided to make another concentrated push today, he doubted he'd find many in the forest. No, what he was looking for was some indication about which caves would make the best hunting grounds, where to set up his own ambushes. He lacked the tools to make anything as intricate as the goblins had used on him, but that was fine. He could kill them himself once he found them.

He scoured the forest, even found a few goblins out and about, killed them, of course, and followed tracks back to various caves. It seemed like most of the goblins were on the west and southwest sides of the valley, with a few scattered ones hailing from the north caves. It was no wonder Curt had chosen one to the east for his workshop.

Luke had a problem with trying to hunt them: his level was too high. It didn't stop him from killing them when he caught up with them, but the little shits started rabbiting as soon as he got close, and the more that happened, the more they got away. Worse, some sort of huge hunting party was roaming the woods, at least thirty goblins strong. There were a few of those warriors in there too, not quite as strong as him but more numerous.

That wasn't the fight Luke was looking for. He knew he needed to find smaller groups to pick off and whittle down numbers, but the goblins knew it too and were denying him that tactic. The trade-off was that they weren't likely to run him down as one big group rumbling through the forest while going slow and making lots of noise. They didn't have any more dogs to track him either, so he felt safe circling wide around them and watching for goblins that strayed too far away.

Getting to them before they could raise an alarm was a different matter. The first time, he got a clean kill in, practically smacking its head off its shoulders before it even realized he was there. The second time, the goblin was about a hundred feet away from the main host and realized Luke was nearby instantly. It immediately ran back and started making noise, which caused all the goblins to start looking in his general direction.

"Damn it, this isn't working. System! Is there any way to hide my XP count so they won't feel me coming?"

"There are several stealth-related skills that do this to some degree. Most suppress XP sensing as a side effect of their attempts to hide the user but do so only imperfectly. The only skill that completely blocks other creatures from sensing your XP will also stop you from sensing theirs. It is known as **[XP Mask]** and costs 20 AP to acquire."

Luke didn't like the sound of that. He still wanted to get a rough sense of when other creatures were near him, especially if they were stronger than him. **[Stealth]** was not on his brother's build, but he was already diverging anyway with the way he was buffing his stats. "How much does **[Stealth]** cost?"

"3 AP for the first rank. This would reduce your effective XP amount by approximately ten percent as long as the other life-form is unaware of your presence. It will do nothing to hide it once you have been discovered. The amount of XP you can hide goes up with each rank, among other benefits."

"I guess that's going on the list then," Luke said. He didn't see any other way to do what he needed to do. There was no way he was going to sneak up on any of those low-level goblins as things currently stood. For the time being, he wasn't going to make any progress in the forest.

But then, if all these goblins were up aboveground, that must have meant there were fewer in the tunnels. It was time to put all the work he'd spent the morning doing to good use.

The tunnels went deeper than he'd thought they would, but Luke no longer needed light to see. The route was straightforward, which wasn't to say there weren't side tunnels or forks, but that the goblins had taken pains to mark the way. At first, he was suspicious of traps. He was, after all, the enemy.

But no, they apparently had uncontested control of their tunnels and had taken the time and effort to smooth out the paths and mark them with odd little symbols carved into the stone. Luke had no idea what they said, but it was easy enough to find the next one in the chain.

The first defensive outpost was about a quarter of a mile away from the surface. It consisted of a wooden barricade spanning the width of the tunnel with slots in it at four and eight feet. The goblins manning it obviously felt him coming because, as soon as they had a clear line of sight, they started shooting at him.

[Twitch Reflexes] had no trouble countering projectiles coming from so far away, and the goblins themselves weren't that accurate. Those crossbows they'd mass-produced really were garbage that way, and after watching them shoot so many bolts in his direction, Luke no longer felt bad about having trouble firing them accurately himself.

He charged the barricade through a hundred feet of straight tunnel so fast that the goblins didn't have time to get off a second volley before he impacted the wood. It shuddered against his body blow but held. Behind it, panicked goblin screams echoed down the tunnel, and the sounds of at least two pairs of feet pattered away from him.

Luke took his mace in both hands and swung at the barricade. Wood splinters went flying, and the head of his weapon punched clean through. He ripped it back out and swung again, and again. On the fifth swing, he'd ripped open a hole wide enough to see through. A screeching goblin jumped in front of the hole and fired off a crossbow from point-blank range.

"Holy shit!" Luke yelped as he fell flat on his ass. The bolt skimmed by and bounced off the ceiling behind him, thankfully missing him completely. He scrambled to his feet and jabbed the mace straight forward to smack into the goblin's chest, then resumed battering the barricade until it collapsed.

The goblins had all fled, all but the one he'd struck. Luke casually finished it by smacking his mace into its face as he walked by and received the confirmation ding to let him know it was dead. Then he sprinted down the tunnel after the runners. Normally, he'd have no problems catching up to them, but the tunnel's ceiling kept getting lower and lower, forcing him to hunch as he moved.

He still thought he was outrunning them, but then he found a new barricade blocking the tunnel. This time, there were four goblins standing in front of it, all of them frantically pounding at the wood and babbling in their own language.

They turned at Luke's approach but were too slow to react to him. He killed them, one after another, without any interference from the goblins behind the barricade. It wasn't until he smashed it down that he realized they'd all fled before he'd even arrived.

The tunnels got far more confusing after that. They crossed over one another, forming intersections at seemingly random locations and, if he wasn't mistaken, sometimes looping over top of and under one another in a giant rats' warren. Every now and then he'd find little chambers off the tunnels, the entrances usually covered with pieces of cloth. Inside would be furniture.

He'd finally found their village, but he didn't find many goblins. They'd all known he was coming and fled from him, which was beyond frustrating. He was trapped in this damn valley, a bunch of goblins wanted to kill him, and when he took the fight to their homes, they all ran in every direction. There was no winning!

Then he turned a corner and found eight goblins in front of him. Half were kneeling, and half were standing behind them. All of them had cross-bows pointed his way. A ninth goblin behind them snapped out something that Luke took to be "Fire!" and they all shot at him.

He didn't try to dodge through that storm of bolts. Instead, he just took a single step backward and let them all bounce off the tunnel wall. Then he was back around the corner and charging as fast as he could with such limited overhead clearance.

Rather than panicking, the goblins all held their ground and reloaded. There was no way they were going to get off a second round before he reached them, but the lead goblin was smirking as he watched Luke run.

They knew something, something that they thought he didn't, something that would turn this around. He could feel their levels; none were above 10 or 11. If he reached them, it was all over. So then, they thought they had some-thing that would stop him from getting that far, and knowing goblins, it was probably a trap of some sort.

Luke didn't see any trip lines or false floors. There were no holes in the walls to fire poison-tipped darts at him. Whatever the trap was, he wasn't going to spot it in the next one and a half seconds before he made contact. So he did the only thing he could think of.

Luke leaped forward, stretching his body just about horizontal and with his mace held in front of him with both hands. His leap carried him into the front rank of goblins and over whatever triggers would set off their traps. He bowled the whole group over, and even though it was eight against one, all he had to do was thrash around with his superior strength and they started dying.

The leader took one look at the chaotic melee and ran, but Luke scooped up one of the few crossbows that had been reloaded, sighted it as best he could, and fired. It didn't hit the goblin center mass, no surprise there. What it did do was sink into the goblin's calf muscle, an arguably even better shot considering his goal was to keep it from running away.

Luke crushed the remaining goblins, got bit once on the arm by a particularly ferocious one, and extracted himself from the pile. He only counted seven dings, so one of them was playing possum on him, but he'd sort that out after he killed the runner.

Luke advanced down the tunnel, caught up with the goblin frantically hobbling away, and crushed its skull with a single horizontal swipe that splattered it against the stone wall. Then he went back to the pile and calmly started crushing heads on the bodies too. It only took two before the living goblin bolted.

Unfortunately for it, it ran directly into the trap that Luke had avoided, and a set of wide pendulum-style blades dropped down from the ceiling. It was most definitely dead, but Luke didn't get a notification for it. "Huh," he said. "Interesting. You'd think it would at least give me half credit."

Shaking his head, he moved deeper into the goblin village.

Name	Luke Bennet
Level	16
XP	14310/15275
AP	0
Bloodline	SysAdmin
Strength	22
Agility	21
Stamina	21
Perception	22
Skills	Mace Mastery (2)
	Sword Mastery (1)
	Unarmed Martialist (1)
	Life Surge (1)
	Peripheral Awareness (1)
	Counter (1)
	Twitch Reflexes (2)
	Survivalist (2)
	First Aid (1)
	Wood Carving (1)
	Leatherworking (2)

CHAPTER 25

It got easier to navigate the tunnels when Luke started thinking of them as streets and giving them names, though *easier* was a relative term. So much of it looked alike that it was by no means simple to determine where he was at, but after half an hour spent wandering around, he thought he had a pretty decent mental map of the place.

What he didn't have was a pile of notifications about all the goblins he'd killed, mostly because he was having problems finding any goblins. The only things he'd found were abandoned chambers and more booby traps. They were a lot easier to spot when he wasn't charging a firing squad, and he'd still missed one. **[Twitch Reflexes]** saved his ass there, and Luke considered that it might be time to push it up another rank with his next level.

His explorations eventually saw him walking into a big cavern, probably four of five hundred feet across and with a ceiling twenty feet overhead. Wary of a trap, Luke scanned the outer edges for anything waiting to ambush him. There was no movement, and he cautiously stepped into it. It was nice to be able to stand up straight for the first time since he'd started his spelunking mission.

The cavern had two balconies ringing it, a feature that he kept a close eye on since he couldn't tell if any goblins were crouched there. There was enough room for a hundred of them to be hiding up out of sight, but it was an easy thing to confirm. He flexed his legs and jumped the eight feet he needed to reach the first balcony. From his new vantage point, he could see that it was empty.

The second balcony was directly overhead and required a bit of acrobatics to reach, but Luke was so strong now that reaching up to grab the edge and doing a one-armed pull-up to haul his body up wasn't any harder than taking the stairs. That balcony was empty too. He walked its length, noted that every twenty or thirty feet there was another room carved out of the stone, and that like everywhere else, it was empty.

Luke lapped the entire cavern twice, once on each balcony, before he returned to ground level. As always, there was plenty of evidence that the goblins had left in a hurry but no sign of where they'd gone. It wasn't until he got down to the ground floor that he finally saw something interesting. After yet another paranoid sweep of the area to confirm that nothing was liable to jump him while he was distracted, Luke returned to a spot on the wall.

In front of him was a metal door, remarkable both for being a huge chunk of metal and for being the only door he'd come across the entire time he was underground. Not only was it metal, but the stone around it had been carved square to accommodate it being there. That was entirely unique. The few barricades Luke had run into had been patchy, ill-fitted things with plenty of gaps and holes around the edges.

There was no handle on it, no latch or keyhole. If not for the fact that he could see the hinges, he would have thought it was an iron panel stuck to the wall. He had no tool for punching through steel other than brute force, and he suspected it might be a lot more work than he was willing to go through to make that happen.

Fortunately, goblins weren't good architects and didn't understand why the hinges went on the inside. Luke rummaged through some of the abandoned chambers until he found a thin piece of metal, then used that to pop the pins off the hinges. The door didn't exactly swing wide-open, but it did fall out of place a little bit, enough for him to get his fingers around it and pull it out of the way.

Behind it was a tunnel and, for the first time, noise. It was maybe ten feet wide but only six feet high. The ceiling hanging so low over his head was annoying but better than being hunched over again. He made his way forward, mace in hand and eyes peeled for traps and ambushes.

Every time he found a new tunnel, he wondered if this was going to be the time the goblins jumped out and attacked him. Every time, he was disappointed, though sometimes there was a nice trap to liven things up. But there was something at the end of this one; he could hear it.

He followed the tunnel as it curved downward in a spiral until it eventually opened to a great room, almost as big as the cavern he'd come from. He'd come in near the top, and there was a sloping path that followed the curve of the room until it reached ground level. There were probably a hundred goblins there, but they didn't look like the ones he'd been fighting. Most of them were under two feet in height, and he doubted they weighed even thirty pounds.

There were a few that were normal sized, but they all seemed to be in a daze and covered in . . . slime?

He wasn't sure, but he thought he might have found a goblin nursery. For the first time since he'd been shoved into this world, Luke found himself with a moral quandary. Every single goblin he'd met had been a murderous little asshole, and he hadn't had any guilt about killing them. This wasn't what he was expecting though, and now he wasn't sure what to do.

While he stood there contemplating the ethical ramifications of turning to the dark side and the irony of his own name, one of the tiny goblins let out a shriek and started running in his direction. Immediately, a hundred faces turned in his direction. The adult goblins stared at him blankly, but the kids went berserk. A tide of two-foot terrors swarmed up the ramp leading to him.

Luke took an involuntary step back into the tunnel and spent a precious second trying to figure out what to do. At first glance, it looked like baby goblins were tiny little murder machines, even more vicious than their progenitors. Then the first one reached him and jumped a full five feet into the air, a feat of agility he'd only seen matched by one of the adults.

Almost reflexively, Luke swatted it with his mace. It bounced off the wall and rolled several times before coming to its feet. Fangs bared, it charged right back in. "What the fuck?!" Luke yelped as he danced backward to avoid its snapping jaws. Any normal goblin would have had its head splattered from either the mace or from the wall, but this one just bounced off both like a rubber ball and came right back at him.

He swung at it again, this time like he was wielding a golf club, and threw it back thirty or forty feet to splatter across the far wall. Except that, once again, it just bounced right off it and fell into the swarm below. He lost track of it as more of them reached him. With him backpedaling the whole way, he fended off their attacks.

Luke reached the main cavern again and twisted his way through the door. Four of the minigoblins leaped through before he managed to shove it closed and drop one of the hinge pins back into place. He could hear the rest of them bouncing against the door as they charged it, a relentless staccato rhythm of blind rage.

There was no time to put the rest of the pins in, and Luke just hoped the door would hold while he dealt with the four that had followed him through. They were already coming for his back, but with room to fight, it was a lot easier to keep them at bay. It was like being up to bat, except the ball was two feet tall and trying to rip his throat out.

He found he had better luck with overhead strikes doing damage as long as he followed through and caught them between the ground and his weapon. If he gave them any room, the little fuckers just bounced away, completely unharmed. For the first time since he'd gotten the mace, he wished he had something with an edge on it.

It was easy enough to keep them at bay simply by swatting them across the room, but that was a losing strategy. He only had to miss once and he'd have a shark mouth of teeth latched on to him, and even if he didn't ever miss, he would get tired eventually. Maybe they would too, but so far they weren't showing any signs of slowing down.

Even the ones with the scrapes from where he'd managed to spike them straight into the ground were still going full tilt. Luke needed to change the game somehow, and the easiest way to do that was to change up his weapon. He leaped up to the balcony overhead and raced across its length, trying to find the room he'd seen that had a small table in it.

He spotted it about a third of the way around the circle and promptly smashed it with his mace. Shards of wood went flying everywhere, leaving him with several jagged wooden legs. Luke scooped them up and returned to the main area, where he found three of the minigoblins had made their way up and were hot on his trail. Luke held the leg with the best point in front of him like a fencer and waited for the goblin to jump.

Then he angled the point in and let it impale itself on the impromptu stake. He'd been afraid it would just bounce off like it did against walls, but between its momentum and the smaller surface area, there was enough pressure to puncture the little bastard. It squealed in what he hoped was pain and deflated like a rubber ball full of gray-green pus.

"What the fuck?" Luke said as the monster turned into a goblin-shaped sac and the ground was covered in the watery liquid. A ding sounded off in his head, confirming to him that he'd gotten the kill.

He didn't have time to check it before another minigoblin reached him. Luke shook the flesh balloon off the jagged table leg and lined himself up for the next one. Predictably, it popped itself too. The third and fourth somehow arrived at the same time, which he handled by simply sidestepping them both and stabbing one from behind.

The damn table leg broke when it rammed into the stone though, and the other ones he had sadly weren't nearly as sharp. Luke picked the best out of the lot and waited for the minigoblin to circle back around again. When it leaped at him, he rammed it with the jagged edge and made sure to take it all the way to the wall so that it would be pinned there and the wood would puncture it.

Four dings meant four kills, and Luke was safe for the moment. He immediately opened his notifications to see what the hell those things were.

[You have slain Proto-Gobling (level 4). 16 XP awarded.]
[You have slain Proto-Gobling (level 4). 16 XP awarded.]
[You have slain Proto-Gobling (level 5). 25 XP awarded.]

[You have slain Proto-Gobling (level 4). 16 XP awarded.]

"System, what the hell is a proto-gobling?" Luke asked.

"The progenitor species that create goblin offspring. Goblins do not reproduce sexually or asexually. Instead, a proto-gobling will grow a goblin inside it, somewhat similar to the cancerous growths that humans die from. In this case, the growth, or goblin, is passed after roughly two months. As long as the proto-gobling has a ready source of food, it will continue to grow new goblins inside it and pass them indefinitely."

"And . . . it's not a goblin itself? Why not?"

"As you have seen, the species itself is very rubbery, not at all sapient, and knows no emotions except for hunger and rage. Proto-goblings will even eat the goblins that grow from them if they go long enough without food."

"This is beyond fucked up," Luke muttered. "And also not why I'm here. Where are the actual goblins that have been trying to kill me?"

As if on cue, six goblins appeared at the far end of the cavern. All of them had crossbows, and all of them were high level. Luke grinned and grabbed his mace in both hands.

Name	Luke Bennet
Level	16
XP	14383/15275
AP	0
Bloodline	SysAdmin
Strength	22
Agility	21
Stamina	21
Perception	22
Skills	Mace Mastery (2)
	Sword Mastery (1)
	Unarmed Martialist (1)
	Life Surge (1)
	Peripheral Awareness (1)
	Counter (1)
	Twitch Reflexes (2)
	Survivalist (2)
	First Aid (1)
	Wood Carving (1)
	Leatherworking (2)

CHAPTER 26

The goblins hadn't seen him yet, a fact Luke fully planned to use to his advantage. He might not have had an actual **[Stealth]** skill, but his agility was higher than their perception, and that had to count for something. That combined with the fact that he was up on the balcony and had a bit of cover from the railing made him think he had good odds of getting the jump on them.

No doubt the goblins knew he was there, somewhere. He had too much XP to avoid being noticed, but they probably wouldn't know exactly where. The goblins spread out into a loose semicircle, crossbows held at the ready. A seventh goblin followed in behind them, this one holding what appeared to be a mutant, roided-out version of a crossbow, so big that it looked ridiculous in the goblin's arms. There were two bows stacked on top of each other, and even from across the chamber, he could see that the bolts were three times thicker than standard.

Before Luke could close in, there was a thump. He paused and cocked his head to the side, unsure what he was hearing. Another thump echoed through the cavern. The goblins were looking around now too. One of them said something and pointed. In unison, the rest turned their crossbows in the same direction.

Thump. Thump. Thump thump.

Luke didn't have an angle on whatever the goblins were looking at, but he knew. The door was still locked, but he'd only replaced one hinge pin. The proto-goblings were pummeling it from the inside, and it was giving way.

The thump turned into a squeal as metal dragged across stone. Seconds later, the first proto-gobling bounced into view. It was running at speed, directly toward the group of goblins on the ground floor. The one with the mutant crossbow snapped out something, and two goblins shot it. Immediately, the proto-gobling flopped down onto the floor, nothing more than a pile of loose skin and pus-like fluid.

That did not seem to calm the goblins down though, and Luke had no trouble imagining why. If one of those little rubber-ball, bouncing fucks was loose, the rest would be right behind it. Sure enough, not two seconds later four more came into view. They closed in on the goblins at a full sprint, heedless and uncaring of their losses as the goblins shot them.

Dozens more came pouring out into the cavern, and the goblins shrieked in fear. The one with the huge crossbow started bellowing over the noise, but it was rapidly losing control of the situation, and it looked like it knew it. Soon enough, the goblin was resorting to smacking its minions to get their attention and yelling directly into their ears.

Far too slowly, the goblins formed up and started backing out of the cave. In Luke's opinion, that was the best possible tactic for them, since it allowed them to concentrate their fire in a single direction instead of having proto-goblings coming at them from every which way. He honestly wished them the best in slaughtering the miniature goblins, if only because he would eventually need to make his way out of the large chamber himself.

He was just lucky that with a more immediate target available to fixate on, the proto-goblings didn't go exploring. Instead they hurled themselves at the goblins in waves and died just as quickly. Judging by the screams Luke heard though, he didn't think the goblins were having it all their own way.

Luke retreated to one of the rooms behind him and put his back to the wall. Never before had he regretted not taking one of those swords from his brother's workshop, but now he needed something sharp and durable. The best he could do was pull out his folding knife and try to sharpen the table legs into points, which was at least easy enough to accomplish. He doubted they'd last through a hundred bouncy boys, but if he was lucky the goblins would thin those numbers considerably before they were overrun.

His only regret was all the XP he was missing out on. There were probably enough monsters there to level him up again, but he doubted he'd survive it if he dropped into the middle of that brawl. Luke would happily settle for the proto-goblings slaughtering their kids, which was kind of a weird thought, but whatever. The toothy bouncy balls were vicious but uncoordinated. If they wiped out the goblins, Luke wouldn't have to worry about being hunted anymore.

Sadly, he doubted that would be the case. Seven goblins had killed at least thirty of them already, and even though they were retreating, he doubted it would be the last he'd see of them. For now though, the plan was simple: wait for the goblins to bait the proto-goblings out of the cavern, then head in a different direction.

One thing he'd learned over the last few days was that Grimshard goblins were the ones least likely to have melee weapons. It seemed like they specialized in ranged attacks, which was not to say none of the other flavors ever had crossbows, just that Grimshards almost always did. That sucked right now because he would love to get another one of those short swords that he'd briefly used if he was going to be fighting proto-goblings.

The noise died down out in the main cavern, and Luke peeked out to check on the situation. It looked like the coast was clear, and he cautiously dropped down to the main floor. When nothing jumped out to attack him, he laughed quietly and shook his head. Even if he didn't kill any more goblins on his way out, he'd still consider it a job well done.

Of course, if he did come across any more goblins, he wouldn't turn down the XP. That would just be dumb. But he wasn't going to go out of his way to look for them now. What he was going to do was start trying to retrace his steps to get out of the maze of tunnels. Hopefully his memory was as good as he thought it was; otherwise he was going to have a problem.

The first few tunnels were familiar, and he made good time. After that, things got frustrating. He was sure he knew where he was going, but every time he got to another intersection, it wasn't what he expected to find. Worse, the proto-goblings had apparently lost their quarry and were running rabid through the tunnels. Twice he had to stop to fend them off when they caught up to him, and the second time one of his sharpened table legs broke.

"Aw, damn it," Luke swore as he examined the shattered wood. "Two left."

They weren't even worth the XP he got for killing them, mostly because he wasn't properly equipped to do so. Every time he saw one of them, he got more annoyed. Every time one of them went by without noticing him, he was relieved. It was hard to even consider them dangerous when there were only one or two, but there were so many that there was always another one somewhere nearby.

Still, it was just a matter of time until he found his way out. He was sure of it. Any minute now something would click and he'd figure out where he was.

"System," Luke said. "I think I'm lost."

Margl was going to gut the Day Hunter, borrow the Bloodbite shaman to heal it back up, and then gut it again. Then he was going to start cutting off fingers, then limbs. He would gouge out the monster's eyes but leave its tongue and its ears so it could hear itself scream.

Perhaps they should have expected it would invade the caves and prepared a better defense, but who could possibly have believed it would be stupid enough to unlock the spawning pit and let the sources just run wild? They'd had to kill half of them already, and it was going to be the work of weeks to round the remaining ones up and shove them back into their hole.

He was busy fuming while he stomped down one of the west tunnels with an escort of four minions. They'd swapped their crossbows for spears, not that he trusted any of them to do more than stick the pointy end forward and hope a source impaled itself on it. As much as it grated to admit it, even to himself, he could use some help from the Bloodbites.

Then he heard a voice, and not a goblin voice. Margl paused and held up a hand. The Day Hunter was nearby and . . . talking to itself? He didn't know who else it could be speaking to. As far as he was aware, it couldn't speak or even understand the goblin tongue. And there was nothing else in the Grimshard tunnels besides goblins to talk to anyway.

The Day Hunter had gained some more levels. It was probably almost as strong as Margl himself now, but fortunately, it was just one monster. He sent his escort guard forward, and they charged into battle. Margl moved in behind them and rounded the corner just in time to see the Day Hunter jumping back and pulling that strange weapon off its back.

It worked the weapon back and forth frantically to block goblin spears, but there was only so much it could do, and it was forced to give ground. Soon they'd have it backed into a corner and they'd bleed it out. Margl grinned and shouldered his spear to pull his double bow off his back.

He sighted the Day Walker down the length of the stock and pulled both triggers. Bolts thicker around than his big toe leaped off the strings to strike the Day Hunter, except somehow the monster dodged! It shouldn't even have been possible to twist a body like that and keep it unbroken, but somehow it did it.

Then its weapon twisted around and shattered one of his escort's faces. Margl cursed under his breath while he pulled new bolts from hip quiver. The double bow was a pain to load and had forced him to put more points than he wanted into strength, but next time he'd hit the Day Hunter for sure. Margl loaded the first bolt in and locked it in place.

A goblin screamed in pain, but Margl ignored it. The whole point of escorts was to stand between him and danger, after all. He finished slipping the second bolt in and whipped the double bow up, only to jerk back in surprise when he realized the Day Hunter was right in front of him. That arm-thick metal rod was coming straight for his face, and there was nothing he could do to save himself besides sacrifice his double bow.

That bought him a second, just long enough to leap back and scoop up his spear. He brandished it at the Day Hunter and looked past the monster to coordinate with his escort, only to find that every single one of them was on the ground. One of them was still twitching, but he wasn't going to be getting back up to help.

It was just Margl left, him against the monster that was slaughtering his tribe. Fear tried to grab him, but he fought free of it with a snarl and hurled himself into the fight. The Day Hunter pushed the spear aside with one hand, its strength monstrous, and brought its weapon up in an underhand swing that caught Margl in the ribs.

His feet left the ground, and he landed on his back. It took a second for his brain to catch up, and by the time it did, the Day Hunter was standing over top of him, weapon in hand and face grim.

That was the last thing Margl ever saw.

Name	Luke Bennet
Level	16
XP	15137/15275
AP	0
Bloodline	SysAdmin
Strength	22
Agility	21
Stamina	21
Perception	22
Skills	Mace Mastery (2)
	Sword Mastery (1)
	Unarmed Martialist (1)
	Life Surge (1)
	Peripheral Awareness (1)
	Counter (1)
	Twitch Reflexes (2)
	Survivalist (2)
	First Aid (1)
	Wood Carving (1)
	Leatherworking (2)

CHAPTER 27

Luke hefted the spear he'd taken from the goblins. It was too bad about that strange crossbow; he'd wanted to examine it closer. Oh well, the spear was the true prize with those freaky little proto-gobling things still running around. He casually stabbed it into the one goblin he'd only clipped when they'd tried to jump him and got another ding.

"And that makes five," he said. "Okay, System, we were talking about how to get the hell out of this place."

"Yes, indeed. I am not able to give you precise directions, but I can inform you that the tunnel you came in through is southeast of your current position."

"That's as accurate as you can be, huh?"

"My apologies, Luke. You do not have—"

"High enough system access," Luke cut him off. "I know, I know. Better than nothing I guess. You're sure about it being southeast though? I could have sworn I needed to go north."

"Completely sure, yes."

Luke sighed. "Fine then. Southeast . . . hmm. Maybe if I go back to that last intersection . . ."

He looked through his notifications and grunted. "Oh, that one was a really high level. That's interesting. It wasn't strong at all. Must have put all its AP into utility skills."

[You have slain Grimshard Goblin (level 10). 102 XP awarded.]
[You have slain Grimshard Goblin (level 11). 123 XP awarded.]
[You have slain Grimshard Goblin (level 11). 123 XP awarded.]
[You have slain Grimshard Goblin (level 15). 231 XP awarded.]

[You have slain Grimshard Goblin (level 10). 102 XP awarded.]

"Damn it. Less than 50 XP to level. Well, I'm sure I'll find something else before I'm done down here."

Luke continued on his way, far more confident now that he had a proper spear. Well, proper might have been stretching it. It was crudely made and sized for a goblin, which meant it was about six feet tall and the head was actually made of stone that had been chipped down to have an edge and a point. Considering he was still stuck in the tunnels though, he appreciated that it wasn't as long as a human-sized spear would be.

He did keep the table legs though, just in case. It was a bit uncomfortable with them stuffed in his belt, but until the spear had proven itself in combat, he wasn't going to discard what he knew would work. For all he knew, the damn head could fall off the shaft the first time he used it, and then he'd be screwed. A big stick wasn't going to kill a bouncy goblin.

Speaking of, he could hear one of those little devils running around somewhere nearby. That distinctive thump sound was a dead giveaway. If it was literally bouncing off the walls, that meant there was probably a goblin nearby too, one who wasn't equipped to deal with its progenitor. Maybe Luke could pull a twofer and finish that level up.

By the time he got there though, the goblin was already dead and the proto-gobling had moved on. He probably could have followed it; it wasn't exactly being quiet, but it was going in the opposite direction that he needed to move, and getting back up to the surface was a higher priority.

"Still southeast?" he asked twenty minutes later.

"No, Luke. More northeast now."

"What? How?!"

"I am not able to map out a path for you. This is all the help I can give you in regard to your current location."

That was frustrating. The tunnels were annoying to walk through, most of them being too small for him to stand fully upright. He'd been sure he was going in the right direction, but it was admittedly hard to keep track underground. The best he could do was try to compensate and keep walking.

As he trudged along, all hunched over and annoyed with the spear but unwilling to abandon it, Luke kept his eyes and ears open for any other ambushes. The goblins in that last tunnel had been trying to sneak up on him, and just because they'd done a bad job didn't mean other goblins wouldn't do better. The longer he spent in the tunnels though, the more convinced he was that the general population had retreated deep, deep underground, beyond his reach.

As long as they stayed down there, that was fine by him. The ones he really wanted to kill were those warriors from his camp raid anyway. Those would be worth excellent XP, and they'd already taken a swing at him once. He supposed they could argue that he'd invaded their home and robbed them, but he'd been kill on sight to every goblin he'd ever met, so in his opinion, they had it coming.

"Oh, hey, this looks familiar," he muttered. "I think . . . left here?"

A few minutes later he came upon the welcome sight of a busted-up wooden barricade. Luke smiled and hurried forward, happy to finally be close to escaping. He practically tripped over a proto-gobling hidden under the collapsed barricade as he rushed by. The thing was just sitting there, gnawing on the wood and ignoring the world, until Luke basically stepped on it.

It hissed angrily, looked up at him, and then sprang at his face. "Whoa!" Luke cried out as he flailed his arms and fell backward on his ass. He scrambled to get the spear up and only managed it by grabbing it right under the tip and jerking it around. The proto-gobling impaled itself and just kept clawing its way down the haft even as its weird blood pus spurted out the back end.

"Ugh," Luke said as he tossed the spear off to the side. "Nasty little bastards."

The proto-gobling gave a final twitch and died just as a set of dings sounded in his head. Luke stood up, reclaimed his spear, and scraped the monster off on a piece of wood. He grinned as he checked his notifications. One kill with two dings could only mean one thing.

[You have slain Proto-Gobling (level 6). 36 XP awarded.]

[Congratulations! You have reached level 17. 17 AP awarded for use.]

"Finally! And exactly enough too. Now, to spend them."

He'd fully planned on buying **[Stealth]**, maybe even two ranks if he could afford it. It was becoming too much of a handicap to have his XP pool announcing his presence to everything around him, and this game of cat and mouse he had going on with every fucking goblin in the whole valley would be a lot easier if he wasn't broadcasting his location to everything that got close enough.

Rank 1 cost him 3 AP, but rank 2 demanded 15. Cursing, Luke went back to his build notes and picked up the final skill from the list his brother recommended acquiring before level 20: **[Power Strike]**. Unlike his other combat abilities, this was an active skill. It allowed him to imbue extra energy into his attacks based on his stamina and was supposed to be a trump card or finisher move.

He wasn't sure about spending 10 AP on it, but Curt had figured out way more shit than Luke had, so he went ahead and bought that too. The last 4 AP got split between strength and perception. His points figured out, Luke's mood brightened immeasurably, and he finished his climb back up to the world of fresh air and trees.

Somehow, it was night. He thought he'd only been down there for a few hours, maybe four or five at most, but it looked like he was way off and it had been closer to ten. Just seeing how dark it was made him feel tired all of a sudden, and he caught himself midyawn. It had taken longer than he wanted, but he had accomplished quite a bit. At least he thought he had. He'd personally killed about two dozen goblins, plus unleashed those little nightmarish proto-goblings on their home base. Those things were vicious; they'd probably kill a few more and would certainly be a pain to corral again.

Now he just needed to make it home unseen. The goblins were probably thickest in the forest right now, so he just circled down the east side of the valley until he got to his own cave and then ducked in. After about twenty minutes of waiting by the ravine and nothing showing up, Luke shrugged and climbed up to his brother's workshop.

It had been a good day, but he was going to stick to fighting topside from now on.

"What do you mean they're all dead?" Gulgok demanded.

"Just what I said. It seems the Day Hunter found its way into their tribal caves and unleashed an entire breeding pit. Grimshard as a tribe is done, and Margl himself is dead. I confirmed that with my own eyes. There are maybe thirty living goblins and an uncounted number of sources running wild."

Gulgok glared at his Right Hand, but the other goblin didn't seem to care. Grumbling to himself under his breath, the boss goblin settled back on his throne. This news changed things. Once the Day Hunter was killed, there would only be two tribes.

For many, many generations, the three powers had kept each other balanced. All of them knew that if one attacked the other, the third would fall on them both once they'd weakened themselves fighting and claim sole control of the valley. Now, suddenly, one of the tribes was broken. Without the breeding pit, it would never ever recover.

Bloodbite was stronger than Bluerock. It always had been, and the Day Hunter had spent an entire day specifically going out of its way to hunt Bluerock patrols. They'd been weakened significantly, and now with Grimshard wiped out, that meant Gulgok was going to win by default. It wasn't a satisfying victory, perhaps, but it would put every single goblin under his control.

That was something to celebrate, but not until the Day Hunter had been tracked down and killed. They would burn its corpse as part of the celebration but only after he'd eaten of its organs and stolen its power. Gulgok needed to make sure he was the one to kill the Day Hunter too. It would be a rich source of XP for him.

The thought that the Day Hunter might actually win never entered his mind. The other tribes were weak. They produced weak warriors and had only held their places by the strength of their numbers. The Bloodbite way was for the strong to devour the weak, to take their power and become the elite, premier goblin warriors of the valley.

"Are there any hunting dogs left among the Bluerock?" he asked his Hand.

"One or two, perhaps. They were being held in reserve as a breeding pair I believe."

"Get them for me. I don't care if you have to shove a knife between Qarsik's ribs first. I want those dogs. Bring handlers for them too. The Day Hunter has done me a great favor; it's only polite that I go hunt it down . . . personally."

Bulgrit's grin matched his own. His Hand knew what that meant. There would be blood soon, and then more blood when they took over the remnants of the other tribes. He was going to be boss of everything, and nothing else in the valley would ever be able to challenge his power.

Gulgok heaved himself off his throne and picked up the massive sword he'd taken from his predecessor when he'd killed him and obtained his current rank as boss. The sword was ancient, a dozen or more generations old, and made from some metal none could identify. It had been taken from the original Day Hunter, and it was only appropriate that it be used to end this new one's life.

Gulgok picked it up with one hand, unbothered by the fact that the blade was as tall as he was. Soon, he would hunt. It would be good. And then he would eat, for he was hungry.

Name	Luke Bennet
Level	17
XP	15275/18255
AP	0
Bloodline	SysAdmin
Strength	24
Agility	21
Stamina	21
Perception	24
Skills	Mace Mastery (2)
	Sword Mastery (1)
	Unarmed Martialist (1)
	Power Strike (1)
	Life Surge (1)
	Peripheral Awareness (1)
	Counter (1)
	Twitch Reflexes (2)
	Stealth (1)
	Survivalist (2)
	First Aid (1)
	Wood Carving (1)
	Leatherworking (2)

Skill	Rank	AP	Prerequisites	Effect
Power Strike	1	10	None	Imbue extra strength into a single attack based on the user's stamina
Stealth	1	3	None	Provides an understanding of how to move silently and avoid being spotted, reduces the amount of XP others can feel from you by 10%

CHAPTER 28

The next few days of Luke's life were miserable. He just couldn't relax any-where, not even safely hidden away in his workshop. He hadn't realized how much his various projects had been keeping him sane until he lost them all. He'd coasted on the initial frenzy of revenge for a day or two, but now it was just stressful to go out.

He wanted the freedom to come and go as he pleased without being hunted, but unless he got strong enough that he felt confident in attacking dozens of goblins at once, he didn't see that happening. The only other options were to leave the valley, which he would gladly do if he could, or to head into the caves for another round of goblin hunting.

Still, for all of that, Luke wasn't just lying there feeling sorry for himself. It sucked being actively hunted, but he needed food and water, needed XP to keep leveling up, and perhaps most of all, he needed sunlight and fresh air. Being able to see in the dark was cool, but being able to see things that weren't stone walls was necessary for his mental well-being.

So even though he knew it was dangerous, and even though he needed to be constantly on guard, Luke spent a great deal of his time out in the valley. It wasn't fun or relaxing, but it was better than sitting in a stone box. The goblins found him several times, which resulted in deaths on their side and occasional injuries on his.

He tried to keep up his elemental grinding, but the arrival of the jumbo elemental was so conspicuous that the goblins took notice and started watch-ing the pass. It didn't matter what time of day or night he showed up; there were always a few goblins looking out for him, and they'd quickly summon more before attacking him.

His sole consolation was that the goblins hadn't come up with any more of those mastiffs. Without the tracking dogs to point the way, he was at least able to enjoy a few hours of relative peace here and there. Red even showed up to keep him company, albeit usually only when he was cooking. The damn freeloader never did anything productive, but Luke figured he still owed the bird for saving him from that cat when he'd first arrived on Aros.

With the loss of his woodworking tools, Luke was back to using a folding knife and his multi-tool. He could still make things, but it really wasn't the same. He also had to go out of his way to be gentle with the tools with his strength stat so high. It felt like he was handling glass instead of steel sometimes, and the fact that the edges had all dulled from overuse didn't help matters.

Still, in the interest of his sanity, he made little art pieces to keep his mind and hands occupied: a small, eight-inch-tall statue of Red to replace the big one he'd been working on was his first project. It wasn't nearly as detailed as his original project, but it made him happy to see Red's form slowly emerge from the wood with each cut.

It was a short-lived happiness, often interrupted by goblin search parties. They were persistent and well armed, and he never saw a group smaller than fifteen. The first time he heard them coming, he snuck away, but **[Stealth]** wasn't strong enough to fully hide him, and they caught up quickly. Luke fought then, using the trees as cover to protect himself from crossbows, slaying goblins left and right. Eventually they broke and ran.

The XP boost was nice but not without cost. He couldn't avoid every attack, and each hit slowed him down, making it harder to dodge the next. The truth was if the goblins had rushed him en masse, they would have killed him quickly and easily. Sooner or later, they were going to realize that.

"So that's another day ruined," he muttered darkly. "And more new holes in my clothes."

Tired and aching, Luke walked back to his cave. It was some small consolation that he'd be back in good health in a matter of hours instead of weeks, but he was getting real tired of hurting. This whole thing with the goblins had to end.

"Today, it ends," Gulgok announced.

He stood in front of his elites, the six most powerful goblins in the valley. All of them were at least level 15. Next to them were a trio of Bluerock goblins who'd been conscripted into service. Each one held a rawhide leash attached to a mastiff, and the dogs themselves had been muzzled to stop their incessant braying.

One of the search parties had made contact with the Day Hunter, and it had slaughtered them, though not without cost. Gulgok stood in the aftermath of the battle, and the dogs had the scent of the monster.

They followed the dogs for half an hour. The handlers grew more and more apprehensive as the Day Hunter failed to materialize in front of them, often glancing back at Gulgok. He was more amused than anything by the amount of fear on display, mostly because they were right to cower. If the dogs failed to flush out the Day Hunter, he would kill the handlers and replace them. The lives of his own tribe meant little to him; the lives of goblins from Bluerock meant even less.

In truth, he would likely kill them at the end either way. That was the fate that awaited almost all the Bluerock goblins, and whatever remained of the Grimshards. Some would have some outstanding skills that he could find a use for, but most would be slaughtered. The new goblins that came from their spawning pit would be part of the Bloodbite tribe and would never know loyalties to anything else.

But first, the Day Hunter. He leveled a glare at the three Bluerock handlers and demanded, "How much longer?"

"We are getting closer, b-boss," one of them said with a stutter. Technically speaking, he wasn't their boss yet, but they knew the end was coming. "We could go faster without the muzzles."

"Idiot. Have you learned nothing from the deaths of your kin? The Day Hunter made a point to seek out these howling beasts and slaughter them. It knows what they are capable of. If it knows we are coming, it will run."

"Or it might come straight to us," Bulgrit said.

Gulgok lashed out, and his Hand took the blow without flinching. "I did not ask for an opinion from you."

One of the scouts they'd deployed around the main hunting formation scurried through the underbrush and approached. It bowed and scraped along the way and hissed out, "Boss! We've found it. The Day Hunter is by the stream, only a few minutes north of here. If we hurry, we can catch it before it leaves."

"We will not rush," Gulgok said. "Circle around. Watch its movements. Do not let it escape."

He wasn't afraid of the Day Hunter, certainly not. But he respected it. It had killed many goblins and grown in level since he'd first laid eyes on it. And now, he would grow from killing it. He followed behind the dogs, flanked by Bloodbite elites, and eagerly gripped the hilt of his sword.

The trees gave way to a small streamside clearing, and there, sitting next to it with that strange metal club, was the Day Hunter. It didn't look surprised to see them. "Tired of running?" Gulgok said. "Good."

Luke's perception was too high for the goblins to sneak up on him. It was also too high for him not to notice the damn dogs they had. Admittedly, they'd gotten a lot closer simply by muzzling the beasts so they wouldn't bark or howl, but he knew they were there. He would have to kill the dogs at least before he escaped, or they'd just keep following him.

The goblins had gotten smarter though, and the dogs were kept on short leashes with a party of high-level goblin warriors. There was even one there that was higher than him, perhaps two. The second one was either the same level as Luke or at most one ahead.

While he waited for the hunters to arrive with their dogs, he kept himself busy ambushing the scouts that were trying to circle around. For once, his higher XP pool wasn't a hindrance. They already knew he was there, and **[Stealth]** did enough at least to keep them from realizing that he was stalking them in turn. One by one, he'd killed them silently over the last few minutes.

Despite all the killing, he was still only halfway to the next level, but if he was right about how strong the goblins coming for him were, they might just be able to push him over. All he had to do was survive and make sure they didn't. They were just goblins; it'd be easy.

Sure it would.

They took their time, but eventually they showed up. Luke had specifically chosen this clearing for two reasons. First, it hugged the riverbank, making it long and narrow. It was as close to a choke point as he was going to get without actually going underground, and doing that would favor the goblins far more than him.

Second, if worse came to worst, he fully planned on jumping into the stream and swimming across it. His stamina was high enough that he could hold his breath for close to an hour now, and being underwater would protect him from crossbow bolts. At least, he hoped it would.

He stood up and turned to face the goblins. His mace was held in both hands in front of him; his feet were set evenly. He knew he was not a grand sight, with his shirt in tatters, his jacket not far behind, his jeans stained with blood and dirt and who knew what else. One of his shoes sported a hole, and his face was covered in scruff.

He was still almost two feet taller than the average goblin, and he'd yet to meet one that could match his strength. Almost all his AP had been spent on combat-related skills and stat increases. While he wasn't in love with the idea of fighting ten more goblins, none of these had crossbows, and they wouldn't be able to come at him more than two at a time.

They parted ways, and the big one came through, the one who was a higher level than him. It said . . . something . . . Luke wasn't sure what. He couldn't make heads or tails of those sounds that came out of their mouths. They sounded like garbage disposals barfing up helium. He didn't bother to respond either. They wouldn't understand him, and besides, everyone there knew what they were there to do.

He raised his mace up in front of him and let out a breath. Despite the adrenaline coursing through him, despite the sound of his heart pounding in his ears, his hands remained steady. This was just another fight, one he was determined to win.

The goblin brought its sword around from where it stuck up over its shoulder. The damn blade was taller than its wielder, and by almost a foot too. It was strange, that sword. If Luke didn't know any better, he'd think it was steel, but the only steel weapons he'd seen so far were the ones hidden away in his brother's workshop.

Then again, it did look like it was a hundred years old. It was etched with time, and its edge had several burrs on it. The hilt had no leather grip, just a core of metal far too long for a goblin's hands. Despite the size and weight, the goblin swung it easily in one hand. With a cruel laugh, it waved the rest of its group back and took a step forward.

That step turned into a run, and the two of them lunged at each other.

Name	Luke Bennet
Level	17
XP	17341/18255
AP	0
Bloodline	SysAdmin
Strength	24
Agility	21
Stamina	21
Perception	24
Skills	Mace Mastery (2)
	Sword Mastery (1)
	Unarmed Martialist (1)
	Power Strike (1)
	Life Surge (1)
	Peripheral Awareness (1)
	Counter (1)
	Twitch Reflexes (2)
	Stealth (1)
	Survivalist (2)
	First Aid (1)
	Wood Carving (1)
	Leatherworking (2)

CHAPTER 29

Luke hadn't forgotten his first few fights, when everything was a higher level than him. He remembered how scared he was, but that memory was dull and faded. He'd killed a thousand monsters in the last few weeks. This was just one more fight.

At least, that's what he thought right up until the goblin brought the sword down on him. Luke swung his mace up to parry the blade and force it aside with plans to follow up by heel kicking the goblin's knee while it was off-balance. Then steel met steel, his mace was thrown back, and it was all he could do to hang on to it.

The goblin's sword bore down, and Luke's leg nearly buckled from the strain of holding it back, even for a second. His arms were going to give out in moments, and he had only a fraction of a second to decide his next move. **[Mace Mastery]** told him how to angle his weapon so that the sword slid down toward the end instead of up to slice off his fingers, but it also told him the weapon could get locked up on the head of the mace itself.

If that happened, there was a very real possibility the goblin would rip his mace out of his hands, and Luke wasn't nearly so confident in himself that he thought his rank 1 **[Unarmed Martialist]** skill would see him to victory.

Mace work alone wasn't going to help him disengage. He tilted the mace, and the sword scraped down the length of the handle. Before it could catch on the head, Luke shoved forward to push the sword back, then turned in a spin that flung him away from the goblin. It wasn't surprised by the move, didn't falter for even a moment. It simply pursued, its sword deadly fast and already coming back at him in a lunge.

Luke had been trying to put some distance between himself and the goblin, give himself that momentary window to react so that he could dodge instead of pitting his strength stat against the monster's. It was obvious from just their one exchange that he was losing there, something that had never really happened to him before.

The goblin had seen through that tactic. Rather than having to shuffle forward to chase him down, it turned its attack into a full-body lunge that was dangerously close to skewering him almost before he even saw the attack. **[Twitch Reflexes]** got him out of the way, but it was **[Unarmed Martialist]** that kept him from falling on his ass doing it.

The goblin kept up the pressure, but Luke could tell it lacked the agility he had. It was compensating for that with sheer skill, or perhaps simply a higher-ranked **[Sword Mastery]** skill. It was hard to tell where the lines blurred between natural skill achieved through study and practice and system-granted skill, especially on another creature.

Either way, Luke settled into a rhythm of dodging or redirecting attacks while his **[Counter]** skill searched for an opening. The goblin might have strength in spades, but Luke was no lightweight either. He could crack skulls quite easily; he just needed the opening. The goblin didn't look like it was going to slip up and make a mistake though.

If that wasn't enough to worry about, there was a full hunting party behind it who could jump in at any moment. It was in Luke's best interest to look like he was losing the fight right up until he killed the goblin with a single decisive blow. That way, they'd be content to stand back and watch their leader beat Luke's ass.

It wasn't much of an act either. The damn goblin was seriously good with that weapon, better than anything else he'd ever fought. It was looking less and less like it was going to make a mistake and trigger **[Counter]**, and if Luke planned on using it, he'd need to make an opening.

The problem with that was that he physically wasn't strong enough to push the sword aside. If the goblin didn't want it to move, it wasn't going to. The best he could do was change the angle of descent by locking his own weapon against it, but then he was so tied up in controlling the sword's angle of attack that he had no way to fight back.

He danced backward, avoiding a series of probing thrusts, any of which he probably could have swatted to the side with ease if it was anyone else holding the sword. He didn't, and the goblin wasn't trying all that hard to make contact. What it was doing was maneuvering him, backing him into a proverbial corner and eliminating his options.

Luke scrambled to find a way out and saw a single possible avenue that would require careful and deliberate setup and leave him vulnerable to a retaliatory attack if he didn't kill the goblin in one blow. Then his foot slipped in the mud, and he went down to one knee. Against nearly anything else, he would have been able to recover but not this goblin.

It was higher level, stronger, just as combat oriented as he was. It probably had a ton of personal experience garnered over years of bloody battles, something Luke was completely outclassed in. He looked up and saw death coming for him in a whistling arc of steel.

He swung his mace up to meet the sword and activated the one thing that might save him. With one foot still solidly planted on the grass, Luke triggered **[Power Strike]**, which streamed up through his arms and doubled his strength. The weapons crashed into each other so hard Luke was momentarily deafened, and even from his position on the ground, he overpowered the goblin's strength and the sword went flying away.

A wave of exhaustion washed over Luke, but he didn't stop. There was no time for stopping. It was now or never. He surged up to his feet and spun once to whip up some momentum before smacking his mace into the goblin's chest. It got its hands up to grab the head of the mace, but it was still reeling from the **[Power Strike]**, and Luke hit it hard enough to throw it through the air, where it slammed into a tree in an explosion of bark and wood shards.

The goblin slumped to the ground with a groan, and two of the warriors leaped forward to defend it. Before they could reach their fallen leader, Luke rushed forward and brought his mace down again. The goblin leader's skull exploded in a shower of gore, and he heard the notification ding in his head.

"Holy shit, that was wild," Luke said, his chest heaving. He'd used **[Power Strike]** a few times before to get a handle on how the skill worked, but this was his first time using it in a fight. It was somehow even more draining. He hadn't wanted to use it precisely because of the side effects. He could still fight, but there were eight more goblins in front of him.

It was too late for their leader, but those other warriors didn't look like they were going to just let Luke go. He straightened up, picked off a chunk of goblin skin that had gotten stuck on his cheek, and said, "I don't suppose you guys want to keep up the one-at-a-time thing?"

Whatever the goblins said, he didn't get a word of it. The intent was clear though. They spread out enough to avoid getting tangled up in one another's attacks, and then on some unseen signal, two swung at the same time. Luke hopped backward out of range and gave silent thanks that they were using normal goblin-sized swords.

When the next set of attacks came, he was pleased to find that they didn't have the same overwhelming strength of their leader. Luke slipped into something closer to his usual style, where he relied on skills like **[Peripheral Awareness]** to keep track of multiple enemies and **[Twitch Reflexes]** to keep him out of the way of incoming attacks. **[Counter]** more than made up for its earlier failures, and he found plenty of openings. The two goblins were both skilled, and Luke worked hard to stay ahead of their attacks, and when he did find an opening, they were quick to dart out of the way. Most of his swings missed completely, and those that did connect were glancing blows.

Even a glancing blow with a weapon as heavy as his wielded by someone with 24 strength could break bones. Things started to go sideways when he broke one of the goblins' arms, and rather than continue to fight, it rotated out to let a new warrior take its place. This one was using a spear instead of a sword, and Luke had to adjust to that new attack vector on the fly.

In a way though, the switch was a blessing. These two goblins weren't nearly as coordinated, and he was easily able to grab the haft of the spear below the head and swing it around with one arm. The goblin went flying with a startled shriek and splashed into the stream. Luke whipped the spear around to crack the remaining goblin in the face, then spun it and skewered the monster before it could recover.

In his experience, goblins were cowardly and usually scattered as soon as he killed a few of them. He was surprised they were still standing their ground, but one or two more kills would probably be enough to cause the rest to flee. The dog handlers looked like they were ready to break already, and only the intimidating presence of that other high-level goblin standing behind them kept them in place.

That one was a strange one. The other warriors were wearing expressions that varied from enraged to predatory. He understood that look; it was one he wore himself quite often. That was the look of someone sizing him up and estimating how much XP they were going to get for killing him. That last goblin though, it didn't look like that. Instead, it looked thoughtful, calculating even.

That worried Luke. It wasn't scared, and it wasn't pissed off. It was planning something. Whatever it was trying to do, it wouldn't be good for Luke if it succeeded. He needed to end the fight, kill the dogs, and get the hell away before the goblins wore him down enough to make a mistake.

The goblin he'd thrown into the water was making its way back out, swimming upstream against the current to try to angle itself behind Luke. That was actually a pretty good strategy he hadn't expected, but it only encouraged him to get a bit aggressive to end the fight quickly. Luke pushed forward, hunched his shoulders to accept the smack of a spear haft on them when the goblin tried to slash at him while he was stepping into range, and brought his mace up in an underhand swing that clipped its chin.

It went up a few feet, then back down in a sprawled, boneless heap. Luke spun in place to meet the attack he knew was coming from the other goblin, only to find it had completely missed the opening to gawk at the remaining goblins. Luke couldn't really blame it, all things considered. The higher-level one had just killed all three of the dog handlers with its axe, and the dogs too!

It stepped forward and brought the axe down on the one whose arm Luke had broken, then it looked back to the fight and smirked. The goblin he'd been fighting shouted something at the traitor, but Luke wasn't about to let the opportunity pass by. He killed it with a single blow to the back of the head, then stepped back warily to keep the swimmer from circling around him while he faced the traitor.

The goblin glanced down at its companion still in the water, its face twisted in clear disgust, and shook its head. It hefted the leader's sword over its shoulder, saluted Luke with its axe, and stepped back into the trees. Luke watched it disappear, then looked over at the single remaining goblin. It floated, stunned into inaction, and the current started carrying it away. The goblin didn't try to fight it anymore, and soon enough it was a hundred feet downstream.

Just like that, Luke was safe. He let out a short laugh full of disbelief, uttered a final, "What the fuck?" to the battleground, and walked away.

Name	Luke Bennet
Level	18
XP	18858/21602
AP	18
Bloodline	SysAdmin
Strength	24
Agility	21
Stamina	21
Perception	24
Skills	Mace Mastery (2)
	Sword Mastery (1)
	Unarmed Martialist (1)
	Power Strike (1)
	Life Surge (1)
	Peripheral Awareness (1)
	Counter (1)
	Twitch Reflexes (2)
	Stealth (1)
	Survivalist (2)
	First Aid (1)
	Wood Carving (1)
	Leatherworking (2)

CHAPTER 30

It was all Bulgrit could do not to cackle when he'd watched his boss get his face demolished by the Day Hunter. For six years he'd been serving that braggart, six years of running errands and performing chores far beneath the dignity of the boss's Right Hand. For six years, he'd felt Gulgok's eyes on his back, sizing him up like a snack, and wondered if today would finally be the day his boss reaped his XP.

And now, suddenly, unbelievably, he was dead. The Day Hunter had freed him from servitude while simultaneously demolishing every conceivable rival he might have left in the valley. All he needed to do now was kill off the last goblin boss and he'd be in charge. That wouldn't even be an issue. Everyone knew Qarsik's build was terrible for direct confrontation. It was a miracle the old schemer had ever held on to his position as Bluerock's boss.

The Day Hunter had proven it was capable of descending into the caves but also that it wasn't good at it. If it hadn't stumbled into the Grimshard breeding pit, it would have killed at most ten or twenty goblins in all its time wandering. The sources had killed many, many more by comparison and were still down there wreaking havoc. Any new goblins that spawned from them would no doubt be slaughtered as soon as they sloughed off their slime coatings.

Now that Bulgrit was the undisputed top goblin in the valley, things were going to change. For one thing, they were going to leave the Day Hunter alone. It was obviously trying to get out of the valley, and Bulgrit intended to let it. As many goblins as the Day Hunter had already killed, he expected the order to stay far, far away from it would be welcomed.

There was one last loose end to take care of first. Bulgrit followed the stream and watched the last of his companions drift closer. As soon as he dragged himself out of the water, Bulgrit stepped out of hiding behind him and, with a single swing of his new sword, detached the last of the elite guard's head from his body.

Blackfut was waiting for him on the other side of the river. "It all went according to plan?" the shaman asked.

Bulgrit grinned. "Exactly so. Did you see the look on Gulgrit's face when he figured out what happened, right before the Day Hunter killed him?"

The two goblins snickered, right up until Bulgrit buried his axe in Blackfut's back. It wouldn't do to leave even a potential rival to his power.

Luke whistled when he checked his notifications. That one goblin had been worth a metric fuckload of XP. Altogether, he'd gotten more than enough to level up again.

[You have assisted in slaying Bloodbite Goblin (level 21). 229 XP awarded.]

    [Congratulations! You have reached level 18. 18 AP awarded for use.]

    [You have slain Bloodbite Goblin (level 15). 231 XP awarded.]

    [You have slain Bloodbite Goblin (level 15). 231 XP awarded.]

    [You have slain Bloodbite Goblin (level 16). 263 XP awarded.]

He honestly wasn't sure what to do with the 18 AP now. He'd picked up all the combat skills Curt had recommended he buy, and his next step was to get them to max rank so that they could unlock further abilities. Until then, the only other thing he could do was push his stats higher. While it was tempting to dump the whole thing into strength, it was approximately one fight too late for that to matter.

"Hey, wait, what the hell does that mean, *assisted?* I didn't see anyone else helping to kill that guy!"

Perhaps it had given partial credit to that goblin who'd betrayed the rest of the hunting party. That didn't make sense to Luke, but he didn't know how else to explain it. He had clearly been the only one fighting the high-level goblin the entire time.

The bullshit system cheating him out of XP aside, he had a few skills that took 15 AP to upgrade, like **[Mace Mastery]** and **[Counter]**, and a few others that only took 10, like **[Peripheral Awareness]** and **[Stealth]**. In the end though, the allure of higher stats was too strong. He split his AP, putting 12 into strength and 6 into agility. If he'd had those stats half an hour ago, that battle probably would have gone quite differently.

As soon as the stats hit, he was knocked flat on his back. "Holy fuck!" he gasped out as every muscle in his body spasmed and tore itself at the same time. It only lasted a few seconds, but those seconds were pure agony. When it was done, Luke sat back up and felt like a stranger in his own body. Casually pushing his hand down to leverage himself upright was enough to leave a three-inch-deep handprint in the ground.

"Oh, that's new," he said, peering down at it. "Uh, System. Is that going to happen again?"

"It's possible," System said, appearing out of thin air next to him. "You boosted your strength significantly. Most people do not put more than a few points into a single stat at any given level. It makes it much easier to adapt to a casually increasing threshold for physical power if it's staggered over months or even years."

"Year?" Luke asked. "It's only been like . . . two weeks? Maybe three?"

"Twenty-six days since I first noticed you on Aros. I am not aware of how long you were here prior to that point."

"So twenty-six then? Wow, longer than I thought. But back to my question: What do you mean months or years between level ups?"

"Some species level up as quickly as you have done. They usually live short and violent lives. Human cultures, on the other hand, almost universally only level up a few times a year, and that rate slows down the stronger they get."

"But why?" Luke asked. "It's not like it's hard to do. I guess it's a little dangerous, but some high-level person could just power level a new kid."

"I am not familiar with this term, *power level.*"

"Oh, uh, it's a gaming term from my world. It's just when a strong person helps a weak person level up quickly."

"I see. An apt description. I will add that to the system lexicon," System said. "You would have to ask such questions yourself. My knowledge of humans is limited primarily to how they interact with the system, not why they make the choices they make."

"Maybe if I ever meet another one," Luke grumbled. Before he could say anything else, a flash of movement overhead caught his eye. He looked up and saw Red alighting on a thick branch overhead, one that creaked with the added weight despite its size. "And where have you been? I could have used some help!"

Red screeched at him and flapped its wings once. Luke glowered up at it. "I don't have any food for you!"

The bird screeched again and shifted its claws on the branch. Muttering to himself, Luke looked around. "Okay, fine, let's see if we can find something. I'm kind of hungry too."

Without Red's appearance, he probably would have gone back into hiding to rest and recover. He hadn't been forced to use **[Life Surge]** this time, but

[Power Strike] also took a toll on his body, and some good food wasn't a bad idea. Well, as good as he was capable of making it.

"Come on then, let's see what's out and about."

For the next two days, Luke didn't see a single sign of goblins anywhere. He even swung by the camp they'd built aboveground, only to find it completely deserted. With all possible caution, he'd crept in, half expecting goblins to jump out at any moment, but every single building was empty. They'd taken all the tools with them, unfortunately, and all the lumber.

That put the final nail in his tree house idea, metaphorically speaking. There were no literal nails, of course. That was kind of the problem. Luke supposed if he really wanted to, he could pick up **[Blacksmithing]** and get his brother's workshop going again. Presumably he'd know what to do with all the leftover stuff in there once he had the skill.

But he didn't want to do that. He wanted to find civilization, talk to another person again, eat properly cooked food, and sleep on a real bed. Since the goblins had completely fucking disappeared, he needed to take advantage of that. He thought he could hit the earth elementals at least three times a day, depending on how ornery the jumbo got about him showing up.

He could feel that he was still far behind the massive earth elemental, though he couldn't say how far. It was stronger than the sword goblin had been, stronger even than Red. Maybe level 30? Higher? He couldn't say for sure. One thing he did know for sure was that he didn't need to actually beat it, just outrun it.

Killing it was preferred though, just in case there was more than one. The last thing he needed was to be running from the jumbo only to have its twin brother pop up in front of him. There was also every chance that the goblins were rallying and would be back topside in force. He needed to take advantage of the free time while he could.

So as much as Luke hated it, he dragged himself up to the pass and killed as many elementals as he could get away with before he got chased off. Then he roamed around the valley, looking for new monsters to fight. Inevitably, they did their best to avoid him. Even if he used **[Stealth]**, the level gap was too much to hide from them. It was no wonder Red was constantly eating his food. Hunting level 3s and 4s was a giant pain in the ass.

Once a few hours had gone by, Luke returned to the pass and killed five more elementals. This time the big one showed up in a hurry and drove him off. He didn't let that deter him from coming back one more time late at night, but it showed up almost immediately, preventing him from getting a single kill.

It looked like the optimal strategy was going to be once every twelve hours or so, and he decided to vary the times a bit just so he wouldn't get too predictable. The elementals didn't seem smart, but the big one was definitely lurking around, watching for him, so there had to be some level of intelligence there. Maybe it was only animal level. He hoped that was the case.

Slowly, he grew stronger. On the morning of the fourth day, he got a level-up ding letting him know he'd hit 19. The points got invested into stats again, this time it was 4 to strength and 5 each to everything else. The kickback wasn't nearly as bad, though he couldn't say he enjoyed it. He resolved to rank up a few skills next level instead.

Before he could get that far, something strange happened. He was halfway across the valley, absently whittling a chunk of wood into the bulky, squat figure of a two-ton raccoon, when the ground started rumbling. At first, he thought it was an earthquake, but then he realized the truth.

"What's got you riled up, big guy?" he muttered as he turned to look at the pass. Perhaps the goblins were the ones trying to flee the valley now. He allowed himself a nasty little laugh at the thought of the big elemental tearing through them.

He couldn't see it through all the trees, but that was hardly an impediment. He leaped straight up, caught a branch some twenty feet overhead, and scrambled up to the top. From there, it was easy to see the pass. About a mile up, farther than he'd ever dared to go, the giant earth elemental was clearly visible.

That would have been a unique occurrence in and of itself. He'd never seen or heard the elemental surface if it wasn't in response to him. The animals living in the valley all stayed far away from the pass leading out, apparently smart enough to know to stay away.

But as he watched, a giant arm formed out of the elemental's body and started flailing around, slamming the ground repeatedly. A second arm joined it, and Luke tilted his head in confusion. It looked like the elemental was fighting something. A second later, he caught a blur of motion as a figure darted out from behind it, barely keeping in front of the massive hands the elemental had manifested.

"Oh, shit!" Luke leaped out of the tree and scrambled out of the hole he made when he landed. He ran at full speed, weaving through the trees and breaking off branches when they got in his way. He had to get to the pass as quickly as possible.

There was a human being up there, fighting for his life.

Name	Luke Bennet
Level	19
XP	23125/25340
AP	0
Bloodline	SysAdmin
Strength	40
Agility	32
Stamina	26
Perception	29
Skills	Mace Mastery (2)
	Sword Mastery (1)
	Unarmed Martialist (1)
	Power Strike (1)
	Life Surge (1)
	Peripheral Awareness (1)
	Counter (1)
	Twitch Reflexes (2)
	Stealth (1)
	Survivalist (2)
	First Aid (1)
	Wood Carving (1)
	Leatherworking (2)

CHAPTER 31

Luke hit the trail at full speed and sprinted toward the battle. Some smaller elementals had already formed, but he didn't have time to take care of them. Instead, he wove a path through and rushed headlong toward the giant elemental up the pass.

The ground shook beneath him, and he felt a growing knot of dread in his stomach as he closed the distance. There was the normal feeling of encountering something with significantly higher XP than him, but there was another facet to it this time. He was charging into a fight he had no chance of winning in hopes of saving the person he'd spotted.

There was every chance that he'd die in the next few minutes. He'd meant to be much stronger, strong enough to fight the giant elemental by himself, before he confronted it. He'd also planned on killing it at that time, but that wasn't necessary today. He just needed to get the other person free, to distract it long enough for them to both run.

Luke approached the fight just in time to see the jumbo elemental form a third arm out of its earthy mass and slam it down. The human it was targeting leaped to the side and swung his sword in an upward two-handed grip. The blade carved a chunk of dirt out of the arm, but that didn't slow the elemental down at all.

Unlike the smaller elementals Luke had been fighting, the big one wasn't man shaped. It was more like a sentient, mobile hill that flowed across the ground and had something vaguely resembling a face on one slope. It formed limbs out of its central mass that lashed out like boneless tendrils and disappeared back in just as quickly. He'd never seen it make more than three at a time, but he didn't trust that to be a hard limit.

Luke rushed in and put his full strength behind the first attack. He even infused it with **[Power Strike]**, just because the elemental didn't appear to have noticed him and he wasn't sure when he'd get another cheap shot in. The mace whistled through the air for a brief instant before a massive boom echoed down the pass.

Literal tons of dirt, sand, and stones blew out the side of the elemental, briefly giving him a view all the way through its mass. He had a second to see the stupefied expression on the other human's face before the elemental condensed its body down to fill the hole, losing a full six feet of its height in the process.

Luke was about to wind up for another swing when a new arm formed directly in front of him and pushed straight forward. He was knocked clear off his feet and tumbled through the air to land a good twenty feet away, a blow that he managed to absorb thanks mostly to his high agility. He was back in the fight immediately and quickly learned that his assumption about the number of arms the elemental could form being higher than three was correct.

It didn't seem to have omnidirectional senses though. Arms lashed out more or less randomly, some completely off target and others easily dodged or blocked. Then the elemental's face popped out of the dirt halfway up, and its attacks became far more coordinated, forcing Luke to give ground and work harder to stay ahead of the flailing limbs.

The stranger took advantage of the fact that Luke had gained its attention and started carving chunks out of the back end, or at least that's what Luke assumed from the noises he heard. Within seconds, the face dissolved back into a featureless slope, and he saw new arms sprouting from the other side of the elemental.

He got in a few powerful strikes, though none as heavy as his initial one that used an actual skill to enhance the blow, then the stranger yelled something just moments before the face reappeared on Luke's side. That forced him to switch his tactics again to a more defensive mindset but allowed the other human to go ham on the elemental's ass.

Luke had no idea what language the other guy was speaking. It definitely wasn't English, and it didn't sound like anything he was familiar with either. It was a bit disappointing to confirm that he wouldn't be able to talk to other humans without picking up some sort of language skill but not really surprising.

When it spun back around, he yelled out his own warning. They quickly figured out what the yelling meant, and after that, it got a lot easier to predict when the elemental was switching sides. Unfortunately, that didn't do much to kill it. It just pulled up more material from the ground to replace lost body mass, and they were hard-pressed to stay ahead of its regeneration.

Luke thought they'd wear it down eventually, assuming their stamina could last long enough, but he recognized that it was going to be a long, long battle. He allowed himself to be cautiously optimistic that, combined with the other human, they would win. Then **[Peripheral Awareness]** caught movement behind him, and he saw four of the regular-sized earth elementals approaching him.

"Shit," Luke swore. The jumbo elemental was facing the other way, which meant Luke could disengage from it, but if he wasn't putting pressure on the big guy's ass, it would be free to focus completely on the stranger. The guy had survived for at least a few minutes before Luke showed up to help, so hopefully he could manage thirty or forty seconds.

Luke broke free of the jumbo and spun in place to meet the smaller elementals. It was easy enough to chop them down; he'd been doing it for a while anyway, and he was a significantly higher level than them. Two or three quick blows targeted at vulnerable joints were enough to break them to pieces. The notification dings sounded in his mind—one, two, three, four—and he spun back to the big guy.

Then he realized that more elementals were forming all around them. There were three coming out of the cliff face to his left, two more crawling out of the ground right next to the big guy, and three over on the stranger's side. No doubt there were dozens more drawn to the fighting but not in sight yet.

Luke knew his own limits. He knew he could manage four more **[Power Strike]**s before he was so exhausted that he wouldn't be able to flee. What he didn't know was whether four would be enough to put the jumbo down. If it wasn't, he'd be fucking himself over completely.

"I don't know if you can understand me," Luke yelled, "but now would be a good time to run away!"

The stranger shouted something back, none of which Luke got. Trying to play a game of charades while they were fighting for their lives didn't seem like a winning proposition, so Luke resigned himself to plan B: beating the ever-loving fuck out of a sentient, malevolent hill, then grabbing the other guy and dragging him along while he made a break for it if the elemental didn't die.

He lined up his first **[Power Strike]** and let it loose on the elemental. Before it could even shift to face him, he hammered it with a second one. Loose dirt and stone rained down across the pass, and the elemental lost a good ten feet off its height. By the time it shifted its face to see him, Luke was already in the air, mace raised overhead and held in both hands, and ready to unleash the third blow.

It came down hard on the elemental's face, blasting its features to pieces and tearing another huge chunk out of its body. Luke rode the attack all the way down to the ground and left a gaping fissure in his wake. The elemental fell forward, trying to rebuild itself and losing more of its size in the process.

Luke had one more in him. He knew he did, but when he tried to pull on the skill, it didn't respond. Wearily, he realized that doing four of them in a row was not the same as doing four of them in a minute and that, despite his earlier tests, he'd overestimated how far his stamina could carry him.

The elemental was much smaller now, more of a fat, squished hill than a looming monstrosity, but it wasn't dead, and he wasn't in much of a position to follow up with another attack. Fortunately, the other guy had been holding on to a trump card too, and he unleashed it while the elemental was still recovering.

The elemental rocked forward, and a rolling wave of dust and dirt washed over Luke. He coughed and stumbled back a few steps, momentarily off guard. Thankfully, not so jumbo was no longer in any condition to follow up. Whatever the stranger was doing, it was carving huge chunks out of the elemental.

And then, so abrupt that Luke wasn't even sure when it happened, the hill collapsed into a pile of loose dirt that rolled out in every direction. A ding sounded in his mind, signifying the end of the fight. Or rather, he realized grimly, the end of the biggest of the elementals but not the many smaller ones approaching. Normally, Luke would have regarded them as easy XP. Right now, he really needed to take a five-minute breather. When the first one reached him, he swatted it away, but he barely had enough strength left in his arm to send it tumbling backward when his attack would normally have broken it into rubble.

The stranger didn't look like he was in much better condition. In fact, he was down on one knee, leaning on his sword to stay upright. "Hey, we can't stay here," Luke said. He knew the guy wouldn't understand the words, but he hoped the tone would convey the meaning.

He jabbed a hand down the trail back into the valley. "Come on, we've got to go."

The elementals closed in on them, but together, the two of them stumbled their way through. Luke pushed aside anything that they couldn't get around, and after a few tense minutes, they outran the small elementals and rounded the boulder that marked the end of the trail.

"Okay," Luke said between breaths. "I think we're safe now. They don't ever seem to come past here. Maybe it wouldn't hurt to get a bit farther away though."

The man regarded him blankly, then said something in that strange language of his. He pointed at Luke, first at his coat, then his pants and his shoes. "What?" Luke said. "Yeah, I guess you wouldn't know what denim is? Why?"

Luke idly wondered what kind of materials humans used on Aros. He only had the goblins to judge off of, and he hoped that their crafting techniques left something to be desired. Then again, considering that the system just dumped knowledge into their heads, maybe it was a lack of material that held them back.

Or maybe they just didn't care, considering the human in front of him was wearing some sort of combination of cotton and leather, with actual metal armor over top of it. The armor itself was stamped with some kind of symbol, a circle made up of a bunch of different-colored lines woven around one another. The same symbol was set into the cross guard of his sword. He'd had a cloak once upon a time, but it was so torn up now that it barely hung down to his waist.

The man kept jabbering, but now it sounded more like he was talking to himself than to Luke. "Uh, dude. You okay there?"

The muttering stopped, and the man forced himself upright. He lifted his sword, regarded Luke grimly, and then lunged forward, point first.

Name	Luke Bennet
Level	19
XP	25337/25340
AP	0
Bloodline	SysAdmin
Strength	40
Agility	32
Stamina	26
Perception	29
Skills	Mace Mastery (2)
	Sword Mastery (1)
	Unarmed Martialist (1)
	Power Strike (1)
	Life Surge (1)
	Peripheral Awareness (1)
	Counter (1)
	Twitch Reflexes (2)
	Stealth (1)
	Survivalist (2)
	First Aid (1)
	Wood Carving (1)
	Leatherworking (2)

CHAPTER 32

oly shit!" Luke yelped. He threw himself backward and to the left, but the stranger just extended the lunge with another step and turned it into a sideways swing. Luke got the handle of his mace up just in time to block the attack, but it hit hard enough to push him back a step. He shoved back and broke the clash.

"What the hell is wrong with you!" Luke shouted. He'd just risked his life to save this guy, somehow miraculously winning a fight they had no business even surviving, and now the asshole was trying to kill him! That was some next-level bullshit.

On the one hand, it wasn't a very good attempt. The man was obviously exhausted and injured. Luke had been threatened by level 10 goblins that had more bite in their moves than this guy did right now. But on the other hand, Luke wasn't really in much better shape. His injuries were superficial, mostly bruises and muscle soreness. His own chain of **[Power Strike]**s was hindering him more than any injuries the jumbo elemental had given him.

The stranger, now mentally tagged as McDickbag by Luke, didn't bother to answer. Maybe it was the language barrier, or maybe he was just using all his processing power to try to murder the shit out of Luke. Either way, McDickbag pushed forward, his sword thrusting at Luke's stomach with each step.

Luke cursed as he gave ground, still not willing to engage McDickbag directly. Whatever misunderstanding was happening here, he'd rather figure out some way to communicate and clear it up than he would kill another human being. Monsters were one thing, even monsters like goblins. Murdering another human was something else.

McDickbag didn't look like he was going to give Luke a choice. His attacks started coming faster, from a wider variety of angles, and hitting harder with each one. There was a glow coming off his exposed skin, faint at first, but with each passing second growing brighter and denser. As the glow grew stronger, so did McDickbag.

Luke could barely keep in front of him, even with **[Twitch Reflexes]** and **[Unarmed Martialist]** helping him dodge. McDickbag was also good enough with his sword that **[Counter]** was giving Luke basically nothing to work with.

The way Luke figured it, there were only two options: play his own trump card or hold out long enough for this glowing spell to wear off. He had no idea what it was though, and it might last minutes or hours. He needed to end the fight, and do it decisively, before McDickbag overwhelmed him.

So Luke pulled the trigger on **[Life Surge]**, even though he knew he'd feel like shit when he was done and he didn't have any stockpiled food to recover with. Those were problems for future Luke to deal with. Present Luke needed to avoid having a dozen new holes poked into him.

As soon as **[Life Surge]** hit, Luke's speed shot up to match McDickbag's. The air was filled with the sound of screeching metal as their weapons smacked against each other, and the ground was covered with splattered blood from where they landed hits. Any slices McDickbag landed disappeared moments later, and the hits Luke tagged him with, hits that should have crushed stone, barely even caused a grimace on the stranger's face.

It was going to come down to whose trump skill gave out first. Luke knew **[Life Surge]** did not last long at all, and he'd activated it a minute after the glowing aura thing his opponent was using. He thought **[Life Surge]** probably gave him a slight edge in strength and speed, and of course regeneration was an awesome perk. Maybe McDickbag's skill lasted longer as a trade-off for granting less power.

Either way, **[Life Surge]** wasn't allowing him to overpower the stranger. It just didn't grant him the kind of power he needed, and he was seconds away from crashing. He fought desperately, hoping against hope to tag McDickbag with a decisive hit, something that would knock the man on his ass without killing him. That last part was optional at this point; Luke was desperate.

Then it happened. The glow winked out, and McDickbag's speed slowed to a crawl. He didn't look surprised at the change, only resigned. Luke saw his mouth moving, though no sounds came out. Whatever he was saying, whomever he was talking to, it wasn't going to save him. Luke's foot flashed up in a kick, courtesy of **[Unarmed Martialist]**, that smashed McDickbag's hand and sent his sword spinning through the air to hit the dirt ten feet away.

Before he could follow up, **[Life Surge]** gave out. Luke stumbled a step, tried to marshal his willpower to take that last swing but couldn't hold the weight of the mace. It tumbled out of his fingers, and he dropped to his hands and knees. It had not been this bad the first time he used the skill, but then he supposed he hadn't dropped **[Power Strike]** four times in a row right before he used it last time either.

McDickbag said something to him, not that Luke understood it. All he could do was stare at the dirt between his hands and pant. He saw the stranger's feet stop in front of him and his shadow raise its arm up. He'd picked his sword back up when Luke wasn't looking.

"Shit. Shit! Move, damn it!"

But he wasn't doing anything more strenuous than flopping on the ground. He should have used **[Life Surge]** to run like hell instead of fighting. His mind was running a million miles a second trying to find a way out, but his limbs were leaden masses that could barely support his body.

Time was up. He'd failed, hadn't even made it a month, let alone traveled the length of Aros to find the God Machine and bring his family back. The very first human he'd ever met was going to kill him, after he'd beaten hundreds of monsters.

A deafening screech rolled over him, so loud that his whole body spasmed and he collapsed face-first into the dirt. In front of him, McDickbag's shadow also flailed around, and a moment later, his feet disappeared from Luke's view. A blast of air flattened him to the ground, and a startled, hoarse cry rang out from overhead.

Luke forced himself to roll onto his back. There, maybe thirty or forty feet in the air, the stranger was struggling in Red's talons. The enormous hawk had grabbed him by the shoulders and was rapidly gaining altitude. McDickbag was punching the bird as hard as the awkward angle allowed, but Red was way too tough to be stopped by that.

And then the human was falling from maybe fifty or sixty feet up. A regular human back on Earth might survive that, albeit with a lot of broken bones. Here on Aros, fortified by stats, Luke doubted it would cause any real harm. But McDickbag was almost as exhausted as Luke himself, and he didn't make that landing well.

He hit with a loud thump, lay still for a long moment, then groaned in pain. Luke would have laughed if the situation wasn't so dire. If there was ever a time to get back on his feet, this was it. But he didn't think he could do it, not even to save his own life.

"No, you stupid asshole. You can do it. Just get up and make it happen," he told himself. It hurt, a lot, but he rolled onto his side and climbed to his knees. Nearby, McDickbag lay sprawled out on the ground, limbs twisted grotesquely. Luke crawled over to his mace, grabbed it in one hand, and stood on wobbly legs.

"I don't know who you are, or what the fuck your problem with me is, but fuck you, man. Fuck you with a cactus."

Then he hobbled over, brought the mace up, and slammed it down on McDickbag's face. Bones crunched and blood exploded outward. A pair of dings sounded in Luke's head, but he was too busy passing out to notice them.

The sun was starting to go down when his eyes opened. Luke was . . . surprisingly not as sore as he'd expected. Most of the exhaustion had come from **[Life Surge]**, which patched up injuries as part of the skill, so other than the fact that he was out-of-his-mind hungry, he was in pretty good condition.

Then he rolled over and saw the corpse of the man who'd tried to kill him. Luke groaned and sat upright. "Good morning to you, fuck head," he said to the corpse.

Then he just kind of stared at it for a bit and thought about what he'd done. He didn't think he felt bad. It was self-defense. The man had been trying to kill him. Or maybe those were justifications. That fight had been over. He could have let McDickbag live.

On the other hand, with stats and who-knew-what skills involved, there was a legitimate possibility the stranger could have gotten back up and finished the job. Luke hadn't considered that though. He'd just been pissed that somebody he'd tried to save had turned on him like that and met lethal force in kind.

The cloak was ruined by the whole busted-skull thing, but it had done a good job of keeping the armor relatively clean. McDickbag had been about the same size, maybe a bit thinner, but when Luke examined the armor, he discovered a lot of straps used for tightening and loosening it. It was a bit ghoulish to rob the dead, but well, he needed armor. That asshole didn't.

So Luke stole it. He took the sword too, and the belt with a leather pouch on it full of gold coins. He didn't feel bad about any of that. The only reason he didn't take the man's boots was that they wouldn't fit him.

His looting finished, he finally turned to his notifications. It was a bit exciting to see what level that jumbo elemental had been. He was figuring it must be at least 50. He flipped through a dozen or so notifications of lesser elemental kills until he found it.

[You have assisted in slaying Goliath Earth Elemental (level 34). 620 XP awarded.]

After that was a more sobering notification.

[You have assisted in slaying Daranite Human Templar (level 23). 277 XP awarded.]

[Congratulations! You have reached level 20. 20 AP awarded for use.]

"Daranite templar? Fuck, you had religion? Some sort of zealot? What was your problem with me though? We killed this fucking elemental together, which the system is totally lying about it being only level 34."

"The system does not lie, Luke," System said, appearing next to him.

Luke rolled his eyes and said, "It's a joke. But since you're here, can you tell me what language this guy was speaking?"

"Thalian," System supplied immediately.

"And that's a popular language? People speak that all over?"

"People speak it in Thalasa," System said. "That is the closest human-claimed territory."

"That's not as reassuring as I'd like it to be. I'm going to have to figure out how to speak that. Is there a skill for that?"

"Indeed. It costs 5 AP."

"Jesus, that's expensive. Least I have the AP for it. I'll come back to that later I guess. For now, I need some food."

Luke started for the forest, intent on finding something and fully willing to eat it raw, damn the risks, if he didn't see it soon enough. A caw brought his attention off to the side, where Red was perched on a rather large rock, four different dead animals piled up below it.

"Goddamn I love that bird," Luke said. "Okay, some wood for a fire and we are in business."

Name	Luke Bennet
Level	20
XP	25614/29492
AP	20
Bloodline	SysAdmin
Strength	40
Agility	32
Stamina	26
Perception	29
Skills	Mace Mastery (2)
	Sword Mastery (1)
	Unarmed Martialist (1)
	Power Strike (1)
	Life Surge (1)
	Peripheral Awareness (1)
	Counter (1)
	Twitch Reflexes (2)
	Stealth (1)
	Survivalist (2)
	First Aid (1)
	Wood Carving (1)
	Leatherworking (2)

Skill	Rank	AP	Prerequisites	Effect
Thalian	1	5	None	Translate speech between the brain and the mouth into the words of a foreign language. Also works on words heard in that language.

CHAPTER 33

Luke sat on the ground next to the shallow grave he'd dug for his brother's remains. "I think this might really be goodbye this time," he said. "I guess we'll see. I might get a mile up the pass and end up turning back when I run into another one of those goliath elementals. I got to say, I'm a bit nervous about making the attempt. Still got 20 AP though. Maybe I should dump it into agility and stamina so I can run away better?"

If he followed Curt's build notes, he really needed to pick up some utility skills and focus on upgrading his combat ones to rank 2 or 3. The build hadn't included spending any AP on language skills though, which Luke was definitely going to do. Curt had thought much higher of Luke's ability to pick up new skills from scratch than he should have.

[Cooking] was on his list to pick up as well. He was quite sick of charred monster meat and raw bitter berries. The only reason he hadn't picked it up already was that, much like **[Wood Carving]**, he doubted the skill would do him much good without tools. He was literally cooking off sticks he'd whittled to a point and skewered slabs of meat on to hang over an open fire.

At least the water was decent, but he really missed carbonation, vegetables, oils, and spices. Mostly, he missed eating things prepared by people who could actually cook. That was one of the things he was most looking forward to when he finally reached human civilization. That and safety, a warm bed, hot water to bathe in, new clothes . . . the list was actually kind of long, once he really thought about it.

"I want you to know that your advice saved my ass. Like a lot. I would never have taken **[Power Strike]** and **[Life Surge]**, you know? I probably wouldn't even have found them. I'm trying to follow this build as closely as possible, but stuff keeps getting in the way. Seems like every time I try to rebalance my stats, I end up having to splurge on stamina or agility because I need it right now. Plus I'm going over budget on skills you wanted me to pick up the hard way."

Luke didn't even need to look at the paper now. He'd read it so many times the information was permanently lodged in his brain. "Wish you were here with me. You'd know what to do. You always knew what to do. Probably why I have this guy." Luke patted the mace next to him. "It's been a lifesaver too."

Curt had given him everything he'd needed to survive so far: the knowledge and tools that synergized and gave him a leg up on practically everything he'd fought. Now he was leaving the valley, leaving the area that Curt had prepared him for. As he understood it, his brother had never made it out, and his builds were made with a lot of ideas and assumptions but no firsthand experience in regard to the rest of the world.

In short, it was time to leave the tutorial. He couldn't expect much in the way of hand-holding, and judging by the fact that the first human he'd ever met had done his level best to murder Luke, he probably needed to be discreet. He suspected he needed a new wardrobe and definitely needed to pick up the local language.

One of those was easy enough, kind of. He went ahead and bought **[Thalian]** for 5 AP but decided to sit on the other 15 AP until he scouted out the pass. If he could just walk through now, he'd dump the AP into a rank up. Otherwise it would go into agility and stamina if needed.

"I guess I'm just stalling now," he said as he stood up. "See ya soon, Curt. You just relax until I get this figured out."

The pile of dirt that was the goliath elemental was right where he remembered it. Luke had to bash his way through four elementals before he reached it, but they were all thankfully of the small variety. Luke jogged past the dirt heap with some amount of trepidation. He half expected it to re-form as he went by, but it remained a loose pile.

He went up another mile before the pass started to level out. It got steadily colder the higher up he went, cold enough that Luke wished his shirt and jacket were still in one piece. His shoe having a hole in it was also surprisingly uncomfortable. He'd mostly gotten used to walking on it, but having the cold hit his foot like that was a nasty surprise.

About four miles into his trek, he found another pile of loose dirt, this time with a corpse next to it. It was a young man, maybe a few years older than Luke. He was dressed in the same type of armor McDickbag had been wearing, the same type Luke was now wearing. Luke eyed the body thoughtfully, then stripped off the boots and compared them to his own shoes.

"Close enough," he muttered, casting his work boots aside. They were a bit too wide for his feet, but the length was good. It was probably about as close as he could reasonably expect to get. The body had been crushed from the waist up though, the armor mangled, head exploded, and arms shattered. Luke emptied the money from the belt pouch into the one he already had and left the rest of the mess behind.

Two miles later, he found two more bodies and three huge dirt piles. "Jesus," he said, looking at the carnage. The fight there had been earth-shattering, literally. Huge fissures ran up the wall and across the pass. Luke had to make a running jump to leap a fifteen-foot-wide crack that completely bisected the trail.

Both bodies were armored with identical equipment. One had a cloak that was still intact, though considerably more stained that he'd prefer. At least it looked like the discoloration was all mud, no blood. The temperature kept dropping as time went by, so Luke stole the cloak off that body. As usual, he looted the gold out of their pouches too.

He had no idea if he was rich now or not, but it certainly seemed like a lot of gold. Plus he'd gotten a pair of boots and a cloak out of it, which he greatly appreciated in light of the continuing temperature drop.

Still, that was five piles of goliath elemental remains he'd encountered now. It was a good thing he hadn't tried that blind run. They would have killed him for sure. He had no idea how close he was to the far end of the pass. He'd probably killed twenty or more of the smaller elementals already, with no end in sight. He needed to make it out before he slept; there was no way he was going to be left in peace.

It was nice XP at least, and nothing had jumped out at him he couldn't handle, so Luke kept running. The pass wound around, mostly easy to navigate with a few rough spots where the trail became narrow or had a drop off on one or both edges. Luke was more nervous than he felt he should be. Most of the time he'd adjusted to having stats, but sometimes something like this happened. He knew he wasn't going to fall, that he could probably walk that trail during a thunderstorm without losing his footing from the wind and rain.

But part of his mind was still looking at the edge and telling him to develop a new fear of heights. He stubbornly ignored it and walked on, a bit slower than necessary and with a lot more worry, but ever forward. At some point in time, the trail started rising again and Luke held his new cloak tightly around him. Apparently high stamina did not make him immune to freezing.

The bright side of things was that he'd killed twenty-six elementals so far, which was about half of a level. If he stopped to fight everything he saw, the number would probably be three times higher. It was tempting, at least in the parts of the pass that he didn't have to worry about falling to his death, but

Luke wanted to tempt fate as little as possible. There was no telling when another jumbo elemental might show up.

It was about four in the afternoon when he ran into a problem. The pass forked. Well, it was more of an intersection than a fork, but neither direction gave much hint as to which way to go. Any previous deviations in the trail had been easily identified and Luke had avoided them since he could clearly see them dead-ending within a thousand feet or so.

Both trails seemed to go miles and miles with no end in sight. One went up, the other down, but Luke had seen the trail rising and falling more than enough to know that just because he wanted to go down the mountain didn't mean the section going down right now was correct. Maybe it was, but he couldn't tell.

"System," he said. "Can you point me in the right direction here?"

"I am only able to tell you that the human lands of Thalasa are northeast of your current location," System replied.

"Neither of these trails goes in that direction," Luke said.

"My apologies, Luke."

He squinted at the blue apparition. "You're not that helpful, you know that?"

"I will not be able to give you more in-depth geographical information at your current level of system access," System said.

"Why do I even bother? Okay, fine. I'll figure it out myself."

"Very well."

Sometimes he got the feeling System was lying to him, that it was making a deliberate choice not to be helpful. If so, there wasn't much Luke could do about it. It was an intangible ghost, completely incapable of interacting with the physical world. Maybe if Luke learned some magic, he might affect it, but he doubted it.

A familiar screeching caw echoed down the left trail, breaking Luke out of his ruminations. He scanned the trail, looking for Red, or at least a darkened silhouette against the sky. There was nothing, but Luke had to pick a direction, and that seemed as good as any. He went left.

After a mile or so, the trail widened until he walked into a thickly for-ested slope. He kept one hand on his mace, just in case something jumped out at him, but trusted his perception to keep him safe. If nothing else, at least he figured there'd be no jumbo elementals with the trees packed so close together.

The smell of cooking caught his attention after a little while, and unlike his own feeble attempts, it actually smelled good. Luke followed his nose and quickly found a small firepit with a metal grill mounted on some poles over it. Several chunks of sizzling meat sat on the metal, so delicious looking that his mouth started watering.

"Uh, hello?" he called out. He didn't want to just jack someone's meal, but hopefully they'd be willing to trade some of the money he'd scavenged for a portion. That was if whoever was the owner of that campfire came back.

He caught a movement with **[Peripheral Awareness]** and looked up. There, perched on a branch overhead, was Red. Next to him, with one hand stroking the feathers on the crown of Red's head, was something shaped like a person but also clearly not. For one thing, it had feathers of its own, and a beak, and those same hawk's eyes. It also had human-shaped arms and legs connected to a human-shaped trunk, though its feet ended in cruelly sharp talons. Wings sprouted from its back and were tightly pulled against its body.

"Oh, um. Hi," Luke called up. "Nice to meet you. I'm Luke."

'*Hello, Luke,*' the thing said, though he heard nothing out loud. Instead, the words appeared in his brain, fully formed and stilted with an unfamiliar accent. '*My name is Kareem.*'

Name	Luke Bennet
Level	20
XP	27239/29492
AP	15
Bloodline	SysAdmin
Strength	40
Agility	32
Stamina	26
Perception	29
Skills	Mace Mastery (2)
	Sword Mastery (1)
	Unarmed Martialist (1)
	Power Strike (1)
	Life Surge (1)
	Peripheral Awareness (1)
	Counter (1)
	Twitch Reflexes (2)
	Stealth (1)
	Survivalist (2)
	First Aid (1)
	Wood Carving (1)
	Leatherworking (2)
	Thalian (1)

Skill	Rank	AP	Prerequisites	Effect
Thalian	1	5	None	Translates speech between the brain and the mouth into the words of a foreign language. Also works on words heard in that language.

CHAPTER 34

Oh, okay. Nope. Don't like that," Luke said. "Can you speak out loud instead of directly into my head?"

The birdman let out a warbling screech, followed by another telepathic message. '*I do not think you could understand my language. And I certainly do not understand yours.*'

"But you're responding to it right now."

'*I am not. I am responding to your thoughts. It is . . . imperfect but far more meaningful a conversation than we could otherwise have.*'

It was also giving Luke a killer headache, and he'd only been talking for thirty seconds. He didn't think he'd survive a full-blown conversation. Any second now, blood was going to start leaking out of his ears and eyeballs, then he'd have a stroke and keel over.

'*Ah, I see. I apologize. Is this better?*' Kareem asked.

The headache didn't disappear or get any better, but it also didn't get any worse. "Kind of," Luke admitted, somewhat begrudgingly. He hadn't actually vocalized any discomfort, and he didn't like that Kareem was apparently reading his mind.

'*Surface thoughts only,*' the birdman assured him. '*Only to facilitate communication.*'

Luke didn't think that made it any better, but he nodded. He supposed there was no need to say it out loud since Kareem was reading it straight out of his brain anyway. The birdman tilted his head in exactly the same way Red did and regarded Luke.

'*It is easier to limit myself to only reading your conversational thoughts when you speak aloud, but it is not strictly necessary.*'

"Okay. So then, it was nice to meet you. I assume you're friends with . . . uh . . . I have been calling it? Him? Red . . ."

'*Him,*' Kareen projected firmly. '*You would not be able to pronounce his real name. I don't know of any human who was able to speak our language. Red is a good name for him.*'

"Red then." Luke nodded at the hawk. "Like I said, it was nice to meet you, and no offense, but I have a ways to go, and I'm not comfortable with this form of communication."

'*I'll keep this brief then,*' Kareen said. '*First, a thank you for sharing your food with my soulbond. Your generosity was noted and appreciated.*'

"You're welcome?" Luke asked as much as he said. That had definitely only started because he was afraid Red was going to kill and eat him, though as time went by he'd started to grow fond of the bird, and there was always more meat than he could eat himself anyway. It hadn't cost him anything, and Red had saved his life, twice. "I really didn't do anything special."

'*It is still appreciated, nonetheless. Second, I wish to give you a warning. I am told that the human who attacked you was marked with the Sign of the Six. You should know that those wearing that mark, the same one on the armor you're wearing now, are considered to be the Voice of the Pantheon. It is their job to enforce Divine Will upon this world. Attacking you clearly implies that they consider you to be an enemy of the gods.*'

"What the fuck did I do to deserve that?" Luke asked, somewhat taken aback.

'*Perhaps because you are from elsewhere. Perhaps they do not want your knowledge and customs to influence this world. I do not know the answer. I merely seek to warn you that your death has likely been mandated by the Pantheon and that you should not expect them to give up after a single failed attempt.*'

Luke thought about how many bodies he'd seen on the trail. If all of them had made it through instead of just one, he wouldn't have stood a chance. Hell, if even two of them had survived, they'd have killed him easily. Maybe if he'd been fresh and they'd been exhausted, he might have gotten lucky, but Luke doubted it.

"What am I supposed to do about that? I'd go home if I could, you know?"

Kareem hopped off his perch and landed in front of Luke in a flutter of feathers. '*I see no evil in you. You do not wish to harm me, and you did not wish to fight the templar who attacked you. The gods surely must know this, and if they still call for your death, your very existence is a threat to them in some way that I cannot fathom. If you cannot flee this world, your only options are to fight or hide.*'

"Fuck. Of course I must be a threat. That makes sense."

His bloodline was called fucking SysAdmin. He was screwing with their system just by being alive. If he actually made it to the command console at the God Machine, he could do all sorts of stuff they wouldn't be happy about. Hell, he'd already made that an express goal of his. Screwing with the system was literally what he was going to do.

"Why didn't they just smite my ass and be done with it though?" he wondered. "Zap me with a lightning bolt or have a tree fall on me or something?"

'*The Covenant. No god may interfere with this world directly. They are all bound by it. Their churches and their faithful carry out their will.*'

That was . . . suspiciously convenient. Luke didn't buy it. If a literal god wasn't doing something, it wasn't because they didn't have permission. There had to be more to it than that. That was if he assumed everything Kareem said was true, and he didn't have any reason to think the birdman was lying to him.

It was a mystery for another time. For now, Luke's takeaway was that by wearing the armor and using the sword, he was impersonating a religious figure with probably a lot of authority, and that meant he probably shouldn't get caught. He might even ditch the armor completely when he did finally reach civilization, but for now he was going to keep wearing it. Some random monster out in the woods wasn't going to care if there was this world's version of a cross or whatever etched into it. The sword was getting dumped into a gully though.

This was a whole new layer of stress he did not need. It wasn't like he was expecting to just hop on a plane and then take a cab to the God Machine after he landed, but the fact that humans would be actively trying to kill him in addition to everything else that moved was more than a little frustrating. The shit part was that he wouldn't even be here if he could help it.

"Okay, so this all sucks. I'll figure something out though. Thank you for letting me know. I could have just walked right into a group of people who wanted to kill me without ever realizing it."

'*I think you may be pleasantly surprised to find that not all humans are enacting the Pantheon's will at every moment, but yes, you should be wary of them. It would be better not to announce your status as an outsider if you can avoid it.*'

"Right, good advice. Thanks again. Listen, not to be rude, but I really do need to get going."

'*One moment,*' Kareem said. He reached up to his wing and plucked a single feather out, then held it out to Luke. '*Take this with you. It has the power to conceal you from all senses. It will only work once, when you have deliberately broken it, and it will only last for a short time. If you find yourself in a perilous situation, it may help you escape.*'

"Oh, damn. There's already been a bunch of times I could have used one of these," Luke said as he accepted the feather. "Are you sure you should be giving this to me? I mean, I know you have a whole wing of them, but still . . ."

Kareem laughed, or at least that's what Luke decided to interpret it as. It was a kind of awkward hiccuping screech, like a nail being skipped across a chalkboard. *'The power comes from inside me. This token is just a physical manifestation of it. I will regenerate it by the time the sun comes up in the morning. It is a small enough thing for me, a gesture of goodwill from me and Red.'*

"Oh, well . . . if you're sure. Thank you again. I do need to get going," Luke said. "Um . . . this is the right way, isn't it? I only took this pass because Red was here."

'It is indeed. Red will guide you to the far end of the pass, but from there you will have to find your own way. If you ever find yourself returning here and you have gained the ability to fly, you should consider visiting our roost. We do not have guests all that often, and we do prefer it that way, but it would be interesting to hear the thoughts of an outsider on this world.'

"I will . . . um . . . keep that in mind," Luke said. He was mentally going over all the skills he'd browsed, trying to remember if there'd been one that let him fly. There couldn't have been, at least not that he'd seen. If he'd found that, it would have stood out as a way to escape the valley. It would probably also be something outrageous like 100 AP to learn.

Luke said his goodbyes, and the birdman flew back into the air. He disappeared beyond the canopy, and Luke looked over at Red, who was still sitting on his perch. The hawk gazed back down at him impassively while Luke adjusted his pack and slipped the feather inside.

"I had no idea you knew psychic bird people," he told Red. "Kinda cool. Not gonna lie. He was nice too, but oh man, does my head hurt now."

Luke took a few minutes to see if the pain would go away; thankfully it did start to subside quickly. He would be more than okay with never seeing Kareem or any other bird person again if it was going to hurt like that just to talk to them. He'd been stabbed and had it hurt less, literally.

Eventually, he ran out of excuses and needed to get moving again. Luke started off at a light jog and picked up speed as the trees thinned out. Occasionally he'd catch glimpses of Red flying overhead through the trees, but for the most part he just tried to keep going in a straight line.

Finally the trail opened up, which was great for putting on speed but sucked because, with the disappearance of all the vegetation, earth elementals started popping up again. Luke wove through them as best he could without slowing down, only occasionally stopping to break a few apart when they blocked his way forward.

Finally, sometime well after the sun had gone down, the ground tilted down, and twenty minutes later he found himself in a new forest. Red cawed overhead and landed nearby. "This it then?" Luke asked. "Eh, I know it is. It got warmer on the way down. Listen buddy, thanks for everything. You really did save my ass a few times, you know? I get that you have to stay with your birdman, your, uh . . . your soulbond I think he said? You want me to see about rustling up some dinner for us before you go back?"

Red cawed again, which Luke took as an affirmative. He spent twenty minutes snooping around the forest until he found something that looked scarily similar to a skunk trundling along. It didn't smell like one though, so he approached with care, clubbed it over the head, and built a quick fire to cook it.

Red got most of the meat raw, and when dinner was over, the bird hopped down onto the ground next to Luke. He gave him a quick peck on the shoulder with his beak, hard enough that Luke felt it even through his new armor, then it flew back off toward the mountains.

"Guess it's just you and me now, System," Luke said. "So, what the fuck is this shit about some gods wanting me dead?"

Name	Luke Bennet
Level	20
XP	28426/29492
AP	15
Bloodline	SysAdmin
Strength	40
Agility	32
Stamina	26
Perception	29
Skills	Mace Mastery (2)
	Sword Mastery (1)
	Unarmed Martialist (1)
	Power Strike (1)
	Life Surge (1)
	Peripheral Awareness (1)
	Counter (1)
	Twitch Reflexes (2)
	Stealth (1)
	Survivalist (2)
	First Aid (1)
	Wood Carving (1)
	Leatherworking (2)
	Thalian (1)

CHAPTER 35

System appeared out of nowhere, as always. "I am not able to speculate on the motivations of the gods or any vendettas they might have against you."

"Don't you give me that bullshit. This has something to do with my being an off-worlder. Tell me what you know."

"What would you like to know about, specifically?" System asked, ignoring the heat in Luke's voice.

"Well, let's start with the gods. Who are they? What do they do? What do they have to do with the God Machine?"

"The gods? Very well. Would you like general information or are you interested in one specific god?"

Luke's eye twitched, and he glared at the apparition. "How the hell am I supposed to know what I'm looking for? I don't know a damn thing about these gods. Let's start with how they're tied to the God Machine."

"They are not. The God Machine, the system itself, is a separate entity from the Pantheon. The God Machine's divine energy permeates this world, though it is a somewhat delicate thing, and the gods dare not act overtly on Aros lest they disrupt it."

"So that's the . . . the thing. The concord the birdman was talking about. No, uh . . . covenant? That sounds right."

"The Covenant is a pact between the various gods of the Pantheon to act only through their intermediaries in order to preserve the world itself. Should any single god wish it, they could destroy this world easily. They avoid this by agreeing not to directly intervene on Aros."

"Plus it'd fuck the whole system up, which would be bad."

"Indeed."

Luke sat down on a convenient rock and scrubbed his hand over his face. "Okay, so, tell me if I've got this right. A bunch of incomprehensibly powerful things want me to go away, and they're sending their minions to kill me? They won't do it themselves because it would piss off their buddies if they interfered, plus it might fuck up the system if they act directly."

"That is essentially correct, though again, I cannot speculate on the reason they are trying to kill you. I can tell you that it is very unusual for the entire Pantheon to agree on something. The Sign of the Six is rarely seen."

"Alright. Cool. Fuck these pricks anyway. Who are they?"

"They are Luos and Zixin, Hestoc and Nuvari, Dar and Ramira."

That meant nothing at all to Luke. Just a bunch of random sounds that he was already forgetting. It was kind of funny; he'd have thought the name of the assholes trying to kill him would stick with him, but nope. It was in one ear and out the other. It didn't really matter anyway, since he wasn't about to go pick a fight with them.

What he needed to watch out for was people with that rainbow ring symbol on them. It was only six colors, one for each god he assumed, and they were woven through one another in a circle instead of being an arch of separate colors, but close enough. Those people would be the humans taking orders from on high, like that guy who'd tried to kill him. Fucking fanatic about it too, more than willing to betray someone who'd saved his life.

Luke didn't want to meet anybody else like that. He just wanted to find the God Machine, access the command console, and get his family back. If he could open the door back home and take everyone with him, that would be the last thing he'd do in Aros. Really, the gods should have just offered him a lift. He'd be home by this time tomorrow, and it would save everyone a lot of effort.

"Is there anything else you'd like to know?" System asked.

"Tons of shit. But you're about useless when it comes to answering questions."

"My apologies. I would like to assist you further, but I am bound by the rules of the system. Your SysAdmin bloodline is not pure enough to grant full access. If you are able to purify it, please consider asking your questions again."

"Well if I ever find someone with the purification ritual skill willing to do it, I'll make sure I get it done," Luke said dryly. "In the meantime, is there anything else you can tell me right now?"

"Certainly. I have the accumulated knowledge of an entire world stored."

"Anything useful to me?"

"Yes. What topic would you like to discuss?"

"Shittiest bloodline ever," Luke muttered before clarifying. "Anything useful and relevant to the conversation?"

"I could tell you more about individual gods, if you would like."

"I don't give a shit about them. Can you tell me about their, uh . . . churches? I guess? The people who worship them, specifically the ones who would be sent to kill me like that guy back in the valley."

"He was a Daranite templar, human, and level 23."

"Yeah, I already know that. I got a notification from the system. From you. What else can you tell me about him?"

"I'm afraid you don't have access to additional information with your current bloodline purity."

"Motherfucker," Luke swore. "You are pissing me off now. Quit running me in circles and tell me something useful. Don't! Don't you fucking say it."

System, who had started to ask what Luke wanted to discuss, closed his mouth. "I am afraid there has been a misunderstanding, Luke. I am not a person. I cannot draw the logical conclusions you do. I can volunteer information about a topic, but I do not possess the ability to make connections or infer from context what specifically you want to know about. I can only answer your immediate questions as thoroughly as I am allowed to with your current access level."

"Like talking to a computer," Luke muttered.

"I do not know what that is," System replied.

"Don't worry about it, doesn't matter. Sorry for yelling at you."

"There is no need to apologize."

"Still. Sorry."

Luke didn't want to be one of those assholes yelling at their phone in public because they couldn't figure out how to make it do what they wanted. System looked like a person, kind of, but it wasn't, and he knew that. He was frustrated and stressed, and what should have been a milestone in having finally escaped Tenebrous Valley was instead starting to sound like he was walking into something even more dangerous.

"You can tell me which direction to go though, right? In a general sense."

"Certainly. Where would you like to go?"

"You said the nearest human city is a few hundred miles away. Which way do I need to go to get there?"

"Valtira is the name of it. It is approximately one hundred ninety miles east of here."

"And the God Machine? If I just decided to walk straight to it, how far would I need to go?"

"That is impossible at your current level. You would need to greatly increase your stamina in order to survive several thousands of miles of walking underwater."

Luke gave System a sharp look. "Where the hell is this thing anyway?"

"The God Machine is located on the continent known to humans as Sastilun. It is in the center of a circle of mountains known as the Crown of the World. To travel there directly from your current location would be a journey of roughly twelve thousand miles, assuming you could move in a straight line and bypass all obstacles."

"Jesus, could they have put this thing any farther away?"

"No. The Door and the God Machine are on the exact opposite ends of the world."

Luke just stared at System for a second. "It was a joke," he said. "Nice to know they're not making this easy or anything. I'm going to assume that was on purpose."

"My apologies, but I am not able to speculate on the motivations of the gods when they built the world."

"Too much of a coincidence otherwise," Luke said, ignoring System. "Okay, can you tell me the best way for someone like me to get there?"

"The most significant form of travel between continents is done by ship. That would likely be the easiest way to reach Sastilun, though not the fastest."

"And what would be the fastest way?" Luke asked.

"[Teleportation]. It would cost 100 AP for the skill alone, not including any other prerequisite skills. It also has a few restrictions that do make it more difficult to use, but once you overcome those hurdles, it would take you less than an hour to traverse the length of the world."

"Shit, even magic teleportation isn't instant? Not that it matters, since I don't have access to it anyway."

"Indeed, nor have you obtained any of the other prerequisites. You do not have intimate knowledge of the location you'd be teleporting to. You would also need at least a few skills to survive the open water between continents, as there are no two places on solid land within range of each other to make the jump in one teleportation."

"Then why the hell are you suggesting it to me?" Luke asked.

"It would be the fastest way to travel if it were available."

"But it's not, so don't suggest it."

"I understand. I will also remove ship travel as a possible suggestion, as you do not have current access to a ship."

"For the love of—no, just no. Okay? No. Leave everything on the list."

"I understand. Is there anything else I can help you with?"

"No. Please, just . . . I need some time to think."

"Very well."

System disappeared, leaving Luke alone in the forest. He sat there for about ten minutes, just mulling things over. Having to go on a cross-continental journey was a bit more than he'd expected. A few thousand miles was one thing, but this was literally the end of the world. Hell, it might even be farther than that. He wasn't sure if Aros was bigger or smaller than Earth.

He could theoretically devote his AP to acquiring everything he needed to teleport himself there, but that would be a huge investment. He was honestly sick of killing monsters, and the thought of a few months chilling on a boat was much more attractive than thousands of kills. He wasn't delusional enough to think that he'd get all the way there without fighting, but still, the thought of grinding out forty or more levels made him want to stab his eyes out with a rusty spoon.

So the trick was getting a ride on a boat across the ocean without attracting the notice of every fucked up religious zealot who'd be happy to slit his throat as soon as they knew who he was. Luke didn't think they were carrying around his picture or anything. The one he'd fought only recognized him from his clothes, and he'd replaced half of them already.

He could find new shirts and pants. That was a nice, easy, accomplishable goal. He'd want to practice speaking the local language, but he'd already spent the AP to obtain that. That reminded him, he was still sitting on 15 AP, and he wasn't sure exactly what he wanted to spend it on. Straight stats didn't feel necessary at the moment, and now that he'd learned more, his backup plan of ranking up a combat skill might not be the best choice either.

"System, is there anything you'd recommend to avoid notice? Any skill to help with that besides **[Stealth]**?"

"**[Disguise]** might help," System said as it reappeared. "It costs 3 AP."

Luke purchased that and said, "What else?"

"It would depend on what you are trying to accomplish. Many skills are situational. Can you tell me more about your goals?"

"Okay, let's start at the beginning. I need to get across the ocean, which means ship travel. Where is the closest place with a port?"

"Valtira," System replied promptly.

"Convenient," Luke said. "So I walk there, spend some of the templar gold I looted from their wallets, er, purses. Whatever. I get a ticket and ride across the ocean. Then I land, start walking, and bang, I'm there."

"That is theoretically possible," System agreed. "I suspect there will be many smaller matters to attend to along the way."

"Sure, but broad strokes. So I need to walk to Valtira. No special skills required. Then I need to catch a ride without getting murdered by some church zealots. So I want to avoid being noticed. What skills do I need?"

Name	Luke Bennet
Level	20
XP	28426/29492
AP	12
Bloodline	SysAdmin
Strength	40
Agility	32
Stamina	26
Perception	29
Skills	Mace Mastery (2)
	Sword Mastery (1)
	Unarmed Martialist (1)
	Power Strike (1)
	Life Surge (1)
	Peripheral Awareness (1)
	Counter (1)
	Twitch Reflexes (2)
	Stealth (1)
	Survivalist (2)
	First Aid (1)
	Wood Carving (1)
	Leatherworking (2)
	Thalian (1)
	Disguise (1)

Skill	Rank	AP	Prerequisites	Effect
Disguise	1	3	None	Decreases chance to be recognized while trying to disguise oneself and reduces the XP others can feel from you by 10%

CHAPTER 36

Luke appreciated Curt's build notes so much more by the time that conversation was done. System only advised on a skill to accomplish a particular task once Luke brought it up and never recommended anything on its own. They wasted close to an hour before Luke decided to walk while he talked.

Some skills were so situational that he couldn't foresee a realistic need to ever take them, but most were general enough that Luke considered spending the AP. **[Deception]** made the list of skills he bought on the extremely likely chance that he needed to lie to someone, though its partner skill **[Intuition]** got shelved. It wasn't that he didn't think anyone would ever try to lie to him, it was just that there was only so much AP to spend.

He didn't need skills like **[Intimidating Presence]**, which magnified the amount of XP awareness people would have of him, but he did consider **[Insignificant Presence]** briefly. Since he wasn't planning on having to hunt a meal for much longer, he held off on purchasing it. **[Stealth]** would already help with that anyway, though it annoyingly only suppressed his XP by 10 percent unless he spent the AP to rank it up, so it wasn't really all that useful.

It did stack with the 10 percent reduction from **[Disguise]**, which was a nice bonus. That only kicked in when he was actually trying to disguise himself, so it was kind of situational, but he figured he was always trying to disguise himself as a non-off-worlder. Hopefully the skill would agree with that logic, since he couldn't imagine too many situations where drawing attention to himself would help.

They went over and discarded dozens of other skills (why had System ever thought **[Fencing]** would help? Or **[Rappelling]**? **[Sleight of Hand]**?) while

Luke walked and System floated next to him. The ghost drifted right through trees and bushes, annoying Luke mightily every time he had to force his way through the underbrush. His stats were too high for it to be a real impediment now, but he didn't care for the idea of walking into the city buck naked after he'd shredded his only set of clothes tromping through the forest.

Despite the terrain, Luke covered ground quickly. Occasionally, he'd have System point out the correct direction and correct course, but with Valtira so far away, he wasn't too worried about missing it just yet. If he ended up walking an extra five or ten miles because he was too far south or north, it wasn't the end of the world. Once he finally broke free from the trees, he expected his speed to triple at minimum anyway.

Day turned to night, and Luke was still in the middle of nowhere. He didn't need much sleep anymore, so he pushed on through and kept walking. Once, he felt something pass nearby, something invisible even to his perception and with so much XP that he could only change course to distance himself farther from it.

He never got a good look at it, but it also didn't seem to care about him, and within a minute, he could no longer feel the creature. It scared the hell out of him though, reminded him that level 20 wasn't all that impressive in the grand scheme of things. Just because he'd beaten some goblin ass did not make him hot shit.

"System, how high do the levels go?"

"The cap is 100," System said. "Though very few creatures actually reach it. Your bloodline allows you to ignore this system limitation."

"Wait, it does? Why?"

"The cap is artificial, enforced by the system itself. Those who created it did not want anything to rise past level 100, but as a SysAdmin, you are not held to this restriction."

"Okay, that doesn't tell me much about why though."

"I apologize, Luke, I—"

"Ugh. Just stop. Stop apologizing all the time. You've done it about a thousand times today."

System must have needed a second to process that. "I understand. I have updated communication protocols to adhere to your instructions."

"Of course you did. Thanks, I guess."

"You're welcome."

"How's our heading looking? Still on track to reach the city?"

"Yes."

Luke grunted and broke through a set of stubborn branches that didn't want to bend far enough out of the way. "Great. Any place to sleep nearby?"

"There is a human village about three miles north of here," System said.

Luke paused, broken branch in his hand, and looked over at System. "There is? Are they going to try to attack me if I go there?"

"I do not know, but the highest-level human there is level 15."

It was weird that System could give him information about whole groups but not individuals, but it was better than getting nothing at all. If the strongest human there was level 15, even if they were combat specialized like him, that was considerably less risky than walking into a whole city.

It would be a good test run to see if he could convincingly act like a native human of Aros. Hopefully nobody would recognize the material of his jeans. He figured it was late, and if whoever he ran into didn't have at least a 20 in perception, they would probably have a hard time seeing fine enough detail to realize the pants weren't normal.

If he'd been thinking, he'd have stolen those too, but then again, taking a dead man's trousers was a bit much. Even if they weren't bloody, some of those bodies had smelled . . . fragrant. He wasn't keen on the idea of laundering the shit stains out of them either. No, he'd take his chances with his own jeans until he could find a better replacement.

"Can we switch to **[Thalian]**?" Luke asked, activating the skill. He was still speaking in English, but something took hold of his mouth. It forced his lips and tongue into the shape needed to speak an unintelligible string of sounds, sounds that he somehow knew were what he was trying to say.

"You are welcome to. I will still be able to understand you," System said. "I am afraid that only you can hear me, and your mind is automatically processing the communication in the way you would best understand it."

"Oh, like the birdman, Kareem?"

"Similar, though on a much more refined level."

There was some truth in that. Despite Kareem's efforts, conversation with him had been actively painful. It had been mildly torturous to talk to the birdman, and Luke had wanted nothing more than to end that conversation as quickly as possible. System, by comparison, was so smooth that he hadn't even realized that it wasn't speaking out loud. Even now, he couldn't tell the difference.

Though it was still sometimes mildly torturous to try to talk to System.

"Cool. Glad it doesn't feel like you're stabbing pens into my eyeballs every time we talk." The feeling like something had grabbed hold of his jaw and was twisting it around wasn't going away. If anything, the opposite was happening. The more he talked, the harder it seemed to twist.

The shit part was that what came out still sounded like English to him, so he didn't think he could get the hang of the language and speak it on his own just by using the skill either. If he didn't want it to feel like someone was violating his face every time he talked, he was going to have to put some serious effort into learning to actually speak Thalian.

For now, it would do, but Luke was not alright with the system taking over his mouth like this. He wondered what he'd hear when someone spoke Thalian back to him. He supposed he'd find out soon enough. The village was close now, he was sure.

"Which way is it again?" he asked.

"Over that way. Less than a mile now."

The forest thinned out the closer he got, until finally he broke free into an open space and found himself near a small field. He circled around it to the road and headed for the center of the village, where he hoped to find someone still awake that could point him toward a motel. Or whatever they called it. At this point, he'd sleep in an alley as long as no one pissed on him to wake him up.

There was one place near the edge of town that still had light coming through the windows. Of course, it was just his luck that it was on the opposite edge of where he'd approached from. It looked like a bar, just judging from what he saw through the open window when he walked by, albeit one lit by candles and lamps and furnished with nothing but hand-carved wooden furniture.

The murmur of conversation died down as he walked by, and he saw at least six people's heads turn to look through the window at him. Luke pulled the cloak tighter around him and made sure it hid the rainbow ring on the breastplate. The door was propped open to let the cool night air in, so he assumed it was fine to walk in.

He smiled. It was a bar. He hadn't gone into too many of them back on Earth, what with the whole being underage thing, but every now and then Lizzie had dragged him and Curt along. She probably drank more than she should have, but Luke wasn't going to begrudge her that. After their mom had died, she'd worked harder than anyone to keep the family stable. If she needed to take the edge off every now and then, well, that was just fine.

Her favorite bar was a place off Band Street where she was on a first-name basis with the owner. That was enough to get Curt and Luke in with her when necessary, which, considering how often Dad worked overtime, was quite a bit. They weren't supposed to drink, of course, but a few of the bartenders were friendly enough to let him have a bit on the side if the place was empty. Specifically, the bartenders who were trying to get into Lizzie's pants.

As far as he knew, not a single one had ever succeeded, and if they had, it definitely wasn't by slipping her little brother the occasional shot of cheap vodka. For all that, he'd spent a lot of hours in bars he was too young to be in, and they were some of his best memories, even if things were a bit fuzzy. He remembered her smile though, and her laughing.

"What can I do for you?" the man behind the bar asked when Luke sat down, not in English. He could hear the words, but it was like someone was translating right over top of them.

"Whatever's on tap," he said in Thalian. "Where can I get a bed for the night?"

The bartender gave him a look that told Luke he'd done something weird, or said something weird. "No beds," the man said slowly. "Town's too small for that."

"Ah," Luke said, trying not to sound too disappointed. "Just a drink then?"

"That I can help you with. No charge."

"What? No charge? Why not?"

"For a Guardian? I couldn't. Even a foreign-born one. You've given enough for the world. Least I can do is give you a drink."

"Oh." Luke was confused. It must have shown on his face. The bartender just smiled at him, patted his shoulder, and slid a clay mug in front of him.

He took an experimental sip. It was warmer than he'd expected, but he supposed he was in a world that didn't know what refrigeration was. There were some spices in there, not anything he was familiar with, but they gave the drink a kind of lingering heat. "Good," he said.

"I'm glad you approve, Guardian."

Whatever that meant. He'd ask System later. Maybe if he was lucky, he'd get an answer. He took another sip, then looked over when a man sat down next to him. He nodded at Luke, then said, "Heard you say you needed a place to stay?"

"Oh, uh, yes."

"Great. I'm Minou. Let's talk."

Name	Luke Bennet
Level	20
XP	28426/29492
AP	9
Bloodline	SysAdmin
Strength	40
Agility	32
Stamina	26
Perception	29
Skills	Mace Mastery (2)
	Sword Mastery (1)
	Unarmed Martialist (1)
	Power Strike (1)
	Life Surge (1)
	Peripheral Awareness (1)
	Counter (1)
	Twitch Reflexes (2)
	Stealth (1)
	Survivalist (2)
	First Aid (1)
	Wood Carving (1)
	Leatherworking (2)
	Thalian (1)
	Disguise (1)
	Deception (1)

Skill	Rank	AP	Prerequisites	Effect
Deception	1	3	None	Increases ability to lie or misdirect with speech and body language

CHAPTER 37

Luke took another sip of his drink and looked Minou over. The man was probably around level 10, which surprised Luke because he looked like he was in his forties. He was dressed in rough homespun, like something the actors in old-timey movies set three hundred years ago might wear.

He was in good shape, but it just looked like the physique of a man who did hard labor for a living, not a man whose body had been fortified with AP invested heavily into stats. Even at level 10, Luke had been in better shape. Compared to his physical capabilities now, he'd been a joke back then, but this guy wasn't even that. He must have invested nearly all his AP into skills.

"Do you have a room for rent?" Luke asked.

Minou nodded eagerly. "Got an extra room for the last three years, since my oldest girl got married, and I'm happy to let you use it as long as you need it."

"One night would be fine. I'm not planning on staying long. Maybe six hours."

"Er, just one night?" The man's face fell. "Ah. That should be fine, yes. That would be fine. You are welcome to stay with my family for the night, Guardian."

Luke struggled not to roll his eyes. "What's it going to cost me?" he asked, dreading hearing the answer. Somehow he doubted it was going to be just money. Luke didn't play a lot of these kinds of video games, but he knew the setup for a side quest when he saw one.

"Well, see, there's this tiny little problem on the farm," Minou said. "More of a speed bump for someone like you."

"No thanks," Luke said.

"But . . . what? I haven't even told you what the problem is yet."

"You need something killed, some big wolf or coyote or fox that's raiding your chickens and pigs."

"I . . . er, yes." The man's face flushed.

"Nope. I want a solid night's sleep, not to hang around for a week playing sheepdog waiting for it to show up. I have other places to be."

Minou seemed to struggle with himself for a few moments. His mouth flopped open and closed repeatedly. Luke just kept sipping his drink. "This is really good," he told the bartender. "Are you sure I can't pay you for it?"

"No, Guardian."

"Why do you keep calling me that? I'm not guarding anything."

The bartender shook his head. "We can all feel your strength. You are young to have that much. You've fought for something important, spent your precious years defending something. That is worthy of respect. I don't know what they call your kind in whatever land you come from, but here, that makes you a Guardian."

Luke took another drink to cover his confusion. He'd had a fairly intense month, sure, but he had trouble believing anyone would take more than a year or two of half-assed effort to catch up to his current level. Probably it could be done in less than six months of weekend hunting.

Then again, maybe the monsters were just less dense outside the valley. There were a lot more people here who'd need to split the XP too, but still, the math didn't add up. There were plenty of people who were ten or twenty years older than him in the bar, and they'd had the other nineteen years that he'd spent on Earth to grind out levels on top of that.

He was missing something that the bartender thought was obvious, some piece of knowledge that everybody knew. If everybody knew, he couldn't afford to ask, not if he wanted to keep his disguise intact. The cloak could only do so much to hide him, and asking stupid questions was a surefire way to get extra attention pointed his way.

They'd already identified him as a foreigner, no doubt from the language skill. Even he could tell that the way his mouth was moving wasn't pronouncing the words correctly compared to what he could hear under the translation coming into his brain. Then there was the fact that everyone around him was a lot darker than he was, enough so that he didn't think it was just the result of spending a lot of time out in the sun. After all, he'd been living outside for the past month and his skin was still lighter than the rest of the room.

Probably the third tell was the fact that this whole village only had maybe thirty or forty houses in it. He doubted there was a person in town over the age of five who didn't know everyone else's name, and probably half their business too. He might have been able to pass as an out-of-towner if it were just that, but everything together was just too much.

it, sucked away too much of their AP into utility skills. He could handle it as long as he was careful.

Wanting to end things quickly, Luke readied a **[Power Strike]** and burst into a sprint. The chimera's lion head roared in challenge, and it bounded forward too. Luke leaped straight into the air, mace held overhead in a two-handed grip, and brought it down on the chimera's face with all the power he could muster.

It left an impressive crater in the farmyard where he landed but didn't even touch the chimera. It pulled up short and spun away as soon as Luke had leaped, had in fact baited him into the attack and then dodged it cleanly. It was smarter than he'd given it credit for.

While he was recovering from the missed attack, it charged in from the side, jaws snapping and claws flashing. Luke let **[Twitch Reflexes]** pull him out of the way and reset his stance. He had definitely underestimated the chimera.

"Goddamn it. I just wanted a night of uninterrupted sleep. Why was that too much to ask for?"

Name	Luke Bennet
Level	20
XP	28426/29492
AP	9
Bloodline	SysAdmin
Strength	40
Agility	32
Stamina	26
Perception	29
Skills	Mace Mastery (2)
	Sword Mastery (1)
	Unarmed Martialist (1)
	Power Strike (1)
	Life Surge (1)
	Peripheral Awareness (1)
	Counter (1)
	Twitch Reflexes (2)
	Stealth (1)
	Survivalist (2)
	First Aid (1)
	Wood Carving (1)
	Leatherworking (2)
	Thalian (1)
	Disguise (1)
	Deception (1)

CHAPTER 38

The chimera was fast and smart. It knew better than to just lock itself into a grapple with Luke. Maybe it would win that, but maybe not. Size didn't mean shit in this world. It had gotten a decent measure of his speed when he'd run at it and probably overestimated his strength based on the attack he'd biffed it on.

The fight ranged across the yard, with the far more mobile chimera taking the lead in keeping at the edge of Luke's range. He chased after it, and it baited him away from the farm. He knew what was happening, but considering how much damage they'd done in under a minute, he was more than happy to get away from the house and barn so that he could really cut loose.

Once they were out past the fields, the fighting intensified. The chimera had a lot more room to pick up speed, and Luke had to admit it was probably faster than he was on a straight run. Without buildings to dodge around or fences to leap over, it switched to doing a sort of drive-by where it would slash or snap at him as it rushed past, hoping to be in and out of his range before he could retaliate.

Luke made it pay for that on its third attempt. He dodged the raking lion's claw that tried to slit him open and smacked its back leg with his mace hard, right in the knee joint. The chimera let out a pain-filled roar and leaped on the strength of its three good legs to put some distance between them.

There was no way in hell Luke was going to let it limp off into the mountains to recover. He took off after it, barely able to gain on it even with its busted knee, and eventually got close enough to take another swing. The chimera was ready for the attack and leaped straight up to dodge. For something so bulky, it was remarkably nimble.

It came down in a pounce, hard and fast. Luke scrambled to dodge, but **[Twitch Reflexes]** couldn't throw him out of the way of something so massive. It buried him in fur and muscle and snapping teeth while he struggled to force its head away from him. 40 strength wasn't just for show though, and despite the fact that the thing had to weigh literal tons, he didn't buckle under the weight.

With one hand tangled up in the chimera's mane and the other still gripping his mace, which he'd positioned across its bottom jaw to force its head up, Luke heaved it to the side. The chimera landed on its flank with a ground-shaking thump, momentarily dazed. Before it could recover, Luke grabbed his mace in both hands and readied another **[Power Strike]**. This one landed home, right across its face.

The bones crumpled, and the chimera went berserk. It hissed and scratched wildly at him, desperate to hurt Luke. Despite the completely ruined jaw and loose-hanging eye, it scrambled back to its feet and charged in. Luke wasn't sure if it knew it was done for and had decided to take him with it or if it was just pissed beyond all reason, but either way, it came at him with a whole new level of ferocity.

He still had **[Life Surge]** in his pocket if he needed it, but the chimera's savage attacks were wild and uncoordinated, displaying none of the cunning it had used earlier. Luke went on the defensive and used his mace to bat away sweeping paws while relying on footwork to keep from being buried under its sheer mass again.

Between its ruined back knee and its crushed face, the chimera wasn't nearly as fast or as accurate as it had been at the start of the fight. Luke tagged it with another **[Power Strike]** about thirty seconds later, that one catching it on its front leg and completely shattering the bone. The chimera staggered and struggled to keep itself upright but didn't relent in its attacks.

From there it was just a matter of finishing it off. It got slower and weaker from pain and blood loss, until eventually it couldn't fight anymore, and it died at the edge of a field. Luke was mostly uninjured aside from a bit of straining to handle the weight when it pounced on him and a triple line going down one arm where a stray claw had raked him while they were grappling. He hadn't even felt it at the time, but it stung like a bitch now. That's what he got for being too lazy to put on the armor.

[You have slain Lion's Head Chimera (level 20). 415 XP awarded.]

[Life Surge] would heal both of those up, but he wanted food on a plate in front of him before he activated it. Luke jogged back to the house and found Minou and his family waiting anxiously at the door for him. He raised a hand in greeting, realized it was covered in blood, and said, "Hey, do you happen to have a shower or tub? Things got messy."

"Of course, Guardian! We'll get it ready for you right away. Kids, start getting buckets of water to heat for our savior."

"Oh, you don't need to go through all the trouble," Luke said. Then he stopped. A hot bath did sound nice. "Well, tell you what, how much would a hot bath and a meal cost me?"

Minou smiled and shook his head. "It is the least we can do. Really, you asked for so little in exchange."

Luke was ushered into their kitchen and sat at the table while they scurried around him and insisted that he need do nothing but wait. Food was placed in front of him, and he took the opportunity to trigger **[Life Surge]** and heal himself up. Then he inhaled the food, only to find a second plate taking its place. That was demolished with similar speed, and soon after, the room he was sleeping in had a large wooden tub filled with steaming-hot water. Minou handed him a bar of soap and asked, "Would you like your clothes laundered?"

"Ha. I don't think the stains are coming out of these," he said. "I've been meaning to replace them. Could you recommend somewhere to buy some new ones in the morning?"

"Ah. I believe we are about the same size. I'll set out a shirt and pants for you to try on. If they fit, take them with my gratitude."

"Oh, come on, that's too much," Luke protested. "You can't give me the literal shirt off your back."

His mouth twisted weirdly when he said that, more so than usual at least, and Minou looked confused. "Sorry," Luke told him. "I don't think that translated right."

"It is fine. Anything we can do, just let us know. Here, let me get those clothes for you and you can get cleaned up."

Luke felt like he was taking advantage of the family, but he tried to see it from their point of view. How many sheep was a meal and a bath worth? Could anybody else have killed that chimera? Probably, but in numbers and at considerable risk. How much peace of mind would Minou have just knowing that a monster wasn't prowling in the night, wondering when it would decide to break into the house instead of eating livestock?

Framed like that, it was a bit easier to accept their generosity. Luke stripped himself down and made sure his jeans and boxers were tucked away. He'd find somewhere else to dispose of the jeans later, assuming he got a decent pair of pants tonight. Then he eased himself into the tub and let out a groan of pure relief at the hot water.

Luke just sat there soaking for a few minutes, his eyes pointed at the ceiling but not seeing anything. Since the minute he'd arrived in Aros, he'd been on his guard. Any second could be his last; there was danger lurking around every corner and behind every bush. Even when he was sleeping, it was troubled.

Exhaustion drove him to bed, and he woke up often at the slightest noise. He knew he wasn't really safe, even in Curt's workshop.

That constant state of awareness, that nervous tension that he never fully managed to shrug off, was draining in more ways than one. Luke was just so Goddamn tired. Lying there in that tub, it hit him all at once. He was going to crack and break long before he made it to the God Machine. Hell, he was already cracking.

Even now, finally back in civilization, he couldn't let himself relax fully. He was having his first bath that wasn't cold stream water in a month, and he couldn't enjoy it. His ears picked up every creaking floorboard, every murmured conversation. He heard Minou in the other room, opening and closing dresser drawers. He heard the animals outside, still unsettled by the chimera attack and huddled together.

It wasn't going to get better. He was heading to a place far more dangerous than the one he'd left behind: a city full of people like that templar intent on hunting him down. None of the rest of his family had accomplished this, and they'd all been older and smarter than him. He was stupid to think he'd make it where they'd all failed.

He wasn't even following his own plan. Curt had laid his whole build out for him long before Luke had even shown up. System was the one pointing him in the right direction. The only thing he was good for was hitting things really hard. Someday something was going to hit him back harder, hard enough that he wasn't going to pick himself back up.

A knock on the door snapped him out of his reverie. "Sir Guardian?" Minou's voice came through the door. "I have your new clothes."

"Thanks," Luke said. "Come on in."

Minou entered and placed them on the dresser. He glanced down at the pile of bloodied clothes and said, "Are you sure you wouldn't like them laundered?"

"No, thank you. Thanks for the replacements, Minou."

"If you're certain then," the farmer said. "When you're done, we'll get the bath drained so you can get back to sleep. Please, stay as long as you'd like."

"Just for the night," Luke said firmly. "I've got a long way to go still."

"As you say," Minou agreed before closing the door.

"A long, long way," Luke muttered to himself before closing his eyes.

He wasn't any sort of psychologist, but he knew he was heading for a breakdown. After just a month, he was completely burned-out. Something had to change if he was going to make it for the long haul. All he could think about was all the close calls. That cat monster that Red had saved him from. That goblin that had almost killed him. The templar . . .

Luke told himself he didn't feel bad about killing another person. It was self-defense. He didn't have a choice. If he'd let the man live, he could have used some healing skill and come after Luke again. It wasn't like there were any police or jail cells to hold him. Even if the templar hadn't had any way to heal himself, Luke wasn't doing him any favors by leaving him alive in that condition. A monster would have finished the man off inside an hour.

He didn't feel bad. The templar had deserved it. There was no reason to hang on to that, to dwell on it and replay it in his mind while he waited to fall asleep, because he didn't feel bad about it.

Now he just needed to find a way to make himself believe that.

Name	Luke Bennet
Level	20
XP	28841/29492
AP	9
Bloodline	SysAdmin
Strength	40
Agility	32
Stamina	26
Perception	29
Skills	Mace Mastery (2)
	Sword Mastery (1)
	Unarmed Martialist (1)
	Power Strike (1)
	Life Surge (1)
	Peripheral Awareness (1)
	Counter (1)
	Twitch Reflexes (2)
	Stealth (1)
	Survivalist (2)
	First Aid (1)
	Wood Carving (1)
	Leatherworking (2)
	Thalian (1)
	Disguise (1)
	Deception (1)

CHAPTER 39

It was a good thing he didn't need eight hours of sleep anymore. When he finally got back to sleep, he only had about two hours until sunrise. Minou and his family were all early risers, even with the night's excitement. Not for the first time early in the morning, Luke cursed his perception stat.

He got himself dressed and stuffed the rags that had been his old clothes into the leather backpack he'd made. His new pants and shirt weren't nearly as comfortable, but they were considerably cleaner, and they blended in. Other than the obvious difference in skin tone, Luke thought he looked just like everyone else.

Minou sent Luke off with a lot of food and an actual waterskin, which he was grateful for. The plastic bottles he'd been using were considerably worse for the wear, all two that were still left. Luke thanked him and, when no one was looking, left a gold coin on the counter. Then he set off for the village and from there to find the road heading east.

He moved at a jog, or at least what he considered to be one now. He was holding a pace of he guessed better than twenty miles an hour without even trying, and that was on a winding dirt track full of ruts and dips. If he pushed himself, he was betting he could run twice as fast for at least five or ten minutes.

Every two hours or so, he'd come across another town. For the most part, they were simple things that looked a lot like the first town he'd visited. Luke slowed down a walk when he got near and tried to be as unobtrusive as possible, though he was foiled by his high XP total. Even with **[Disguise]** and **[Stealth]** helping to mitigate it, at least as much as **[Stealth]** could help in the middle of the day on an open road, people noticed his presence when he walked by.

He got a few strange looks, but more than one person made a sign with their hand that it took him a few repetitions to recognize as some sort of gesture of respect, or maybe a salute. It kind of reminded him of those people back home who were all about thanking people for their service. Lizzie had a friend who had been part of the army, said it always made him uncomfortable because his job had taken him nowhere near the front lines ever.

That's what it was like. He didn't know these people. He wasn't fighting for them, and he had no idea why they kept looking at him like that, calling him Guardian, and thanking him. He'd thought it was the armor he'd stolen at first, but he'd been extra careful to make sure it wasn't visible at all, and he still caught people doing it.

After the third town, Luke started circling off the roads rather than walking through them. It actually took him about the same amount of time to go wide through fields and trees as it did to walk down the street, and it was distinctly less conspicuous. Very few monsters or animals even stopped to look at him when he went by. Most of them either froze or ran at his passing, and he never encountered anything that he would place above level 15.

He was about 650 XP short of his next level, and he was 1 AP short of bumping up his **[Disguise]** skill another rank. He wanted every advantage he could get before he actually walked into Valtira, so he detoured away from the road and started looking for monsters. He wasn't looking for anything as challenging as the chimera, just three or four weaker monsters he could steamroll to get his next infusion of AP and buff some skill ranks.

That hunt took far longer than he'd expected and made Luke reconsider just how dangerous the rest of the world was based on his limited experience in Tenebrous Valley. Things were more spread out on the other side of the pass, and with that space there was a lot less pressure forcing things to level up. His hunt took him miles and miles from the road.

He eventually found a pair of level 14 bears, both of which put the chimera to shame in terms of sheer size but had nothing on it when it came to speed. They attacked on sight too, which Luke appreciated. He didn't feel guilty about killing a pair of man-eaters, even if he was the one who'd intruded on their territory.

A part of him wanted to stop and build new hide-tanning racks, to butcher the bears as best he was able and make something useful out of the hides. He reminded himself that he was no longer trapped far from civilization and didn't need to do that kind of stuff anymore. He just needed the XP.

Reluctantly, he moved on. The mountains he'd come out of had followed him, always to the south, curving around the land and blocking out the horizon. By his logic, he'd come from the mountains, the chimera had come from the mountains, Red had come from the mountains. If he went that way, that's where things got stronger. He hoped he didn't need to go too far to get the last few kills he needed.

Twenty minutes later, he could safely say he no longer needed to go searching for monsters. He ducked behind a tree just as a large rock, really more of a small boulder, went flying by. It hit the next tree down the line, broke off a handful of branches, and crashed into the trunk hard enough that Luke could actually see the whole tree tilt a few degrees.

"Nope, nope nope nopenopenope. Fuck all of this," Luke said. The ogre roared in response and started stamping down the slope toward his position. Each step shook the ground. Luke scrambled away from the monster, weaving through trees and hoping that the next rock to come flying down his way didn't catch him by surprise. There was only so much **[Peripheral Awareness]** and **[Twitch Reflexes]** could do against a boulder half the size of his body that he wouldn't see until it crashed through the branches and hit him.

The monster was maybe level 15 or 16. He probably could have killed it without too much trouble, despite its overwhelming strength. Or maybe it was some sort of rock-throwing skill that made it faster. Luke wasn't sure, but either way, he could have worked around that.

A second and then third miniature boulder crashed through the foliage nearby, lobbed by the ogre's two buddies. All three of them crashed down the mountainside in pursuit, their enraged bellowing clearly marking their positions. If they'd just spread a bit farther apart, he thought he could isolate one long enough to bring it down.

They didn't do that, unfortunately. In fact, the noise seemed to draw them to one another, and Luke was left with no other choice but to keep running to stay ahead of them. While he ran, he schemed. The ogres were strong, but they didn't seem that smart. It was a dumb plan to just pit his raw power against theirs, to play to their strengths.

There was a small ravine he'd noted on his way up that he steered the chase to. It was maybe fifteen feet across, easily jumpable as long as he wasn't blundering wildly through the trees. Luke crossed it without a problem and made sure to make plenty of noise so that the ogres would pursue. With any luck, they'd burst right out of the trees at full speed, cross the three or four feet of open space next to the ravine, and tumble headfirst right into it.

He wasn't going to stick around to find out. If all three of them did manage to jump the ravine, or even just two of them, he didn't want to be anywhere near where they landed. If he split them up, well, it would depend on the split. He didn't see a lot of point in planning out his next twelve moves when it all depended on whether or not this part worked.

He heard a surprised yell echo through the trees, followed by a massive thump and the crack of rocks breaking. Luke grinned and listened for the sounds of the other ones falling. A few seconds later, he heard the massive crash of one of them landing, presumably having jumped the ravine. There was no third crash, which Luke assumed meant the last one had stopped in time and wasn't keen on trying to jump it.

With the pack thoroughly separated, he doubled back to see if he could close in on the one ogre who'd stuck the landing and ambush it. [Stealth] helped a little here, though it seemed to want him to take a route that was both convoluted and significantly longer than necessary. He couldn't really figure out why it pushed him to go that way at first, but as soon as he narrowed down his thought process from "not being seen" to "not being seen by the ogre," everything straightened itself out.

Luke filed that trick away to be examined later for possible exploitation. The skill was trying to help him avoid being seen by everything, or maybe just everything his perception had fed him but that he hadn't had the time to consciously sort out. Either way, he wanted to know a bit more about how the skill worked to see if he could use it to detect things as well.

That was a problem for another time. Luke ghosted through the woods as quietly as he could until he found the ogre, which wasn't hard. Unlike him, it made no effort to conceal its presence, and no effort to wait for the other two to catch up. It stomped through the trees, shoving whole trunks aside and tearing up roots where it needed to.

It definitely had a higher strength on top of being at least eleven feet tall with proportionate arms. Getting a solid hit in on a vulnerable area was going to be a challenge if Luke fought fair. So he instead did his best to guess which trees the ogre would pass by, scrambled up one, and waited. A minute later, the ogre pushed a nearby tree out of its way, and Luke tensed to make the jump.

His guess was off slightly; it took a path between two trees to the left, but Luke could still make that jump. His big problem was going to be that he wouldn't get that nice clean swing at the back of its head he was going for, and if it had anything like his own [Peripheral Awareness], there was every chance that it would see him in the air. He did not want to get caught midjump, unable to dodge.

On the bright side, his agility was definitely higher than the ogre's. It passed by, stepping into what Luke judged to be the perfect position, and he leaped off the tree. The branch he'd been squatting on shattered from the force, but he was already in the air. The ogre started to turn, its eyes wide in surprise, when Luke brought his mace down on its skull with all his might.

It was like bashing a mountain. The steel groaned and deformed, its formerly straight haft now twisted out at an angle. Reverberations stronger than

Luke had ever felt went through his hands and up his arms, so intense that he almost dropped the weapon in both pain and surprise. Then he crashed into the ogre's chest, and they both went down.

Fortunately, Luke landed on top, and the ogre didn't make a move to grab him. It lay there on the ground in a heap, its limbs twitching and eyes rolled up into the back of its head. Luke stared at it a moment, then looked to his mace. There . . . probably wasn't any way of fixing that. He tried to bend it back straight, and he mostly succeeded, but it was still very obviously damaged.

"Ah, damn it," he said. Then he stalked over to the ogre and slammed the mace down onto its face a few times. It started to bend again. Luke cursed his luck and delivered one final blow, finishing off both the mace and the ogre at the same time.

[You have slain Black Pine Hill Giant (level 17). 298 XP awarded.]
[Congratulations! You have reached level 21. 21 AP awarded for use.]
"Giant? Shouldn't you be, like, twice as tall then?"

He regarded the broken mace and sighed. At least he'd gotten the level he needed to increase the ranks on a few skills.

Name	Luke Bennet
Level	21
XP	29501/34079
AP	30
Bloodline	SysAdmin
Strength	40
Agility	32
Stamina	26
Perception	29
Skills	Mace Mastery (2)
	Sword Mastery (1)
	Unarmed Martialist (1)
	Power Strike (1)
	Life Surge (1)
	Peripheral Awareness (1)
	Counter (1)
	Twitch Reflexes (2)
	Stealth (1)
	Survivalist (2)
	First Aid (1)
	Wood Carving (1)
	Leatherworking (2)
	Thalian (1)
	Disguise (1)
	Deception (1)

CHAPTER 40

As much as it pained him to spend the AP on it, Luke couldn't help but feel that utility skills would serve him better in a human city than combat skills would. He wanted to upgrade **[Mace Mastery]**, but seeing as he no longer had a mace, that was probably not the best route to take. The loss of his weapon was enough to convince him not to even try going after the other two ogres. Or giants. Whatever.

With 30 AP to spend, upgrading **[Thalian]** to rank 2 seemed like the best use. That ran him 15 AP, and another 10 would go into either **[Deception]** or **[Disguise]**. He was leaning toward **[Disguise]** just for the increased XP-sense reduction. That last 5 AP would either go into a brand-new skill or directly into his stats or be spent on an upgrade to **[Unarmed Martialist]**.

In the end, he decided that with 25 AP going into utility skills and his main weapon broken beyond any real usefulness, he could justify putting a few points into the skill that was probably going to be most helpful to him if he got attacked before he was able to find a new weapon. **[Unarmed Martialist]** got the upgrade.

Luke was somewhat disappointed to learn that the amount of XP **[Disguise]** hid only went from 10 percent to 15 with the increased rank, but every little bit helped. Still, if he'd known, he might have put the points elsewhere.

It was a more somber jog back to the road and into Valtira. The city itself wasn't as big as Luke had thought it would be. He spied it from the road, just a wide, sprawling collection of one- and two-story houses and streets that stretched out as far as he could see. The whole region was heavily forested, but around the city it had been cleared out for miles and miles. Most of the open land was being used for farming, but the farther east he went, the more clumps of houses started popping up until finally the farms died out completely.

There were maybe two or three miles of dense urban sprawl before the city hit the water, though Luke wasn't sure if *dense* or *urban* were appropriate words to use. It looked more like a busy little town than a true city to him, but compared to the sizes of the other places he'd been through, he could see why people thought it was a city. If it had a population of more than a hundred thousand, he'd be surprised.

He could see eight different roads leading into the western half of the city and an impressive number of ships docked on the east side. Hopefully he'd be able to score a ride on one of them without attracting any undue attention, but before that, he needed to see if he could find someone to repair his weapon.

Luke followed the road into Valtira, not stopping until there were buildings all around him and dozens upon dozens of people walking the streets. He kept his cloak pulled tight to hide his armor even though he'd splattered mud across the rainbow-circle insignia to cover it. There were a few people wearing armor, their version of police he figured, with clubs on some sort of leather loop tied to their belts, but they were the only ones.

They were also, one and all, no higher than level 15. Even that was being generous. Some of them were as low as level 10 or 11. Despite Luke's **[Disguise]** skill helping to suppress his own XP, he still stood out far more than he wanted. The last thing he needed was anyone noticing that the armor he wore looked different than the police standard-issue.

At least as it got more crowded, it was harder for people to pick out that it was him. He didn't realize it at first, having never had a problem differentiating what he was feeling from each individual member of a group, but that obviously was not the case now. He constantly saw people's heads moving around, scanning the crowd, and passing over him without any sort of realization. Some of them still guessed correctly, but with so many bodies on the streets, he was able to maintain some anonymity. The police still unerringly picked him out, a feat he suspected was due to a higher perception than average.

None of them hassled him though, which was good enough for Luke's purposes. He only had two objectives: repair his weapon and get on a ship. If he could do that without getting into trouble, he'd call it a successful day. Unfortunately, that meant he needed to do something he'd been avoiding so far: actually talk to someone.

He found what appeared to be some kind of a business district, or at least it was a clump of streets that had a lot of different storefronts on it, and snagged a person at random. "Excuse me," he said, "Can you tell me where I can buy weapons?"

The man's eyes widened slightly when Luke started talking to him but otherwise didn't betray any emotion. "Two blocks that way, then right for another three blocks. The place is called Donaley's. You can't miss it."

"Thanks," Luke told him. He could see the man staring at him thanks to **[Peripheral Awareness]** as he walked away. Probably the guy just had enough perception to notice Luke's level. Or maybe even a rank 2 language skill wasn't strong enough to convince anyone he was a native.

He found Donaley's easily enough, and the random stranger was right, it was impossible to miss. The outside was painted neon blue, literally. It actually glowed, and the words *Donaley's Alchemical Blacksmithing* were inscribed in what appeared to be glittering golden letters above the door. Luke didn't know what that meant, but he was already there, so he went inside.

There was a . . . thing . . . in there. It looked human, kind of, except that it was at most two feet tall and proportioned like a bobblehead, and it zipped around the interior of the store through no discernable means that Luke could see. There wasn't a bit of hair on its head, and it had overly large ears with a nose to match.

"Who-o-oh! What's this, a customer?" the thing said, its voice buzzing in Luke's ears as it flew a few circles around him. "We do love customers. Hey, Donaley! You got someone out here on the showroom floor!"

"Um." Luke didn't want to be rude, but this thing was way too far into his personal space, and despite how fast it was, he was pretty sure he could tag it with a solid swat if he needed to. His fingers twitched, which was all it took for the buzzing thing to shoot off across the room, where it veered away from a wall mere fractions of a second before splattering itself across the wood paneling.

"I'm coming, I'm coming!" a voice grumped out from a back room. A regular-sized, human-proportioned person kicked open the door and marched into the room. He scowled at the buzzing thing before turning to face Luke. "What can I help you with?"

"I need to replace—gah!" Luke was interrupted by the buzzing thing zooming back around him to do a few more laps, one of which probably would have tweaked his nose if he hadn't leaned back out of the way. "I need to repl—do you mind?!"

The buzzing thing landed on Luke's head, prompting him to drop into a low crouch and snap one arm up to swat it away. It scooted through the air, ricocheted off a shield mounted on the far wall, and landed in a heap next to a display rack full of swords of all shapes and sizes.

"I, er, sorry," Luke said. Rank 2 **[Unarmed Martialist]** was going to take a bit of getting used to. "I didn't mean to just . . . you know . . . do that."

"Hahahaha! Pips deserved it," the human said. "Annoying little bastard. Don't worry about him; he's practically indestructible anyway. What were you saying?"

Luke shrugged off his pack and pulled it out from under his cloak. He flipped the top open and pulled out the two broken pieces of his mace. "Snapped this in half earlier today. I was hoping you might be able to fix it or replace it."

"Hmm, let me get a look at it. Bring it on over to the counter here, please."

Luke joined the human at the counter and waited patiently while he looked it over. "Rough work, but good quality. Never seen steel quite like this. Old too. I'd rate it for about 25 strength, maybe 30 if you're gentle. To do this to it though, I'm guessing you're probably closer to 40 normally, maybe 60 with an active skill. There's some stress cracks going through here that don't line up with the big break in the middle."

"That's . . . surprisingly accurate," Luke said. "I guess I've just outgrown it then."

"A little bit, yeah. Not to worry though, I've got a few pieces that'll handle a 40 strength all day long and take upward of 75 in a pinch. That should last you a good long while, assuming you got the coin to pay for it. Something like that's not cheap."

"How expensive is not cheap?" Luke asked. "I do have kind of a budget here."

Specifically, he'd counted them up, and he had twenty gold coins left exactly, but he had no idea how much that was actually worth. He could only hope that was enough to replace his broken weapon and get a ride across the ocean. If he could only afford one, Luke wasn't sure which he'd choose. He could double down on **[Unarmed Martialist]**, he supposed, but he wasn't keen on losing his range or on splitting his knuckles every day.

"Depends on how you want it, but cheapest one I've got that's rated for 40 strength is nine gold, and I want to be clear up front when I say that's good Kingdom gold, not whatever they've minted where you're from. If you got foreign money, I'll have to bring out the scales and make sure it's not alloyed."

Luke produced a gold coin out of his money pouch and held it up. The shopkeeper glanced at it, nodded once, and said, "Good. That'll make it easier. If you'll follow me then."

The showroom, as Pips had called it, wasn't all that big. It had a few racks with various types of weapons, all of which were what the shopkeeper described as display pieces. "You're looking for another mace?" he asked. "I've got two that'll work for you, but I've got four different kinds of swords, an axe or three, and a halberd that'd do some damage for someone with your strength."

"Just maces, I think. I've got skills tied to the type."

"Figured," the shopkeeper said. "But it doesn't hurt to ask. Okay, this wall here has the different kinds I make. On the left here are your choices, flanged, spiked, what have you. On the right is material. Everything from basic steel to living steel, stone wood, blood silver, even dead steel."

The living steel looked the most like Luke's own broken weapon, though there were some differences even he could see. It had a different texture and wasn't colored quite the same, though he didn't know what that meant. Stone wood looked exactly like he'd expect: a petrified log carved into the shape of a weapon. Blood silver, on the other hand, creeped him out. It was shiny, but with veins of color running through it that pulsed slightly.

At the far end, they had one single example of dead steel. It was a matte-black piece, devoid of ornamentation. Wavy ridges ran up and down the haft, interspersed with small, thorny spikes. The head was a wider fluted bar with its own curving thorns, bigger than the ones on the bottom. The very air around the mace was cold, though the weapon itself was unnaturally warm. Just looking at it made Luke uncomfortable in a way he couldn't quite put words to.

"Downright creepy, isn't it?" Pips said, popping up next to Luke's face.

Name	Luke Bennet
Level	21
XP	29501/34079
AP	0
Bloodline	SysAdmin
Strength	40
Agility	32
Stamina	26
Perception	29
Skills	Mace Mastery (2)
	Sword Mastery (1)
	Unarmed Martialist (2)
	Power Strike (1)
	Life Surge (1)
	Peripheral Awareness (1)
	Counter (1)
	Twitch Reflexes (2)
	Stealth (1)
	Survivalist (2)
	First Aid (1)
	Wood Carving (1)
	Leatherworking (2)
	Thalian (2)
	Disguise (2)
	Deception (1)

Skill	Rank	AP	Prerequisites	Effect
Unarmed Martialist	2	5	Rank 1	Increases ability to deflect or dodge attacks, as well as strike at vital spots
Thalian	2	15	Rank 1	Grants literacy and makes speech more natural, helps smooth over accents
Disguise	2	10	Rank 1	XP suppression is increased to 15%

CHAPTER 41

Pips bounced off the far wall, all the while cackling madly. Donaley barely spared them a glance before shaking his head. "Pips, don't you have anything better to do?"

"Nope," Pips said, popping back up to its feet and buzzing through the air again.

Luke resolved to ignore the tiny thing, though he was curious about what they were. It felt like it'd be rude to ask and also something he probably would already know if he wasn't an off-worlder. The best thing to do was just ignore Pips.

"Anyway," the shopkeeper said, shooing Pips away again. "That last one is dead steel, like I said. My old man got it off a dark revenant years ago. Not sure how much you know about dead steel, but it's great for people with high strength. Not only is it strong, it regenerates. For dark revenants, the armor is actually part of their body and will regrow if damaged. When it's properly harvested and treated, weapons made out of that steel will retain that property."

"It's kind of edgy, don't you think?" Luke said.

"Edgy? I guess. It's not really that sharp, but with all those little spikes, it can bite down on something if you need it to. Rips them right apart when you pull the mace back out."

That wasn't really what Luke meant, but he didn't bother to correct Donaley. Instead, he said, "How much is it though? It sure looks expensive, maybe more than I've got on me."

"Thirty gold, firm," the shopkeeper said, no trace of hesitation in his voice.

"Too much," Luke replied. "If it were half that, I'd think about it, but even that would be tight."

"Hmm, pure blood silver's probably going to be too soft for someone with your strength. Stone wood might hold, but it's so light that it'd be a waste." Donaley scratched at his chin while he stared at the wall. "What I'd really like to sell you is a weapon with a blood silver core braided with living steel. With the right bonding catalyst, you'd have something flexible enough not to break the first time you slam it down but still resilient and heavy enough to let you leverage your full strength."

"That sounds good, but again, budget."

"I don't have any maces in stock made that way. Got a sword, if you're interested, but I really doubt it. It's that one right there, with the basket handle and the thin blade."

Luke followed Donaley's gesture to see a sword nestled into a display rack with a long, thin blade that looked like it was made of chrome and tinged red. It was something he pictured a fencer using, or maybe a too-handsome pirate in a movie. He expected agility would be more useful than pure strength for a weapon like that, though he did have **[Sword Mastery]** as well and a 32 in his agility stat. He probably could use it effectively.

"I could make you a mace the same way, if you can wait a week."

"That . . . might be acceptable. I'm not sure how long I'll be in town."

"Go on over and test that sword out. Get a feel for the metal. You can damn near bend that blade down to touch the hilt and it'll snap back into place. Then after you do that, tell me it's not worth waiting a week."

Luke did as he was told. The sword's handle was perhaps a bit too small for him, or rather the basket guarding his fingers was a bit too tight, but after using those swords he'd looted from the goblins, it was nothing he couldn't deal with. He gave it a few experimental slashes and jabs, but he could tell right away that it was far lighter than what he was looking for.

That wasn't what he was supposed to test though. He brought the blade up near his face and peered at the metal. "Living steel is porous," Donaley said from across the room. "Takes well to the bonding process. It lets the core metal seep into it, all the way through it."

Sure enough, he could see the pattern in the steel, and he could see little spots of brighter red where the blood silver had seeped in. Without his perception, he doubted he'd ever have noticed; it all would have been just a reflective red sheen on the metal. Luke put some slight pressure on the blade and watched it flex. He increased the pressure until it bent almost ninety degrees. The steel started to crack, but the red silver just filled the gaps and forced the steel back into shape once he released the metal. A few seconds later, he couldn't tell that there had ever been anything wrong.

"That's amazing," Luke told the shopkeeper.

"Yes, quite. Would you like to talk about a custom order?"

"Let's talk price first."

"Mace uses a great deal more metal than a sword does. Eighteen gold."

"Too high," Luke said. He didn't know how much a boat ticket was going to cost, but he was betting more than two gold, and that wasn't including things like food. He liked food, and he liked it cooked by someone else if possible. "Twelve."

"Ridiculous. I'd be losing money on the material alone, not even looking at the labor."

"Fourteen then, and that's as high as I can go. If you won't take it, I'll have to find something else."

"Fourteen . . . and I'll take your old mace. I want to study it and see if I can figure out what went into the forging process."

Luke hesitated there. The weapon was kind of junk now, but Curt had made it, and it had kept him alive for weeks now. It had sentimental value, but at the same time, he needed to live so he could get Curt back. "Deal. Half of the money and the mace up front, half upon delivery."

"It's a deal! It's a deal!" Pips shouted while bouncing around the room. Donaley clotheslined it as it were going by, sending the pint-size thing into a spin that ended with it crashing into the floor.

"Swear to Hestoc, if you weren't so useful, I'd have booted your ass out years ago."

Pips's enthusiasm was not diminished in any way by that declaration, but the two humans both ignored them while they completed their business. "You want the new one shaped to match this one?" Donaley asked, gesturing toward the broken mace.

"If you can, yes. That'd be great."

"Sure, no problem. Might not look the exact same, but it'll be close."

"Thanks," Luke said.

"Like I said, no problem. Easy enough to do. Now, get on out of here and I'll see you in a week. Don't forget to bring the other half of the money!"

Myla was so surprised at the front door of her house being thrown open that she nearly nicked her finger with her knife. That would be a disaster, since she was in the middle of dissecting a ribbon toad's poison gland so she could drain the fluid out. It wouldn't be immediately fatal, and she did have an antidote on hand as any competent poisoner should, but her master would be . . . displeased.

She set the knife aside carefully and wiped her hands clean of blood while she sorted through what her perception was telling her. Two people had entered the house, one in armor. The other was wearing something with layers, judging by the swish of cloth on cloth. They walked confidently, which told her they were either fools or incredibly dangerous. No one with any sense barged into an inquisitor's home, not if they valued their lives. That went double if the inquisitor in question was their master of poisons, Adrevald Lath. There were maybe four or five other people in the entire Inquisition Department who outranked him, and all of them respected him and his talents far too much to rudely barge into his home.

This was likely a visit from someone inside the church hierarchy, but not part of the actual Inquisition itself. Considering that one of the intruders was heavily clothed and the other was in armor, they were probably a priest and a templar. She was so sure, she'd bet her favorite stiletto on it. Well, maybe not. It was a gift from her master, after all. It was precious to her.

A twitch of her legs was all it took for her to leap the eight feet to the ceiling and enter the secret passage there. She crept forward, silent and blade held at the ready, until she was over the foyer. One of the maids was standing there, scraping and bowing in front of a tall man with thinning gray hair and a bad comb-over.

Though she'd never spoken to him personally, she recognized him immediately. The armored man standing behind him and slightly to the left was new to her, but she didn't suppose he mattered. He was muscle, there to keep his boss safe.

Her favorite stiletto would remain in her possession, it seemed.

Myla dropped down from the ceiling behind the two men, one hand trailing against the wall to help control her descent. She landed without a sound, blade held down against her leg. "Hello, Cardinal Gnox," she said smoothly, interrupting the maid.

The templar reacted immediately, which was somewhat admirable she supposed. His sword cleared its sheath and whipped around in an arc, where it would have sliced her skull off at the nose if she'd let it. Instead the knife she was holding came up, flicked forward to smack the base of the sword, and knocked it straight up into the air. The templar managed to keep hold of it, but he was thrown off-balance in the act.

It would have been trivially easy to put the knife in his throat then, but Myla restrained herself. It was best not to make enemies of the other branches of the church, and moreover, her master would be upset if she stained his foyer with blood. He was rather fond of several of the paintings hung on display. Myla was confident she could angle the blood down and away from them, but it was best to let the intruder live.

"As I was saying," she continued as if a man hadn't just tried to reflexively murder her. "What can I help you with today, cardinal?"

"Ah, yes, the apprentice. Where is your master, girl?" Gnox stared down his nose at her. She was used to that. At barely five feet tall, everyone looked down on her. Most didn't manage it with quite the same level of contempt as he did, but she'd seen worse from more dangerous people.

"I'm afraid he is unavailable at the moment," Myla said smoothly. She knew better than to reveal even a hint of Master Lath's business, even to high-ranking members of the church. "Is there something I can do to assist you?"

"There is an apostate running around, still breathing the air that the gods have gifted this world. He needs to be scrubbed from existence, lest his heresy taint us all."

"I'm sure there are many apostates," Myla said. "What makes this one so special that Cardinal Gnox himself comes to request the services of an inquisitor?"

"I request nothing!" Gnox hissed. "I demand that you and your master do your jobs before you find the blades of the Inquisition turned on you!"

Myla gave him a blank stare. "Mm-hmm. Interesting. What did this guy do anyway?"

"Does it matter? Do you doubt my word?"

"Of course not, cardinal. I would never."

Something in her tone must have tipped him off because the man's eye started twitching. No doubt the threats would start spewing out any second now, which would likely spell the end of his career. Master Lath did not tolerate disrespect, not toward himself, and not toward his apprentice.

Surprisingly, Cardinal Gnox mastered his emotions. "He killed a patrol of templars," he said, his voice tight and strained.

Myla found herself nodding along. It didn't take much to get on the church's bad side, or rather, on the bad sides of some power-hungry individuals within the church, which was the same thing. Inquisitors didn't take orders from cardinals though. But in this case, if the man really had slain templars, she would gladly hunt him down.

"Tell me, what does he look like, and where might I find him?"

Name	Luke Bennet
Level	21
XP	29501/34079
AP	0
Bloodline	SysAdmin
Strength	40
Agility	32
Stamina	26
Perception	29
Skills	Mace Mastery (2)
	Sword Mastery (1)
	Unarmed Martialist (2)
	Power Strike (1)
	Life Surge (1)
	Peripheral Awareness (1)
	Counter (1)
	Twitch Reflexes (2)
	Stealth (1)
	Survivalist (2)
	First Aid (1)
	Wood Carving (1)
	Leatherworking (2)
	Thalian (2)
	Disguise (2)
	Deception (1)

CHAPTER 42

With his weapons issue sorted, kind of, Luke started working on securing passage on a ship. That turned out to be decidedly more difficult. He made his way through the city until he reached the docks, then started asking around for ships willing to take on passengers. Most of the dockhands and sailors didn't know, didn't care, and weren't impressed with the amount of XP they could feel coming off him.

More than once he was threatened with violence, and on two different occasions someone actually did take a swing at him. Luke fended off the attacks and left in a hurry. He wasn't eager to start a dockside brawl that might get him arrested, even if he was confident that he'd win. It was amazing how few people were above level 10. That had to mean something. It wasn't hard to gain levels, but it was rare for him to meet anyone higher than him.

He'd chalked it up as low-population-village life the first few times he'd seen other humans, but now he was in a big city, and it was still everywhere. It maybe made sense that the average level would be lower since people would specialize in their work and not everybody needed to go hunting monsters or defending the city, but that should mean that there were a few people who were much higher level.

It had only been a few hours since he'd arrived in Valtira. There probably were people like that, and he just hadn't run across them. Still, it was an odd coincidence. Something funky was happening there, but it was a mystery for another day. For now, he needed to find a sailor who wasn't an idiot, an asshole, or both.

Walking around questioning random people who were working wasn't the solution he needed, but he wasn't sure who he needed to be talking to instead.

There was no internet to look up the answer, no website to get a customer-service number, nowhere to fill out an order form, and nowhere to put in a credit card number.

Which meant he needed to find new problem-solving methods, and he didn't have a clue what they were. So far, he'd just been asking random people, but he seemed to have found a cross section of the population who were all perpetually pissed off and unhelpful. Maybe he could find someone dock adjacent who'd be more approachable.

"Move it, you jackass!" someone yelled at him.

Luke looked over and saw a dockworker with a heavy-looking barrel balanced on his shoulder. He glared at Luke and pointed toward the nearby warehouse. It wasn't like Luke was even in his way either. There was plenty of room to go around, but everyone on the docks acted like this.

"Piss off," he told the dockworker. "You can walk around."

The barrel hit the ground with a thump, and the dockworker stomped forward to crowd his space. "What was that, you little shit?"

"Are you serious with this?" Luke asked. "What's with every one of you pricks down here looking for a fight?"

The dockworker didn't answer. Instead, he swung at Luke, a full-body, twist-at-the-hips, all-the-weight-behind-it right hook. It came nowhere near hitting Luke, thanks to **[Unarmed Martialist]**. He slapped it aside with one hand and popped the dockworker in the face with a quick jab, just hard enough to rock the man back on his heels.

"Must be a cultural thing," Luke said. "Look, I'm really not interested in a fight. I'm just trying to find a ship that's taking passengers."

The dockworker's response was a blistering string of cursing that started in Thalian and quickly transitioned into another language Luke didn't know. He thought it might even have switched to a third somewhere in the middle, but by then he was too busy blocking punches to pay much attention.

"Just stop," he said. The dockworker had maybe half his strength and none of his agility. Luke wasn't going to get hit, and even if he did, it wasn't going to hurt.

"What, you too chickenshit to fight back?" the dockworker spat out. "Come on, you fish fucker. Why not take a real swing?"

"I'd really rather not."

He blocked a few more attacks, tripped the dockworker up, and sent him sprawling with a planted foot to the ass. Before the crusty old bastard could get back on his feet, Luke turned and walked away. He ducked down the first alley he saw, hoping the dockworker wouldn't follow him. A few had tried that, but he figured with the cargo being there, the man wouldn't stray too far away.

"You should have just knocked him for a loop," a new voice said.

Luke started and spun in place. He wasn't used to people sneaking up on him, but there, sitting on an empty crate, was a strange, small woman with bright-blue eyes and long, strawberry blonde hair that she'd tied into a literal knot behind her head. It took Luke a moment to process what he was seeing, since she was barely over four feet tall but otherwise looked like a normal person. She was dressed much the same as the dockworkers themselves, except on her the clothes were far too big and also far more ragged and threadbare. He could see toes through the spots in her shoes where the soles had come loose.

"One across the jaw, one to the balls, then kick him in the back of the head when he's down," the girl said.

"What good would that do? I kick his ass, six of his buddies come to his rescue. Then I'm running. Even if I'd stayed and fought and won somehow, so what?"

The girl shook her head and hopped off the crate. "You don't get how it works down here. That's why you can't get anyone to talk to you."

"That so?" Luke asked. "What am I doing wrong then?"

"You have a foreign accent. Your skin is too pale. Half your outfit is home-spun farmer clothes, but you're also wearing a templar's armor, boots, and cloak. Whatever game you're playing, they don't want to get dragged into it."

When she put it that way, it made a lot of sense to Luke. He hadn't real-ized the stuff he'd pulled off those dead guys was that recognizable. None of the farmers he'd talked to had remarked on it, but he guessed the church didn't send a lot of enforcers out to minor farming communities. They probably had a heavy presence in the city itself, heavy enough that people recognized their outfits.

He needed a whole new wardrobe, which meant spending more money. That meant he needed a way to make money, since he suspected he was already going to come up short on a boat ticket, but now he had even more expenses on top of that.

"Why are you telling me this?" Luke asked.

"Simple. You don't know what you're doing. I know what you need to do. I need money. You have money."

"So, what? You want to be my tour guide? And how do you know I have any money?"

"You're looking to book passage on a ship, so you must have at least a little money, or you're a complete idiot. I figure it's not that you're stupid, it's just that you're not from around here. You don't know how things work, and you could use the expertise of someone who does. So you want some help or not?"

"Depends what it's going to cost me," Luke said. He wasn't sure he trusted the strange woman to actually be helpful, but her guesses had been surprisingly insightful so far. Plus it wasn't like he'd had any luck. As long as she wasn't asking for outrageous sums of money, he might as well see if her advice was worth anything.

"Tell you what. I know where you can unload that templar gear. I'll go with you, make sure you get a good price. I get half what you make off it, and I'll help you find some stuff to blend in and show you where you can make money fast."

Since he had no idea what the gear was worth, he'd have no clue if he was getting ripped off when he went to flip it. Any deal where this lady got a percentage of what it sold for was good; it meant she'd try to get as much as she could for it. Or that she was running a scam with the pawnshop and was just trying to trick him into thinking he could trust her.

Luke had no way to know for sure, but the fact was he was hopelessly ignorant about even the most basic of things. He had no idea if he had a lot of money or a little, though he suspected that the weapon he'd commissioned was worth a lot, which probably meant he had a decent amount leftover. It would be so easy to lose it overnight just by getting ripped off by someone who smelled a sucker.

"What's your name?" he asked.

"Zea."

It was probably a fake name, or a nickname. Or hell, now that he considered it, every new name he'd learned so far was . . . weird. He supposed her name could really just be Zea.

"Zea? Nice to meet you."

"What's yours?"

It wasn't clever, or original, but he figured it would work. "Sucal."

"That's a weird name."

Luke scowled. "No one asked you."

"You should pick a better fake name."

"Goddamn it," Luke muttered. "Fine, what should my name be?"

"Something common enough that no one will remember how weird it is," Zea said seriously. "Maybe Ellis?"

"Eh . . ."

"Torgin? Ferdart? Vyndus? Cendran?"

"Stop, stop. Just pick one." Luke did not like Zea's evil grin, so he quickly amended, "One that isn't stupid and is commonly used."

"You're no fun," she pouted. "Fine, for real then? How about . . . Aldrick?"

"Sure, fine. I'm Aldrick as far as anyone in this city is concerned," Luke agreed.

"Great, nice to meet you, Aldrick. Now, let's get rid of that temple gear before the wrong person notices and sics an inquisitor on your trail."

"Maybe we should find at least some replacement shoes first," Luke said.

"Get 'em at the pawnshop. You need to get out of that stuff right away. You should honestly bundle up the armor and the boots inside the cloak, which you need to turn inside out, and carry it so that nobody sees."

"Seems like that would draw a lot of attention," Luke said. "Better to be mistaken for a templar than caught with contraband."

"Oh, sure," Zea agreed. She waved a hand toward the market district. "Over there. Where we're going, someone might try to kill you if they think you're doing a church raid."

"What the fuck is a church raid?" Luke asked. The name was certainly evocative enough that he had ideas, but he hoped he was wrong.

"What's it sound like?" Zea gave him a flat stare. "Church types come through, looking for heathens and blasphemers to abduct and do gods only know what to them. You see a squad of templars coming, you get the hell out of the way and pray you're not interesting enough for them to chase you down."

"Jesus Christ, that's fucking barbaric. And the people just . . . let them?"

Zea started laughing. "Gods, you must be from really, really far away. Come on, foreigner. Let's get you taken care of so I can get my money and you don't get killed. Maybe you can tell me how you ended up with half a templar's kit to begin with on the way."

"Looted some dead bodies. I needed new shoes," Luke said.

Zea sucked in a hissing breath and shook her head. "Take them off and walk barefoot. It's not going to kill you." She wiggled her toes to accentuate her point. "If a whole brute squad got killed, the church'll be looking for someone to blame. They'll come down on you like Dar himself marked you to die."

Luke had no idea what that meant, but he figured it was probably bad. Hopefully the walk wouldn't be too far though. He kicked off the boots, undid the straps to the armor, laid it all on his cloak, then tied it up into a bundle and threw it over his shoulder. "You'd better be right about all this, kid."

"Kid?"

"Uh . . ."

"I'm not a kid. I'm twenty-three."

"Shortest twenty-three-year-old I've ever met," Luke said.

"I'm a dwifkin, idiot."

"Oh, right."

Whatever the hell that was.

Name	Luke Bennet
Level	21
XP	29501/34079
AP	0
Bloodline	SysAdmin
Strength	40
Agility	32
Stamina	26
Perception	29
Skills	Mace Mastery (2)
	Sword Mastery (1)
	Unarmed Martialist (2)
	Power Strike (1)
	Life Surge (1)
	Peripheral Awareness (1)
	Counter (1)
	Twitch Reflexes (2)
	Stealth (1)
	Survivalist (2)
	First Aid (1)
	Wood Carving (1)
	Leatherworking (2)
	Thalian (2)
	Disguise (2)
	Deception (1)

CHAPTER 43

Zea handled the bargaining. Luke, on her orders, just stayed back and kept his mouth shut. The pawnbroker squinted at him a few times but didn't say anything about it. When it was all said and done, he stashed the bundle away and dropped nine silver coins into Zea's hand. She handed over three to Luke and stuck the rest in a little pouch she wore around her neck on a string.

"That doesn't look like half," he said.

"It's half minus the cost of your new boots," she shot back. "Just give him a minute."

The pawnbroker came back with a pair of low-cut boots that came up to Luke's ankles. There were cracks in the leather, but they were still solid enough to last for a little while. More importantly, they were about the same size as the one's he'd traded away.

Luke slipped into them, did a quick lap around the room, and nodded at the broker. They weren't as good as the boots he'd traded in, but if Zea was to be believed, he'd be a lot less conspicuous. At least, he'd be less likely to get targeted by church enforcers. There was nothing he could do about his level. Anyone with any decent amount of perception was going to pick him out of a crowd.

"Come on," she said.

Once they were back on the street, Zea led him a few blocks over before he asked, "Where are we going?"

"I said I'd show you where to make money, didn't I?"

"Oh, yeah. I guess you did. What kind of money are we talking about anyway, and what would I be doing?"

"Big, strong guy like you, the best place is the fight clubs."

"I thought you didn't talk about those kinds of places," Luke said with a smirk.

"What? No, why wouldn't I? They're not a secret. If no one knew about them, there'd be no money in it."

Luke groaned. If ever there was anything to drive home that he was in a new world, that was it right there. Forget the monsters and the levels and all that crap; the fact that not one single person would ever get any pop-culture reference he made, ever, was the real kicker. It really drove home how much he missed his old life. That and indoor plumbing. And toilet paper. God he missed toilet paper.

"Never mind," he said. "It's a joke from where I'm from."

"Weird foreigner humor. You should probably just let me do the talking when we get there."

"Hold on there. I didn't agree to this."

Zea spun in place and jabbed a finger at him. "You got anything useful besides combat skills?"

"I, er, [Leatherworking] and [Wood Carving]?"

"They'd better be at least rank 3, and even then, you're going to need raw materials and buyers before you make any money."

"[Leatherworking] is rank 2. [Wood Carving] is 1," Luke admitted.

Zea nodded along. "That's my point. You're good for fighting, not good at much else."

"I feel like I should be offended."

Zea shrugged and made a point of looking Luke over. "Do what you want. This is how you get money quick."

"How much does it cost to sail across the ocean anyway?" Luke asked.

"Why would you want to?"

Luke just gave her a look, and she rolled her eyes. "Fine, fine. I don't know. Fifty gold? Sixty? A hundred?"

There was no getting around it. He needed money, and he was going to be in Valtira for a while trying to get that much. Then again, Zea sounded more like she was guessing than like she actually knew. Maybe it would be less, significantly less. Unless she was off by a ton though, he didn't have near enough.

"Fuck me. Fine. Fight clubs. Which way?"

"Come on, foreigner. Let's go make some money!"

Luke had the sneaking suspicion that talking him into fighting was what Zea was after all along, but he had to admit that so far she'd been an excellent source of assistance. He followed her down the street as she navigated toward the seedier side of the city. The walls got dirtier, the streets got narrower, and it started to smell like shit and dead fish.

He half expected a street gang to jump out from around the corner and try to mug him, but either the city wasn't as dangerous as he'd expected or Zea was weaving around trouble spots. Considering the irregular twists and turns their route took, he had his suspicions that it was the latter. Before he could ask her about it, she stopped in front of a grimy door and pounded on it three times.

A moment later, someone pounded from the other side, and she hit it twice more. The door swung open to reveal a fat man in a grease-stained shirt with a mop of unruly black hair on his head. "What?" he asked.

"Got a fighter for you," Zea said, jerking a thumb at Luke. "Goes by Aldrick. I'm managing him."

"Your fighters are shit," the fat man told her.

"This one's different. Just feel the XP coming off him."

Fatty gave Luke a once-over, shrugged, and said, "Doesn't mean shit. So he stupidly piled on a bunch of XP. Doesn't mean his build is any good."

"So? Put him through an audition and then set the odds to favor the house."

"I—" Luke started to say, but Zea cut him off.

"I got this. You just wait."

Fatty snickered. "You're a mouthy one, you know that?"

"Fuck you," she said. "You want him or not? I can always take him over to Faye's."

"Screw her. Bring him in, we'll give him the once-over. If he's a flop, we can at least use him for an opener."

"Deal." Zea turned to Luke. "You need to fight a private match so they can get a feel for how to bill you, who to match you up against, so on. The better you show, the more money we make, so don't sandbag, got it?"

"Yeah," Luke said quietly. He gave Zea a searching look when she turned back to talk to Fatty again. Once again, he wondered just what a dwifkin was and if there was any way for him to find out without it being suspicious that he'd even asked.

There were obviously lots of people who weren't standard humans. That bobblehead person at the weapon store could talk too, and he still didn't have a clue what it was. That was the problem with not knowing stuff: he didn't know what it was common to not know and what would attract attention.

It was annoying because Luke really wanted to know what Fatty meant when he'd said it was stupid to pile on XP. It seemed like everyone was a lower level than they could be, and he guessed it could be on purpose, but why was it stupid to raise his level? It was just another of those things that was driving him crazy, but he didn't dare ask for clarification.

Zea finished up whatever her conversation was and poked Luke in the hip. "Huh? Oh, are you done now?" he asked.

"Ha. Barely even started, but come on. Let's get you into a pit so you can show off a bit, that way I've got some negotiating leverage."

Luke followed Zea and Fatty into the building. It was bigger than he'd expected, but only because someone had knocked out the wall between it and what he'd taken for a warehouse next to it. The front portion was a bar of some sort, and the other side, which was twice as big, was taken up by a twenty-foot-wide pit. Bleachers circled it, four seats high, mostly empty right now.

"The real fights don't start until the evening," Fatty explained, noticing the unasked question on Luke's face. "Hop down into that pit on the left side and I'll go grab someone for you to trade punches with."

There were no stairs or anything, but Luke didn't have an issue with jumping the eight feet to the ground. It was kind of soft anyway, a bit spongier than solid ground should be. He wasn't quite sure what to make of that, so he chalked it up to a purposeful design to cut down on injuries if someone took a bad fall. It was still solid enough that he didn't think it would affect his footwork.

Zea sat on the edge of the pit and watched him. "What do you think?" she asked.

Luke shrugged. "It's fine, I guess. Softer than I'm used to moving on, but it's not a big deal. Got any advice on this? Should I drag it out or drop them fast?"

Zea snorted. "If Sideon brings back who I'm thinking he will, you're just going to want to try not to get your ass kicked too bad to walk away after."

"Your confidence in me is touching," Luke told her.

"I don't know you that well."

"Didn't slow you down from trying to make money off me."

"We're both winning here. You badly need some direction, and I badly need more money."

That was true enough, if he went by what she was wearing. She looked like a homeless orphan, but he was starting to suspect the outfit was more camouflage than because she couldn't afford better. There was no way someone as smart and proactive as her was just scraping by, wearing clothes that came out of the garbage and hitting up foreigners for help.

"I'm just saying, you haven't seen me fight yet," he told her.

Zea looked over her shoulder at something Luke couldn't see from where he was standing in the pit. "Figured," she said. "You want some advice? Guard your nuts."

"What? Why would I need to..."

"You heard me," Zea said. "You ever want to have kids, you'll listen."

"What the fuck are you talking about?" Not punching his opponent in the crotch was pretty standard fight etiquette where Luke came from.

Then Fatty, or Sideon, Luke supposed, appeared next to Zea. "He ready?" he asked, nodding down at Luke.

"Ready as he'll ever be," Zea said.

They both snickered at that, an evil little laugh that Luke was not at all comfortable with. He was confused though; Fatty was supposed to bring out someone for him to spar with, and there was no one. Hopefully they weren't expecting him to do shadowboxing or something, unless it was some sort of ploy to weaken Zea's negotiating position.

Then a little boy he hadn't noticed hopped down into the pit in front him. The kid was even shorter than Zea. He had long black hair that he'd tied back at the nape of his neck and wore heavy boots and tight pants held in place with a metal-studded belt.

"This the guy?" the kid asked, raising his hands. "He looks like a pushover."

"Um . . ."

"Oh great, one of those assholes. Thinks a dwifkin can't fight just because we're small. Gods help me, I love putting shitheads like you in your place."

"What? No, that's not it. I just . . . haven't done this before."

"Done what before?" the not-kid asked. "Fight? You're in for a bad time, buddy. Don't worry, I won't break anything permanently."

Luke was more confused than anything. The guy was maybe level 10, and that was being generous. The lower levels kind of all blurred together to his perception, but he wouldn't be surprised if the not-kid's actual level was as low as 7. Luke shot a glance over at Zea, who just smirked back at him.

"Remember what I told you," she said.

"Uh . . . not really sure if . . . I mean, you know, what are the rules?"

"Rules?" the not-kid said. "Don't kill each other. Try not to break anything too expensive to fix."

"That's it?"

"You talk too much," Fatty said. "Kick his ass around the ring for a bit, Zammin."

"Wait, wha—!"

Name	Luke Bennet
Level	21
XP	29501/34079
AP	0
Bloodline	SysAdmin
Strength	40
Agility	32
Stamina	26
Perception	29
Skills	Mace Mastery (2)
	Sword Mastery (1)
	Unarmed Martialist (2)
	Power Strike (1)
	Life Surge (1)
	Peripheral Awareness (1)
	Counter (1)
	Twitch Reflexes (2)
	Stealth (1)
	Survivalist (2)
	First Aid (1)
	Wood Carving (1)
	Leatherworking (2)
	Thalian (2)
	Disguise (2)
	Deception (1)

CHAPTER 44

[Twitch Reflexes] was Luke's new best friend. One moment, Zammin was standing in front of him, maybe five feet away; the next, the diminutive fighter was a foot in front of him with his fist driving into Luke's outer thigh. And the only reason it was just his thigh taking the blow instead of Zammin's intended target was that beautiful, beautiful skill: **[Twitch Reflexes]**.

Luke resolved right then and there that his next level's AP was going to be devoted toward bringing that skill up to rank 3. It had saved his ass so many times, and he was sure with another rank and a few more points into agility, he'd have dodged the cock shot completely.

"Dirty fucking pool, you little asshole," he growled, lashing out with a knee. If it had connected, it probably would have knocked a few of Zammin's teeth out, but the dwifkin was so damn fast that Luke whiffed it completely. A spike of pain shot through him when the little fucker punched the inside of his attacking knee, and the only reason Luke remained standing was his tremendous strength stat helping him resist the blow.

It didn't seem possible. The pint-size fighter was a fraction of his level. Even if he'd invested every single AP he had into agility, there was no way he was beating out Luke's perception. Impossible or not, that was exactly what was happening. He couldn't keep up with Zammin's movements at all. **[Twitch Reflexes]** protected the family jewels, something Zammin targeted liberally, but otherwise wasn't much use in getting Luke out of the way.

[Unarmed Martialist] had something to say about that. He couldn't keep up with Zammin, for whatever reason, but he could and did limit the other fighter's avenues of attack. It didn't help him land a blow of his own, but it did help him protect himself. If he was going to win this fight, he needed to come up with something clever.

"See," Zea said. "Look how well he's doing."

"He's getting his ass kicked," Fatty argued. "He hasn't even touched Zammin."

"Well no shit. Nobody touches Zammin! But he's still on his feet, and he blocked that first punch to the balls."

Luke lost track of the argument—or maybe it was a negotiation—after that, when the little testicle terrorist came back for another flyby. He twisted his leg to block the punch, then hopped up about six inches into the air to avoid a kick to the ankles. His foot lashed out, and he planted it firmly on the leg supporting Zammin's weight. The dwifkin yelped in surprise and pain and retaliated with an uppercut right toward his favorite target.

"Getting predictable, shithead," Luke said, pivoting the heel grinding into Zammin's upper thigh so that he could twist to take the punch. Then he leaned forward and put all his weight squarely on the dwifkin, who collapsed with a yelp and a loud snapping sound.

Luke landed with most of his weight on his back foot while his leading foot pinned Zammin to the ground by the leg. "I think it's broken," he called up to Zea and Fatty. "You want to call it here?"

"Holy shit," Fatty breathed out. Zea just grinned.

Luke saw a flicker of movement, **[Twitch Reflexes]** tried to throw him to the side, and something clamped onto his ankle before he could move. There was a tiny fraction of a second between Luke realizing that Zammin had grabbed hold of him with one hand and the dwifkin fighter's other hand driving hard into Luke's nuts.

Luke fell back, an almost inaudible squeal of pain escaping his lips. Zammin wasn't that strong, thank God, but even a 5 or 6 in his strength stat would match a full-grown earthling in good shape. And the little fucker didn't hold back, at all. It took a lot of willpower not to throw up all over the floor.

"Ha! The Nut Devil strikes again!" Zammin yelled from where he was lying on the ground. The fact that his leg was broken didn't seem to bother him at all.

"I told you we're not calling you that!" Fatty yelled down at him. "Someone else is already using that name."

"Oh, come on! It's the perfect name for me. Who's the other fucker who's using it? I'll pay him a visit and we can determine who the true Nut Devil is."

"I said no."

Luke groaned and steadied himself. He'd been hurt before; hell, he'd been stabbed and shot more than once. This pain wasn't exactly worse, but it was different. He took a deep breath in, then back out, in, out. Slowly, he straightened out. Zammin was still sitting on the ground, his broken leg sticking out at a funny angle.

Luke took two running steps and then, leg fully cocked back, unloaded a kick into Zammin's crotch so hard that it lifted the fighter off the ground and threw him across the pit. He skidded a few feet across the ground before flopping over, laughing hysterically.

"Hahahahahahaha! I love it! This guy is awesome. Hire him, Sideon."

"We'll see," Fatty said. He turned back to Zea and said, "Okay, the human's got some style. Audience would probably love it. He's not fast enough to do a good fight with Zammin, but we could put him against a few of the upper ranks as a newcomer and clean up on the bets early on. He does good enough, maybe we put them back in the ring together. With a bit of practice, they could choreograph something that people will pay to see."

"Hey, is this fight over now?" Luke asked.

"Hmm? Yeah, sure. Go get yourself a beer or something."

The beer tasted like shit. Luke found himself missing that spiced drink and wishing he'd gotten the name of it. Maybe if he described it to the bartender, she'd know what he was talking about. He was just about to get up and follow through on that plan, when Zammin slid into the chair on the other side of the table.

"Hi there. Ugh, one second, the lever is stuck," the dwifkin said.

Something popped, and the chair rose up an inch before stopping. "Zixin take you, you piece of shit! Death on your family to the ninth degree!" Zammin roared, hopping back out of the chair.

He kicked something under the seat, Luke heard a piece of metal squeal, and the chair rose up another foot. As if nothing had happened at all, Zammin calmly climbed back into the seat and looked at Luke. "Right, like I was saying. Hi."

"Um . . . hi."

"Your manager is raking Sideon over the coals. Very ferocious." Zammin waggled his eyebrows as he spoke.

"Look, no offense, but my balls still ache, and this beer is piss water. Do you need something?"

Zammin reached across the table, plucked Luke's beer out of his hands, and took a drink. "Oh, yuck. That is nasty. Let's get something better."

"Hey. You can't just . . . You know what, fuck it. I don't even care. It's not like I was going to finish it anyway."

"I'll be right back. You just wait here."

Luke watched, bemused, as Zammin weaved through tables that he could barely see over, approached the bar, and loudly demanded two flagons of something called black burrow stout. Then he carried them back over, each one about the same size as his head, plopped them onto the table, and hopped back into his seat.

"Right, take a sip of that and tell me you don't love it," the diminutive fighter ordered.

The liquid was pitch-black and thick like melted chocolate. At least, that's what it looked like. It was hard to tell if it was even moving inside the flagon. Almost hesitantly, Luke took a drink. It was incredibly bitter. "Oh, Goddamn," he said. "That's something."

"What, you don't like it?" Zammin asked.

"I didn't say that, just that it's a lot." Luke took another sip. "Is this even alcoholic?"

"Oh, incredibly so," Zammin said happily. "At least, it is for humans. You probably shouldn't finish that if your stamina is under 30."

"Eh, close enough."

Zammin shrugged and took a long pull from his own flagon, an act that looked ridiculous to Luke. When he set it back down, he leaned back in his chair with a happy sigh. "I wasn't sure about you at first, but after the match, well, you're alright for a tall-boy."

Luke took another drink. Still bitter, but he was warming up to it. "Thanks, I guess. Uh, weird question, but are you wearing a cup?"

"A cup?"

"A . . . uh . . ." Luke gestured toward his crotch. "Armor?"

"Oh, a codpiece? Always."

That explained the weird resistance at the end of that kick. He hadn't been sure if it was dwifkin biology or not.

"So anyway, wanted to talk to you about your fights. Sideon always wants to put the new guy up against Tantoro. The regulars expect it, so it's pretty much mandatory."

"Okay, thanks for the warning, I guess?" It didn't mean too much to Luke since he had no clue who the hell Tantoro was, but he appreciated the gesture. Admittedly, he'd appreciate it more if his balls didn't hurt. Though the stout was a good start. The flagon was half-empty already.

"It's not a warning," Zammin said. "Well, kind of. Tantoro isn't human either. He has . . . different customs. Don't be shocked when you meet him. Also, he doesn't have the stats to take a full shot like that, so maybe go a bit easy on him, yeah? It's supposed to be fun, not deadly."

"Yeah, I got ya. Speaking of which, how's the leg? I thought I broke that."

"Oh, you did. Hurt like a bitch. I've got it splinted now."

"You're just walking around on it? That's crazy."

"It'll heal. No big deal." Zammin eyed Luke's flagon. "Are you sure you should be drinking that? You don't sound like a man with a high stamina stat to me."

"I, uh, I guess I never really dealt with having to heal up big injuries like that. I've got a fast-healing skill."

"Those are expensive," Zammin said. "But good to know. Means I don't have to go easy on you when we fight for real."

Luke choked on his drink. "That wasn't for real?" he asked, wiping his mouth off on his sleeve.

"Nah, that was just playing around."

"Jesus."

Zammin was already faster than he could handle. If that was just him screwing around, Luke was completely outclassed. He eyed the dwifkin dubiously. Maybe he was using some sort of skill to hide his level. Luke was doing the same, it was just that his wasn't very effective. The conversation so far had been casual, and they'd both dropped a few hints as to their skill sets, but Luke wasn't sure how rude it would be to just ask like that.

Zammin emptied his flagon out in one long pull. "Gods, that's good stuff," he said. "Alright, I've got stuff to do. Good to meet you, tall-boy. Looks like your manager's about done anyway. See you at the fights."

"You too," Luke said. He stood up when Zammin walked away and turned toward Zea, who was threading her way between the tables toward him. As soon as he got his feet under him though, the whole world tilted, and Luke staggered. He grabbed onto the back of his chair desperately, just trying to hold his balance.

"Holy shit, that just hit me all at once."

"Black burrow stout?" Zea asked, sniffing the flagon. "You dumbass. Come on, let's find you a place to sleep it off. I'll tell you all about how rich we're going to be tomorrow."

"Not sure I can walk that far," Luke admitted, his head spinning. He'd never drunk anything that hit him that hard, or that quick. He'd been perfectly fine until a few seconds ago when he stood up. "And it's only . . . afternoon?"

"You're done for the day now, trust me. And you can't sleep here, so try. If I have to get someone to carry you out of here, I'm making you pay for it."

"Okay, okay. Just give me a minute." Luke took a couple of breaths. "I got this. Let's go."

He made it four steps before he tripped over a chair.

"Gods damn it," Zea muttered. "Come on, back upright. Let's try it again. Fucking Zammin."

Name	Luke Bennet
Level	21
XP	29501/34079
AP	0
Bloodline	SysAdmin
Strength	40
Agility	32
Stamina	26
Perception	29
Skills	Mace Mastery (2)
	Sword Mastery (1)
	Unarmed Martialist (2)
	Power Strike (1)
	Life Surge (1)
	Peripheral Awareness (1)
	Counter (1)
	Twitch Reflexes (2)
	Stealth (1)
	Survivalist (2)
	First Aid (1)
	Wood Carving (1)
	Leatherworking (2)
	Thalian (2)
	Disguise (2)
	Deception (1)

CHAPTER 45

Luke groaned and rolled over in bed. His head wasn't exactly pounding, but the sunlight stabbing at his eyelids was not welcome. He pulled the blanket over his head and tried to go back to sleep, but now that he was awake, his bladder was demanding attention. "Goddamn it," Luke muttered, kicking the blanket off and sitting up.

He stopped and looked around blearily. Wherever he was, he didn't recognize it and also had no idea how he'd gotten there. It was a small room, barely wide enough for the bed, with a window he couldn't stick his head through and a door that was maybe six feet tall. Everything felt small and cramped, which told him that his current situation probably had something to do with Zea.

He had to literally crawl out of the bed before he could stand up, and even then, he felt like he was going to smack his head on the ceiling. It had a few inches of clearance, thankfully, but it was claustrophobia-inducing to be in such a small room, like he was some misplaced giant. The door's handle was set much lower than he was used to as well, forcing him to bend forward to turn it.

The hallway wasn't much better. It needed an extra foot or two of width so that he didn't have to hunch his shoulders together. Luke shuffled down the hallway, passing by numerous closed doors that were all too small and all too close together. Before he made it to the end of the hall, one of them opened, and Zea stepped out.

"I thought I heard something large and heavy thumping out here."

"Yeah, hi. Where are we?"

"The Brick Stouthouse. You paid for our rooms, by the way."

"I did? I don't remember that at all."

"Least you could do," Zea told him.

Luke took a second to study her. Her body was . . . *tense* maybe wasn't the right word, but he couldn't think of a better description. If he didn't know any better, he'd have said she was afraid of him. "Look, whatever I said last night, that was just the alcohol talking."

"Oh, you said plenty."

"I did? I'm sorry?"

Zea laughed, but she didn't sound amused. "We should talk."

"In a minute, yeah. I need to piss right now. Where's the bathroom?"

That last word didn't come out quite right. He could feel his language skill twisting it around to translate it but couldn't figure out exactly what he'd said. It was like when the skill was only rank 1 and every word he said felt like an invisible hand had grabbed his jaw and was working it around to form the sounds it wanted.

"End of the hall," she said, pointing at a door that was somehow even smaller than the rest. "Come to my room when you're done."

Zea stepped aside but left her door open, and Luke squeezed himself down the hallway into what was essentially a linen closet, except with a bench that had a hole carved into the middle of it. There was no running water, or even water of any kind. There was a stack of something kind of like paper, fibrous and strong enough not to tear easily. That was depressingly all too common.

Luke finished his business and shuffled back to Zea's room, where she was seated on her bed. "Close the door," she told him.

"Okay."

Luke made himself comfortable on the floor while Zea stared at him silently. Her hands fiddled with the hem of her shirt while she watched him, and her leg bounced up and down. Now that he really got a look at her, she looked exhausted.

"So," she began slowly. "You're an off-worlder."

Luke shot straight upright. "What?"

"You told me last night you got the templar stuff off a brute squad that tried to kill you. And that you think it's because you're an off-worlder."

"Shit," Luke swore. "I'm never drinking with Zammin again."

"That means you're an apostate, an enemy of the gods, forever hunted by the church, and to be killed on sight. Anyone aiding you would also be killed."

"I didn't ask for any of this," he told her darkly.

It was no wonder she was so afraid. They didn't know each other that well, and he'd apparently blurted out a secret that someone might be willing to kill to protect. She was wondering whether she was going to walk out of the room alive or if he'd leave her corpse in the bed and flee. He could have told her she had nothing to worry about, but coming from him, he could understand why she might not believe it.

"You think I asked to be poor and homeless? That's the crap hand life dealt me," she said with a bitter laugh. "I guess it's still better than yours."

"Gee, thanks. What now?"

"You tell me. I still need the money. Are you still willing to fight?"

Luke shrugged. "I need money too."

"What happens when the next templar or inquisitor shows up?"

"Maybe we'll get lucky and it won't happen."

Zea shook her head and said, "You don't know what you're talking about. I didn't get the whole story, but they sent a squad out into the wilderness to hunt you down. How did they even know about you?"

"I don't know. The gods, I guess? Seems like a god-level thing to know about."

"Lucky for you that the Covenant exists then, huh?"

"Sure. I'm so lucky," Luke agreed.

"Sorry, I didn't mean it that way."

"Look, I wasn't planning on telling anyone about this. It doesn't really change anything, so how about we just pretend you never found out and we'll get on with our business? If some church asshole shows up before I've got the money I need, you can just scamper off and leave me to fend for myself."

"It doesn't really work like that. If you're in the middle of a fight and the church raids the place, they'll arrest everyone they can. Nobody will be safe, not the staff, not the audience, not the other fighter. For something like this, they do not do half measures. They already sent five people to kill you."

"So what then, we split up here?"

"No. I'm in it now, whether I want to be or not. Might as well ride it out and see how things turn out."

Luke leaned back against a wall and blew out a noisy sigh. "I'm sorry. This all sucks. I get it. I'll try not to involve you in anything else. I'll fight, we'll get paid, then I'll piss off before any trouble comes down on you."

"You really trying to sail across the ocean?" Zea asked.

"Yeah. Why?"

"That's going to be a lot harder than just catching a ship going up or down the coast. You'll need to go north. Intercontinental trade ships make the crossing where the water is colder. It's a shorter trip, and there's less chance of being attacked there."

"Fuck me." Luke smacked the back of his head against the wall in frustration. "There's always another step, isn't there? So I'm going to need passage on at least two ships, not one."

"Probably. What are you going to do when you get there?"

"Start walking until I get to the place I'm looking for."

Zea opened her mouth, thought better of it, and closed it. It was probably better that way anyway. The less she knew, the less she'd be involved. He assumed that meant she'd be safer, but the way she talked, Luke was kind of wondering if anybody around him was safe. She made it sound like they'd just indiscriminately abduct anyone they thought was connected to him, and maybe that was true. If so, the church was pretty fucking evil, as far as Luke was concerned.

"Since you know anyway," Luke said, "do you mind if I ask a few questions?"

"Oh. Uh, sure, I guess."

"Okay, first off, what's up with everyone's level being so low? That's been bugging me ever since I started running into other humans. I find random animals all the time with higher levels. I've seen goblins over level 20. But most humans don't make it past 10. Even the cops aren't that strong. The one templar that tried to kill me was only around 22 or 23."

Zea just stared at him, her mouth open. "Oh gods, you don't know. Of course you don't. Why would you?"

Luke didn't like the sound of this. "Don't know what?"

"People try to keep their level low because the more XP you have, the faster you go insane and have to be put down. People who get too high a level often are killed even if their minds aren't broken yet, while they can still cooperate. No one wants a level 50 terrorizing the country, forcing other people to level up just so someone is strong enough to stop them."

"I'm sorry," Luke said, trying to keep his voice level and calm. "I'm going to need you to repeat that."

There was something off about this job. Cardinal Gnox had kept a lot of information back, which was perhaps expected but frustrating nonetheless. It wasn't like she wasn't going to find out anyway, so him hiding it was disrespectful toward her and her master. She had to wonder if he'd seriously thought he could keep something like this a secret, and after that thought, she wondered who it was above the cardinal who'd commanded it be handled that way.

Politics aside, there was an actual apostate to find. Someone near the top of the hierarchy had received a divine revelation directing them toward the target. A whole brute squad had failed to take the apostate out, and two of them had been over level 30. Even if the apostate hadn't been an apostate, someone with that many levels was practically a target just because of the threat they represented.

There was a reason only inquisitors were allowed to level that high. Only they had the training and mental fortitude needed to resist the corrupting, insanity-inducing effects of high XP. Even then, without the blessings of the gods, they too would fail in time. The thought of some random apostate being in the high 30s or even 40s was . . . troubling.

Cardinal Gnox had to have known all of this, but he hadn't bothered to share the details with Myla. She'd wasted precious time confirming facts she should have known before she'd even started, and when this was all over, she'd be paying the cardinal a visit to discuss exactly how bad of a mess he'd made trying to play games with an inquisitor. For now though, she needed to find the apostate.

She thought she had a lead to follow, but only time would tell how it panned out. Some templar gear had shown up on the underground markets. There wasn't much, and maybe it was a dead end. Thefts did happen, and not every templar made it home from every job safely. It could be unrelated to the mysterious apostate, but she chased it down anyway.

And then Myla saw it. "I knew it," she said, staring down at the breastplate in her hands. It wasn't much to look at, just standard-issue armor, and not even in particularly great condition. Whoever had owned it hadn't taken care of it that well. That didn't matter though.

What was important was the symbol stamped into it. It was an after addition, clearly tacked on years after the armor had been forged. Six circles, their lines weaving through one another and every one a different color, gleamed brightly near the top of the breastplate. The Sign of the Six.

Whoever had originally owned the breastplate had been on a literal mission from a god, as ordained by a cardinal or perhaps even higher. An apostate hunt could certainly qualify, especially one as high level and dangerous as this one.

Myla had a thread. Now she just needed to pull on it and see what came unraveled.

Name	Luke Bennet
Level	21
XP	29501/34079
AP	0
Bloodline	SysAdmin
Strength	40
Agility	32
Stamina	26
Perception	29
Skills	Mace Mastery (2)
	Sword Mastery (1)
	Unarmed Martialist (2)
	Power Strike (1)
	Life Surge (1)
	Peripheral Awareness (1)
	Counter (1)
	Twitch Reflexes (2)
	Stealth (1)
	Survivalist (2)
	First Aid (1)
	Wood Carving (1)
	Leatherworking (2)
	Thalian (2)
	Disguise (2)
	Deception (1)

CHAPTER 46

Luke scrubbed at his beard with his hands and tried to hold on to his temper. Fucking System had to know this but had never bothered to mention it to him. It wasn't like Luke had been shy about his leveling plans, but not once had that rat bastard ever so much as hinted that too many levels could have negative consequences.

And it wasn't just because Luke didn't ask the right questions either. He knew that Curt had asked System a million questions when he was figuring out builds and taking down notes. He would have been smart enough to sniff out something like this, which meant System had actively concealed it. If Curt had known, it would have been all over that notebook in big, bold letters, underlined, probably an entire page all on its own just with the warning.

"Okay, let's say that I'm level 21, hypothetically speaking."

"Hypothetically," Zea said.

"How fucked am I?"

She shrugged. "I don't know the numbers for humans. You'll make it to middle age if you never gain another level. Maybe you'll get old enough to retire, but I wouldn't count on it."

"Shit. Shit. Fuck."

He couldn't do this as a level 21. Hell, even if he wanted to, there were going to be more monsters between him and the God Machine. He would level up involuntarily just from having to fight his way there. Unless there was a way to not get XP. "Can you kill monsters without getting XP? Is there a skill that stops that or something?"

"Not that I'm aware of. If there was anything, it would be a blessing from a god, but . . . uh . . . you know, what with the whole apostate thing, I kind of don't think they'd give it to you, even if it does exist."

"Okay, I'm completely screwed then. Let's say I've got to get to level 40. What's my life expectancy look like?"

"Fucking grim," Zea said. "Middle age is probably a goal you shouldn't expect to obtain. Even if you haven't gone around the bend, people will feel that amount of XP on you and report it. You'll have hunters on your ass immediately."

All that really told him was that at some point in time, that XP-masking skill would stop being optional. The percentage cuts from stuff like [Disguise] and [Stealth] weren't going to cut it, not that they were doing much to help him already. Not going to the God Machine wasn't an option, not if he wanted to get his family back. That meant more levels, which meant hiding those levels.

He wasn't keen on the other half of that skill, the one that stopped him from feeling out anything else's XP, but he supposed he'd eventually be a high enough level that it didn't even matter. If he was level 50, what difference did it make if whatever he was fighting was 20 or 30? Still, he thought he'd hold off on that skill for as long as he could.

"Okay, this is a problem, but I can work around this. I just need to get to the God Machine and change how the system works before I lose my marbles."

"You can't change how the system works," Zea objected.

"Sure I can," Luke said. "That's the whole point. I have a bloodline called SysAdmin that gives me greater system access."

"That's . . . blasphemy. Only the gods can alter the system."

"Well now you know why they want to kill me," Luke told her.

"Holy shit, this is . . . it's insane. There's no way you can really do this. And bringing someone back from the dead is functionally impossible anyway."

"Why's that?" Luke asked. If System had lied to him about this too, he was going to find a way to wring that insubstantial prick's neck.

"I mean, the skill for it exists. It's in the system, but it's one of those things that are impossible to obtain. You'd never grind out enough AP to buy everything you needed for it without succumbing to XP madness first, and it would take centuries to learn all the skills on your own."

"If it's in the system, I can get it," Luke said firmly. "I just need to get to the command console, and my bloodline will do the rest."

Zea flopped backward on the bed and stared up at the ceiling. "This is insane," she said. "There's no way. You can't do this. It's impossible. Fuck." She sat back up and threw a glare at Luke. "I just wanted to make some easy cash managing a few fights off some human who had more levels than brains."

Luke couldn't help himself; he started laughing. "Sorry to disappoint. You can still do that though. I need the money too."

Sometimes it was hard to take Zea seriously. She was barely four feet tall, maybe four three or four four at most and kind of adorable. Right now, she wasn't adorable. She just stared at him, her face expressionless and her eyes cold, and judged him. He could see the gears turning, the thoughts running through her head while she weighed the risks.

He could feel himself tensing up. The way he saw this going, if she wasn't in, then she was out and going to sell him to the church. If she decided she wanted nothing to do with his shit show of a life, she was smart enough that she wouldn't announce her intentions, and he probably wouldn't realize what she'd done until it was too late.

No matter what she chose to do, he was going to have to trust her. It was no wonder she was so nervous. She'd been ten steps ahead of him and realized where this conversation was going to end up before she'd even started it. If he tried to kill her, he gave himself good odds that he'd succeed. Just by being there and having the conversation, she'd placed a measure of trust in him.

"You don't have to stick around if you don't want to," Luke said. "I appreciate the help you've given me already. If this is too hot to handle, I won't blame you if you walk away. And I won't try to go after you or anything. Just . . . keep your mouth shut about me, please? I promise I'm just trying to raise boat money, and then I'll be on the other side of the world. I won't cause any problems for you."

"Oh, shut up," Zea said, hopping off the bed. "You think I'm going to let a big payday like you get away after I've already put in the work? All I have to do now is make sure you show up for your fights and collect my money."

Luke let out a breath he hadn't realized he'd been holding. "Thanks," he said.

"Yeah, well, you're just so pathetic."

"Me? Please, your shirt is more holes than shirt at this point."

"Well you'd better not go down with the first punch tomorrow, or I won't be able to buy a new one!"

"Please. Zammin practically begged me to take it easy on the guy. No way I lose."

"He did what?" Zea asked, any trace of playfulness gone from her voice.

"Er, that's what we were talking about when we were drinking yesterday. He said the first guy I'll fight against doesn't have the stamina to take heavy hits, and I should pull my punches so I don't hurt him too bad."

"Oh, he did, did he?"

"Yes?"

"And who did he say you were fighting?"

"Uh . . . To . . . Tom . . . Tomtaco? That's not it. Hmm."

"Tantoro," Zea said flatly.

"Yeah, I think that was it," Luke agreed.

"Tantoro is the second-best fighter on their roster. You absolutely should not be holding back when you fight him. He's not as fast as Zammin, but he's considerably stronger, and he's been fighting for over a decade."

"You're a lot more serious about this than you were yesterday," Luke said.

"Yesterday was tryouts. Now we're in business, and I make more money when you win."

"Speaking of money, how much are we talking about here?"

"Not as much as you want, I'm sure. Five silver a fight, three to you and two to me."

"Uh . . . that doesn't seem like a lot. Pretend I don't know anything and tell me how much gold that is."

"Ten silver to a gold, assuming MSW is followed. Oh, sorry, Merchant Standard Weight. Obviously if a coin has more metal in it, it's worth more."

Luke did some quick math in his head. "So ten fights is three gold. And I'm going to need maybe a hundred. That's over three hundred fights? How often do I fight?"

"Maybe twice in a night," Zea said.

"Shit. That's . . . what, a few months just to make that much money, not counting how much I'll need to live off of. Zea, it's probably not a good idea for me to be in Valtira that long. I was hoping to be here for a week at most."

She barked out a laugh and shook her head. "That was pretty naive of you. There is no way you're making a year or two of common man's wages in a week. Even if you wanted to start hunting monsters, you still wouldn't make close to that, not even if you took every job there was."

"There's nothing I can do?" he said.

"Nothing I could help you with, at least. I can't imagine anyone who's not the heir to a large merchant family or a noble's house having that kind of money."

"Okay, well . . . what if I got hired onto a ship instead of paying for passage?"

Zea shrugged. "Maybe if you can convince someone to take a chance on you, but do you have any of the skills for it?"

"I don't. No. But I could go gain a level or two and pick them up?"

Poor Curt's build was getting further and further away from being a reality. At this point, Luke was using it more as a loose guideline than anything. He'd probably need an extra 100 AP to cover everything he was supposed to pick up, and he was nowhere near his goal. At the rate he was needing to pick up extra skills, he'd be lucky if it was only 100 AP.

"You have no idea how psychotic you sound when you say that. 'Oh yeah, I'll just go trade five or six years of my life to avoid having to actually learn anything on my own.' Fucking crazy."

"Hey, it's a crazy situation," Luke said defensively. "I don't have years to spend on this."

"Okay, yeah, that's true, but just don't talk like that out in public."

"Right. Fuck. It's so stressful not knowing what I can and can't talk about."

"Well let's go over a few things," Zea said. "Uh . . . man, explaining this all is weird. It's like trying to teach a child, except if you screw up, nobody's going to think you're just a precocious little tyke."

"Well let's start with the basics," Luke said. "What's rude to do in public? What's rude no matter where you're at?"

"Okay, basics. Um, let's start with system etiquette. It's rude to talk about someone else's level, stats, or skills. It's intimate information."

"I get the stats and skills, but the level? I mean, we can all sense it anyway."

"No, we can't," Zea said. "Your perception must be really high if you get more than a vague feeling of higher or lower level off an individual person."

"Oh yeah, I did notice that. Okay, so don't mention anything about system stuff. What else?"

"No, it's not that you can't . . . it's just like . . . you wouldn't talk about your neighbor's sex life just because you can hear them fucking through the walls, would you? But in a more abstract sense, you might talk about the act of sex itself."

"I'm not comfortable with this metaphor," Luke said.

She just smirked at him. Then she kept on talking about sex. Luke groaned and buried his face in his hands.

Name	Luke Bennet
Level	21
XP	29501/34079
AP	0
Bloodline	SysAdmin
Strength	40
Agility	32
Stamina	26
Perception	29
Skills	Mace Mastery (2)
	Sword Mastery (1)
	Unarmed Martialist (2)
	Power Strike (1)
	Life Surge (1)
	Peripheral Awareness (1)
	Counter (1)
	Twitch Reflexes (2)
	Stealth (1)
	Survivalist (2)
	First Aid (1)
	Wood Carving (1)
	Leatherworking (2)
	Thalian (2)
	Disguise (2)
	Deception (1)

CHAPTER 47

Luke followed Zea into the fight club, which he'd learned was named the Bloody Harbor on account of how close it was to the docks and how often it was frequented by sailors. It was practically empty early in the day, but he'd been told it would be filled to the rafters in the evening. That was apparently a good thing, since larger crowds meant more money in bets. That wouldn't matter to Zea yet, since they needed to get paid a few times before she had the cash to bet with.

Gambling was her idea for increasing their income. Luke didn't love the scheme, but it'd be a few days before he had to deal with it anyway. He wasn't about to let her know about the money he already had, if only because most of it was already reserved for Donaley.

"I started poking around the docks like you wanted," Zea told him while they waited for Fatty to show up. "I don't think you're going to get work as a sailor unless you can impress someone important who's willing to vouch for you, but I do have some good news. I overestimated how much it was going to cost by a lot. Kind of."

"What does that even mean?" Luke asked.

"There's no such thing as an ocean-bound ship docked in Valtira. They just don't make the trip from this port, which makes sense really, when you consider that you can go a thousand miles north of here and shave two thousand miles off the journey. The continents are way closer up there, and I guess sailing cold water is less dangerous."

"Oh, I see. So we're talking about a trip north of here. Damn, a thousand miles though. I guess I could walk it. If there were decent roads the whole way and nothing bad happened, I could do that in a few weeks. Maybe even less."

"I don't think so. A thousand miles is the ship route. The land route is almost double that on account of the Skymaw Mountains. You've got to go the whole way around them. There are no safe passes, from what I can tell."

Luke shuddered at the idea of hitting up a mountain pass. The last thing he needed was to encounter another jumbo elemental. That thing had been the most terrifying, overwhelmingly powerful monster he'd ever met. It served as a stern reminder that, whatever the risks involved, Luke needed to gain a lot more levels.

"So the first leg of the journey is to get up north to a place called Sicanti. For that trip, fifteen gold. Maybe twenty if you get a big cabin on an expensive passenger ship. From there to cross the ocean is going to be more, maybe thirty or forty. The closest port I could find is in Naldrin."

That was still a lot, but maybe it wasn't as bad as he thought. He'd sleep in a hammock with the crew if that's what he had to do and it saved him some money. Once he actually got to the eastern continent, he'd walk the whole way, barring any other options. But it still looked like he needed to come up with fifty gold at minimum just to get across the ocean.

He'd rather not do that in Valtira, so he set his first goal at fifteen. That was only a few weeks of fighting, maybe a bit less if they got real lucky with the bets. Then he'd get the hell out of there before the hammer of the gods came down on his head. Once he made it to the next port, he'd worry about funding the intercontinental trip.

"There you are," a new voice cut in. Luke looked over and saw Fatty making his way over to them. He frowned and tried to remember the man's name. It started with a *V* or *C* maybe. No, that didn't sound right.

"What's his name again?" he asked Zea in a whisper.

"Sideon."

"Oh, right." Damn, he'd been way off.

"Come on, I want you back in the staff area until your fight starts. You've got half an hour."

"Uh, alright. That's okay, Zea?"

"Yeah. Normal stuff. Remember what I told you about not trusting that rat fucker Zammin."

Sideon started laughing and clapped Luke on the shoulder. "Come on, Aldrick. Let's get you ready to fight."

Luke momentarily blanked, until he remembered that he'd given that alias out. He followed Fatty out of the bar part of the building and past the pits. There were already a few people sitting on the bleachers bullshitting, and he saw a pair of guys down in one of the pits circling each other.

"Ignore them," Fatty said when he saw Luke looking. "They're just warming up. It's not an official show unless you can place a bet. Speaking of, are you going to be wanting to put some money on your own fight?"

"Zea said she'd handle all the betting."

"Oh, I'm sure she did. Smart woman, that one, even if she does cuss like a sailor sometimes. All fighters have the right to bet their fight fee on their own match though. Double or nothing. I promise you, you're not going to get better odds with the bookies."

Luke took a second to consider that. It might piss Zea off, but he didn't really care. It was his money. "You mean my cut or the whole thing?" he asked.

"Your cut," Fatty said seriously. "Don't go gambling money that's not yours. I'd hate to have to send the boys around to teach you that lesson."

"Fair policy. Alright. Just my cut of the fight fee. Zea can bet her own money when and where she wants."

"That's a good lad! Nice and confident!" Fatty started laughing, and his belly rolls jiggled. Luke honestly couldn't figure out how the man was so big. The system provided them with stats! Without even trying, Luke was more yoked than anybody he'd ever seen in his life. He looked like a Goddamn movie star after they were done airbrushing the photos. Well, maybe not his face. But his abs! The abs were amazingly defined.

No one else was quite as chunky as Sideon, or really, chunky at all. Most everyone was in extremely good shape, and Luke wasn't just looking at the other fighters. Everyone he'd met had been some variation of fit, except for this guy. He kind of wanted to ask where Sideon put all his AP, but mindful of the conversation he'd had with Zea, he kept it to himself.

"Alright, here we are," Fatty said, leading Luke into the back room. There were five other people there, two men and three women, including Zammin. "Someone will come to get you when it's your turn. Probably . . . third round, I think."

"Tall-boy!" Zammin called out, racing over. "You showed up. Good. Come on, let me introduce you."

The dwifkin grabbed Luke's hand before he could even start to protest and dragged him forward. He couldn't have done it if Luke fought him, but he let himself be hauled around until he was standing in front of a man, of a sort. He was somewhere over seven feet tall and probably weighed three times as much as Luke. His skin was apple green, and there wasn't a single strand of hair anywhere on his body, which was entirely naked. Thick, corded muscles stood out on his . . . everything.

"This is Tantoro," Zammin said.

"You are very naked," Luke said.

"Yeah, you should see it from my angle," Zammin said. "It's a cultural thing, I think."

Tantoro made a low rumbling noise, like two rocks scraping together, and said, "We wear only the hides of our own kills, and only if the kill's level equals our own. I have grown too old and too strong and cannot afford to take on more of the curse."

"Well, that's . . . I don't know what to say here." Luke looked over at Zammin, who shrugged back.

"Ostals have a lot of rules. I don't know. Makes it easy to unleash the ballbuster on him."

"So you are the new fighter. Strong, for one so young," Tantoro said.

Luke had learned not to rely too strongly on his XP sense, but Tantoro didn't give off much stronger of an aura than Zammin did. In fact, none of the fighters did. He didn't think there was a single one of them over level 15. Maybe XP-hiding skills were more common than he'd thought. Or maybe the levels were accurate, and they just had higher-ranked skills honed over years of use.

"That happens sometimes with humans," one of the women said. Luke glanced over at her, and his brow furrowed. She looked as human as he did, except for a pair of horns growing out of her hair and the electric-green color of her eyes. She ignored the look and kept talking, "They get overeager, addicted to the AP. Why worry about the consequences years down the road? Foolish."

"Not quite what happened to me, but okay," Luke said.

"Ignore her," Zammin advised. "No one plans for the future like Revara."

Before anyone else could reply, Fatty came in with two more humans. Both were in their twenties, both looked nervous, and neither of them said a word. "We'll call you up in a few minutes," Fatty told them. "First fight of the night. Just as soon as everyone gets seated."

"Ooh, openers. We haven't had new ones in weeks," Zammin said. "That must be why your fight got bumped back."

"That or because Tantoro refused to do another opener against a no-name," Revara pointed out.

"The fight fee is too low," the big green guy agreed. "Though now that I've met you, I look forward to our match."

"Same, I guess?" Luke said. He didn't actually like fighting that much, truth be told. That didn't seem like the kind of trivia that would go over well with this crowd, so he kept it to himself.

Zammin made introductions for the new trio, though Luke promptly forgot most of their names. The other two newcomers were low level, maybe 7 or 8 he thought. It was no wonder they were the opening act. They both looked like farmers, and Luke was willing to bet their AP hadn't been spent on combat skills.

Fatty showed back up after a few minutes and dragged them off. "This is boring," Zammin said. "I hate waiting for last billing."

"Feel free to trade with me," another fighter said. She was vaguely human-shaped, except what visible skin she had was dark blue with red-and-green markings on it. Luke wasn't sure if it was natural or some kind of tattoo. Her hair was blindingly silver, cut short and split by two horns coming up out of her head.

"Yeah, I'd love that last billing bonus. What's that, an extra six silver?"

Zammin shrugged. "I wouldn't mind if Sideon wasn't so much of a hard-ass about keeping us all here waiting."

"Well he wouldn't be if you'd ever showed up for your matches on time. So thanks for fucking that one up for all of us."

The noise picked up, and the fighters all stopped talking. About two minutes later, it got quiet again. "Quick fight," one of them commented.

"Newbies. They're not going to last, no matter who won."

There was a chorus of agreement around the room, except from Luke. Tantoro looked over at him and shook his head. "No fight promoter wants a fight that only lasts a minute or two. That's why they went out first. They are a preshow."

Fatty showed back up and hauled off two of the ladies, including the one with the blue skin. "Settle in," Tantoro advised Luke. "These two always take at least half an hour. Then it will be our turn. It will be fun."

Luke looked up at the big green fighter, who was sitting calmly and serenely, listening to the sounds of the crowd. "Yeah. Fun."

Name	Luke Bennet
Level	21
XP	29501/34079
AP	0
Bloodline	SysAdmin
Strength	40
Agility	32
Stamina	26
Perception	29
Skills	Mace Mastery (2)
	Sword Mastery (1)
	Unarmed Martialist (2)
	Power Strike (1)
	Life Surge (1)
	Peripheral Awareness (1)
	Counter (1)
	Twitch Reflexes (2)
	Stealth (1)
	Survivalist (2)
	First Aid (1)
	Wood Carving (1)
	Leatherworking (2)
	Thalian (2)
	Disguise (2)
	Deception (1)

CHAPTER 48

Luke walked behind Tantoro as they followed Fatty out of the back room. The previous fight had gone on even longer than anticipated, which didn't seem to surprise any of the other fighters, but now it was finally his turn. He was about to step foot into the ring with a seven-foot-tall naked, hairless green man.

They passed through a gap in the bleachers and hopped down into the pit. Tantoro walked over to the halfway point and stood there, hands crossed over his chest while the crowd cheered for him. Luke glanced around and saw, perhaps not surprisingly, more than a few women cheering. In fact, they were the ones howling the loudest.

"Alright, folks!" Fatty yelled, cutting through the noise, "We all know who's here for this fight, so pipe down and let's get it started. We've got another new fighter for you, as you can see. Aldrick here sparred against Zammin himself and held his own. He even got a good hit or two in, so let that serve as his credentials. But no reason to take my word for it, not when you can see him in action yourselves."

The crowd started cheering again, though to be fair, the loudest were a group of women positioned at the front row along the centerline of the pit. Fatty let the noise wash over them for a second before cutting in, "Will this newcomer give our resident exhibitionist a challenge? Or will he be crushed into the dirt?! Let's find out!"

Luke glanced around at the bleachers again, looked over at Fatty, who had a hand raised up in the air, then to his opponent. Tantoro was now visibly aroused, which brought some heat to Luke's cheeks. "Are you for real with that?" he asked.

"Battle is in my people's blood. It is only with the utmost willpower that we live to see old age."

That was not a sufficient explanation to start a fight while at full mast, not in Luke's mind at least. The refusal to wear any sort of clothes did not help matters, though Tantoro's fan club seemed to like it.

"And fight!" Fatty bellowed.

Tantoro charged forward, his arms open wide and his stance low. He was set to tackle Luke, something that Luke wanted to avoid at all costs. Even if he outmuscled the green man, size and leverage were important advantages, not to mention . . . other considerations.

Luke leaped backward to dodge Tantoro's grab, skirted around to the side, and flicked a low kick at the other fighter's knee. Tantoro shifted expertly, not even trying to dodge the attack, and instead caught it on the meat of his leg. When Luke's foot connected, the ostal fighter surged forward, pushing back on the offending limb and trying to throw Luke off-balance.

Luke hopped backward to help disperse the unexpected countermomentum and keep his balance. That tiny break in his defenses was all the opening Tantoro needed to close the distance again, and this time he got Luke's arm around the biceps with one of his giant hands. He heaved, pulling Luke toward him, and tried to wrap his human opponent in a bear hug.

Luke was having none of that. He might have been able to plant his feet and resist Tantoro's pull, but that would leave him vulnerable to a follow-up attack, and unfortunately, **[Twitch Reflexes]** wasn't doing much to help. Tantoro's attacks were fast but also very visible, which left the skill very little to work with. **[Unarmed Martialist]** was pulling most of the weight in this fight by helping Luke predict oncoming attacks before they started and respond accordingly.

[Counter] also had something to say, namely that in response to the pull on Luke's arm, he needed to jump forward with it and plant both knees in Tantoro's chest. Luke didn't even have time to think about whether that was a good idea before his legs started moving. He slammed into the other fighter as hard as he could, which was more than enough to send Tantoro staggering backward but not enough to actually get free of the vise grip on his arm.

Luke dropped down, found his face uncomfortably close to a flopping green sausage, and pivoted in place. Tantoro had to either twist with Luke to keep his hold or let go. The ostal didn't have his feet set to move with Luke and didn't have the leverage to prevent the spin. Luke broke free, completed the pivot with another kick at Tantoro's knee, and darted out of the big man's reach.

They went back and forth for a few minutes, Tantoro's greater range giving him an advantage, but Luke's higher agility helped him even it out. He knew he had a higher strength stat than his opponent did, but he was also confident that if Tantoro managed to take it to a grapple, he'd lose anyway. **[Unarmed Martialist]** would be of limited help and the rest of his skill set would be basically worthless. It would come down to pure muscle power on his end against what he suspected was a highly ranked grappling skill.

Luke got in a few good punches, one right on Tantoro's face that split his lip, but the green man's defenses were superb and his reactions quick enough to keep Luke from really setting himself and putting his full power behind any single attack. He could technically use **[Power Strike]** without a weapon, but he never had and wasn't sure what kind of feedback it would give him. Plus this wasn't a fight to the death, and accidents could happen.

Then misfortune struck. Throughout the day, the pit had been torn up and churned, and this last fight hadn't helped matters. Luke's foot slipped just enough that he had to catch his balance, just enough that Tantoro managed to clap both of his hands down on Luke's shoulders and drag him forward. The big man threw himself backward, taking Luke with him.

He hit his back, Luke pulled in close, and continued to roll until he was on top of the human. Luke struggled to rise; he knew he could lift the weight if he could just get his limbs coordinated. Tantoro wasn't having any of that though. He expertly kicked Luke's legs out to keep him from getting back up to his knees and pushed him belly down into the ground.

"It was an excellent fight, my new friend!" Tantoro said from his position on Luke's back. "Quite exciting, and you are most slippery prey!"

Considering the position he was pinned in and the fact that he could feel the ostal's erection grinding against him, Luke felt entirely justified being creeped out. "Man, we are not friends," Luke said. "Maybe if you put a pair of pants on."

He wasn't going to escape on his strength stat alone. Agility was basically out the window with the compromising position he was stuck in. It was time to play the trump card. Luke kicked **[Life Surge]** on and felt power shoot through him like lightning. With a roar, he heaved and, heedless of the joint lock Tantoro had on his arm, swung his whole body around.

There was a look of comic surprise on Tantoro's face as Luke threw him with the strength of one arm alone, but before he could recover, Luke sprang on him with a dropkick to the chest, followed by a solid pummeling with his fists. Tantoro got his arms up to guard his face, but Luke still slipped in a good blow every few swings.

By the time **[Life Surge]** gave out, Luke was on his feet, chest heaving, while Fatty screamed something in the background that was completely drowned out by the crowd. The only part of it he got for sure was that the fight was over, and he was pretty sure he'd won. Tantoro lay on the ground groaning, and Luke reached down to help him up.

"Good . . . fight," Tantoro said again. "Surprised me . . . at the end. Come, help me out, please."

Luke gave his defeated opponent a boost, then wearily climbed out of the pit after him. They both trudged through the gap in the bleachers toward the waiting room, the deafening sounds of the fans chasing along behind them.

Myla considered the three new human fighters at the Harbor. The first two were obviously amateurs, unlikely to be her target. They were farm boys who thought they were good at bare-knuckle brawling and had little in the way of ability. They were also both obviously low level, so low that she could disqualify them by that alone. If either of them, or even both together, had killed an entire brute squad of templars, their levels would be higher just from the XP gained in that one fight.

Of course there were ways around that. The system didn't tend to reward indirect killings, at least if the person setting the trap was far enough removed from the actual kill. She had more reason than most to know that a clever mind could trump a strong arm, after all.

Still, she doubted they were who she was looking for. The man from the third fight, Aldrick, was more likely to be her target. He was a higher level, for one thing, though again not high enough to beat even one templar in a fight, let alone five. He was reasonably clever, though in her estimation he could stand a year or two of training to learn how to really fight instead of relying on his skills.

The most damning piece of evidence was the manager though. She was one of the little folk, or dwifkin as they called themselves, and if the testimony that had led her to the pawnbroker was correct, the breastplate had been sold by a human and a shorty. It was a suspicious coincidence, even though she didn't see how the human could have possibly survived an encounter with the brute squad.

The problem was that the information wasn't really reliable. It made no mention of any of the weapons or other armor, and if someone was stupid enough to sell stolen temple gear, she would have expected them to sell all of it. The description of the seller had also been muddled so much that about the only things she was sure of were that the human was male and the shorty was probably a female dwifkin.

If not for the Sign of the Six on it, she would have thought the sellers had just gotten into a storeroom somewhere or broke into a templar's house and taken it as part of the loot. Equipment with a Sign inscribed on it wasn't easy to come by, even if it was forged. People knew better than to copy something like that. She had sent the piece in to be appraised, just to confirm, but she was confident it was genuine.

Myla left the Bloody Harbor, still mulling things over. She would watch for now, follow up on a few other possible leads, and see if she could find a better candidate. This one fit some of the facts but not enough. That wouldn't stop some inquisitors, but she prided herself on bringing in the right criminal the first time and never having to make the wrong person disappear to cover up mistakes.

Mistakes were for amateurs, after all. She was the apprentice of the greatest inquisitor who'd ever lived. She couldn't bring shame on her master's name with slipshod work. So she would watch, and she would wait. Once she was sure she had the right target, she would move.

The human left the Harbor an hour later, strangely sober after his victory. She would have expected him to celebrate. His opponent had been a tough one, and his last-second upset had been the talk of the bar. Myla ghosted along after him, silent, practically invisible, determined to see where he was going and what he was up to.

Name	Luke Bennet
Level	21
XP	29501/34079
AP	0
Bloodline	SysAdmin
Strength	40
Agility	32
Stamina	26
Perception	29
Skills	Mace Mastery (2)
	Sword Mastery (1)
	Unarmed Martialist (2)
	Power Strike (1)
	Life Surge (1)
	Peripheral Awareness (1)
	Counter (1)
	Twitch Reflexes (2)
	Stealth (1)
	Survivalist (2)
	First Aid (1)
	Wood Carving (1)
	Leatherworking (2)
	Thalian (2)
	Disguise (2)
	Deception (1)

CHAPTER 49

After his first go with black burrow stout the other night, Luke had declined to participate in the end-of-the-night celebration. He'd scarfed down half his winnings in food, much to the amusement of the other fighters, and then left to find a place to sleep. The last thing he wanted was to spend another night in a dwifkin-sized hotel.

At Zea's recommendation, he headed for the north side of the docks. The places there were rough and ugly, both the buildings and the people. It was mostly sailors and dockworkers and the kinds of people who dealt with them. The first streetwalker to take a pass at him left Luke completely flabbergasted.

Eventually he found a place, though he couldn't begin to guess what it was called. There was a sign, but at this point it was just a slab of wood with some random spots of faded blue paint on it. Either way, the room was cheap. Once he got in though, he knew why.

"Okay, this is disgusting," he said, surveying the bed. Thanks in large part to his high perception, he could see the bugs crawling on it and the stains of questionable origin. It would be cleaner and probably safer to sleep in an alley. There would definitely be less chance of him catching something.

Luke marched right back out and demanded his money back, which got him laughed at until he hauled the asshole over the counter by the collar of his shirt. "Let me make this clear. I'm not staying in this diseased shithole. Give me back my money before I break your fucking nose."

A bouncer tapped him on the shoulder. "I'm not looking for a fight here," Luke said without taking his eyes off the manager or whatever he was. "I just decided not to stay, and I'd like my money back. I was in the room for all of thirty seconds. This shouldn't be a fight."

"I wouldn't if I were you," one of the sailors sitting at a nearby table said. "That's the guy who beat Tantoro earlier tonight."

The bouncer, one fist cocked back, hesitated and glanced around for help. There was another guy across the bar, but he just shook his head. The manager, seeing no backup coming, fumbled the coins out of a pouch and passed them over to Luke. "Here, take it. Just get the hell out of here if you're not staying!"

"Thanks," Luke said. "And don't worry. You couldn't pay me to sleep here."

Now in a foul mood, tired, and already feeling hungry again, Luke stalked out of the shitheap hotel and into the cool evening air. He scoured the streets for another place to stay, but now that he knew the signs, he walked right back out of every single one he tried without a word. Eventually, he decided to settle on just a place to eat. It would hardly be the first night he spent outside, after all.

Evening gave way to night, and the streets emptied out. Lamps and candles were visible in most of the unshuttered windows, not that it mattered much to Luke. He had no trouble picking out fine details in the dark anymore, especially on a night with the moon so full in the sky. He settled down on a side street, back against the wall of some sort of workshop. He could hear a few people in there, talking about something while they worked, though he couldn't make out what they were saying.

As uncomfortably small as the dwifkin place had been, he was half-tempted to go back there. At least it was clean. He'd probably already be on his way if he knew which direction to go. He kind of missed being back in the valley, where he at least knew where everything was. He didn't miss those damn goblins constantly trying to murder him though, or having nobody to talk to except System.

That reminded Luke, he needed to have a conversation with that bastard about the whole XP-madness thing. He'd find somewhere more private than a random street though, just in case anyone was nearby listening. That wasn't something he wanted to try to explain, that he was apparently talking to himself.

The door to the workshop he was leaning against opened, and a young woman stepped out. She looked like she was about Luke's age, pretty, wearing the same kind of rough homespun look that so many people on this side of the city sported. Her hair was black and wavy, and tied into a braid that hung halfway down her back.

She turned in Luke's direction and immediately flinched back. "Oh! I'm sorry, I didn't realize there was someone out here. Are you okay?"

"Fine," Luke said. "Just passing some time while I decide what to do."

"You should probably go home and get some dinner in you."

"If only. I'm afraid I'm new to the city and don't have a home yet. I tried finding a place to stay, but let's just say the quality of the beds for rent around here isn't up to my standards."

"Well you know what they say about inns. Cheap, clean, available. Pick two."

Luke snorted. "Yeah, that sounds about right."

"Did you try the places over by the temple district?" the girl asked, sitting down next to him.

"I, uh . . . no. I'm working over by the docks, so . . ."

"Yeah, well, no surprise everything is lousy over here, right? The inns over by the church are a lot nicer, and not too expensive. Probably more than they cost here, but how much are a good meal and a clean bed worth to you?"

"More than I would have thought an hour ago," Luke said with all honesty.

He didn't love the idea of skulking around churches and temples, but then again, he was just some random guy looking for a place to sleep. It wouldn't be too suspicious if he rented a room over there, and besides, it was the last place any pursuers from the church would expect him to go. Maybe if they were circulating his picture and description, it would be different.

"There you go then. I actually live over that way myself. Do you want to walk with me? I'll point out some of the good inns."

"Are you sure that's okay? You don't even know me," Luke said.

"Well that's easy enough to fix. What's your name?"

"Aldrick," Luke lied. He'd been called it enough times over the past day that he didn't even have to think about it this time.

"Nice to meet you, Aldrick. I'm Myla. Now come on, I'll show you the good inns."

"You're an idiot," Zea said. "What the fuck made you think finding an inn near a church was a good idea?"

"I was thinking I didn't want to sleep in a bug-infested shithole and have to pay for the privilege," Luke replied.

"There are plenty of places to get a room for the night outside the temple district that don't have lice."

"Can I do it for eight copper a night or less?"

Zea thought about that for a moment. "Well, no. Probably not."

"Then you tell me where I'm supposed to sleep."

"Ugh, come with me after tonight's match. I'll show you where all of us homeless people sleep."

Luke stopped walking and stared at her. After a few steps, she noticed and turned around to face him, hands on her hips. "What?" she demanded.

"Why are you still sleeping on the streets? I thought you were making good money as my manager."

Zea just started laughing. "It's going to be a few weeks before I can afford to get a place of my own. Lots of places won't rent to a dwifkin, you know?"

"I don't," Luke admitted.

"Oh, right. Doesn't matter. Point is I'm not keen on blowing half my wages on a room every night. I'll save up for a bit, then find a place to rent by the month."

"How much would that cost?" Luke asked.

"Depends on the place, but probably two gold up front and another one each month. Maybe two and a half, depending on how they prorate the month."

"And a room is a silver a night for something clean," Luke said. "So about three gold a month. Okay, let's go find rooms."

Zea regarded him skeptically and said, "Just like that, huh? You earn some gold last night I don't know about?"

"Less earned and more already had it," he said. He'd gotten his own neck pouch the other night after he'd caught a pickpocket going for the one on his belt. Thank God for high perception. Myla had almost screamed when he'd spun on the guy and clocked him. Fortunately, it had been easy to calm her back down.

Luke fished two gold out of it and handed them to her. "You got anything pressing to do right now?" he asked.

Her eyes glittered as she regarded the coins. "You tricky son of a bitch. You know I was talking about the rate for one room, right?"

"Will they care if we share it?"

Zea's head snapped up, and her face colored. "Sh-share it?" she gulped.

"Is that a problem?"

"It's . . . No. It's fine. You're paying for it after all."

"I feel like it's a problem."

"No, it's just . . . not customary to share a private room with someone you're not betrothed to unless they're family."

"Ah, yeah, I get that. But, desperate times, right?"

"Don't mock my people's customs," Zea snapped.

"Whoa there." Luke held both hands up. "I'm not trying to make fun of you. I'm just saying, we're both tight on money. We both need a place to sleep. It's not ideal, but I've been sleeping under trees and in caves for most of the last month. I don't mind a floor."

"That's . . . no, you're paying. You should take the bed."

Luke shrugged. "Maybe we'll share it. Switch who gets it each day or something."

Zea's face somehow got even redder. She just nodded sharply once and started walking again. After a moment, Luke hurried to catch up to her. Fortunately, it wasn't hard given how small her legs were.

"So we'll find a new place to stay. I've got a fight this afternoon and then another one this evening. Anything else we need to take care of?"

"Nope," Zea said, picking up the pace and keeping her eyes pointed down at the street.

"Zea, are you sure this is okay? I didn't mean to do something inappropriate here."

"It's fine. Let's not talk about it anymore. In fact, if you trust me, I'll go find a place, and you can head over to the Harbor so you're not late for your match."

Truth be told, he was a bit hesitant about giving her that much money, but she hadn't screwed him over yet. "Okay," he agreed. "I'll see you later."

His match was against a human this time, but Luke beat him pretty easily. He drew it out for a few minutes, just to please the crowd. That was Zammin's recommendation, and it made sense to Luke, but he didn't like how hard he had to fight against his skills to pull it off. **[Counter]** especially wanted him to beat the guy's ass with every bad punch he threw.

Luke was walking out of the back room, having just stuffed his fee into the neck pouch, when he spotted someone he recognized. "Myla!" he said with a smile. "What are you doing here?"

"You made the fights sound so exciting last night, I had to splurge a little to see this one," she said. "You were amazing."

"I don't know about amazing," Luke said. He lowered his voice, "I don't think the guy I was fighting had much experience. He made me look good."

She slapped a hand against his shoulder and said, "Don't be modest. Hey, do you want to get lunch?"

"I . . . sure. That sounds good."

"Great!" She grabbed his arm and pulled. "Come on, let's go!"

Luke let her lead him across the room. He caught sight of Zammin over by the bar, watching them thoughtfully. He grinned at the dwifkin, who just shook his head and smirked back.

Name	Luke Bennet
Level	21
XP	29501/34079
AP	0
Bloodline	SysAdmin
Strength	40
Agility	32
Stamina	26
Perception	29
Skills	Mace Mastery (2)
	Sword Mastery (1)
	Unarmed Martialist (2)
	Power Strike (1)
	Life Surge (1)
	Peripheral Awareness (1)
	Counter (1)
	Twitch Reflexes (2)
	Stealth (1)
	Survivalist (2)
	First Aid (1)
	Wood Carving (1)
	Leatherworking (2)
	Thalian (2)
	Disguise (2)
	Deception (1)

CHAPTER 50

Zea entered the Harbor and scanned the place. Aldrick was nowhere in sight, of course, because that would have been too easy. She still couldn't believe he'd just casually suggested moving in together like that, as if they hadn't just met a few days ago and knew practically nothing about each other.

Though, she supposed from his perspective, that wasn't true. She knew his biggest secret, something that would get him killed if the wrong people found out. It wasn't like there was much she could do with it, not if she didn't want to end up locked away in a cell under the nearest church with him. But still, she could see why he might have decided he might as well trust her completely.

But gods help her, she'd nearly passed out from shock when he'd suggested that. Things like that just *weren't done* between a young dwifkin lass and a man, let alone a human one. If anyone ever found out, she'd die of embarrassment. And he'd been so casual about it, like it was no big deal! Fucking ignorant off-worlder asshole.

Then he'd gone and handed her the money, told her he trusted her, and just went on his way. The temptation to just take the gold and run for it was awfully strong, to get some distance from the most wanted apostate in the country, possibly the whole world. Smart Zea would have run and not looked back. She'd salvaged as much as it was reasonable to expect from the whole situation; it was time to extract herself before it blew up in her face.

Too bad she wasn't smart Zea. No, she was dumb, stupid, idiot Zea who'd actually gone and found a room for rent, and a big one too. At least, she thought it was. It was hard to tell what humans considered big. Everything about them was too big already. If it wasn't enough space to . . . to share . . . then she'd just let him have it and find something else for herself.

"Hey there, what's got you blushing so hard today?" Zammin said, popping up next to her.

She nearly punched him on reflex, not that it would have had a prayer of actually hurting him. "Nothing! What do you want?"

"To be nosy and hear the latest gossip."

"Ugh. Go away, Zammin. Actually, tell me where Sideon is, then go away."

"Not here right now. He went out about twenty minutes ago, said he'd be back in an hour. Want to have a drink with me and wait for him?"

"No, no, I do not."

"Aw, don't be like that. Your guy's already gone too, left with a girl on his arm."

"Oh? He did?"

Zea wasn't sure why she cared, or why she had a sudden spike of irrational jealousy. She was not soft on a human, especially not one as dangerous and touched in the head as Aldrick. Hell, she didn't even know his real name. He could go fuck whoever he wanted, as long as he was back on time and won his fights. She couldn't give less of a shit.

"Yeah, real pretty. Knew how to move too, which is weird because I thought I knew all the fighters who slum it down here on this side of the city, but I didn't recognize her."

Icy dread clawed its way into the pit of Zea's stomach. She could think of several reasons someone who knew how to handle themselves in a fight but wasn't instantly recognizable in the fight scene would be interested in Aldrick, and none of them were good. The absolute best-case scenario was she was just some rando looking for a quick fuck before she moved on, but it was a lot more likely that whoever this bitch was, she was looking for someone she thought needed killing.

"You okay?" Zammin asked. "You look pale."

"Describe her to me," Zea demanded. "As much detail as you can remember."

"Hey, no need to get jealous. He's a human anyway. I'm sure you'd rather spend some time with a man of my stature."

"This isn't a fucking joke, Zammin! What did she look like?"

"Okay, okay. Calm down. Zixin's tits, lady. Let me see. She had black hair . . ."

The accent was subtle, but it was there. Aldrick wasn't a native. That wasn't enough to prove anything in and of itself, but combined with a few other discreet probes Myla had launched under the guise of casual conversation, it was obvious that the man didn't know a thing about Valtira's culture. He hadn't been born there, or anywhere else that she could figure.

It was harder to ask the questions she wanted to ask while under the guise of a mild-mannered seamstress's apprentice, but Myla didn't have a rank 4 **[Disguise]** skill for nothing. Aldrick never suspected that she was anything other than what she'd presented herself as.

The more she listened to him talk, the more certain she became. He was the one who'd sold the armor, which meant he was somehow connected with the deaths of an entire templar brute squad. Normally, that would be enough right then and there to arrest him and throw him in a dungeon to be interrogated, but there was the shorty girl too.

There might be even more she didn't know about yet, and if her suspicions were correct, he wasn't just some heretic who'd committed sacrilege against the church. He was an off-worlder, and his influence had to be torn out root and stem. Anyone he was working with needed to be killed; anyone who knew who he was and hadn't turned him in was an apostate too.

She would get them all, but it would take time. After they'd finished eating, she'd pretended to return to work but had instead gone straight home. She needed some more tools, better equipment, stronger poisons. And she'd need a night to question him fully without anyone missing him. Depending on what she learned, she might have to place him back into his life without him being any the wiser. That would require some specialized poisons that she didn't have on hand.

The only solution was of course to prepare them. Before she could even get started, the front door banged open and someone barged in. It took her less than a second to recognize the voice of Cardinal Gnox. Myla suppressed a sigh and leaped up to the hidden passage in the ceiling. Depending on why he was at her house and what he had to say, she might lead with the knife this time.

"Where is he?" Gnox yelled at the poor housekeeper.

"Cardinal, please! He's not back yet. I can't tell you wh—eeeeh! Let go! Let go!"

Myla crossed the intervening distance in an instant and produced a thin needle, which she promptly jammed into Gnox's elbow. He let out a gasp of pain, and the housekeeper pulled her shirt out of his fingers. If Myla had done it right, his arm would be numb down from the point of impact to the tips of his fingers. The way Gnox cradled the arm to his chest suggested she'd hit the spot exactly right. That was good; Master Lath had wanted her to practice the technique while he was away.

"Why are you assaulting this poor girl?" Myla asked calmly. "And why are you barging into my home?"

"You little bitch," Gnox said. "I'll have your head for this."

"I doubt it," Myla told him blandly. If she'd been an ordinary inquisitor, he would probably have been correct. She wasn't though, and he damn well ought to know that. Myla was starting to get the impression that Gnox wasn't all that bright.

"Go fetch your master this instant," the cardinal snapped. "We'll be having words about your behavior and his failure to appear as summoned."

"I'm afraid he is not available at the moment, not even to you, Cardinal Gnox. I will certainly relay the details of your visit to him as the earliest opportunity. All the details of your visit." She let a hint of threat seep into those last words, and it looked like the buffoon had enough wits about him at least to grasp the implications.

"This is unacceptable. His services are required, and he works to our schedule, not the other way around. The Will of the Six is made manifest through me!"

Perhaps she'd overestimated his wits after all. The idiot just wasn't getting it. "I understand, cardinal, but that does not change the fact that he is already hard at work and is not available for you to speak with. I suggest you leave and attend to your other duties. When Master Lath is available, I'm sure he will speak to you."

"No! Tell him to get out here right now."

A knife appeared in Myla's hands. "I am at the limits of my patience. You will leave, now. You do not have the authority you think you have in this house. If you require a second demonstration of this, I will make sure it is one that leaves a permanent reminder for you."

Gnox sputtered in fury, but he spun on his heel and stomped out of the house.

"That impudent little bitch! Who does she think she is?" Gnox snarled as he strode along. His templar escort remained silent behind him. "We're going to speak with Jemil immediately. Come on."

"Yes, cardinal," the templar said.

The two of them entered the Grand Holy Cathedral, dedicated to all six gods, and paced through its intricate and convoluted passages. Gnox knew where he was going; he had after all been a cardinal for going on five years now. The better part of his forty years had been spent in service to the church, and the last half a decade at the Grand Holy Cathedral specifically.

The underground section of the cathedral that was controlled by the Inquisition Department was far less opulent than the upper chambers. That was to be expected. It was after all part dungeon, part confessional chambers, and part training grounds for prospective new inquisitors. Head Inquisitor Jemil's offices were thankfully near the front, so Gnox would be spared the smell of the confessionals.

He shoved the door open and barged in without knocking. Cardinals didn't do things like that. It was already stretching propriety that he personally traveled to see someone. By all rights, a servant should fetch whomever he wished to speak to and bring them to Gnox's own offices. For the head inquisitor though, and for their master of poisons, Gnox wasn't quite so bold as to demand that they attend him.

Jemil was hunched over his desk, scribbling away at something or other. He looked up at the sudden interruption and the barest hint of a frown creased his face. "May I help you, Cardinal Gnox?" he asked.

"You damn well may," Gnox said, stalking across the room and flopping down into the chair opposite Jemil. "One of your inquisitors needs to be pulled in for behavior corrections. She assaulted me and then further threatened me."

"Oh really?" Jemil sat up straight and put his quill down. "Please, tell me all the details."

Gnox laid out the encounter in short, terse statements, how he'd gone to recruit Master Lath, for the second time no less, and been turned away by his apprentice, how she'd stabbed him with a needle and spouted ridiculous threats.

When he was done, Jemil sighed and pinched the bridge of his nose between his fingers. "Cardinal Gnox," he began slowly, "are you in fact the world's biggest fucking idiot?"

"Excuse me?" Gnox said, half standing and leaning forward.

"Did it ever occur to you that maybe our master of poisons isn't available to attend your every whim because he is an exceedingly busy man and we've already got him working elsewhere?"

"But this is the voice of the gods! Whatever he's doing couldn't possibly be more important. The Sign of the Six itself stands behind this mission."

"Be that as it may, no one is going to be able to get word to Lath until he finishes his current job. Unless the gods themselves deign to whisper in his ear and bid him return to us. He. Is. Unavailable. Do you understand?"

"Fine, but what about the girl? She needs to be punished."

"You will not go anywhere near Lath's apprentice. If I find out you have, I will take you to confession myself. Do you understand me?"

Jemil rose to his full height while he was speaking, and all the XP he kept hidden away with various skills unfolded around him. Gnox caught his hands trembling against the desk. His eyes darted away from the head inquisitor, flicked across the room, and then came back.

"I said, do you understand me?" Jemil asked again.

"I . . . I understand."

"Good. Get the hell out of my office."

Name	Luke Bennet
Level	21
XP	29501/34079
AP	0
Bloodline	SysAdmin
Strength	40
Agility	32
Stamina	26
Perception	29
Skills	Mace Mastery (2)
	Sword Mastery (1)
	Unarmed Martialist (2)
	Power Strike (1)
	Life Surge (1)
	Peripheral Awareness (1)
	Counter (1)
	Twitch Reflexes (2)
	Stealth (1)
	Survivalist (2)
	First Aid (1)
	Wood Carving (1)
	Leatherworking (2)
	Thalian (2)
	Disguise (2)
	Deception (1)

CHAPTER 51

Luke walked into the Bloody Harbor about half an hour before his fight was scheduled to start. Fatty wanted them there earlier, but he wasn't going to sit around in a room next to naked Tantoro trying to avoid looking at a big green pickle while he listened to other people fight.

Before he'd even made it halfway across the floor, Zea cut through the crowd and practically tackled him. Well, she tried at any rate. She was kind of lightweight and small, and he could now lift a thousand pounds over his head. It was more like she ran into a telephone pole than anything.

"There you are," she said, still clinging to his pants. "Come with me!"

"What? Stop. Stop! What's going on?" Luke said, not moving while she tugged at the fabric.

"Shut up and do what I tell you to!"

"Okay . . ."

Luke let himself be led off to the least crowded part of the building, the corner near the betting booth. Since there were no fights going on just yet, it was relatively empty. "What's going on?" Luke asked once she stopped dragging him across the floor. "The fights haven't even started yet. Your money is safe."

"Fuck the money," Zea said. That alone told Luke that it was serious. "Who's this girl you're hanging out with?"

"I . . . what?"

Zea glared at him, and Luke said, "Just a girl I met. She saw me fight and asked if I wanted to get lunch. Why, are you jealous?"

"No, I'm not fucking jealous, you moron! What did you tell her? Is this the same girl who steered you into an inn near a church?"

"Tell her about what? And yeah, that's her. We just kind of chatted while we ate. Zea, what is wrong with you?"

"Me!" she practically screeched. "What is wrong with you?! Are you trying to get the attention of an inquisitor?"

"I have no idea what that is," Luke admitted.

"Luos save me from this man's stupidity," Zea muttered. "Or maybe don't. I guess you guys are all kind of pissed that he exists. Fuck, what a mess."

"Zea, I need you to calm down and explain to me what you're so upset about. Use small words, please."

The dwifkin looked like she was ready to leap up and strangle him, but Luke still wasn't sure why. He could admit that, looking back on it, sleeping in an inn down the street from a church probably wasn't the best idea, but nothing had happened. He'd learned his lesson and wasn't going to do it again, but as far as mistakes went, he didn't see the issue as long as he didn't repeat it.

"The girl is part of the church. She goes to the church. She works with the church. She could be a fucking inquisitor for all we know. Maybe you've forgotten, but they would really like to kill you, and probably me by association. So please, for the love of all that is holy, just see a rent girl if you need to get your rocks off that bad."

Luke wanted to laugh, but he was smart enough to realize it would set Zea off if he did. She already looked like she was about to explode. "Okay. I think you're overreacting. She's a seamstress. Hell, I met her coming out of a workshop. I don't think the big, scary inquisitors spend their free time making shirts and scarves. You make it sound like they're some sort of gestapo secret police."

His mouth twisted awkwardly at the end of that last sentence, and he wondered what his skill had translated that as. Judging by the look on Zea's face, he guessed it was accurate enough. She was pissed, but underneath that, she was afraid. "That is exactly what they are like," she hissed. "Get it through that thick skull of yours. If the church catches you, they are going to kill you. So quit fucking around with them and steer clear."

"I still think you're probably overreacting, but you're right. The stakes are crazy high here. You know she knows where I fight though, right? What do you want me to do if she shows back up?"

"Make excuses. Tell her you're too busy right now. Put that perception stat of yours to work and make sure she's not following you home. I swear if you lead the Inquisition to me, I will kill you myself."

"Fine. I'll figure something out. Please, just relax."

Zea started muttering under her breath and shooting dark looks at Luke, but she didn't say anything else until he started walking away. Then she grabbed the hem of his shirt and said, "Don't forget and do something stupid."

"I won't."

"Oh, and I found a place. I'll take you around tonight. You're busy after the fight, no time to hang out with seamstresses. And no drinking!"

"I won't," Luke said again. After that crap Zammin had plied him with, he didn't think he'd be drinking again anytime soon. There was too much variation in the strengths of drinks, a cultural artifact of people having wildly different tolerances thanks to stamina and the multitude of different species living in Valtira.

"It's about time you showed up," Fatty said from near the door to the waiting room when Luke walked over.

"Yeah, I was getting chewed out by my manager."

Fatty snickered. "Got a mouth on her. Real feisty. Kind of hot, eh?"

"Not having this conversation. Not now, not ever."

"Didn't think you were such a prude, kid. You one of those species purists who think it's a sin to knock boots with anyone who isn't human?"

Luke hadn't even considered that. Truth be told, the majority of nonhumans he'd met he only saw at the fight club. Most of the population of Valtira outside places like this was human. Once he thought about it, that seemed kind of weird, but he wasn't going to worry about it now.

"I have no opinions on interspecies relations."

"Sure seems like you do," Fatty said. "Why don't you go in there and tell Zammin he can't get any because he's not six feet tall. See what he has to say about it. I bet when I call your name to come fight, you'll be walking funny."

Luke shoved past the man without another word and walked into the waiting room. He flopped down onto a bench, crossed his arms, and leaned back to look up at the ceiling. "Rough day, stud?" Zammin said. "Guess your girl didn't take care of you?"

"Zammin, please, just shut up."

The dwifkin laughed. "And your manager's all the way up your ass, too, right? I don't know what her problem is, but as soon as she heard you went out with another woman, she lost her shit. Kind of surprised she'd be jealous about something like that."

"You don't know what you're talking about. So stop talking."

Now everyone in the room was looking at them. All other conversations had ceased, and the little nut-cracking asshole standing on the bench next to him loved the attention. "It's okay. You can work your frustrations out in the pit," Zammin said. "Hey, did you know that you're fighting Kalishka tonight? Do you think your manager will get jealous if you start wrestling with her like you did with Tantoro the first night?"

"Oh, fuck off, Zammin," Kalishka said from the other side of the room. "At least he's not going after the genitals of everyone who sets foot in the pit with him."

"I do what I have to do to win. It's not my fault all the tall-boys put their weak spots right at such a punchable level. Besides, if you had dicks in your face all day, every day, you'd want to punch them too."

The two started bickering, which Luke was honestly thankful for. It drew the attention away from him until the door opened twenty minutes later and the first pair of fighters got called out. The room slowly cleared out as fight after fight until it was just Zammin, Tantoro, Kalishka, and Luke.

"Are you alright?" Tantoro asked Luke.

"Yeah, fine. Just got a lot of stuff on my mind."

"I see. May I offer you some advice?"

"Sure, why not?"

"Forget about all of that for the next twenty minutes. Respect your opponent and focus your attention on her. We all know your trick now, and you will find Kalishka quick to take advantage of any lapse in your concentration."

Luke glanced over at the woman. She grinned back. He shuddered. Luke hadn't caught her fight against Zammin, but from what he'd heard, she'd made the champ work for his win. It was probably because he couldn't cock punch his way to victory with her.

Soon enough, it was Luke's turn. Kalishka stood up when Fatty called their names and offered Luke a hand to pull him to his feet. Before he could take it, Tantoro's own green fingers closed around his wrists. "Do not," he said.

"Spoilsport," Kalishka told him.

"Wait until the fight begins. It would not be fair otherwise."

"A good fight shouldn't be fair."

"What are you guys talking about?" Luke asked. "And can I have my arm back, please?"

"You will see once she touches you. It would also not be fair to tell you her tactics," Tantoro told Luke.

"So don't let her touch me. Got it. Alright, let's do this thing."

He followed Kalishka into the pit and looked around. The lighting wasn't great, with most of it being shone directly into the pit from hanging lamp poles stationed around the bleachers. That actually made it harder to see than pure darkness would, but Luke was pretty sure Myla was nowhere to be found.

Maybe that was a good thing, or maybe Zea was just overreacting. Either way, it was an argument diverted for one night. He realized he'd missed Fatty's rousing introductory speech, but honestly, it was the same thing every time. Luke didn't understand why people got excited about it. It wasn't like they hadn't heard it before.

He turned his attention to Kalishka. Whatever weird thing was going on with her, no one was willing to tell him about it. His only clue came from Tantoro, and it wasn't one that was all that helpful. Given the nature of the fights, it was impossible not to be touched by the other fighter. They didn't wear armor, not even padded leather. They didn't have weapons. If nothing else, he was going to have to touch her in order to hit her.

"Fighters, are you ready!" Fatty bellowed out.

They both signaled with a raised hand that they were. Luke was less confident about this fight for some reason, even though Kalishka was smaller and appeared human. Tantoro had been more intimidating but also more straightforward, and Luke had faith in his stats.

He was afraid this fight was going to be some sort of mind fuckery like that one time with the goblins when they'd laid a literal curse on him that stole away his perception. That was a lot harder to predict and react to, and his skills did nothing to help him in a situation like that. If something like that was her trick, he could find himself going down hard and quick.

Zammin had beaten her though, and that meant Luke could do it too. He just needed to copy the dwifkin's fighting style. He'd go in aggressive, fast, hard, overwhelming. Her tricks wouldn't matter if he took her down before she got a chance to use them. That was the plan. It would work. Definitely. Probably.

"Begin!"

Name	Luke Bennet
Level	21
XP	29501/34079
AP	0
Bloodline	SysAdmin
Strength	40
Agility	32
Stamina	26
Perception	29
Skills	Mace Mastery (2)
	Sword Mastery (1)
	Unarmed Martialist (2)
	Power Strike (1)
	Life Surge (1)
	Peripheral Awareness (1)
	Counter (1)
	Twitch Reflexes (2)
	Stealth (1)
	Survivalist (2)
	First Aid (1)
	Wood Carving (1)
	Leatherworking (2)
	Thalian (2)
	Disguise (2)
	Deception (1)

CHAPTER 52

Kalishka didn't waste a second in closing the distance. She led with an out-stretched hand, and only **[Twitch Reflexes]** kept Luke out of the way. He faded back and sidestepped her grasping lunge, which didn't slow Kalishka down at all. Smoothly, she pivoted off her lead foot and swept her other leg around to crack against Luke's shin.

The blow was surprisingly weak, coming from the number-three-ranked fighter at the Harbor. Whatever her style was, it didn't focus on strength like Tantoro or agility like Zammin. Considering how quickly her fight had ended against Zammin the other night, he didn't suspect stamina was her high stat either. The only conclusion he had left was that she was a balanced fighter like himself or that all her stats were garbage and she'd spent her AP on skills instead.

So far, he wasn't seeing anything that supported any use of combat skills. It was only seconds into the fight though, so that didn't mean anything. He just wished he knew what she was trying to do. It involved her touching him, obviously, but without the strength to back it up, it couldn't be a grapple. Maybe she was a magic user. Luke didn't know much about them other than that just gaining the ability to use magic consumed tons of AP, not even counting the spells themselves.

He should have asked Zea, but the conversation had been focused on other things, and he hadn't gotten the chance. He was sure she knew though. She was plenty familiar with the stable of fighters that entertained the patrons of the Harbor.

Kalishka pursued Luke across the pit while he backed away from her and tried to find an opening that would allow him to land a blow without her touching him in return. Her style was too fluid for that, unfortunately. Her attacks weren't trying to hurt him, just make contact, and it was a hell of a lot harder to dodge someone who just needed to tag him once than it was to trade blows and blocks with someone aiming for vulnerable points.

It was inevitable that she was going to touch him sooner or later, so Luke decided to trade it for as much as he could get. Kalishka wasn't stupid; she knew his strategy as soon as he stopped running. Her next attack was a feint, but Luke went with it anyway. When she tried to pull back and come at him from a different angle that would prevent him from pushing through her guard, Luke just chased her down.

He knew the attack was going to be light, and he was willing to trade a little damage to his arm if it meant getting a solid body blow in. Kalishka's hand slapped down onto his fist to push it aside, and she grinned triumphantly. That grin disappeared an instant later when he activated **[Power Strike]** and blew past her attempts to deflect him. The punch landed squarely in her stomach, strong enough to pick her up off the ground and throw her across the pit to slam into the wall.

"Oooooh! That looks like it hurt!" Fatty roared over the crowd. "Who knew he was holding back this whole time!"

Kalishka pulled herself back upright, but her whole body was shaking, and she wobbled in place. "Didn't know you could hit that hard," she said. "I'll enjoy paying you back for it."

"I could do it again if you want, but I'm afraid I'd kill you," Luke said. "You could give up though."

The wobbling stopped, and she stood up straight. "No, I don't think that's necessary."

"Quick recovery at least," Luke said.

She smirked and said, "Must be the high stamina. But it's nothing compared to the strength."

"Huh?"

He'd gotten a feel for her strength and agility during the opening few seconds of the fight. Unless she'd been sandbagging or had some skill he didn't know about yet, neither were that high. He would be able to outmuscle her easily if it came down to a slugfest.

Kalishka took a deep breath, then rocketed forward so fast that Luke almost missed it. **[Twitch Reflexes]** kicked in, and he threw himself to the side, then turned that movement into a spinning kick aimed for her hip using **[Counter]**. Somehow, Kalishka was already out of range and coming around for another attack.

She was definitely stronger than she'd been a minute ago. Luke blocked some of her attacks, only to find himself grimacing in pain and his bones creaking from the impact. There were going to be a few spectacular bruises on his arms pretty soon, and his opponent was showing no signs of letting up.

She was as fast as him, maybe even a bit more. Luke didn't get it. If she was this fast the whole time, there was no reason for her to hold back. The only logical answer was that she wasn't. Somehow, touching him had increased her stats. Or had his dropped? They didn't feel any different, but Luke risked a moment of distraction to call up his status and confirm they were at normal levels.

Nothing had changed, and there was no status ailment like that one time he'd been cursed. Whatever she'd done had been a buff to her, not something that affected him. But holy hell, she was kicking his ass now. It was all Luke could do to keep up with her attacks, even with four different skills working to keep him safe.

Kalishka came at him from every angle at once, displaying an agility higher than anything he'd seen from anyone else combined with flawless technique. **[Peripheral Awareness]** wasn't something that normally saw a lot of action in a one-on-one fight, but in this case, she struck like lightning, often skipping off to one side and throwing punches and kicks in such rapid succession and so far outside the normal range of vision that he could barely track them.

Worse, he couldn't afford to ignore the blows. A single one that got through unguarded could be the one that dropped him. Kalishka was faster and stronger, and she didn't appear to be tiring. Her face was set into a wicked smirk.

Luke blocked a strike to the left, ducked under a follow-up from her right, then threw himself backward to avoid a knee that almost connected with his nose. **[Counter]** flared once again as he landed on his back and both feet shot out to catch Kalishka in the chest. She flew backward but landed with grace and rolled right back to her feet.

"You are very strong," she said. "I like that. It's intoxicating having stats this high."

"Well then you won't mind if I stop holding back," Luke told her as he climbed back upright himself. He set his feet and brought his arms up.

"Please, don't limit yourself on my account. I can take it," she practically purred.

"Okay then. If you're sure."

Then they clashed again. Luke triggered **[Life Surge]** to pump his strength and agility even higher, then pummeled her with a one-two **[Power Strike]** combo. Kalishka tried to block the first one, but he broke through her defenses, and the second caught her cleanly. Once again, she went flying across the pit to smack into the wall.

Luke didn't wait for her to get back to her feet. He was on her in an instant and stomping down as hard as he could. She jerked her head to the side, wrapped her arms around his leg, and heaved. Even from such an awkward position, there was so much strength in her upper body that she threw him up into the air. Luke twisted to reorient himself for a landing and slammed down onto her with both feet.

She rolled, just barely fast enough to avoid him, and he drove his feet down into the dirt hard enough that it came up to his knees. Luke ripped one leg out, then the other, and climbed back up to the pit's floor. That was all the time Kalishka needed to regain her feet, but she was starting to tire now.

Luke charged in with only seconds left before **[Life Surge]** gave out. He slung vicious punches one after another, hoping to tag her with a knockout blow before it was too late. He even hit her once too, but then his skill gave out, and exhaustion flooded his limbs. Kalishka noted the change immediately and, with a desperate grimace, cocked an arm back, then slugged him right in the face.

Luke went down to one knee, shook his head, and tried to get back up. His limbs were lead now though, and it was all he could do to keep from blacking out while the world spun around him. He saw a leg coming at him, impossibly fast, or maybe he was just impossibly slow to react. It connected with his shoulder and shoved him sideways with a flash of pain.

Before the leg could disappear, he grabbed the ankle with his hand. Then Luke brought his arm up and around, leg still attached to the rest of Kalishka's body, and swung her overhead to slam her face-first into the ground. A second later, he fell over on top of her, and everything went dark. The last thing he heard was the ding of a system notification.

"Holy crap," Zea said. She was too poor to attend fights regularly, but she'd still seen her fair share. That had been without a doubt the most vicious, no-holds-barred, knockdown fight she had ever seen. Aldrick and Kalishka had gone at it like madmen and beat the bloody hell out of each other. She had no idea how either had still been standing halfway through.

The crowd loved it. There was blood all over the pit, and Aldrick had stomped a hole more than a foot deep into it. It was probably a good thing that attack had missed; she could very easily imagine it crushing Kalishka's ribs and killing her. But every blow, right down to the end, had driven the spectators into a rabid frenzy of cheering and screaming.

Sideon himself was yelling so loud his whole face had gone red, but she couldn't hear a word he was saying. Whatever it was, he looked excited. She just hoped that would translate into good medical care for Aldrick, otherwise tonight's fight was going to be a loss. It was going to cost two or even three times as much as he'd made to patch him back up, and he was going to be down for at least the next four days while he recovered.

They had to get two other fighters to remove Aldrick and Kalishka from the pit since neither were in any shape to climb out on their own. Hell, it was a minute or two before Kalishka even woke up to find Aldrick passed out on top of her. She groaned and heaved, which was barely enough to roll the other fighter's weight to the side so he'd flop onto the ground.

That was what woke Aldrick up, but he just lay there in silence, his eyes blank and staring up at the ceiling. After the pair had been dragged back to the fighters' waiting room, Zea circled around the outside of the room and followed them in. She found them both laid out on the floor with Zammin and Tantoro looking down at them.

"Looks like you two had fun, huh?" Zammin was saying when Zea walked in.

"Ha," Kalishka gasped out. "Jealous?"

"Nah. You look like shit. I prefer being beautiful."

"Fuck . . . you."

"You're too tall for me."

"Sideon wanted me to let you know once you were coherent that he has a healer coming around to look at you in a few minutes," Tantoro cut in. "You should try not to move too much until then."

Zea squatted down next to Aldrick's head and looked down at him. "I've said it before, but it bears repeating. You are an idiot."

He laughed, but it was a halting, painful thing. Maybe he'd learn his damn lesson, but somehow Zea doubted it.

Name	Luke Bennet
Level	21
XP	29756/34079
AP	0
Bloodline	SysAdmin
Strength	40
Agility	32
Stamina	26
Perception	29
Skills	Mace Mastery (2)
	Sword Mastery (1)
	Unarmed Martialist (2)
	Power Strike (1)
	Life Surge (1)
	Peripheral Awareness (1)
	Counter (2)
	Twitch Reflexes (2)
	Stealth (1)
	Survivalist (2)
	First Aid (1)
	Wood Carving (1)
	Leatherworking (2)
	Thalian (2)
	Disguise (2)
	Deception (1)

Skill	Rank	AP	Prerequisites	Effect
Counter	2	15	Rank 1	Increases reaction speed when countering an opponent's attack

CHAPTER 53

The first thing Luke did when he woke back up was panic over the notification he'd received right before passing out. He was afraid he'd killed Kalishka, but as soon as he checked it, that fear dissolved.

[Congratulations! Counter has reached rank 2. 250 XP awarded.]

It was still a warning to him though. The fights could get vicious, but they'd gone too far. Toward the end, neither was holding back, and both were determined to win. It had been a fight to the death, and the only reason they'd survived was that they both ran out of steam at roughly the same time.

"I've said it before, but it bears repeating. You are an idiot," Zea said, crouching over him.

Luke tried to laugh but ended up just wincing. "I know. Good thing I've got you looking out for me."

Zea rolled her eyes. "Not if you're going to do dumb shit like this. Neither of you made money off that fight."

"What? Why not?" After a performance like that, Fatty ought to be giving him a bonus on top of his normal fight fee.

"It's all going to go to the healer, and then some more besides."

"Fuck that," Luke said. "I'll heal just fine on my own."

"Maybe, but would you do it fast enough to fight again tomorrow?"

"Ah, well." Luke stopped to consider it. "Probably?"

"No, you will not," she said, kicking his shoulder lightly. Luke grunted and shifted with the impact. "You'll be lucky if you can walk home tonight."

"Aldrick," Kalishka said from her spot on the floor next to him. "Could I ask you for a favor?"

"Not really in much of a position to do stuff for other people right now," he said. Between **[Life Surge]** and all the **[Power Strike]** attacks, he was thoroughly drained.

"Just hold my hand so I can copy your stamina," she said, reaching out for him.

"What?"

"It's my bloodline, Mirror Fiend. It lets me copy stats from things I touch, briefly. Your stamina is a lot higher than mine. I'll heal faster if I can borrow it."

"That's so fucking unfair," Luke grumbled. All his bloodline did was give him an annoying adviser who refused to answer anything but the most basic questions. Theoretically, he could do more with it but only at one particular spot in the whole world. More or less worthless.

Kalishka put her hand on Luke's and shuddered. Her breathing evened out after a few seconds, and she said, "Thank you."

"This isn't going to do anything to me, is it?"

"No, it doesn't hurt you, other than me knowing your stats, I guess. I know all the fighters' stats sooner or later. Don't worry though, I won't tell anybody."

"I'm kind of surprised you want my stamina and not Tantoro's. His has got to be higher."

"That'd be telling," she said, "But he's going to be out in the pit in a few minutes, and I figure we can lie here together for the next hour until it doesn't hurt so damn much just to breathe."

"I hope it was worth it," Zea said.

"Sure," Luke said. "Ranked up one of my skills. Good fight."

"You did?" Zammin asked, shooting to his feet. "That's awesome! We need to celebrate tonight."

Kalishka groaned. "Not tonight. Maybe tomorrow."

The door opened, and Fatty stuck his head in. "We're ready for the next fight. Going to be impossible to top that last one though. I sent someone out to get a healer to look at you two."

"Don't need it," Luke said. "I'll be fine soon."

Fatty snorted. "On the house. Next time you two fight, I'll more than make it all back."

Everyone in the room stared at the fight promoter in surprise. Luke hadn't gotten the impression that the man had a generous bone in his body, and judging by the slack-jawed reactions of everyone else, they seemed to agree.

"What?" he asked. "If I could get the rest of you to fight like that, I would keep a healer on staff to patch you back up afterward. Hell, we'd need to move the Harbor to a bigger building to hold the crowds."

Fatty left and took both Zammin and Tantoro with him. Zea admonished both Luke and Kalishka for being so reckless, then followed the others out. She closed the door behind her and cut most of the noise from the crowd. Luke let out a sight and shifted in place.

"You're really good," he said. "I'm glad you don't go for the nut shots like Zammin."

Kalishka snorted. "He does it as part of his image. When he first started, it was a tactic he employed to eke out wins against stronger opponents. Now he does not need it, but the crowd expects it, so he plays it up for them anyway."

"I'm pretty sure he enjoys it. When I sparred with him before I started, he went out of his way to tag me once then too. Nobody was around except Fa—er, Sideon, and my manager."

Kalishka started laughing, then choked and winced. "Owwww. My ribs are all messed up. Do not make me laugh again."

Luke really wanted to activate **[Life Surge]** again, but his belly was still gnawing on his spine from the last time he used it. It was probably best to wait until he had a good meal in him. They lay there in silence, both beat up but with wounds closing at least fifty times faster than they should have, maybe more. Luke could see a bruise on his forearm from a blocked punch changing colors every few minutes, rapidly going from red to a dark purple. Within half an hour, it was yellowing, and by the time the healer showed up, it was completely gone.

Every few minutes, he felt Kalishka brush his hand with her own as she renewed her Mirror Fiend ability to copy his stats. "You know," he said one time, "that ability is completely unfair. You could just put all your AP into skills and beat anybody with it."

"It's not so easy as all of that. I have to figure out how to work my own body when my stats change so much instantly. I've gotten pretty good at that, but it's still a challenge sometimes, like for example when someone has a ridiculously high strength and agility and stamina and perception. The noise . . . it was overwhelming. How do you live like that?"

"You start to filter it out after a while," Luke told her. "And the rest, you just get used to it. You could crush an egg in your bare hands, but that doesn't stop you from picking one up and handling it, does it?"

"No, but there's just so much energy. Even now, I am barely able to move, but I want to get up and run. I want to climb buildings and do backflips off roofs. The only thing stopping me is that it hurts too much. How do you deal with having this much energy all the time?"

"Well," Luke said slowly, drawing the word out, "I joined a fight club so I could beat the crap out of people in a pit while a hundred other people watch and get paid for it."

Kalishka started laughing again, then cut off with a wince and glared at him. Luke grinned back, but before either could say something, the door opened and a young woman walked in. She was probably four or five years older than Luke, dressed in simple unadorned pants and a shirt, and was wearing too many rings and bracelets for his taste. They clinked against one another as she walked, which she didn't even seem to notice.

"Ooooh, that's annoying," Kalishka said, and Luke could see her eye twitching with each clink.

"You get used to it," he told her again. "It's all background noise eventually."

"What are you two whispering about over there?" the woman asked.

"Guess her perception isn't very high if she can't hear us," Luke said.

"Well we're barely audible at all."

"True. It would be rude to not answer." Luke craned his neck to look at the woman. "Just discussing the burden of having higher-than-average perception. I'm Aldrick. Are you the healer?"

"I am. My name is Ortessa Maldalva. Are either of you in immediate danger?

Luke and Kalishka exchanged glances. Simultaneously, they said, "No?"

"We'll start with you then," she said, stepping over to Luke. "If you'll just hold still for a minute here . . ."

She started muttering under her breath while she worked, though it wasn't hard to pick out what she was saying anyway. "Internal bleeding . . . muscle tear . . . dislocated . . . fractured rib, not completely broken . . ."

When she finished, she announced her findings. "You'll need to take it easy for a few days. I'd guess you'll be fine again even without intervention in under two weeks. We'll try to speed that up to a week. Now, let me look at your friend here."

Luke doubted it would take a week. He doubted he'd even have a problem fighting again tomorrow. All he needed was a good meal and a good night's sleep, but he wasn't going to turn down help, especially if Fatty was covering the tab. Or rather, Sideon. It really wasn't nice to call the man that, even if it was true.

Kalishka got a similar diagnosis, though with the added distinction of a minor concussion and three broken ribs, as well as a torn ligament. Luke didn't know shit about medicine, but he was pretty sure a lot of those injuries were lifelong problems that people never fully recovered from. Whatever this world had going on in terms of health care, it was miles ahead of Earth's technology.

Ortessa activated some sort of skill that made Luke start to glow green with generous splashes of red over his injuries. Slowly, the green started to bleed over, shrinking the red spots down at irregular rates. After a minute, she cut the skill and started channeling it to Kalishka instead.

"There you go. How are you feeling?"

"Better," Kalishka said. "It doesn't hurt as much anymore."

"Good. You'll need to avoid anything strenuous for the next few days, but by this time next week, you should be ready to recklessly risk your life pummeling each other for the amusement of the unwashed masses again."

It did feel better, though not by all that much in Luke's opinion. He thought the healer had spent a little more time on Kalishka than on him, but then again, she'd been the one to lose that fight. Probably. He'd landed on her at least, which meant she went down first. That should mean the winner's fee was his, by his way of thinking.

After Ortessa left, clinking with every step, Kalishka reached out and grabbed Luke's hand again. "Whew, that is much more comfortable with all the extra stamina," she said. "I'd rather just hang around with you than have the healer."

"Well you got both, at least for now. I'm just waiting for that last fight to be over and the crowds to filter out so I can get a meal."

Luke wondered why the healer didn't just heal them fully. There was probably a reason for it, but as always, he didn't dare ask. Maybe Zea could tell him. He made a mental note to add that to his list of questions to ask once he got home, wherever that was. Hopefully his manager wouldn't go off without him.

The sound of cheering picked up outside the room, signaling that the fight had either ended or was almost done. "Who do you think will win?" Luke asked.

"Zammin," Kalishka said without hesitation. "Tantoro almost never beats Zammin. He's too slippery to get a hold of, but Tantoro is so tough that it takes Zammin forever to wear him down. Their fights take ages, but the audience loves it."

"Tantoro must have balls of steel to jump down into the pit with a guy whose main combat strategy is 'punch them in the groin.'"

Kalishka started laughing, this time without the wince. "Ha, yes, it's quite the matchup. We do always seem to have more women than usual whenever Tantoro fights."

"I still wish he'd put on a pair of pants."

Kalishka threw him a haunted look that suggested she'd had her own traumatic experience fighting the naked wrestler. "Me too, Aldrick. Me too."

Name	Luke Bennet
Level	21
XP	29751/34079
AP	0
Bloodline	SysAdmin
Strength	40
Agility	32
Stamina	26
Perception	29
Skills	Mace Mastery (2)
	Sword Mastery (1)
	Unarmed Martialist (2)
	Power Strike (1)
	Life Surge (1)
	Peripheral Awareness (1)
	Counter (?)
	Twitch Reflexes (2)
	Stealth (1)
	Survivalist (2)
	First Aid (1)
	Wood Carving (1)
	Leatherworking (2)
	Thalian (2)
	Disguise (2)
	Deception (1)

CHAPTER 54

Luke laid on the floor and stared up at the ceiling while Zea sat on the bed. He'd gotten a meal on his way out of the Harbor, then stopped at a street vendor for a second one while following Zea to their new home. Rather than eat it on the spot, he'd taken it with him and, only once behind closed doors, triggered **[Life Surge]** while devouring it. He still wasn't at 100 percent, but he figured he'd be able to fight tomorrow.

"This is weird," Zea said, gesturing back and forth between them.

"I guess. I'm not really thinking about it."

"Well I am."

"Have you tried not thinking about it?" Luke asked dryly.

"Have you tried not being a dick about it?"

Luke sat up and turned to face her. "I'm sorry. Look, I don't understand why this is such a big deal for you, but it obviously is. Is there anything I can do to make this easier for you?"

"No, it's just . . . I mean, I've slept in rooms with other people before, but I didn't have a choice, and it wasn't just two people. This feels . . ." She trailed off, before finishing lamely, "Improper."

"Would you feel better if I told you that you're not my type?"

Zea snorted. "No. Just forget about it, alright? I'm just stuck in my own head. Are you sure you don't want the bed? You got beat to hell and back barely two hours ago."

"Nah, I'm fine. Between high stamina, the healer, and my own skills, I'll be ready to fight again tomorrow."

"Bullshit you will," Zea said. She hopped off the bed and stomped over to look at him. With a frown, she poked his arm and said, "Huh. How about that? Bruises are all gone."

"Yeah, why do you think I'm eating so much food?"

"I don't know. Humans always eat a lot of food. I just figured you ate more than usual."

"Four times more than usual?" Luke asked with a laugh. "It's not Thanksgiving."

"I don't know what . . . that word you said . . . means."

Luke waved the implied question off. "Just a holiday from back home that revolves heavily around family gatherings and food. Ignore me."

"Oh. That sounds nice. Dwifkin have something like that. It's not limited to just family though. Once a year, there's a communal feast day that any dwifkin can attend. We all bring something to add to the table and spend the evening catching up with old friends or making new ones."

"So a giant potluck then," Luke said.

"Kind of, except more than that. It's hard to explain. For us, the world is big. Everything is too big, too hard to handle. It's rare to find things sized for us, so we have this place, a kind of sanctuary, where everything is made for dwifkin, where the foods are just for us, our traditional dishes. It's a place where we don't have to make any concessions to humans."

"I think I understand," Luke said softly. "It's hard being an outsider, being different from everyone around you. It sets you apart. You don't get the inside jokes or know what people are talking about. There's stuff that everyone takes for granted, but you don't have it. It's lonely."

Zea nodded. "That's part of it. I miss going to those."

"Why don't you?" Luke asked, surprised.

She spread her arms, showing off her ratty, tattered old clothes. They weren't the ones she'd been wearing when they'd first met, but they weren't in much better condition. "I used to, when I was younger, before my family died and I ended up here. I don't even know where they gather in this city, and I definitely couldn't bring in a dish. I've been living on scraps for years."

"Oh. That's shit."

"Yeah."

"Well, let's talk about something a bit cheerier," Luke said. "You've got to be building up a nice little pile of silver from managing the fights. What are you going to spend it on?"

Zea snorted. "That's cheerier? I need to pay you back for fronting the gold for this room. Then, warm clothes for when it starts to get cold. If you're still around by then, I'll see about saving up for something else."

"You don't think I'll still be saving for a boat ticket by then?" Luke asked.

"Nah, I think you'll be getting tortured in a church dungeon somewhere because you're doing stupid shit like sleeping in inns on Religious Row and trying to stick your dick in a girl who has really obvious ties to the clergy."

"Mmm . . . cheery indeed. I still think you're overreacting about Myla. I'm telling you she works as a seamstress. I doubt she has a lot of pull with the guys at the church. Also I'm not trying to sleep with her."

"You don't have to be part of the church hierarchy to report someone to an inquisitor. Even if she's not, all you need to do is slip up and say something stupid, again, like you did to me."

"In my defense, I was extremely drunk," Luke said.

"Well, don't do that again. But also you do know that you look like you're not from around here, yeah? Your skin is too light. You have a noticeable accent when you say certain words. I can see that sometimes you have no idea what's going on when any twelve-year-old would be following the situation without a problem. It's really obvious."

"To you, maybe. I don't think anyone else has realized that I'm . . . you know."

"Maybe not, but my point is that you already slipped up, and believe me, I considered turning you in. If you weren't making me money, I would have."

"Nah. You wouldn't."

Zea let out a huff and shoved him. "You know I'm not joking when I say if they catch you, they'll kill me too, right?"

That was a sobering thought right there. "I won't say anything. Just pretend you didn't know if it comes down to it."

"The inquisitors won't care. I wouldn't be surprised if they kill me, the landlord, Sideon, every person you've fought against in the pit, the on-site bookie, and half the audience."

"Jesus."

What that really told Luke, more than anything, was that he needed to leave town. Sooner was better than later. Tomorrow he would stop at Donaley's and see how his new weapon was coming along. After that, he'd need to take a good, long look at his options. "A trip north by boat isn't the only way to go, is it?" he asked. "Maybe it's better if I walk. I could be out of the city by the end of the week."

"You could . . . It's dangerous though, and it's a long trip."

"Something to think about, I guess." Luke rested his head against the wall and stared off at nothing. "Look, you've helped me a lot, way more than you needed to. Thanks for that. I'll try to get out of your hair as soon as possible. If the church does find out about me, I don't want them coming down on you too."

Zea lifted herself back onto the bed, which was almost funny to watch. It was a normal-height bed, but for her, it involved hopping up to sit her butt on the mattress. He could see how it would be frustrating to live in a world of giants, where everything was a stretch to reach or a struggle to use. She noticed him watching and tossed a glare his way.

With a smirk, Luke said, "Don't worry, you made it look easy."

"Shut up."

"Will do." He was getting tired anyway. "Thanks again. I think I'm going to go to sleep now."

Zea ripped the blanket off the bed and threw it at him. "Here. At least have some padding and something to keep you warm."

Luke smiled and wrapped the blanket around his shoulders. "Thanks, Zea."

"You're welcome. Now get some rest. I need you in top form so I can make more money off you."

"You got it, boss."

Zea reached over and extinguished the candle on the windowsill, not that the lack of light hindered his vision in any way. He saw her crawl under the sheet and pull it tight around her before he closed his own eyes and laid down. As tired as he was, sleep was an elusive beast that night. Despite his claims of good health, his injuries did still ache. Added to that was the memory of that man with the rainbow ring on his armor trying to kill him, and of his mace crushing the man's face. He still couldn't get that image out of his brain.

One hour turned into two, and still he couldn't keep his eyes closed. Normally, that would have been fine. Anymore, he was down to three or four hours of sleep a night anyway, but right now, he needed the rest. It looked like it wasn't going to happen, not with everything crowding in on his thoughts.

Luke sighed and opened his eyes. He walked over to the shutters and opened them up, then leaned on the sill and looked out. The world was so different to what he was used to, even now after weeks and weeks on Aros. Hell, he could see the stars. They probably weren't the same stars as Earth's, but he wouldn't know. It was pretty hard to see them at all back home.

It was quiet though. There were no trucks rumbling down the streets, no foot traffic stumbling home drunk from the bars. Well, there might have been, but none directly in front of him. It was dark, and cool, and just different from everything he was used to. Part of him wondered if he was insane to think he'd ever get back home. A different part wondered if he even wanted to.

It wasn't like he'd had a lot going on there. Manual-labor job, no girlfriend, family all disappearing one by one. At least he'd solved that mystery. This whole XP-madness thing was an unpleasant surprise, but hell, he had SysAdmin powers. Maybe he could fix it. He'd ask System later when he finally got a moment with no one else around.

He could probably get away with it in front of Zea. She already knew he was an off-worlder anyway, but it felt weird to talk to his imaginary friend while there was someone else there. It wasn't like there was much he could do about it either way right now, since the best-case scenario would no doubt involve going to the God Machine and accessing the command console, like always.

A stray breeze gusted through the window around him and chilled the room. Off to the side, he saw Zea shiver and clutch the sheet tighter around her. Smiling slightly, he closed the shutters, unslung the blanket from his shoulders, and draped it over the bed. As it settled on her, she cracked one eye open and looked up at him.

"Sorry," he said. "Just having some trouble sleeping is all."

Before he could walk away, her hand shot out and grabbed his shirt. "I'm cold now," she grumbled.

"I won't open the window back up. Sorry again."

She didn't let go. "No. I'm cold."

"What?"

"Get in the bed, dummy."

Luke froze for a second, then sat down on the edge of the bed. Zea scooted over toward the wall to make room for him and held the blanket up. Slowly, Luke stretched himself out along the length of the bed, which he had to admit was far more comfortable than the floor. He felt the blanket drape across him, and she scooted back closer.

"Holy crap," he yelped quietly. It was like a block of ice was pressed up against him.

"Sorry. It's a dwifkin thing."

It didn't take long before she warmed back up, but when he went to get back out of the bed, her hand tightened onto his shirt again. Luke relaxed and lay still, eyes closed. Finally, he fell asleep.

Name	Luke Bennet
Level	21
XP	29751/34079
AP	0
Bloodline	SysAdmin
Strength	40
Agility	32
Stamina	26
Perception	29
Skills	Mace Mastery (2)
	Sword Mastery (1)
	Unarmed Martialist (2)
	Power Strike (1)
	Life Surge (1)
	Peripheral Awareness (1)
	Counter (2)
	Twitch Reflexes (2)
	Stealth (1)
	Survivalist (2)
	First Aid (1)
	Wood Carving (1)
	Leatherworking (2)
	Thalian (2)
	Disguise (2)
	Deception (1)

CHAPTER 55

Luke woke up to find Zea practically lying on top of him and snoring softly. It wasn't possible to slide out of bed without moving her, but, well, he really needed to pee. She groaned softly when he relocated her, cracked one eye open to glare at him, then shot up right, her eyes wide and mouth hanging open.

"You . . . and I . . . we didn't . . ." She trailed off.

Luke laughed softly and shook his head. "Nothing like that. Your dignity is safe."

She threw the pillow at his head. Luke let it bounce off his face before he stood up. His injuries had continued to heal at a tremendous rate throughout the night, so much so that he didn't think he needed another **[Life Surge]** now.

"You look better," she said. "Still hurting?"

"I wouldn't want to go another round with Kalishka right now, but I could handle some light exercise."

Zea's cheeks flushed, and she looked away. "Ah, hrmm, well, that's good. Maybe you'll be ready for a fight this evening. That's the only light exercise you're getting."

It took Luke's brain a second to catch up. "You know, you keep protesting like this, I'm going to start to wonder."

"Please. Man human–woman dwifkin pairings never work out. You'd split me in half."

Now it was Luke's turn to blush. He'd been joking and hadn't expected anything other than the pillow chucked at his head again. "I, uh, I didn't mean anything by it," he said. "But you're right . . . You're a little bit too small for my tastes."

"Right. Exactly. The logistics don't work out. So let's talk about something else please."

"Right."

Neither of them looked at each other, and neither of them said anything. Luke scratched the back of his head and glanced over at the shuttered window. It was just a little bit past dawn, probably too early for anything to be open yet. He could maybe find a bakery or something and grab breakfast. Despite all the food he'd put away, he was still hungry from all the regenerating he'd done last night.

"You want to get breakfast? Then after I have an order for a custom weapon that's still a few days away from being finished I want to check up on today," Luke said. "I might see if a bit of coin can get it done faster. I feel like it would be better if I had it with me just in case something happens."

There were plenty of people who walked around armed, though it was admittedly the minority. It might make him stand out a little bit, but he didn't think it would draw that much attention. He'd just be one more of the maybe 10 or 15 percent of noncop people walking around with some kind of weapon.

Zea started to answer, interrupted herself with a yawn, and said, "It's too early for breakfast. Maybe in an hour or two. And stop pacing back and forth. You're making me agitated just watching you."

He hadn't even realized he was doing it. "Sorry," he said as he sat down on the edge of the bed. "Just stress, I think. You're right, I haven't been making good decisions. That needs to change."

Zea crawled across the bed and plopped down on his lap. "Shut it," she said before Luke could comment. "I'm cold again."

"My fault for letting all the heat out."

"Yeah, it was."

Luke moved backward so that his back was resting against the wall, then pulled the blanket up over them. His high stamina helped him ignore it, but it really was kind of cold that early in the morning. There was no furnace pumping warm air into the room or fireplace. The window didn't even have glass. It was just wooden shutters latched closed but with gaps around the edges that let in the early-morning light.

Zea didn't have his stats. If he didn't miss his guess, she was maybe level 10 or 11. It was no wonder she was so cold. He wondered how she'd survived the cold nights on the streets. It must have been a miserable experience for her. He wrapped his arms around her and felt her momentarily stiffen at the movement, then relax against him again.

"You're warm," she murmured softly. "Good for something after all."

"That's me," Luke said, "human furnace, amateur fighter, and abomination in the eyes of the gods."

"And don't you forget it."

Luke smiled, but there was still one problem: he still really needed to piss.

"So . . . don't yell at me, but . . ."

Luke ended up going out for food on his own, but he brought enough back to share. It turned out that freshly baked and still-warm bread was a much better meal than he'd expected, though he was willing to admit that after a month of relying on his own cooking abilities, almost anything tasted good by comparison. Zea's only complaint was cleaning the crumbs out of the bed.

"You think that weapon place will be open this early?" Luke said.

"Maybe. I guess it doesn't hurt to go by and find out. I'll go over to the Harbor and see if Sideon can fit you in for a lunch fight. Think you can meet me there around noon?"

"Yeah, no problem."

Zea looked him up and down and said, "You sure you're ready to fight again? Nobody would blame you for taking a day or two off."

"As long as it's not someone at the top of the rankings, I should be fine," Luke said.

"Alright. I'll tell him you want an easy match, maybe against a first timer. It won't pay much, but better than nothing. And Luke, stay away from the church girl. She's trouble. I mean it."

"Why, Zea? Are you jealous?"

Zea hopped to her feet, grabbed Luke's collar, and jerked him around to face her. "This isn't a joke. I don't need you getting yourself killed or dragging me along with you."

That was probably the worst part of it. If Luke was captured and killed, there was a chance that all his new friends and coworkers would get dragged into it too. He tried not to spend too much time thinking about that, but it was one of the reasons he wanted to put a rush on his new mace, and one of the reasons he was considering leaving Valtira on foot instead of by boat.

Her face was inches away from his, her eyes hard and glaring at him. "Tell me that you understand it's not a joke, that they are deadly serious about hunting down and killing apostates."

"I understand," he said. He looked her in the eyes and tried not to think about how close she was. Damn **[Peripheral Awareness]** anyway for making it so easy to see her lips.

She growled, then pulled him forward into a kiss. His eyes widened in surprise, but he didn't fight her. "And I'm not jealous," she said as she let him go.

"I . . . but . . . you said . . . with the splitting apart," he stammered.

"Well not from that, idiot!"

"Right, uh, yeah. I knew that."

"Go run your errands. Meet me at the Harbor around noon."

Luke left Zea behind in the room. He was equal parts confused and excited. All he could think about was that she was much curvier than he'd expected underneath the human-sized clothes she wore, and how much he enjoyed how feisty she was.

Luke needed to stop and ask for directions twice to find Donaley's again, but he did eventually make his way to the shop. Donaley's Alchemical Blacksmithing was just as he remembered it, with one notable exception. Pips was nowhere to be found, which was just fine by Luke. That thing was annoying anyway. He still hadn't figured out what exactly Pips was either.

"Donaley?" Luke called out from the showroom floor. "Your front door was unlocked. I hope you're here."

"In the back," Donaley yelled. "Come on back, just mind your step."

Luke pushed through the door behind the counter and found himself in a workshop of some kind, except all the tables were filled with glasswork instead of tools. The back end looked more like what he expected a smithy to look like, only with some sort of weird apparatus suspended over the anvil.

Donaley stood at it, holding a dagger made of some shiny material that glowed blue with a pair of tongs. The apparatus hanging overhead dribbled a liquid, also glowing blue, one drop at a time while Donaley moved it around. With each drop, he ran some sort of stone across the length of the blade, then flipped it so the next drop splashed onto the other side.

"Sorry, you caught me at a bad time. I can't stop in the middle of this process, or it'll ruin the whole thing. You had the blood-silver-core mace, right? The one braided with living steel?"

"That's me," Luke said. "I'm just checking to see how much longer until it's ready."

Donaley shrugged with one shoulder. The other one held the dagger steady with the tongs. "Two days, at least. Maybe three."

"Any way I can speed that up?" Luke asked.

The smith glanced up from his work and grinned at Luke. "Sure, if you got the extra gold to spend. I'd also need the rest of the order up front."

"I still owe you seven. Call it eight if you can have it ready tomorrow?"

"Deal. Just put the money on that bench over there. I'll get started on the core bonding for your piece as soon as I'm done with this one."

Luke counted the coins out, pressing each one down hard enough to clink so Donaley could hear it. "So, what's special about the dagger?" he asked.

"Ever sharp," the smith said. "Won't rust, won't shatter. Good hunting knife, not bad for defending yourself either. You interested?"

"You're not making it for somebody?" Luke asked, surprised.

"Nah, this is a showroom piece. They sell pretty fast. People like them because a good knife is always handy, and one that you don't have to do any maintenance on is even better. There's four more out on the floor right now. I make them in my spare time when I'm waiting for something to cure but don't have time to do a big project."

"Huh, that's cool. How much?"

"Eight silver, nine if you want a sheath with it," Donaley said without hesitation.

Luke could make the sheath himself, but he didn't have the tools or materials for it. He did still have the knife he'd taken from Curt's workshop though. "Hmm . . . you ever figure anything out from that mace I traded you?"

"Little bit, yeah. It was pretty damaged but still clever the way the steel was made. Why?"

"I've got a hunting knife already that was made the same way. I'm not sure how it compares to what you're making now."

Donaley turned the blade over again and wiped another dab of the blue liquid across it with the stone. "It's an interesting forging technique; never seen anything exactly like that. Good steel, but there's no comparison between that and something that's been alchemically treated. Now, if you wanted me to upgrade that knife with this same treatment, I could do that for four silver."

"How long does that process take?" Luke asked.

"Twenty minutes, unless a nosy customer won't stop asking me questions."

Luke's biggest concern with handing over the knife would be that he'd be down to precisely zero weapons if he walked out of the shop without it. He could stand to wait twenty minutes though. Counting out four more silver next to the gold he'd already put on the counter, he said, "Let's do it. I'll just stay out of your way. You mind if I wait in the showroom until it's done?"

"You want it right now? Yeah, fine. Give me half an hour. Got to finish this one first."

Luke stepped back out of the workshop and looked around the showroom. It was kind of crap security to just have the door unlocked and nobody watching it. It was a wonder no one had robbed him yet.

"Oh hi, you're back!" Pips said, popping up from behind a stand that Luke could have sworn there was no room behind. "Are you here for another weapon? What is it this time? A sword maybe? Everyone looks fashionable with a good sword."

Luke groaned. It was going to be a long half an hour.

Name	Luke Bennet
Level	21
XP	29751/34079
AP	0
Bloodline	SysAdmin
Strength	40
Agility	32
Stamina	26
Perception	29
Skills	Mace Mastery (2)
	Sword Mastery (1)
	Unarmed Martialist (2)
	Power Strike (1)
	Life Surge (1)
	Peripheral Awareness (1)
	Counter (2)
	Twitch Reflexes (2)
	Stealth (1)
	Survivalist (2)
	First Aid (1)
	Wood Carving (1)
	Leatherworking (2)
	Thalian (2)
	Disguise (2)
	Deception (1)

CHAPTER 56

Zea and Zammin sat at one of the tables with the adjustable-height chairs with a pair of mugs in front of them. She didn't drink very often, both because she couldn't afford it and because she needed to keep her wits about her. Today had her frazzled though, too many emotions churning inside her and rebelling against what she knew were the smart, rational choices.

"There is no way he's ready to fight again," Zammin said. "Him and Kalishka beat the hell out of each other. I don't care how high his stamina is."

Zea shrugged. "He said he didn't want to fight against you, but he wouldn't mind some 'light exercise.'"

The other dwifkin smirked and wiggled his eyebrows. "Going to give him some light exercise then?"

She coughed and took a drink from her mug. "Ah, no. I don't think so."

Zammin stared at her for a second, then started snickering. "I was just joking, but now . . . well, Aldrick's a handsome enough guy, I guess. Bit tall for my tastes, but don't let that stop you." The fighter sobered and said, "I don't judge anyone for that, but I won't tell anyone if you don't want. I know not everyone is accepting of crossing the species line, but fuck them. If he makes you happy, that's good enough."

"It doesn't matter," Zea said. "He's not going to be around for much longer anyway. Saving up some money, and then he's back on the road. Even if he was interested, it wouldn't work out. And why would he want to be with a woman he couldn't even sleep with?"

Zammin looked down at his beer while he thought about what he wanted to say. "I don't really know how to say this delicately Zea, but . . . why do you even want to stay in Valtira? You've been struggling and scraping by for years. Once every few months, you come around and it seems like every time, you look worse and you're more bitter. I know you've got some coin in your pocket now and that Aldrick's the reason.

"You've been a lot happier these last few days than I've seen you in the last decade. Maybe if he thinks he's going, you should talk to him about staying. Or maybe you should go with him. Whatever makes the two of you happy."

Zea had good reasons for not wanting to stay too close to Aldrick, but she couldn't explain those to Zammin. Even mentioning that he was leaving town soon was probably saying too much. But, well, the contract she'd negotiated with Sideon had been on a per-fight basis, with no obligation to continue from either party. She'd made sure to include that so he didn't come after her for money if Aldrick flaked on her.

"And besides," Zammin said, interrupting her musing. "That whole size thing is mostly overblown anyway. My sister dated a human guy for a while, said they just had to do a lot of foreplay and then ease in slowly."

Zea's head snapped up, and she stared at the fighter in open-mouthed horror. "Your whole family is way too open about stuff. I don't want to talk about this. Just drink your damn beer."

Zammin cackled while she glared at him, drawing a few glances from other tables. Fortunately, the bar portion was mostly empty this time of day. The Harbor itself didn't have many customers, and the few that were there were almost all sitting around one of the pits eating off plates balanced on their laps while a pair of day laborers duked it out for a few silver and a free tankard to the winner.

"Speaking of tall-boys, yours just walked in," Zammin said, nodding toward the door. "And damn, you weren't kidding. That does not look like a man who got the shit beat out of him yesterday."

Aldrick was walking easy, with no hint of a limp or pain in his breathing. He nodded toward a few of the regulars who recognized him and made his way over to where Zea was sitting. "Hey there, boss. Am I late?"

"No," she said. "Still got half an hour before the lunch rush starts. Just some amateurs filling the pit right now. How'd the errand go?"

"Good. I got the guy to put a rush order on it, so the new weapon will be ready tomorrow. I'm looking forward to having it again."

"Oh, new weapon?" Zammin cut in. "What'd you get?"

"Heavy mace with a blood silver core braided to living steel."

The dwifkin fighter let out a low whistle. "That's an expensive piece. Must have set you back at least fifteen gold."

"About that, yeah."

"If you need something like that . . ." Zammin eyed him up. "Hmm. 50 strength?"

"Not quite," Aldrick said with a smile. "Maybe in a level or two."

"You're still gaining levels? Are you insane?" Zea said.

"I'm not strong enough to do what needs done yet, so . . . yeah, I guess maybe I'm a little crazy."

"You must have lofty ambitions," Zammin said. "You're going to put yourself into an early grave if you keep it up though. I doubt you're going to live much past sixty with all the XP you've got now. And it gets worse even faster when you get more."

Sideon walked over, interrupting any further discussion, and said, "I didn't believe your manager when she said you were ready to fight, but look at you." He slapped Aldrick on the shoulder and laughed. "Sturdy as a rock. Alright, let me walk you through what I'm thinking for the lunch fights. I don't have anyone for you to fight except Zammin here, but Zea said you wanted to take it easy for a day before getting back into the heavy stuff. So here's the idea."

He held up a set of fetters with about a foot of chain connecting them. "We're going to give you some handicaps like this, maybe do your hands if we need to, and I'll offer a prize if anyone manages to knock you down. You'll be facing a bunch of dockworkers today, which means they spent their AP on strength and stamina and not much else. I think you should be able to take 'em no problem."

"What's the fee look like?" Aldrick asked, glancing over at Zea. It might have been her imagination, but she thought his eyes lingered on her a bit too long, and his cheeks were a bit red.

"Standard for this kind of fight," she answered. "The guys taking shots at you will pay half a silver to enter. Any of them win, they get five silver. Each one you take out without losing past ten gets you half a silver. If you're still standing at the end, you get another two silver."

"So if I go through let's say twenty of these without losing, that's seven total. That's not bad for what sounds like a pretty easy afternoon," Aldrick said.

"Not bad at all," Sideon agreed.

"Just remember that you're going to be handicapped," Zea said. "And if not enough people try, they'll add more handicaps until someone gets tempted. You'll be fighting at a disadvantage."

Aldrick reached out to pick up the fetters. "I'm assuming you don't want me to break these," he said.

Sideon started laughing. "Like you could!"

Zammin grinned over his mug but didn't say anything. Zea knew what he was thinking though. If Aldrick was custom ordering alchemically bonded weapons to keep up with his strength, there was no way those plain steel fetters were going to stand up to him. "If you damage them, it'll come out of your fee to replace them."

Aldrick winced but nodded. "If you've got something stronger, that might be better. These are kind of . . . flimsy."

"Try," Sideon said smugly.

"Are you sure?"

The fight promoter just nodded. With a shrug, Aldrick took the fetters in both hands and pulled until one of the links snapped. "Holy crap," Sideon yelped. "I . . . I'll see if we have anything stronger. Just try not to accidentally jerk your leg when you're in the pit, okay?"

Sideon led Aldrick toward the fighters' waiting room, leaving Zea alone again with Zammin. "Hmm . . . that one's got something strange going on. Could be fun though. Just think about what I said, okay? What's going to make you happy?" He frowned down at his mug. "Damn. Empty."

Luke felt like he was wearing construction paper cuffs. Every time he took a shuffling step, he was afraid a link was going to snap, but Fatty didn't have anything better. Sideon. Sideon didn't have anything better. He really needed to stop calling the man that.

They'd set it up just like Sideon had said they would, and a few of the guys who'd seen last night's fight had been keen to take a swing at him. Luke wasn't sure if they thought it'd be an easy payday because of how bad last night's fight was or if they just wanted to say they'd gotten into the pit to fight him.

Either way, the hardest part was not breaking the damn fetters. [Twitch Reflexes] was doing its level best to trip him up there, but they'd managed to get a decent run of contenders without having to shackle his hands together, so Luke was mostly dodging around the issue by blocking attacks with his hands.

That got harder when Sideon started letting them into the pit two at a time to fight, but it just meant more money for Luke when he swatted them down. Even when they upped it to three, he had to hold back and not blast people away with one shot. Sideon had made it very clear that if he did that, nobody else would want to try. They'd know they didn't have a shot in hell at winning.

His final match was one he had to agree to first, a five-on-one rumble that he'd only gone with on the condition that his fetters be switched for a pair with an extra foot of chain. He doubted he'd be able to make it look good while standing still, and he wasn't interested in paying the repair costs.

The fights weren't challenging, but the pay was decent. He ended up with a gold coin at the end, which ironically beat out his fee from his fight with Kalishka. Apparently, there were a lot of people who would pay good silver to take a swing at him if they thought he couldn't really fight back.

"You want a big fight this evening?" Sideon asked, after unlocking the fetters so Luke could climb back out of the pit. He turned around and gave the fat man a hand up, then shook his head.

"Not unless Zea scheduled me for one."

"She didn't. I asked, but she said you wanted to recover some more. You look fine to me though. If you think you're up for it, I'll go talk to her about setting one up."

"Not tonight," Luke said. "I'm still a bit sore. It wouldn't be a good fight. If I actually had to try against the top-ranked guys, you'd see me hitting a wall pretty quick. These guys today . . . you know, not fighters, plus I had plenty of time between each round."

"No problem at all. When you're ready, send the shorty around and I'll get something set up for you."

"Thanks," Luke said. "I think I'm going to grab lunch now. See you around."

He found Zea still seated at the same table, though Zammin had disappeared sometime in the middle of the lunch event. "I'm going to get something to eat. Want to come?"

"Actually, I was thinking . . . I've almost got enough to cover my half of the rent now, but I kind of want to get out of these rags and get a proper bath. Feels like I haven't had one in years. And, uh . . . you kind of need a bath too. Why don't you grab something to eat on the way? I'm going to pick up some clothes and we can go to a bathhouse?"

"What?" Luke asked, his eyebrows shooting up. "Like, together?"

"Not in the same tub! Not even in the same room," she said. "But yes, we're both . . . fragrant."

"Okay, it's a date."

"It's not a date."

"If you say so."

"I'm already regretting inviting you along. Maybe you should just go find a bathhouse on your own."

"Sure. Give me the key so I can get into the room?"

"Stupid room," Zea muttered. "Why couldn't they have two keys for it? Okay, fine, let's go together."

Name	Luke Bennet
Level	21
XP	29751/34079
AP	0
Bloodline	SysAdmin
Strength	40
Agility	32
Stamina	26
Perception	29
Skills	Mace Mastery (2)
	Sword Mastery (1)
	Unarmed Martialist (2)
	Power Strike (1)
	Life Surge (1)
	Peripheral Awareness (1)
	Counter (2)
	Twitch Reflexes (2)
	Stealth (1)
	Survivalist (2)
	First Aid (1)
	Wood Carving (1)
	Leatherworking (2)
	Thalian (2)
	Disguise (2)
	Deception (1)

CHAPTER 57

Shopping wasn't really Luke's thing. Luckily for him, Zea seemed to know exactly what she was looking for. He had no idea what it was, but he dutifully followed along behind her until she ventured into some sort of dwifkin specialty store. He took one look at the size of the door and how low the ceilings were and told her he'd wait outside.

When she came out twenty minutes later, she had a package wrapped in some sort of paper and held with twine in her hands. Her eyes sparkled, and she hugged it close to her chest. "All set," she said.

"You're still wearing those rags?

"I want to get a bath first." She eyed Luke up and down and added, "We'll choose one with a laundering service. You've been wearing the same clothes since you got here, haven't you? I don't think you even own a second pair."

"That's true," he said. "Maybe I should get a spare outfit too. It'd be nice to at least have one other thing to wear, just so I'm not naked while I get the first one cleaned."

"Something like that. Come on, let's get cleaned up and then we can figure out what the next month is going to be like."

The bathhouse was divided into two sections. The men's side at least had an open pool that was a quarter-silver, as they called the small nail-sized coins, or for a half-silver he could get a private room. Luke wasn't exactly shy and would have gone for the pool, except that the laundering service wasn't available without renting a private room.

So he sucked it up, paid the extra coin, and let the attendant lead him down a tiled hallway into a room with a tub that was sized like a hot tub. He stripped out of his clothes, wrapped himself in the towel they'd provided, and handed the soiled clothing through the door to the waiting attendant.

"Thanks," he said. "How long will it be until they're ready?"

"About an hour. Most of that is drying time, so we can't really do it much faster."

"That's fine, I guess."

Luke wondered what kind of skills related to doing laundry. Maybe there was an actual [Launder] skill that sped the process up. Or maybe they just did it the old-fashioned way, on a washboard with muscles made strong and tireless through the power of stats, and then hung things up near a fire to dry.

Once he was alone in the tub, he took a few minutes to scrub himself clean, then went still and just listened. There were noises coming from everywhere around him, the sounds of men splashing in their own rooms, a conversation between two of the employees about restocking the empty rooms and getting more fuel for the furnaces built under the main floor.

"System," Luke said quietly.

"Yes, Luke?"

"I've got a lot of questions that've been building up."

"I will do my best to answer them," the apparition said.

"First of all, why the fuck didn't you tell me about XP madness?"

"Several reasons, but foremost among them is that you did not ask."

Luke groaned. He hadn't talked to System in a few days and had started to forget how much of a pain it was to get information out of him. He was no substitute for an actual person. "Will it be a problem for me?"

"If you are able to further purify your bloodline or if you can access the command console and increase your SysAdmin privileges, I do not see why it would impede your stated goal."

"And if I don't do that?" Luke asked. "If I gave up and just lived out my life here, how many years would I have left?"

"Assuming you never gained another point of XP, which would be quite unlikely, I predict you would live to be around seventy years of age before the affliction becomes noticeable to people."

That didn't match with what others had told him, but they were also operating under some incorrect assumptions. He'd gone close to two decades before he ever gained his first point of XP, which seemed like something that was probably unusual and might have an effect on how much time he had left. The XP just plain had less time to do . . . whatever it was that it did.

"Why does this happen?" Luke asked.

"Ah, that is a complicated answer. I suppose the easiest way to explain it is to say that XP congeals together, which is bad for the host. The more XP there is in one place, the more it becomes a single solid chunk. Cycling XP and keeping it broken apart so that it does not congeal is the true function of the God Machine."

"And . . . that drives people crazy?"

"No. They are not crazy. They are merely hearing the god in the machine."

Luke sat upright and looked over at System. "What in the fuck does that mean? That sounds bad."

"That is what XP is, Luke, little pieces of the god trapped inside the machine and being cycled around, moved from one mortal being to another in endless variations and combinations, all in an effort to keep it from reforming back into the god it's all part of."

"Jesus. There's something living trapped in there? That's . . . sadistic. Why does this exist?"

"I am not able to speculate on the motivations of the Pantheon. My apologies."

That did tell him that the gods were behind all this crap. He already knew that though, really. Of course they'd made the system and had control over it. This just told him the *how* of the whole thing. They'd sacrificed one of their own to serve as the source of power for the whole system.

"Can you tell me anything about the god trapped in the system?" Luke asked. "Did they deserve it? Were they an evil god? Or did they just draw the short straw?"

"The god in the machine was never part of the original Pantheon. They were an interloper from beyond the Pantheon's sphere of influence."

Luke took that to mean that some other god had intruded on the Pantheon, and then they either couldn't kill it or refused to, so they trapped it instead. He had to imagine that the god in the machine was pissed about that. Their . . . being . . . he guessed, was being divvied up into little chunks and handed out to mortals.

"So then . . . XP is a fragment of a god. Every single point is its own piece. What are you then? Are you the warden of the prison?"

"I am not," System said. "It would be more accurate to say that I am the prison itself. I am the machine. If anything, you are the warden."

"Me?"

"You have the SysAdmin bloodline. You are a descendent of the first warden. You can change the rules."

"Damn it," Luke muttered. "This is all so completely fucked."

He sank down into the water until only his eyes and nose were still exposed to the air. Steam rose from vents spaced around the walls, keeping the room warm and obscuring his view of everything but System, who somehow still appeared to just be superimposed on the world instead of part of it.

Sometimes it all felt like a bad dream. Other times it was a cruel joke. Right now it was just fucking crazy. He didn't want to go up against gods. He didn't want to fight monsters. He just wanted the people this world had taken from him back and to go home. He supposed he wouldn't mind keeping some of his stats, but if they really were little god pieces fortifying his body, he probably should give them back.

The gods had some reason for trapping another god inside a machine and cutting it into individual cells, but Luke wondered if he'd agree with them. Was the god in the machine an invader, come to destroy? Or was the Pantheon just a bunch of selfish assholes who hated the idea of any other divine beings intruding on its territory?

A knock on the door interrupted his thoughts. "Sir?" the attendant said. "Your clothes are ready."

Luke moved around so that the important bits were more or less covered and said, "Thanks, you can bring them in."

The attendant slipped into the room and set a pile of clothes on a bench built into the wall, right above where he'd left his boots and neck pouch. Luke leaned over and snagged the coin pouch, picked out another quarter-silver piece and flicked it over to the attendant, who caught it with a surprised blink.

"What's this?" the boy asked, confused.

"Call it a tip for such quick service."

"Ah, sir. Thank you? Is there anything else you require?"

"Nope. When I'm done, I just get dressed, leave the towel in here, and leave?"

"Yes, sir. If you do need anything else, please let me know."

"Actually, do you have a shaving kit or something for customers?"

"Certainly, sir, there is a station to have a barber attend to you if you'd like. I can wait for you to get dressed and show you the way?"

"Thanks. That would be perfect."

The attendant stepped outside, and Luke sighed. If it had been an hour already, then Zea was probably already done and waiting for him. She'd just have to wait a few more minutes. He had a month's growth on his face, and he wouldn't say no to a haircut either.

The clothes were clean and dry. That didn't necessarily mean they were comfortable though. Now that he had them back on, he was reminded just how rough they were compared to modern clothes, how much they made him itch. There was no help for that though, not right now at least.

Luke followed the attendant down the hall to what looked something like a barbershop with two women stationed there, each looking after their own chair. One was occupied by a thick, dark-haired man with a gnarly beard, but the other was empty. The attendant gestured for Luke to take a seat and said, "Do not worry about paying, sir. You already have."

He held up the quarter-silver and smiled. Luke wanted to object, to tell him that the tip had been for him, but the truth was tipping had been more of an impulse than a smart use of his money. So he let the stylist do her thing, and in just a few minutes, his hair was trimmed back, and his face was smooth again.

"There you go, handsome," she said, winking at him.

"Er . . . thanks." Luke wasn't sure what else to say. He wasn't really very good at flirting and was kind of preoccupied with other stuff anyway. After extracting himself from the chair, he made his way out of the bathhouse and back to the street, where he did not find Zea.

Either she was still in there and he hadn't needed to rush, or she'd left without him. Neither would really surprise Luke. While he was standing there trying to figure out how rude it would be to use his high perception to find Zea if she was still in the baths, someone poked him in the hip and said, "Why are you just staring off into space?"

"Huh? Oh!"

Zea had changed into her new clothes, which were apparently a sleeveless blue shift dress that came down to her calves and was belted at her waist, some sort of shawl that was thrown over her shoulders, and a pair of new, sturdy shoes. Her strawberry blonde hair was combed out straight for the first time since he'd met her.

"You . . . you look good," he said.

She smiled up at him and said, "Thanks. I wish I could say the same, but you look like you bit into a lemon. Baths are supposed to be relaxing, you know?"

"Yeah, I guess I screwed that up. I got some bad news, and it's kind of on my mind."

"In the baths?" Zea looked skeptical. "From who?"

"I'll tell you later," Luke said. "It's kind of a private matter."

"Oh. It's serious?"

"Yeah."

"Alright, let's get going. You can tell me all about it later."

Name	Luke Bennet
Level	21
XP	29751/34079
AP	0
Bloodline	SysAdmin
Strength	40
Agility	32
Stamina	26
Perception	29
Skills	Mace Mastery (2)
	Sword Mastery (1)
	Unarmed Martialist (2)
	Power Strike (1)
	Life Surge (1)
	Peripheral Awareness (1)
	Counter (2)
	Twitch Reflexes (2)
	Stealth (1)
	Survivalist (2)
	First Aid (1)
	Wood Carving (1)
	Leatherworking (2)
	Thalian (2)
	Disguise (2)
	Deception (1)

CHAPTER 58

You need to stop using that skill if you want to save any money up," Zea said as she watched Luke stuff some food into his bag.

Luke shrugged, bit down into an apple, and held it with his teeth while he closed the bag. "I don't think it matters all that much," he said. "Pretty sure the whole boat idea is a nonstarter. It would be faster to walk than to try to save up money to take a ship."

They started walking away from the stall, and she said, "What about money for travel expenses?"

"Hunt and cook for myself. That's what I was doing before I got here." He paused. "I am not a good cook, but it was edible, and I never got sick from it."

"How do you not have at least rank 1 [Cooking]?"

"Never spent the AP on it," Luke said.

"Well yeah. Nobody buys it. You should just get it from, you know, cooking stuff."

"I am not a good cook," Luke repeated, staring straight ahead.

"Even still, that's almost an achievement on its own to still not have gotten the skill for it."

"Zea," Luke said softly.

"Hmm? Oh! Oh, sorry."

Maybe if he'd lived nineteen years with the system, he'd have already picked it up naturally, but after only a month, and all of that spent without access to whatever passed for a kitchen in this world, Luke hadn't quite managed to acquire very many skills on his own.

They didn't talk much for the rest of the walk. The room Zea had rented was in what Luke thought of as an old-timey apartment. It had a common hallway and two stories. There was a public toilet, which was a step up from using a chamber pot or an outhouse at least. Zea had the keys to both the front door and to the room they were sharing.

Whoever had built it was smart enough to put the stairs right by the entrance, which beat out the designs of a lot of inns, according to Zea. It was one of the reasons she'd picked the place. They went up to the second floor and walked down the hallway to room twenty-one, where she let them both in and locked the door behind her.

"Sorry," she said. "I wasn't thinking. I shouldn't have mentioned—"

Luke cut her off with an upraised finger and cocked his head to the side. "Both rooms on either side are empty, but there's someone in the room directly under this one," he said in a low voice. "And someone two rooms over that way. No, two people."

"Wow, your perception must be very high to be able to tell that. Can you understand what they're saying in those rooms?"

"I hear so much stuff that people don't think anyone would overhear. It's amazing that you all have this stat your entire life and everyone thinks they've got privacy just because they closed a door."

"In all fairness, most people don't raise it past 8 or 10. Yours is . . . higher? I'm sorry, that's rude. Forget I asked."

"29," Luke said.

"Fuck me, that's insane. How do you deal with hearing just . . . all of that, all the time?"

"Don't have much of a choice, I guess. You get used to it, but I've been thinking I might head out of the city for some time away from all the noise as soon as I have a weapon to defend myself with again."

"I'm not even sure why you need a weapon," Zea said. "I've seen you fight just fine without one."

"I only started doing that here. My weapon broke a few hours outside the city. Slammed it on a giant's skull and snapped it."

"You are scary as fuck, you know that?"

Luke blinked and focused his eyes on her. "I'm sorry. I'm not trying to be."

Zea hopped on the bed and pulled the blanket over to cover her legs. "It's okay. I don't think you'd try to hurt me. You can be scary at other people. I know you're gentle. Now, can you tell me what got you in such a bad mood at the bathhouse?"

"Oh, that. Just some off-worlder stuff. Are you sure you want to know?" Luke sank down to his butt and put his back against the wall opposite her.

"If you think it's safe to tell me, I guess. I'm already up to my ass in this whole mess anyway."

He took a second to compose his thoughts and try to structure it all into a coherent sentence. "First, I guess I need to tell you that I have a bloodline that lets me talk to the system itself. It can manifest as a ghost thing that's only visible to me. I was talking to it today, asked it about XP madness."

"I've never heard of a bloodline that does that," Zea said.

"I guess only off-worlders have it. Anyway, the important thing is that I found out what the system is. It's a god, trapped by the other gods in the Pantheon. XP is little bits of god stuff carved out of it and cycled through us mortals, and XP madness is what happens when you get too much XP together for too long a time and it starts to reconnect itself. Then you hear the voice of the trapped god, and I guess that drives people crazy?"

"Wow. Okay. That's not in the scriptures," Zea said. "I wonder if the gods tell anyone that. There are people who are supposed to be immune to XP madness, the ones who carry out divine will and are blessed by the gods."

"System thinks I could be, if not immune to it, able to . . . turn it off, I guess? With my bloodline. I just need to purify it enough to gain access to the ability or go to the physical location of the prison of this god, and once I'm there, I can just . . . do whatever I want."

"That's why you're trying to cross the ocean," Zea said. "To get to this prison."

"Right. As long as I do it before I go crazy, I can fix everything. System thinks I've got about fifty years left if I don't ever gain another point of XP."

Zea flopped backward on the bed and looked up at the ceiling. "Yeah right. Like that'll happen. You're fucking crazy," she whispered. Luke didn't know if he was supposed to hear that. He definitely wasn't supposed to hear the next part. "At least he doesn't know any better. I'm crazy *and* stupid."

"Why's that?" Luke asked.

Zea flinched and said, "You just pretend you can't hear me when I don't want you to."

"Okay, I can do that."

"Stupid Zammin," she muttered to herself again.

Neither of them said anything for a while. Zea obviously had a lot on her mind, and Luke was content to just sit there and watch her legs kick back and forth over the edge of the bed. He was going to miss her when he left. She was his first real friend since arriving on Aros, his only real friend, actually. He was friendly with some of the other fighters, but he wasn't close to them.

He'd liked Zea pretty much the instant he met her, though not so much that he would have told her he was an off-worlder if not for being falling down drunk. He could see why drunk Luke had made that call, but he hadn't been doing her any favors. She had a lot of unnecessary stress from carrying that one around. It would have been far kinder to maintain a professional relationship instead of letting his problems splash over onto hers.

"When are you leaving?" she asked.

"A few days, maybe a week. I want to get a bit more money built up for both of us."

"That's . . . quick, but I get it."

"Going to miss me when I'm gone?" he teased.

She sat upright, kicked the blankets off, and stood up. "Yes," she said simply. Then she crossed the room, pushed his arm out of the way, and plopped down on his lap. Luke smiled softly and wrapped his other arm around her.

"I'll miss you too."

"I was talking to Zammin before your afternoon fights," she said. "You know what he told me? Hell, maybe you do, with those ears."

"No, too much background noise, and I try not to eavesdrop."

"He said I've been a lot happier this last week than he's seen me in years, that whatever we've got going on, I should hang on to it. I'm pretty sure he meant I should keep you here, but that's not a possibility."

"I thought about it," Luke admitted. "Or of coming back to find you when I was done, if I can't go back home. Or maybe even if I can."

"Please, like you could find anything without me around to show you where it is."

"True enough."

They shared a laugh at that, though it was a quiet, subdued one. "It's going to be a long, long journey," she said. "Very dangerous. Some of the monsters out there . . . even you're not strong enough to fight them."

"I'll get stronger," he said. "Don't really have a choice."

"Yeah, you're crazy. You need to pick up some skills to hide your XP before someone decides you need to die just for being too high level."

"I have skills that do that," Luke said. "Two of them, actually. **[Stealth]** and **[Disguise]**."

"Better rank them up higher and find another couple."

"I'll add it to my list."

"Good. It would suck if you died."

"I agree. I'll do my best not to."

"Good." Zea snuggled in closer.

"Are you going to be alright once I'm gone?" Luke asked. "Did you get enough seed money to get whatever schemes you come up with going?"

"Oh, don't worry about me. I'll survive," she said. "Always do. This dress probably won't make it though. It'll be rags once I'm back to living on the streets."

"That's a shame. It's a nice dress. You look very pretty. Have you considered not living on the streets so that it stays in good condition?"

"It's not that easy, jerk."

"I know . . . Is there anything I can do to help?"

"You just win as many fights as you can so I can keep making money off you."

"I can do that," Luke said with a laugh.

At least, he could for a little while. It would be enough to get her the money for maybe another month's rent and food. If she was careful with it, maybe she could turn it into something bigger. He wondered why she was living on the streets and what she'd done for money before finding him. It seemed rude to ask though, so he kept his mouth shut.

"You really think I look pretty?" she asked suddenly.

"I really do."

"Well, good. That's because I am. You, on the other hand, are too tall to be handsome."

"Makes sense to me," Luke said with a nod.

"But you are wonderfully warm. I'll give you that. This floor, however, isn't. So I am going back to the bed. Come on."

Luke dusted his butt off as he stood up. Zea waited for him to climb into bed and set his back against the wall before crawling over to sit on him again. This time she pulled the blanket up around her. "How did you ever survive on the streets before?" he asked. "Sorry, that was insensitive."

"The winters are mild this far south, but it's still pretty miserable. There's a reason there aren't a lot of dwifkin in Valtira. We just aren't made for the cold. If you go another few hundred miles south down the coast, we almost outnumber the humans."

Which meant there was no way she'd be interested in going even farther north with him. She'd freeze to death before they got halfway. He hadn't even considered that when he was listing all the reasons it would be a bad idea to ask if she wanted to come.

Zea squirmed on his lap and pulled the shawl off. "It's a very nice dress, but it's not as comfortable as I'd like," she said. "Plus if I slept in it, it would get all wrinkled."

"Uh . . ." Luke said dumbly.

"You'll keep me warm, right?"

"Uh," Luke said again.

"Hey." She scowled up at him. "Keeping me warm is your job right now."

"Right. Yeah. I guess I have no choice."

"Good." Zea reached up to wrap her hand around the back of his head to pull his face down toward hers. Just before their lips met, she whispered, "Keep me warm all night."

Name	Luke Bennet
Level	21
XP	29751/34079
AP	0
Bloodline	SysAdmin
Strength	40
Agility	32
Stamina	26
Perception	29
Skills	Mace Mastery (2)
	Sword Mastery (1)
	Unarmed Martialist (2)
	Power Strike (1)
	Life Surge (1)
	Peripheral Awareness (1)
	Counter (2)
	Twitch Reflexes (2)
	Stealth (1)
	Survivalist (2)
	First Aid (1)
	Wood Carving (1)
	Leatherworking (2)
	Thalian (2)
	Disguise (2)
	Deception (1)

CHAPTER 59

The viscous liquid dripped into the vial while Myla counted. For a man Aldrick's size, two drops per ten stamina should be enough. She'd watched him fight once and thought she had good estimates of his stats, but there was always a measure of guesswork in something like this. Four drops would probably suffice, perhaps five, but she upped the dose to six to be safe. Any higher and she'd risk the poison overwhelming him, which defeated the point.

There was always a chance it wouldn't work. He'd exhibited some sort of temporary-enhancement ability, which could either burn through the poison or make it even more effective, depending on how the skill functioned. If it suppressed the poison while it was active, then the crash afterward might leave him significantly more vulnerable to it. If that was the case, the poison could very well kill him.

That wasn't the desired result, but Myla considered it an acceptable risk. If all went according to the plan, she would drug him, abduct him, and interrogate him. The poison, derived from the milk of a sankapor viper, would leave him delirious and too scattered to think of lying when she asked her questions, and if necessary, she could dump him somewhere and let him wake up thinking he had a bad hangover.

Ideally, the rot he represented hadn't spread too far, and the inquisitors could scoop up any allies he'd made in one fell swoop. Then Aldrick could be disposed of without ever leaving the confessional. If she was lucky, all the paranoia and extra preparations had been a waste of time. If not . . . it was important to keep up the facade that Aldrick was operating unknown to the church until they'd rooted out every last member of his cult.

Myla bottled up the poison. It was a cloudy white color on its own, but it wouldn't be noticeable once she poured it into a drink. All she needed to do now was put on her seamstress outfit again, find him after one of his fights, and invite him out for lunch. He'd accepted eagerly enough the first time; she doubted it would be difficult to get him alone again.

And if for some reason it was, there were other ways of gaining access to his food and drink. **[Disguise]** was an extremely flexible skill, and she had plenty of practice with it. It was a point of pride to her that she'd gotten it all the way up to rank 3 without spending a single point of AP, though Master Lath had insisted that it would take many, many years of effort to reach rank 4 and that she needed to spend the 50 AP on the upgrade instead.

That still rankled, but she wouldn't disobey his instructions. It seemed like a waste to dump a tenth of her total AP into one single skill rank, but those were her orders, and she trusted her master to know what was best. He'd created the path of the poisoner himself, after all. No one in the world knew its intricacies better than him.

She heard an inquisitor approaching a few seconds before a knock came at the door. Myla spent a moment cleaning up her workstation before answering the knock. "Yes?"

"Ma'am," the inquisitor said. "I've handed off watch to Inquisitor Mekan."

"Ah, that late already?" There were no windows in the workshop, not with so many of her mixtures and concoctions being vulnerable to light. She often found herself losing track of the time when she was working. "Very well. Anything to report?"

"He visited an alchemical-weapons shop early in the day and participated in a round of gimmick matches where he allowed himself to be shackled while fighting challengers. There were eight fights, one of which had five opponents, and he cleanly won all of them. After that, he left with the half-sized manager to run errands. They spent the night in bed together again, this time engaging in sexual activities."

The inquisitor's mouth twisted in distaste at the end of his report. Myla could understand his feelings; to sleep with something that wasn't even human was . . . disgusting, like lying with a monster. If the church had gotten its way, nonhumans wouldn't be allowed in Valtira, or any other human city. Soldiers should have been dispatched to drive the invasive species out of human-claimed territory decades ago. That hadn't happened, unfortunately.

Regardless of her personal feelings, an inquisitor mastered herself and betrayed nothing on her face. This man hadn't learned that lesson yet, apparently, and she made a mental note to speak with his master about putting a focus on increasing his control. If he wore his emotions so openly, he'd never rank up **[Deception]**.

"Thank you. Where is he now?"

"As of half an hour ago, the human told the half size that he had planned on picking up his new weapon today before meeting her at the fight club he works at."

"Perfect. If there's nothing else, you may go," she said.

"Ma'am."

If Aldrick's tastes swung that way, she might have to reevaluate her plans. She'd thought he was quite smitten with her seamstress persona, but perhaps not. It wasn't time to retire the disguise just yet, but she wouldn't be surprised if he declined her asking him out for a lunch date. There was a hard limit to how much **[Disguise]** could alter her appearance, and removing about a foot from her height was well past that limit.

There were other ways to capture him without attracting attention from any of his allies or followers. They just weren't as convenient. Regardless, she'd have him in a confessional before the end of the night and, if necessary, slipped back into his life without ever realizing he'd lost a few hours of it.

Myla returned to her workbench to complete her preparations.

It took all Luke's willpower to get out of that bed in the morning when the alternative was snuggling with a still-naked Zea, which would inevitably lead back to sex again, and it was really, really good sex. But eventually, despite her pouting, he forced himself to get dressed.

"Do you want to come with me?" he asked.

"No," came the muffled response from under the blanket. Her hand shot out and snagged the waist of his trousers. "Want you to come back to bed."

"The sun's up. I've got errands to run. I'm sure you do too?"

"No, I'm on vacation. I haven't gotten laid in five years, you're out of here soon, and I want all the dick I can get before that happens."

She tried to pull him back onto the bed, but she was nowhere near strong enough to move him if he didn't want to move. That meant of course that he feigned losing his balance and shuffled a few steps closer. Zea's head popped out from under the blanket to regard him suspiciously as he sat down next to her.

He pulled her into his arms, blanket and all, and kissed her deeply. "You stay here and keep the bed warm for me. I'll be back in an hour or two. And then, well, I guess we should figure out some definite plans and take advantage of however much time we have left."

"Ugh. Fine. Hurry back."

"I will," he promised, kissing her again. Then there was some more kissing, and roaming hands, and it took Luke another forty minutes before he actually managed to get all of his clothes on and leave. It was totally worth it.

* * *

"I was wondering if I was going to see you today," Donaley said when Luke walked in. "Usually when someone pays that much for a rush order just to get something a day or two early, they show up first thing in the morning to pick it up."

"Yeah, I was, uh, going to, but . . . something popped up."

"It's fine. Been a slow day anyway. Come over here, I've got your mace all ready for you. You were wearing a back harness for the old one right? You got it with you?"

"I was, and no, I didn't think to bring it," Luke said. "I have had a very energetic morning, and it slipped my mind."

"No big deal. Not to put too fine a point on it, but your old one looked like it was done by an apprentice anyway, and a beauty like this should have a master's work to hold it. I've got a few adjustable ones if you'd like to buy something that'll really show the old girl off."

Apparently, maces were girls. Or maybe all weapons were female in Donaley's mind. Luke would have thought as phallic as they all looked, it would have been the other way around. Or maybe it was like boats. He decided it was best to just play along until he was out of the shop and then promptly forget the whole idea of gendered weapons.

"Sure, I'll take a look," he said. He doubted he'd buy anything, considering he had a perfectly serviceable harness already, but it didn't hurt to be polite.

Donaley pulled out a mace from under the counter and placed it in front of Luke. He grinned when he saw Luke's jaw drop and gestured for him to pick it up.

"Holy shit, this thing is gorgeous," Luke said, holding it in front of him. It was heavier than his old mace but not by enough to make a real difference considering how much strength he had now. The haft was a few inches longer, but the head was almost a replica of the one Curt had forged. The real difference was that the metal looked like gleaming chrome with a red cast to it. If he really looked closely at it, he could see the little veins of blood silver entwined in the living steel.

"You want to test it out?" Donaley asked slyly.

"Hell yes, I do. Do you have stuff around here I can hit?"

"Come with me," the smith said. He opened a door Luke hadn't seen before and led the way down a flight of stairs into a basement where a series of training dummies had been set up like a row of scarecrows. "Take a swing at that one all the way on the left. It's reinforced with dead steel, so don't worry about breaking it. Anything that comes off will grow back."

"You're sure this won't break my weapon?" Luke asked, suddenly apprehensive. He could still clearly picture the last time he'd swung his old mace and bent it a full ninety degrees.

"It'll be fine," Donaley scoffed.

Tentatively, Luke moved into position, set his feet, and took a half-hearted swing. The metal rang out, and the mace bounced back. He could feel the reverberations down the body of the mace, but they were not anywhere as strong as he'd expected. His old mace had practically vibrated out of his hands when he'd fought that high-level goblin with the huge sword.

"Put some effort into it," Donaley said. "I thought you were supposed to be strong. This'll handle a full-strength swing from anyone under 50 strength without any problems. You'll start to see some damage around 70 or 75 strength, but it won't really break short of 85."

Luke struck the black-plated dummy again, this time with considerably more force behind it. A crease appeared in the armor, but otherwise the dummy was unharmed. The mace itself didn't have so much as a blemish on it. "Okay, time to test it for real," he said.

He took hold of it in both hands, spared a moment to marvel at how well the grip fit him, activated **[Power Strike]**, and struck the dummy so hard that it flew across the basement and broke apart against the wall.

"Oh shit, sorry," Luke said. He looked over his shoulder and saw Donaley chuckling.

The mace itself had a crack running down the handle and seemed a bit crooked, but even as he watched, the crack was filled with something that looked like red mercury. It quickly hardened, and as it did, it jerked the body back into alignment. A few moments later, it was impossible to tell that there'd ever been any damage there.

"That is fucking awesome," Luke said.

"Course it is. I made it, didn't I? Come on now, let's go look at a harness for you. Don't worry about the dummy. I'll put it back together later after it finishes repairing itself."

Name	Luke Bennet
Level	21
XP	29751/34079
AP	0
Bloodline	SysAdmin
Strength	40
Agility	32
Stamina	26
Perception	29
Skills	Mace Mastery (2)
	Sword Mastery (1)
	Unarmed Martialist (2)
	Power Strike (1)
	Life Surge (1)
	Peripheral Awareness (1)
	Counter (2)
	Twitch Reflexes (2)
	Stealth (1)
	Survivalist (2)
	First Aid (1)
	Wood Carving (1)
	Leatherworking (2)
	Thalian (2)
	Disguise (2)
	Deception (1)

CHAPTER 60

Despite his earlier predictions that he wouldn't want to buy a nice harness when he could simply make his own with his **[Leatherworking]** skill, Luke had to admit that the stuff Donaley had for sale was way, way better than the thing he'd made. It was kind of the same design, except it was adjustable with a few straps and was modular. It could have sword sheaths attached across the back in two different directions or on either hip, for example.

It could also do axes or knives, even a whole bandolier mounted on his chest if throwing knives were something Luke wanted. Since he really only had the one knife, not counting the fold-out one and his multi-tool, he passed on those options and just bought the base harness with the back-mounting accessory.

It rode with the head on his shoulder and required him to reach around behind his hip to grab the handle, then lift up and pull out to release the mace. At first, it was a bit awkward, but Luke quickly found that having the head sitting up by his shoulder where the weight wouldn't swing around was actually a lot more comfortable.

He did have some concerns that someone might pluck the damn thing right off his back when he wasn't looking, which were perhaps a bit irrational considering how high his perception was, but Donaley put that fear to rest too. He showed Luke how to lock the collar that held the mace to his shoulder into place, a feat that he doubted he could do with one hand, even if it wasn't currently attached to his back.

"Mind you," Donaley said, "this isn't something you'd want to do out in the field when a monster might jump you at any moment, but it's not like you're going to be brandishing this thing casually around town, right? If you do find yourself needing a weapon of convenience, there's always the knife."

Luke thought that was probably correct, although he could think of one or two scenarios where having his weapon unavailable to draw would be a problem. It was far more likely that someone would try to steal it than that someone would try to murder him and he'd be unable to defend himself without the mace. He wanted it more for monster killing than anything.

"Right, how much do I owe you for the harness?" he asked.

"Two and a quarter-silver," Donaley told him immediately.

Luke paid it without hesitation. He wasn't rich by any means, and he hadn't been planning on buying this, but it was so much better than the one he'd cobbled together, and he was still flush from that lunch round yesterday. Sideon had told him not to expect profits like that regularly, if ever, but he figured he could afford to treat himself just a little bit.

On a whim, he bought an extra knife and stuck it in his backpack. Maybe he wouldn't find a use for it, but maybe, just maybe, Zea would want to come with him. He knew the answer was going to be no when he did finally ask, but he was going to keep hoping anyway. Besides, she ought to have a way to defend herself if she needed to.

Luke had gotten used to getting the occasional, or not-so-occasional, stare when someone clocked him as the source of a large amount of XP. Nobody had said anything about it while he was going about his business, and he'd learned to ignore it. He didn't expect that to change when he left Donaley's, but he learned better almost immediately.

A general ripple of unease went through the crowd as he passed through it. It seemed that a guy with high XP was unusual but not worth confronting, but a guy with high XP and a visible weapon was a different story. No less than three of the cops who patrolled the streets closed in on him within a block of the weapon shop.

"Here now, what're you up to?" the boldest of the trio asked. He sounded nervous, but with two of his buddies flanking him, he held his ground.

"Nothing, sir," Luke said, doing his best not to set any of them off. The last thing he needed was a bunch of jumpy cops deciding to use excessive force on him. He wasn't even sure if it would be worse to let them beat on him or fight back.

"What's with the weapon?" the cop asked.

"Just got it from Donaley's," Luke said, waving a hand vaguely in the direction of the building.

"I hope you're not planning on causing any trouble. Just because you've got some XP doesn't mean you can do whatever you want."

"No, sir. Nothing like that. Is there a problem with having a weapon? I see a lot of people walking around with them."

"It's not the weapon, so much," the cop said. He was calming down now that Luke was being cooperative. He probably felt like he was in control of the situation, that the risk of a violence was decreasing with each passing second. "It's just . . . you have to understand what it looks like when someone that strong walks around with a weapon like that. That's not something you get for a street brawl. That's a weapon designed to kill."

"It is," Luke agreed. "I'm leaving town soon, on foot. I need to be able to defend myself against anything that might attack me on the road."

"True enough, but look at it from my perspective, son. You're not on the road right now."

"Well I'm sorry, but it doesn't really fit in my backpack, you know? Look, I've got the collar locked on it." Luke turned at the waist to show the weapon's harness to the cops. "I couldn't use it right now even if I wanted to."

That wasn't really true, of course. The harness was just leather. If he absolutely had to defend himself, he could rip the weapon free. But he hoped it would set the cop at ease if he said that he couldn't, and that seemed to be working. He noted a slight relaxing of posture and an overall lessening of twitchiness.

"That thing is a damn beaut," one of the cops said.

"Bet it cost a bundle too," the other backup added.

The one who'd been talking to Luke frowned at his two coworkers but didn't say anything to them. "Alright, here's what I want you to do. I'm going to put a seal on it so any other guards who see you will know you've spoken to someone. But you take that thing straight home and leave it there until you're on your way out of town, alright?"

"A seal?" Luke asked, wondering if this random dude who was maybe level 12 actually knew magic of some kind.

Instead, the guy produced some sort of yellow paper ribbon that he looped around the collar and harness. One end was covered in some sort of sticky glue, and he pressed it to the ribbon to turn it into one solid strip. There'd be no way to pull the weapon without first breaking the paper. Then he pulled out some sort of stamp thing and a bit of ink, carefully poured a few drops of ink into it, and pushed it against the paper.

"There you go. All official. Like I said, straight home, understand?" the cop told him.

"Yes, sir."

"Heh. Sir, I like that. Alright, get on out of here."

The cops, er, guards, walked off, verbally patting one another on the back for doing such a good job diffusing a volatile situation. Luke rolled his eyes and started walking again. The stares didn't lessen, but the next time a guard stopped him, he just showed the woman the paper ribbon with the ink stamp on it, and she sent him on his way.

That pattern repeated itself every four or five blocks with various degrees of hostility until Luke got sick of it and started taking back alleys instead of main streets. It was a winding route, one that sometimes smelled foul, but the alleys didn't have anyone patrolling them, at least not anyone affiliated with the law.

A few times he caught sight of some of the locals peering at him; once a few even gathered and started following him. Luke put an end to that by coming to a complete stop and turning to stare directly at where they thought they were hiding. The thugs scattered immediately, and he was on his way again.

The first thing he noticed upon walking through the door was the lump under the blankets and the dress still sitting unmoved on the floor. Luke grinned and paused to listen to the sound of snoring coming from the bed. In all fairness, he had woken her up in the middle of the night and interrupted her sleep.

Luke undid the straps on the harness and set it against the wall, then kicked off his boots and crawled under the blankets. Zea groaned and cracked one eye open to glare at him. "Don't let all the warmth out."

"Sorry."

"And why are you wearing clothes? I thought we went over this already."

"I thought maybe we could talk about some stuff."

"Unnggghhh. Fine." Zea scooted closer and wrapped herself around him. With her head resting on his chest, she said, "What are we talking about?"

"I think I'm going to leave tomorrow or the next day."

"What? That soon? I thought you'd stay at least until the end of the week."

"I want to, but . . . I can't stay forever, you know. And if I can't get a boat, then it's time to start walking again." That was kind of a crazy thought to him, to just walk over a thousand miles, but when he considered how fast a light jog was for him now and how many hours he could do that nonstop, it didn't seem too bad. More like boring, or at least he hoped so. Boring meant nothing was attacking him.

As much as he was dreading hearing the answer, Luke had to ask. "Do you want to come with me?"

"Go with you?" Zea repeated. "I . . . You know I can't really handle the cold like you humans do. I'd need to get a whole new outfit for cold weather, definitely some thicker boots, a fur-lined cloak. I wonder if I could get one of those emergency warming potions alchemists make. Probably too expensive."

Luke blinked down at her. It sounded like she was considering it. He'd expected her to scoff at the idea and make a sarcastic quip. "We could get you all of those things," he said slowly.

"It would be expensive. I don't have that much money. Are you sure you want someone like me with you though? I don't walk as fast as humans, and I know your stats are way higher than mine. You'll move much faster without me."

"Of course I want to be with you," he said. "You are without a doubt the coolest person on this planet."

"I . . . Hey, are you making a joke about me being cold?"

Luke laughed. "No, sorry. It's an expression from my language that I don't think translates right. It means you are my favorite person, the best person I've met since I got here, the best person there is."

"It's a bit late to be trying to flatter your way into my pants, don't you think? As you can see, I'm not wearing any."

"Don't you try to distract me with your body! We're having a serious discussion," he said. That didn't stop him from taking a peek under the blanket.

Zea slapped a hand against his chest in reprimand, but she was smiling. "I'll think about it, okay? Ask me again tomorrow."

"I will."

"Now, what is that thing you've brought back with you? It's huge." She cut Luke off before he could even start to speak. "No, not that! I mean that weapon sitting over there on the floor."

Name	Luke Bennet
Level	21
XP	29751/34079
AP	0
Bloodline	SysAdmin
Strength	40
Agility	32
Stamina	26
Perception	29
Skills	Mace Mastery (2)
	Sword Mastery (1)
	Unarmed Martialist (2)
	Power Strike (1)
	Life Surge (1)
	Peripheral Awareness (1)
	Counter (2)
	Twitch Reflexes (2)
	Stealth (1)
	Survivalist (2)
	First Aid (1)
	Wood Carving (1)
	Leatherworking (2)
	Thalian (2)
	Disguise (2)
	Deception (1)

CHAPTER 61

Luke had a goal, and he was going to keep moving toward it, but he knew himself well enough to know that if he didn't take care of himself along the way, he'd crash and burn long before he hit the finish line. He'd rather it took an extra year because he wasn't rushing forward at breakneck speed than never get there at all.

He wasn't worried about the idea of the journey taking an extra few weeks if Zea went with him, not if it meant he got to spend more time with her. He'd been alone for a month already, not counting System. And Luke did not count System. That would have been like saying he was never lonely because his phone's voice assistant counted as a friend.

He had some concerns about the amount of cold-weather clothes Zea said she needed, mostly in the figuring-out-how-to-pay-for-it department. She had even less money than he did, so that would be on him to come up with the cash.

"What can I do that's extremely lucrative, even if it's only short-term?" he asked. "There's got to be stuff that needs killing. The world is full of monsters."

"You would draw all the wrong sorts of attention looking for work like that," Zea told him. "The people who volunteer for those kinds of jobs are either desperate or insane, and they are screened heavily, then watched closely after to make sure they're not building up too much XP. Honestly, how did you even get to the level you're at now?"

"When I first got here, I was trapped in a valley in the mountains. There were a lot of goblins that tried to kill me, and some earth elementals that tried to kill everything that got close to them. And then one human made it in. The rest of his group died in the pass, but he got all the way to the end. I even saved his life by helping him fight off the giant elemental there. And then he tried to kill me too."

"Oh. That sucks."

"It does, yes." Luke didn't want to talk about the person he'd killed. "How much do you think you could get for a round against Zammin?"

"On short notice? Maybe seven or eight silver? If we had some time to properly hype it up and scheduled it for later in the week, a whole gold at least. I can float the idea by Sideon and see if he bites. You're popular for a new fighter, but your matches against the big names have been really close. People don't have a lot of confidence in you winning moving forward now that you've revealed some of your skills. I'm sure there are plenty of people who'd like to watch Zammin kick you in the balls, but I'm not sure Sideon would pay a premier fee for it."

"What if I won?"

Zea snorted. "You're not that good."

"Ouch."

Zea was probably right about that. He'd managed to take the dwifkin fighter in that sparring match, but Zammin was just so damn fast that it took everything Luke had just to stay on the defensive. And the little asshole wasn't above fighting dirty either, which was a big problem considering his size. Luke would need a lot of practice to rank his skills up manually or an infusion of XP to level up a few times.

"There's got to be something we can do, even if it's a one-time thing."

"I can't think of anything legal, and I don't want you getting tangled up with anything illegal and drawing the wrong kind of attention to us."

"Us?"

"Shut it," Zea said.

Luke smiled. "I like us."

Zea sighed and said, "For however long it lasts. Alright, let me go. I'll go talk to Sideon about a Zammin fight and see if we can work out something."

Luke watched her bend over to pick up her dress off the floor, smiled at the bit of extra wiggle in her ass. "You keep that up and you're not going to make it out of the room."

She tossed a smirk over her shoulder before standing back up right and putting the dress on. "Behave yourself. What are you going to do today?"

"I'm not sure yet. Want me to meet you at the Harbor around noon?"

"Yeah. I'll have something figured out. You interested in a lunch fight if I can swing it?"

"Sure. More money never hurt anyone, right?"

"Exactly. Good to see I picked an industrious fighter to manage."

"It's good to have such an excellent manager working hard to get me new fights."

Zea crawled up onto the bed and tackled Luke, or at least she tried to. There was no way she was budging him if he didn't play along, so he promptly fell backward and landed with her on his chest. She kissed him, then said, "I mean it. Behave yourself. The church has got something going on. Rumor is a few inquisitors have been spotted in the rougher parts of town and extra templars are being put on rotation. Some people think they might be gearing up to do a purge."

"I don't like the sound of that."

"If we're lucky, it has nothing to do with you, but it won't matter if you get caught up in it anyway. If we're not lucky . . . Well, either way, it's probably a good idea not to stick around town too much longer. But since you're still here, don't do anything to draw attention to yourself."

"Doesn't fighting these fights do that?" Luke asked.

"Nah, there's probably twenty or thirty fight clubs by the docks alone. As long as we stick to those and you don't try to get into one of the fancy ones in the noble districts, it won't draw too much attention. Zammin told me they're a lot more thorough about vetting who they let into those clubs."

"Bet the pay is better too."

"Probably," Zea agreed. "But it's not an option. So don't get any stupid ideas."

"Where would I be without you?" Luke said.

"Probably sitting in an inquisitor's cell getting your fingers snipped off one at a time and your dick smashed with a hammer. Which would be a shameful waste."

She said it so casually, like it was a joke, but Luke figured that was probably exactly what happened to people the church got ahold of and locked away. That was all sorts of fucked up in his mind, and he didn't understand why society as a whole let them get away with that sort of behavior.

But really, when he thought about it, it was simple. If the gods could grant people immunity to XP madness, then the church would always have the highest-level people. Might made right. Even if most of them weren't immune, there was never a shortage of religious zealots willing to spend their lives on a holy crusade. Luke couldn't even imagine how much more intense that would be in a world like Aros where God wasn't an abstract concept that maybe existed or maybe didn't, but there was actual, tangible proof of the divine.

"I'll try to keep everything intact down there until you're done with it," Luke said.

"See that you do," Zea said primly. "Okay, I'm going now. I'll see you around noon."

"Yes, ma'am."

* * *

Luke spent the rest of his time shopping. Now that his new mace was safely stowed away under the bed in their room, he received much less attention from just about everybody. Nobody tried to stop him in the streets anymore, though he did still get the occasional stare.

It took a bit of doing to find the stores that sold dwifkin-sized clothing, but Luke vaguely knew what area to start searching in. He found the shop Zea had bought her dress at and worked his way around the area from there. Eventually he came up with warm pants and a shirt in her size, as well as a dwifkin-sized cloak with fur lining around the hood. Once he got a good look at it, he realized all their clothing had lining in it, and it made him shudder to think of how much she'd suffered wearing literal rags.

Luke got a lot of funny looks shopping in dwifkin stores and actually got kicked out of one when he inquired about buying clothes for a dwifkin woman. There was no mystery there; the owner was a bigot who thought it was disgusting for a human and a dwifkin to have anything to do with each other. He knew because the jackass made a point of telling him, very loudly, with some amount of spittle. Luke didn't even get the chance to lie about the relationship, not that he wanted to.

He'd long ago learned the lesson that some people were just assholes who weren't worth the effort to even think about, let alone to try to get them to be better people. Luke just went somewhere else where the shopkeeper was either less bigoted or valued money enough to keep his mouth shut about it.

The only reasonably priced thing left on the list was boots, but he'd learned firsthand how uncomfortable shoes that didn't fit could be, especially the ones made on Aros that had probably been handcrafted to fit someone else's feet. If Zea decided to come with him, she'd need to get that done herself. If not, he'd try to leave her enough money to do it anyway.

She was already going to bitch him out for spending money on her, but that was fine. It was a small price to pay to make sure that no matter what happened, she wouldn't freeze when the weather turned cold. He definitely wasn't going to tell her about it until he left though. In fact, maybe not even then. He might just leave it as a surprise for her to find if she stayed.

Luke didn't want to get his hopes up, but she hadn't immediately said no. He'd feel better about this whole church-purge thing if they were long gone from the city when that swept through. There was no doubt in his mind that the poor districts would be hit hard by that, and they weren't exactly living in an upper-class neighborhood right now.

With about an hour to spare, Luke stowed his surprise presents under the bed, safely tucked up and hidden behind his harness, where he could quite easily see them but hoped the shadows would keep them safe from her lower perception. If she did spot them, he'd hear about it.

As Luke was making his way to the Bloody Harbor, he caught a flicker of motion out of the corner of his eye. It was a man turning a corner behind him, which wasn't anything unusual by itself. What was strange was that Luke was pretty sure he'd seen the guy before when he'd been thrown out of that one dwifkin shop. He'd stood out because it was a dwifkin neighborhood and there were only a handful of humans in it.

When he turned to look closer, the man was gone. It could have just been a coincidence, or he could be mistaken. The city wasn't really that big, not by the standards he was used to anyway. Even if it was the same guy, that didn't mean he had anything to do with Luke. Still, it didn't hurt to be extra vigilant, and Luke resolved to keep an eye out for anything suspicious.

"Aldrick," a woman called out.

Luke followed the sound and saw Myla walking straight toward him through the crowd. "Oh, hello," he said. "What are you up to?"

"I have the day off, and I thought I'd see if you wanted to get lunch again," she said as she came to a stop in front of him.

"Oh, uh . . . I'm kind of on my way in to work right now."

"That's fine. I don't mind waiting an hour or so for you to be free. Why don't I come with you?"

"Myla, look. Um. I kind of started seeing someone recently."

She regarded him easily, with one eyebrow crooked. "And? Are you one of those guys who can't have friends that are women just because you're in a relationship?"

"No! I'm not. Just . . . uh, sure, I guess. If you don't mind waiting."

"Not at all," Myla said, beaming at him. "Come on, let's go."

Luke allowed himself to be led toward the Harbor. Somehow, this was going to blow up in his face, he just knew it.

Name	Luke Bennet
Level	21
XP	29751/34079
AP	0
Bloodline	SysAdmin
Strength	40
Agility	32
Stamina	26
Perception	29
Skills	Mace Mastery (2)
	Sword Mastery (1)
	Unarmed Martialist (2)
	Power Strike (1)
	Life Surge (1)
	Peripheral Awareness (1)
	Counter (2)
	Twitch Reflexes (2)
	Stealth (1)
	Survivalist (2)
	First Aid (1)
	Wood Carving (1)
	Leatherworking (2)
	Thalian (2)
	Disguise (2)
	Deception (1)

CHAPTER 62

Three days was the earliest Sideon was willing to go on a match between Aldrick and Zammin. He wasn't wrong to take that stance, since the longer they hyped it up, the better the turnout would be, but the fight fees wouldn't change based on that. So it helped him, but didn't help Zea and Aldrick. She couldn't really blame him though; it wasn't like Sideon knew who Aldrick was or how quickly he wanted to leave.

Three days wasn't too long though, and it would give Zea time to decide what she wanted to do and gather supplies if needed. That one was going to take a lot of thinking. On the one hand, Zammin had been right: she was miserable in Valtira and pretty much always had been. She was only there to hide, and she'd done that quite well. It had been years since she'd caught even a whiff of anyone looking for her. At this point, she had very few reasons to stay.

But she also couldn't go back south. That would just be stupid. Going north was equally stupid, so she was stuck in Valtira mostly by inertia. And life in Valtira sucked for her. At least it had before she'd met Aldrick. She was making bank off his fights, enough to live for a week or more every night. Zea had a warmish bed to sleep in, and her new roommate was doing an excellent job of making it even warmer. She had a roof over her head and food to eat. She'd even gotten new clothes, a hot bath, and a haircut that didn't involve hacking the end off with a knife for the first time in years.

At the same time, Aldrick's status as an off-worlder apostate meant there was practically nowhere more dangerous to stand than right next to him. She liked the guy, but regardless of her personal feelings, the church would come down on him like a bolt of lightning if they ever figured out who he was, and her too just for being associated with him.

That was a pretty big drawback to traveling with Aldrick, the colder climate notwithstanding. That wasn't even getting into crossing the literal ocean, which, if half the stories the sailors told was true, might be even more dangerous than staying in Valtira with the church hunting for him. But if he could do what he said he could, if that bloodline of his really worked that way, maybe he could reset her back to level 1, let her level up right. Even better, if he could just change her skills directly and refund the AP she'd lost, that would let her keep all the progress she'd earned on her own.

It was tempting. She liked Aldrick, didn't mind the idea of traveling with him, and would tolerate the cold if she had to, but the risks were insane. Even if he could make it across the ocean to Sastilun, there were no guarantees. She figured she needed to talk to him first about that anyway. Lying to him about her reasons for going wasn't going to do anyone any favors.

There wasn't much to do but bet on the fights between a bunch of no-names in the pit while she waited for Aldrick to show up, and Zea didn't want to risk the money if she was going to need it for traveling expenses. She wondered if she could get back some of what they'd paid to rent the room if they only ended up using it for a week. It wasn't exactly a cost-efficient investment at that point.

The more she considered it, the more she realized she was making plans for leaving, despite there being a few good reasons to stay and a lot of reasons to not go. Yes, she liked Aldrick, and yes, she would love to be relieved of some of the skills that she'd been forced to take, but the odds of that working out in her favor had to be practically nonexistent. And still, for some reason, she was considering it.

And then the idiot himself walked into the Harbor with none other than the church girl with him. Zea felt her eye start to twitch as she watched him say something to the girl and point her toward a table. Then Aldrick scanned the place, spotted Zea, and walked over to her.

"I need your help," he said in a low voice.

"It's hard to help someone who doesn't listen. How many warnings do you need?"

"It's not my fault! She found me. She already knows I fight here. I tried to shake her off, but she was insistent, and I didn't want to draw attention to myself. Isn't it better not to make a scene that might end up with people from the church looking at me?"

"I suppose." Zea was still annoyed. "So what do you want me to do?"

"Help me cut her loose? I already told her I was seeing someone now, but that didn't do it."

"Oh, you are, are you?"

Aldrick looked confused there. "Well, kind of, yeah? Sorry if I'm making some assumptions here, but I thought that was the best way to kill her interest in me. It just, you know, didn't work."

"What does she think you're doing now?"

"I told her I'm talking to my manager because this is where I fight, and of course I need to touch base and find out if I'm doing any fights. Speaking of which, am I?"

"No." Zea scowled. "I tried, but Sideon won't do the big fight for at least three days, and he wants you to stay out of the pit to build up anticipation."

"Shit, is it even worth it at that point? We could make more doing a few smaller fights every day."

"Well I do have some good news there. I managed to get a two-gold fight fee for the wait, so that's not an issue."

"Oh, nice! Total or just my cut?"

"Total. Sideon's not that generous. Still, it would be good seed money."

Zea didn't comment on it, but she knew Aldrick had some money from before they'd met. He held it pretty closely, which was probably smart. She didn't know how much it was, but she figured since he was bothering with fighting in the first place, it couldn't be a life-altering amount. It would take a fair bit of coin to travel a few thousand miles on foot, probably more than he had. Another reason not to go with him.

"So no fight today then, or tomorrow. And then the fight with Zammin?"

"No. It's a three-day wait, and then the fight's on the fourth day. That's why it's worth four times as much as your normal fight."

"Not really a lot of incentive to even do it then," Aldrick said. "Maybe I could fight somewhere else during those off days?"

"Not if you want to fight here. Your contract means you're exclusive to the Bloody Harbor. If it gets back to Sideon that you're fighting in any other club, he'll ban you, probably me too. So don't do that."

"Got it. Okay, so we're waiting on that. Four days. That's not so bad, I guess. I can use the time to work on something else." Aldrick ran a hand through his hair and blew out a sigh. "What about Myla?"

"Not much I can do to help you," Zea said. "I don't have anything to keep you busy with. Just give me the room key, have some lunch, and try not to do or say anything stupid or incriminating."

"Right. Okay, I can do this." Aldrick fished the key out of his neck pouch and left it on the table. "Fuck, I do not want to do this now. It was a lot easier to talk to her before I was afraid she was a church spy."

"You'll be fine," Zea said. "Probably."

"Thanks," Aldrick said, rolling his eyes. "Your confidence in me is overwhelming."

*   *   *

Luke sat down at the table across from Myla. "Hi," he said. "I guess I don't have a fight today. The guy who runs that side of the business has one for me in a few days, but no work right now. So, lunch?"

Myla smiled. "Lunch would be fantastic. I was maybe lying a bit when I said I didn't mind waiting to eat. I just thought it was worth waiting for good company. Did you want to eat here or . . . ?"

"Oh, I'm not picky if you want to go somewhere else."

Luke spared a moment to wonder why the girls back on Earth were never as forward as the ones on Aros seemed to be. No one had ever asked him out prior to getting shunted through a doorway into another world. Then again, he was in fantastic shape now. It wasn't like he'd been a butterball back home, but still, he was completely shredded here.

Plus he figured he had a sexy foreign accent now, and that had to help. Everyone loved a sexy foreign accent. It was too bad for Myla that he considered himself extremely taken, even if only for a few more days before he left. She was very obviously interested in him, which he sadly had to view with suspicion. Even if not for her ties to the church, he would have had to rebuff any advances she might make. He was uncomfortable enough just doing lunch.

She didn't try to take him back toward the church, thankfully. Instead, they went to a bakery with an outdoor patio. "I love the bread they make here," Myla told him. "Just add some butter or jam. And they even have fresh juice or wine to go with it."

She directed him to a table near the back, where there were a few small trees growing to give the illusion of privacy. "I'll go grab us something," she said. "My treat. I invited you out after all."

"Are you sure?" Luke asked.

"Oh, yes. Just wait here, I'll be back in a minute."

Luke settled into the chair and looked around. Despite it being lunchtime, there were only three other people out on the patio, a couple at one table nearby and a man sitting by himself. Luke made an effort not to look directly at any of them and to keep his facial expression neutral. **[Deception]** kicked in to help, but he wasn't sure that he managed it.

There was something off about those three people. The guy sitting by himself was pretending to be reading something, but his eyes weren't moving. He was just staring blankly at the book in his hand, occasionally turning the page. Luke also noticed that he'd angled it to see a good portion of the patio out of the corner of his eye. Whoever that guy was, he wasn't there to enjoy his lunch.

The couple was a different story. They had eyes only for each other, but the woman's bracelet was a coil that went up her forearm and was sharpened. He heard it scrape across the table when she moved her arm carelessly and could actually see the small peel of paint and wood come up. Both of them pretended not to see it, but he noted a tenseness in the man's leg when it happened. It would have been less suspicious to acknowledge the accident, unless they didn't want to call attention to the concealed weapon.

Luke focused on listening for a few seconds and did his best to ignore the three people. He wanted to know if there was anyone else around that he couldn't see. Other than the murmur of conversation inside the bakery where Myla was getting their meal and the chatter of the couple, there was nothing but the normal background noise of the city.

He wasn't convinced. Casually, Luke looked over toward where Myla was standing and took in some of the background details. The screen of trees wasn't enough to hide anybody in, not unless they had some sort of skill to assist, but he trusted his perception to tell him. He hadn't been debuffed in any way. But the whole thing had him tense.

He was in danger, somehow. They'd wandered into the middle of something they shouldn't have. Or he'd been led into it.

Myla returned with a tray held in both hands. She set it down on the table between them and said, "Let's eat!"

Name	Luke Bennet
Level	21
XP	29751/34079
AP	0
Bloodline	SysAdmin
Strength	40
Agility	32
Stamina	26
Perception	29
Skills	Mace Mastery (2)
	Sword Mastery (1)
	Unarmed Martialist (2)
	Power Strike (1)
	Life Surge (1)
	Peripheral Awareness (1)
	Counter (2)
	Twitch Reflexes (2)
	Stealth (1)
	Survivalist (2)
	First Aid (1)
	Wood Carving (1)
	Leatherworking (2)
	Thalian (2)
	Disguise (2)
	Deception (1)

CHAPTER 63

The way Luke saw it, they'd either wandered into something meant for someone else and Myla was completely innocent of any malicious intent, or she'd led him into a trap on purpose and was an excellent actor. The third possibility, that someone had known where they'd eat lunch and managed to clear the whole place out to set it up for a trap in literally minutes, seemed too unlikely to consider.

If it was a trap, then it was probably the church. They knew about his existence, as evidenced by the fact that a templar brute squad had been dispatched to Tenebrous Valley to murder him, and he supposed it wasn't impossible for another divine message to come down and paint them a picture of him so they knew exactly who they were looking for. That would just be his luck.

"Why don't we walk while we eat?" Luke threw out, just to see what she'd say.

"Oh. Um, we can do that," Myla said, clearly surprised. She didn't seem to be against the idea though. "Did you have somewhere in particular in mind?"

Her hands started moving, shuffling the meal into a kind of sandwich using the bread as a plate. It barely took a moment for her to finish, then she grabbed her cup and took a drink. "I usually save my drink for the end, but it's fun to do things differently every now and then, right?"

"Yeah, exactly. You should mix things up occasionally to keep life from getting stale."

Luke picked up his own cup, which smelled like some sort of wine, and took a sip. It was a bit sweeter than he liked, but it wasn't bad. He used the motion of drinking to hide taking another look around and confirming that no one had moved from their seats.

Myla took another long drink and frowned. "Maybe I can ask if we can walk with the cups if I promise to bring them back later. I think I'd still like to save a little for after I'm done eating."

"Sure," Luke said. He took another sip and stood up. "The food does look good though."

It was kind of weird. Bread as a meal wasn't something he'd enjoyed growing up. It was an unfortunate necessity some weeks but not something to look forward to. On Aros, it was different. There were a lot more spices baked into it, and it was always fresh. It was a cornerstone of the meal, there more often than not, and he'd grown to appreciate it a lot more than the old thinly sliced bread in a bag he'd had as a kid.

It was just one of a truly overwhelming number of changes he'd been hit with all at once. The food was different, the buildings were different, the people were different. Indoor plumbing was a thing of the past, and he had to go to a special building just to get hot water to bathe with. Boredom took on a whole new level without phones and the internet.

There were good things to balance it out, of course. Stats were amazing, though the whole XP madness kind of put a damper on that. Skills were neat but also uncomfortable to use. His body moving on its own like that creeped him right the fuck out. It was getting better as he grew more accustomed to the movements, and moot of his skills related to fighting didn't jar him mentally anymore, but he doubted he'd ever fully be comfortable with the sensation.

"Luke, I believe you should check your notifications. You indicated that this type is a high priority to you."

"I . . . what?"

System was standing in front of him, right behind Myla, who was watching him intently. He hadn't noticed that she'd stopped doing anything else. The other three people were also watching him openly now for some reason. Luke was more confused about why System had appeared and what notification he was talking about, but he checked anyway.

[You have been afflicted by the following condition: Poison—Draught of Waking Dreams (1H22M).]

That wasn't good. Once System pointed it out, Luke realized that he'd been mumbling all his thoughts out loud for the past minute or so, ever since he'd taken a sip of the wine. "You poisoned me," he said.

"Oh? That's unusual. I wonder if I made a mistake. No one ever realizes they've ingested this particular type of poison. That's why I went out of my way to make it." Myla sounded annoyed now. "Or is it that your stamina is just that high? Either way, the whole plan's gone out the window. Get him inside so we can question him."

Luke tried to move, but everything felt sluggish. He could barely even focus on the movements of the people around him, barely felt when two of them grabbed his arms and started frog-marching him into the bakery. "That smells really good," he mumbled.

"Yes, they do make good food. I love eating here," Myla said casually. "It's a shame you wanted to go for a walk. I would have liked to enjoy my meal before we got to this part."

"We could still eat," he said.

"Ah, no, I'm afraid not. Time is of the essence. Given how lucid you are, I don't imagine the poison will last more than an hour or so. Tell me, was it some sort of poison-resistance skill or simply high stamina that saved you? I tried to account for stamina, but it's difficult to guess correctly."

"No, no. Not that," Luke said. He tried to reach for a roll sitting on a display shelf, only to find that something was stopping him. Frowning, he jerked his arm free, and the man holding him stumbled forward.

Luke ignored him to grab the roll and take a bite. "God, that's delicious. If it had just a bit of butter in it . . ."

The man recaptured Luke's arm with a grunt of effort and tried to twist it back behind him. Luke flexed and dragged him forward again to take another bite. He kind of wished he'd gone along with Myla's plan now too. He'd already fucked up by drinking the drugged wine, and this next part would go better if he had a good solid meal in him.

"Look, what is it you wanted to ask me?" he asked, finishing off the roll and reaching for another.

"Let's talk in the back," Myla said, gesturing toward a door that had even more delicious smells coming from it.

Luke's hand wavered over the next roll, then snagged a whole loaf of bread instead. It was hard to focus on what Myla was saying, hard to even remember what he was doing. The hardest thing though was keeping himself from saying his thoughts out loud. He suspected that was the primary purpose of the poison, to get him to just say whatever he was thinking when they questioned him.

It probably worked a lot better when the victim wasn't aware that they'd been poisoned. That must be hard to pull off when the system went and told people that they'd been afflicted with a status effect. Then again, maybe it was just him. He had made modifications to his status, after all. Plus his whole bloodline was tied up in system stuff anyway. He would try to remember to ask about it later.

For now, Luke devoured the loaf of bread, barely even stopping to chew it. "So good," he said, which was true, but that wasn't why he was gorging himself on it. "I like it right here better."

"I really must insist. It would be better for everyone if you cooperated."

Luke triggered **[Life Surge]** and felt his head start to clear up immediately. He checked his status to confirm that the poison had been burned away, only to find that it was still present, but now read: **[Condition: Poison—Draught of Waking Dreams (18M42S)]**. That probably explained why things were feeling a lot less foggy but not completely normal.

Myla noticed immediately and snapped, "Grab him!" A knife appeared in her hand as if by magic, and she lashed out at him, but Luke leaned backward to avoid it. The man on his right drove a fist into his side, no doubt aiming for his kidneys, but his skills were kicking in now. He shifted his lean into a measured step back, slapped the hand down and away from him, and stomped the heel of his back foot down on the toes belonging to the man on the left.

Even with the poison still making things muddled, Luke was cognizant enough to be aware that he was in a bad position. There were four of them surrounding him, and he had no weapon. He needed to break free and run. Luke didn't try to go on the offensive, not when all he needed to do was bodycheck a guy who was already off-balance and then hustle out through the bakery's front door.

He lifted his foot just enough to hook it around the guy's ankles, then slammed into him with his shoulder, which had the dual benefits of knocking the guy on his ass and getting Luke farther away from Myla's knife. She was already closing the distance, this time leading with the point of the knife, and he could see some sort of wet coating on it. Getting hit by that was probably a bad idea for more than one reason.

Luke hopped over the man he'd knocked down, swiped a muffin on the fly, and rushed out into the street. He didn't stop to pick a direction, since there wasn't really anywhere safe to run to. The goal was simply to lose his pursuers. That turned out to be more difficult than he expected.

All four of them burst out of the bakery, but only three went after him as he sprinted down the street. Myla took one look at his retreating form and went back inside. Somehow, that made him feel even less safe not knowing where she was or what she was doing. He couldn't take the time to backtrack and confront her, not that he wanted to.

Two of his would-be kidnappers were obviously not built for speed. They struggled through the crowds, and Luke quickly left them behind. One of the men, the one who'd been pretending to read a book, either had some sort of movement skill or was getting by like Luke on raw agility because, if anything, he was closing the gap.

Luke wondered if he had the strength to match too. He took a running leap and jumped as hard as he could, over the roof of a single-story house. It was only about twelve feet straight up, and he thought if he'd timed it better, he might have cleared the whole roof to land in the next street over, but instead he landed near the peak. He skittered across the roof and leaped the entire street to land on the one opposite of where he'd started.

Now with two streets between him and his pursuers, Luke hopped back down to the ground and started moving again. He was heading toward the busier business district near the docks, and though he wasn't quite sure where he was, he thought he could figure it out if he turned and walked toward the water until he saw something familiar.

That plan depended on him having shaken his pursuers, but there was no telling if that had even happened. For all he knew, there were dozens more people in disguise watching him. There was no help for it; it was time to leave the city. Before he could do that, he needed his supplies. They were locked behind a door he didn't have a key to right now, but Luke was okay with breaking it down. Hopefully that wouldn't reflect badly on Zea, but there was no choice.

He just needed to make sure he didn't lead Myla and her minions straight there first.

Name	Luke Bennet
Level	21
XP	29751/34079
AP	0
Bloodline	SysAdmin
Strength	40
Agility	32
Stamina	26
Perception	29
Skills	Mace Mastery (2)
	Sword Mastery (1)
	Unarmed Martialist (2)
	Power Strike (1)
	Life Surge (1)
	Peripheral Awareness (1)
	Counter (2)
	Twitch Reflexes (2)
	Stealth (1)
	Survivalist (2)
	First Aid (1)
	Wood Carving (1)
	Leatherworking (2)
	Thalian (2)
	Disguise (2)
	Deception (1)

CHAPTER 64

Zea told herself that she wasn't committing to anything when she bought the bag. It was only sensible to have something like that, especially considering she was still kind of homeless. She had a place to stay, for now, but she was under no illusions that she'd have enough money to pay for the rent next month. Even if she did, it would likely be all her money, leaving her penniless again. It would be far better to save that money for food and other necessary supplies.

So she bought a bag to hold her meager possessions. Her dress would go into it soon, and she'd be back to rags. The money stayed in her neck pouch, safe from all but the nimblest of pickpockets. She was going to pick up a few other things, perhaps a nice warm cloak. That also was not committing to anything, as a warm cloak was invaluable during the winter months, and she already had the bag to store it in until she needed it.

Zea didn't make it to cloak shopping though. Her afternoon was interrupted by the sight of a human barreling down a street, only for him to abruptly leap so high into the air that he cleared the eaves of the house a block away. If she didn't know any better, she'd have thought that was Aldrick. It couldn't be though because he was taking that church hussy out to lunch so that he didn't arouse suspicion.

Part of Zea had been tempted to follow him, but she reined that back in and told herself that it wasn't really her business. Besides, he hadn't been completely wrong in his logic, though she thought he might have come up with that idea with only half his blood going to his brain.

On the off chance that his plan had backfired spectacularly, she started toward the nearest alley to try to get a better look at the man who'd jumped onto a roof. Before she got halfway there, another man went flying by, heedless of anyone else who might be in his way. Zea barely managed to dodge to the side in time to avoid being kicked.

Her heart in her throat now, she raced around the corner just in time to see the first man somehow leap completely across the street to land on another roof. There was no doubt about his identity now, which meant that the worst had happened. Aldrick had done something, or said something, or was maybe just plain unlucky, but at least one person was after him.

She had no idea where he was going, but she'd never keep up. He ran like the wind, leaving both her and his pursuer behind. Soon enough, the city guard was involved, and since they weren't detaining the man who'd been chasing Aldrick, that meant he was someone important. Zea slipped away as soon as she saw the guards showing up and working with the pursuer.

If there was anywhere in the city she might find him, it was their room. He had left an extremely expensive weapon there, one that he might come back for. She didn't think she would if she were in his place, but Aldrick wasn't the smartest man she'd ever met. Kind of the opposite, really. All heart, too trusting. The city would have eaten him alive if she'd let him do whatever he wanted.

If it had been her, she would have cut her losses and run, but it was entirely possible that she could catch up to him at their room if she was fast enough. At least, she hoped that was the case. Zea walked as quickly as she could without attracting attention and silently prayed that she was right, and that she wasn't too late.

Luke dropped back to street level after a few more jumps. He called upon all the knowledge he'd gained from **[Disguise]** and **[Deception]** to help him hide, and the big thing that jumped out to him when he activated the skills was that he was far too conspicuous. He needed to blend in with the crowd, so he dropped down onto a side street, ran toward the closest main road, and as soon as he was there, slowed himself down to a walk and did his best to just merge into traffic.

There was only so much he could do since his high XP marked him as unusual to anybody with even a halfway decent perception, but at least this way he wasn't actively advertising his presence. Luke walked as quickly as he could, weaving between slower people and occasionally forcing his way past someone with a hastily muttered apology. Neither of his skills liked that, but he couldn't afford to get bogged down by every window-shopper and casual stroller crowding up the place.

The last of the poison burned itself out while he walked, which was a relief in and of itself. Its effect had grown weaker as the timer counted down, but it wasn't until it was fully gone that he really started to trust himself to make good decisions and maintain awareness of the world around him. He started moving in a wide circle through the city, sometimes ignoring the main thoroughfares in favor of side streets and small, winding alleys that were nothing more than dirt trails between buildings.

Normally, Luke avoided places like that. He wasn't looking for a fight with a street gang, and Zea had been adamant that it was worth the extra time to go around places with bad reputations. Today he didn't have that time, so he cut straight through them without a thought. He needed out of the city, but he didn't think he'd survive without a good weapon.

As much as he wanted to just make a run for it, there was no choice but to circle back. Hopefully Myla and her flunkies didn't know where he lived, but he wouldn't put it past them. He'd need to approach carefully and keep his eyes peeled. It was almost guaranteed to be a trap, and he didn't have any weapon at all to rely on.

Luke made his way back to the one-room apartment he'd rented with Zea and spent some time circling around it, just to see who was loitering around and keeping an eye on the front door. The fact that he didn't find anyone didn't reassure him, but his perception was high, hopefully high enough to spot any hidden watchers.

An uncomfortable nagging feeling told him that they'd probably been watching him prior to making their move, that Myla had somehow found him days ago and had been spying on him ever since. Trusting in his perception might not be the right move. If for no other reason than that, he'd have to be quick. In, grab his stuff, and out. In a pinch, he'd settle for just the mace, but fortunately, he'd been paranoid enough to keep everything packed and ready to go at a moment's notice.

Luke slipped inside and took the stairs four at a time. He ran down the hall toward his room, fully prepared to knock the door down, only to find it was already unlocked and open. Zea was standing there, huffing and puffing as she stuffed the clothes he'd bought her into a bag.

"What are you doing?" Luke asked.

She froze, then relaxed when she recognized the voice, and spun to face him. "I saw you running, figured you'd gotten into trouble if you were jumping across the roofs. This was the only place I was sure I'd find you."

Shit. She'd run toward danger. "You shouldn't be here. They're after me, but they'll take you too if they find us together."

"It's too late. I'm your manager. That church girl knows that. I'm liable to be picked up too."

"Then why are you here?" Luke asked. "You should be hiding somewhere where they won't find you."

She looked down at the bag she'd been packing, then back up at Luke. "You're an idiot," she said with a snort. "Here, get this harness strapped on so we can go."

Despite the danger, Luke's heart fluttered. "We?"

Before she could reply, **[Twitch Reflexes]** activated, and he threw himself sideways. A dart of some kind whipped past his head and buried itself in the wall behind him. Luke blinked at the dart, then traced its trajectory back. Despite the shutters being closed, someone had thrown it through the small gap with such precision that he hadn't even heard it clip the wood.

"Holy shit!" Zea yelped, staring at the dart with her mouth hanging open.

Luke dove for the floor and scrambled to grab his bag. "Here," he said, rummaging through it until he came up with a feather. "Take this. The guy I got it from said you have to deliberately break it, and it will conceal you from all senses for a short time. I'm not sure what that means, but you use it so they can't catch you."

"Wait!" Zea grabbed at his sleeve. "You get out of Valtira as fast as you can. Don't stop to let me catch up. There's a town forty miles north of here called Landston. I'll get there as fast as I can. Be careful."

"I will, I promise. We'll get through this, okay?"

"Of course we will. Who the hell do you think you're talking to?"

Luke smiled. "You're amazing, you know that?"

"Yeah," Zea said, one eyebrow cocked. "I do."

"I'm going out through the window," Luke said, the harness firmly strapped to him and his mace freed from it. "Gonna catch whoever threw that fucking thing in the face with this mace. Then I'm running at top speed. Hopefully they all chase me."

He took a step back, centered the window, and took a running leap forward. Wood shattered and exploded out in every direction. Crouched on the roof opposite his room was a woman wearing some sort of armor with a bandolier of throwing knives across her chest. She had a blowgun in her hand, held up to her lips, and as soon as their eyes met, her cheeks puffed out.

Luke twisted in midair, every single point of agility he had working to keep control of his limbs, and somehow, miraculously, the second dart missed. By forcing him to dodge, he was no longer any sort of coordinated, and he smacked into the roof without ever getting a shot at the woman.

Luke rolled to his feet and spun to face Myla, who'd produced a dagger in one hand and a throwing knife in the other. "Foolish to stand and fight," she said.

"Seemed like I owed you one," Luke told her, though he agreed. There was no telling what poison was on that knife. But he wasn't just going to let her put it in his back. He had to at least disable her before he made a break for it.

It was hard to get a feel for her. She obviously had a few skills reducing how much XP she appeared to have, but he wasn't going to underestimate that. The first few passes would be defensive. He had a longer weapon, and he was pretty sure he was faster and stronger, but he wasn't going to take anything for granted.

Three people climbed up onto the roof, all of them in full armor and wielding swords or axes. Silently, they fanned out to circle around Luke. "Fucking heretic," one of them said softly as she raised her blade up to skewer him.

"Screw this," Luke said. There was no chance he was taking this fight. He'd have to take his chances with getting shot in the back and hope that if he needed to use **[Life Surge]** again that it wouldn't kill him to do so.

Luke turned and sprinted for the edge of the roof.

Name	Luke Bennet
Level	21
XP	29751/34079
AP	0
Bloodline	SysAdmin
Strength	40
Agility	32
Stamina	26
Perception	29
Skills	Mace Mastery (2)
	Sword Mastery (1)
	Unarmed Martialist (2)
	Power Strike (1)
	Life Surge (1)
	Peripheral Awareness (1)
	Counter (2)
	Twitch Reflexes (2)
	Stealth (1)
	Survivalist (2)
	First Aid (1)
	Wood Carving (1)
	Leatherworking (2)
	Thalian (2)
	Disguise (2)
	Deception (1)

CHAPTER 65

Before he'd gained skills that moved his body for him in battle, Luke might have been surprised at being attacked from behind. Well, probably not in this case, since obviously the church wasn't just going to let him go. But despite only being on Aros for a few months, he'd spent a lot of his time fighting, and if his matches had been good for anything, it was teaching him the difference between an animal or monster and an intelligent, reasoning person.

So he didn't need a skill to tell him that running in a straight line directly away from them was an excellent way to get shot in the back. Luke never would have considered the acrobatics he was about to perform back when he'd lived on Earth, especially not with a weapon held in one hand, but now he knew he could do it.

His sprint lasted all of five steps before he rolled forward into a one-handed handspring that converted his forward momentum into lateral movement. Myla's throwing knife cracked against the roof tiles, splitting one into multiple pieces where it impacted, and clattered away to land in the street. Luke was only dimly aware of that, having spotted the damage when he turned his handspring into a cartwheel to get his feet back under him, and brought his mace up in an underhanded swing to catch the templar in front of him off guard.

[Unarmed Martialist] didn't like the maneuver, not at all. It was flashy, a little desperate, and riddled with holes. The only reason it worked was that no one was expecting him to shift from escape back to offense. His swing caught the surprised templar in the stomach so hard that the man let out an explosive grunt and was lifted clear off his feet. He suffered the same fate as Myla's throwing knife had: he crashed into the tiles on his back, cracked a few of them, and then slid off the roof to land in the street below.

Luke followed right behind the man, except he'd planned to jump to the next roof. That was foiled by another knife, barely dodged when **[Twitch Reflexes]** shifted him out of the way. Suddenly off-balance, which was probably better than a poisoned knife stuck in his leg, Luke tumbled over the edge of the roof and landed right next to the templar.

He took the landing better, but the templar had armor to protect him from the mace strike and enough stamina to stand back up. He'd also kept hold of his sword, and Luke was forced into a desperate roll to dodge the descending blade. The templar kept the pressure up with a lightning-fast series of stabs and slashes all designed to lock Luke into his position on the ground. He blocked as best he could, gritted his teeth when the templar slipped past his guard and left a bloody gash across his ribs, and kicked out at the man's ankles to try to trip him up.

The templar was too good for that, and Luke didn't have time for an opportunity to present itself. There were three more people less than twenty feet away, all of them looking to kill him or worse, and he doubted they'd be afraid to make the jump down to street level. So when the templar's next overhead slash came down on Luke, he parried it with a **[Power Strike]** and threw the surprised man's sword so far into the air that it cleared the eaves of the nearby house.

Luke scrambled to his feet and dashed away. **[Mace Mastery]** and **[Unarmed Martialist]** both protested at the wasted openings he let go by running instead of fighting, but Luke wasn't interested in finishing the duel. Winning beat losing by a thin margin, but not getting caught blew both options out of the water. So he ran, turning **[Unarmed Martialist]** toward helping him keep his balance with top-notch footwork while he scrambled through the crowds.

It quickly became clear to the bystanders that some sort of bad shit was going down, and the streets started to clear out. Luke briefly considered moving with the flow and trying to hide, but now he had at least four people in pursuit, and Myla had already cut him off once. Admittedly, he'd been going to a location she might be familiar with, but if she'd found him by making assumptions instead of chasing after him, that just meant she wasn't stupid. In a way, that was kind of worse.

Luke was banking on superior stats to get him out of trouble. He was ridiculously outnumbered, and hiding didn't seem like a good plan. It was time to find out just how fast he could go and how long he could keep it up. He'd experimented some on the roads out of town, and he knew he was fast but not how well he stacked up to everyone else.

He ran for all he was worth, mace held up near the head and tucked close to his body to keep it from catching on things. He sprinted where he could, wove through the few people who hadn't gotten the message to get the fuck off the streets, and took detours around knots of guards that appeared in front of him.

All the way, he kept catching flickers of movement with **[Peripheral Awareness]**. Whatever it was, it was keeping pace with him, and he had a sneaking suspicion it was someone with an agility-based build, someone who maybe worked as a church assassin and had spent a bit too much time studying him.

What he couldn't figure out was why she wasn't trying to stop him. His best guess was that she was keeping pace with him to keep tabs on his location as he fled. Maybe she had some sort of magical cell phone and was sending out group texts to coordinate with his other pursuers. If that was the case, the only thing he could do was stop running and attack, except he never actually saw anyone there.

Luke's mad dash down various streets eventually brought him to the edge of the city. He hadn't paid much attention to which way he was going other than generally north when possible and was a bit surprised to see how far west the guards and templars had managed to push him. That wasn't a big deal though; he could course correct by cutting through the woods and farmlands surrounding Valtira once he was safe.

He darted past the last two houses at the edge of the city and felt his eyes widen as **[Peripheral Awareness]** screamed at him. There were at least thirty guards or templars armed with crossbows, all pointed in his direction. It was the goblin trap in the woods all over again.

But Luke wasn't the same guy he'd been back then, and this trap wasn't as well constructed. If they fired now, they'd be shooting at one another. They knew it too, so almost all of them hesitated to pull the trigger. The few that did were far too late to hit him, as he'd already skidded to a stop and darted back into the city. Shouts rang out behind him as he fled the foiled trap.

Luke jumped a roof rather than run all the way to the next side street. He landed on the peak for a moment, then threw himself forward. Below him, a startled woman working in her garden gawked as his shadow crossed over her. Luke spent just enough time looking down to confirm she wasn't a secret church spy about to attack him, then returned his focus to sticking the landing onto the next roof.

He heard the guards scrambling after him and had a mental image of a dozen crossbow bolts sticking out of his back with the next jump. Even at this speed, he had no chance of outrunning a bolt. His only options were to put enough distance between him and the guards that even the luckiest shot would fall short or to put enough buildings between them that they couldn't shoot him. The problem with that second option was he was trying to get out of the city, not run deeper in.

So Luke jumped, then he jumped again, and again. By the fifth roof, he thought he'd gained enough distance to sneak a glance behind him. The templars had outrun the guards, but there were only five of them compared to the thirty or forty they'd numbered before. That was already a definite improvement, one that he liked even better when he realized that none of them held ranged weapons.

His last jump took him back to ground level. He rolled with the impact, sprang back to his feet, and sprinted for the tree line a few thousand feet away. Unless someone uber-badass appeared to take a swing at him, Luke was in the clear now. All he needed to do was break line of sight on the remaining templars in the forest and circle around to start heading north.

It wasn't an ideal scenario, not really. Way too many people knew what he looked like, and he was worried about the collateral damage the Bloody Harbor was going to suffer for associating with him, but there wasn't a lot he could do about that. If there was any sort of instant communication between cities, there would be people watching out for him. Hopefully, that wasn't the case, and he could outrun news of him being an apostate.

Probably the gods would dick him over somehow. He didn't believe a word of that hands-off Covenant crap anyway. Luke was going to have to be very careful about his future moves now, but he was sure Zea knew what to do. The church had been focused completely on him; there was no reason to think she hadn't gotten away safe. Plus she had that magic-feather thing.

If they'd hurt her, he'd tear their limbs off with his bare hands.

For now, he was going to continue with the plan. He'd meet her up the road in Landston. If she didn't show up, he would slaughter a thousand monsters until he was the biggest monster of them all, then come back and rip apart the church until he found her. Nobody would be able to stop him. That was how power worked in this craptastic fucking world, right?

Luke ghosted through the tree line, easily slipping around the brush and ducking under tangled branches. Once he was hidden out of sight, he slowed down both because the terrain forced it and to catch his breath. He turned north and started looking for a game trail to follow, one that was widened from human hunter using it. As soon as he stumbled across one, he could put on the speed again.

He felt an impact on his back, then two more so close behind that at first he thought it was a fist punching him. Only once he staggered forward and spun in place did he realize there was no one standing behind him. He didn't need the system notification that pinged to tell him what happened, but he checked it anyway.

[You have been afflicted by the following condition: Poison—Night Stalker's Venom (7M31S).]

"Why wait until I thought I was clear?" Luke asked. "Is it some kind of game?"

"No," Myla said. She appeared from the trees, the blowgun in her hand. She was far more disheveled than he'd expected. "It's probably better this way. Out here, your heresy can't spread to infect anyone else."

The poison was fast acting, already spreading to his limbs. Everything felt heavy and numb. He tried to move his fingers, but they barely twitched. "Some kind of paralytic," he said, his voice slurred. He wanted her to think it was working.

It was, but not so much that he couldn't move. He could drop the mace to help sell the act, but then he'd be relying on his fists to fight her off. No, he just needed her to get closer so he could clobber her with a solid **[Power Strike]**–infused hit. Once he put her down, he would be back on his way.

But Myla didn't get any closer. She just pulled a new dart out of a hip pouch and fitted it into the blowgun. "It's nothing personal," she told him. "From my understanding, you off-worlders don't come here voluntarily, but that doesn't change anything. I can't let you break the foundations of our world, accidental or otherwise."

Then she brought the blowgun up to her lips and lined it up to fire.

Name	Luke Bennet
Level	21
XP	29751/34079
AP	0
Bloodline	SysAdmin
Strength	40
Agility	32
Stamina	26
Perception	29
Skills	Mace Mastery (2)
	Sword Mastery (1)
	Unarmed Martialist (2)
	Power Strike (1)
	Life Surge (1)
	Peripheral Awareness (1)
	Counter (2)
	Twitch Reflexes (2)
	Stealth (1)
	Survivalist (2)
	First Aid (1)
	Wood Carving (1)
	Leatherworking (2)
	Thalian (2)
	Disguise (2)
	Deception (1)

CHAPTER 66

The effects of the first **[Life Surge]** hadn't hit Luke too hard. He'd been tired, but it turned out the effects of regular full meals did a lot to mitigate the insane amounts of hunger it generated. Having less to heal also reduced the draw-backs. But if he used it again so quickly, there was going to be hell to pay afterward.

Luke could still move, so he held off on that strategy. Killing Myla and then collapsing next to her body where the rest of the church templars could find him wasn't a winning move. He had enough of a lead to wait out a seven-minute debuff timer. All he had to do was survive against Myla without her shooting any more darts into him.

"Fuck," Luke said.

The dart shot out of the end of the blowgun, and Luke's arm snapped up. It shouldn't have been possible, but perception let him see it, and between agility and **[Twitch Reflexes]**, he was quick enough to block it. The dart ricocheted off the mace and stuck into a tree. Myla's eyes widened in surprise as she tracked its path.

"How many more you got?" he said. "What if you can't hit me with another one?"

"More than enough," she told him, fishing another dart out.

He hated to admit it, but deflecting that shot had been as much luck as it was skill. He could barely feel the mace in his hand now, and his muscles didn't want to respond when he told them to move. If he gave Myla the time to take another shot at him, there was a very real chance that she'd hit him.

So he charged her. It was an awkward, stiff-legged gait, but it ate up the distance in a second, and he timed it perfectly so that he made impact in that moment between loading the dart and bringing the blowgun up to her mouth. That way, she couldn't just stick him with it when he got close.

That didn't stop her from pulling a knife to stab him instead, but Luke was counting on that. His right foot slammed down a full two feet in front of her, arresting all his momentum and preventing him from impaling himself on the blade. She leaned into the thrust, perhaps intent on delivering the venomous payload coating the blade, and Luke's mace whipped around, fully infused with a **[Power Strike]**, to crack into her elbow.

Myla screamed as the bones snapped and the joint was crushed. The knife went flying off into a nearby bush, but rather than scramble to get away or chase it down, she raised the blowgun back up to her lips and fired from close range. The dart shot out and sunk into Luke's chest.

[Condition: Poison—Night Stalker's Venom (10M19S)]

The mace tumbled out of Luke's hand as another dose of paralytic hit him. It was all he could do to stay upright with that one sticking in him. He weakly raised a hand to paw at the dart, trying to pull it out and failing. It started getting harder to breathe, and he felt dizzy.

"The poison can affect your heart if it's injected too close," Myla said, panting while she spoke. She cradled her ruined arm close to her stomach, and the blowgun was sitting in the dirt between them. "I didn't want to kill you, but if the alternative is letting you go . . ."

"Fuck . . . you . . ." Luke gasped out. It wasn't like she had an altruistic motive in taking him alive. Idly, he wondered if she had some sort of antivenom in that bag that would reverse the poison. He didn't suppose it mattered though. He was out of options. The only thing left was to get himself into a position where he could hit her with explosive force as soon as he triggered **[Life Surge]**. He'd find out if the aftereffects were going to kill him soon enough.

He let himself drop to one knee but kept his foot under him, ready to push him upward into the most brutal uppercut he could manage. Myla watched him drop, her face expressionless. At least she wasn't enjoying it, though it might have been easier for him if she was. He could have hated her for the sadism of it all then.

[Life Surge] shot through him, shocking his body into motion and burning away the remaining poison. Luke sprang up, his feet leading the way, and caught the church woman in the chest, right under the bandolier of throwing knives. He hit her so hard they both went into the air. She flew away and landed flat on her back, and he ended up spinning in place once to bleed off some momentum before he landed back on his feet.

Something broke inside Myla when he hit her. He didn't know what, but she was coughing up blood. That didn't stop her from scrambling back to her feet, and Luke found himself idly wondering exactly how much stamina she had. He wasn't sure he'd have been able to get back up from a hit like that.

He sprinted forward, intent on finishing the fight before his skill gave out. If she was still standing when that happened, it was over. There was no way he was going to still be on his feet. One way or another, it was going to be decided in the next half a minute.

But Myla didn't meet his charge. She didn't even pull one of the throwing knives to attack him. Instead, she spent a fraction of a second examining him, just long enough for him to take two steps in her direction, and then she turned and fled.

He chased after her, but it was more for appearances than because he had any hope of actually catching her. Even if he did, by the time he was within arm's reach, it was likely that all he'd accomplish was passing out at her feet. So he rattled some branches, stomped around, and made some noise while she ran.

And then he let her go. No doubt she'd be back, probably with some new poison that he wouldn't see coming until it was too late. Maybe she'd have reinforcements again. He'd need to do some serious leveling very quickly if he wanted to survive the next encounter.

He opened his pack, saw that most of the food had been crushed in the various scuffles he'd been in over the last hour or so, shrugged, and started gobbling it down as fast as he could. **[Life Surge]** gave out a few seconds into gorging himself, and the wave of vertigo that followed it almost knocked him back off his feet again.

Luke was honestly just happy that he didn't pass out. He'd really been expecting it to drop him on his ass, and then he'd probably wake up in a cell somewhere. Or maybe he wouldn't wake up. Ever. But that didn't happen, so he went through all the food he'd purchased in a few minutes, and when it was gone, he felt a little bit better, not really good, but better.

Before he left, he scooped up the blowgun and stuck it in his bag. There was no sense in leaving it behind, after all. If was small and easy enough to carry and might be worth something. Then, after securing his mace back in its spot on his harness, he started wearily trudging through the woods, one foot in front of the other, utterly spent and too tired to even watch for predators. Red could have landed on his head at that point, and he wouldn't have realized until he felt the talons sink in.

Day faded into night, and Luke curled up in some giant burrow he found. An animal had dug it out under a mass of gnarled old tree roots, but it didn't smell like anything had lived there for a long time. If it did, well, tough shit. He was borrowing it for the night.

* * *

His stomach woke him up, no surprise there. Luke almost wished something had tried to come into the burrow overnight while he recovered, just so he wouldn't have to go hunting in the morning. He was starving, but there was nothing left in his backpack to eat.

Before he set out, Luke took a minute to center himself and make sure he had his priorities in order. His most immediate need was sustenance, not because he couldn't handle an empty belly, but because **[Life Surge]** was his trump card. It had saved his ass multiple times, usually in literal life-and-death moments. He needed to be able to use it without worrying about passing out after. That meant food, and lots of it.

Once he was back in fighting shape, his next priority was to start moving north and find some monsters in need of a good smiting along the way. If it was just him and Myla in an open field with no tricks, he thought he could take her, but he knew that wasn't how it would happen. It would be him shitting his guts out after she poisoned his lunch and her garroting him from where she'd been waiting on top of the outhouse.

So he needed more stamina to resist her next poisoning attempt and more perception to keep track of her. Strength and agility were probably fine as they were, unless she brought along friends. Running had worked well the first time, but they might lay a better trap for him. He was well aware that if he hadn't been able to shrug off that poison, they'd have had him dead to rights in the bakery.

More AP for higher stats was a must, but Luke was honestly considering holding it to buy a rank up for **[Life Surge]** instead. It was insanely expensive at 100 AP for the rank 2 version, but there wasn't a doubt in his mind that it would be worth it. The question was whether or not he could afford to sit on close to five levels worth of AP while he saved up.

That was a decision he could put off for a little while at least, since he was a bit over 4000 XP short of leveling up, and he wasn't sure where he'd find the monsters he needed to cover that. He knew where some were if he was willing to go in the wrong direction, but Zea was heading north, and she was expecting him in Landston. If he knew exactly where that was, he might have considered going on an expedition back toward the mountains, but knowing him, he'd likely get lost in the woods, and he wasn't about to get onto the roads.

Though once he thought about it, he realized he did have an easy way to make sure he could get back to Landston. "System," he said. "Can you tell me which direction Landston is from here?"

"Certainly, Luke. It is approximately forty-three miles in that direction," System said, appearing in front of him and pointing past Luke's left shoulder.

"Perfect. Okay, I need something to eat, and while I'm looking for that, I want to ask you about some skills."

"What would you like to know?"

"Well, for starters, is there such a thing as a poison-resistance skill? Because that would be really fucking handy to have right about now."

"There are, yes. There are actually quite a few of them, though they are statistically almost never purchased with AP. The rare individuals who acquire them generally do so naturally, by being exposed to the poison repeatedly."

"Why not?" Luke said. "Deliberately exposing yourself to poisons seems like a great way to die."

"I can only speculate, but I believe it is because while the resistances are individually cheap, there are a great many of them, one thousand eight hundred and fourteen, to be precise."

"What the fuck? Why are there so many?"

"One for each type of poison," System explained.

"Damn it, so if you don't know what kind of poison you're dealing with, it's pretty useless."

"An increase to your stamina may serve you better if you are expecting to be poisoned but are unsure of what kind of poison you'll be subjected to," System said.

"Great. Okay, so that's off the table. Let's talk about combat skills designed for fighting large groups of opponents and maybe some stuff that works at range. I've been having problems dealing with people who have crossbows lately."

"Indeed. Let me start with a few defensive options that you may find useful . . ."

Name	Luke Bennet
Level	21
XP	29751/34079
AP	0
Bloodline	SysAdmin
Strength	40
Agility	32
Stamina	26
Perception	29
Skills	Mace Mastery (2)
	Sword Mastery (1)
	Unarmed Martialist (2)
	Power Strike (1)
	Life Surge (1)
	Peripheral Awareness (1)
	Counter (2)
	Twitch Reflexes (2)
	Stealth (1)
	Survivalist (2)
	First Aid (1)
	Wood Carving (1)
	Leatherworking (2)
	Thalian (2)
	Disguise (2)
	Deception (1)

CHAPTER 67

The mountains had been a fantastic source of monsters for Luke to hunt, just based on his brief time spent scouring them before he'd ventured into Valtira. Landston was in the opposite direction though, so he reluctantly gave up the idea and started searching for game trails that would take him generally north.

Despite the difficulty of navigating the woods, he still made it the full forty miles in a single day. Being able to just force his way through thick underbrush or leap crevices and gullies that he stumbled across helped keep him going in the right direction, and he was sure that not getting lost from having to go around obstacles sped up the process.

Luke had no intention whatsoever of actually staying in Landston. It was too close to Valtira, and since Myla wasn't an idiot, he was sure she'd made it back to the city alive and was sending messenger pigeons or whatever they used to spread around his description. His mace was distinctive enough that it would be a dead giveaway if anyone was on the lookout for it.

Instead, he circled the town twice. It wasn't that big, maybe a hundred or so homes and some larger businesses near the south end. There was a manse on the north side, walled in and with a pair of security guards standing at the front gate. Luke immediately crossed that off his list of places Zea might potentially be and focused more on watching Main Street and keeping an eye on the people coming and going from what he thought was the inn.

He wasn't expecting her to have beaten him there. It was technically possible, but she was smart, and she would be cautious. She didn't have his stats, and she didn't have the money to call a cab, or hire a carriage, whatever. It would probably be a few days before she showed up. Not for the first time, Luke wished he had his phone. It would have been really convenient if he could just text her and get an update.

Since that wasn't an option, and he wasn't going to be waiting in the town, or even setting foot in it if he could avoid it, Luke decided to explore the deep woods far away from civilization. With any luck, he'd find something lurking in there that was worth a nice chunk of XP without being overwhelmingly powerful.

What he found was a giant pig with way too many spurs growing out of its body and three sets of tusks hanging off its face. When Luke stumbled across it, it had its snout buried in the guts of something that might have once been some sort of large deer, or elk, or moose, maybe. It was mostly a slurry of bone, fur, meat, and blood at this point.

The pig spun in place, agile for something that was easily eight feet tall at the shoulder and as long as a truck. A pair of black eyes peered out from under a heavy brow lined with sharp little spikes, focused on Luke. It lowered its head, snorted, and rushed forward.

Pigsly was about level 15, if Luke had to guess. It wasn't going to be worth a huge amount of experience, and it could definitely fuck up his day if he wasn't careful, but this was exactly the kind of thing he was looking for. Luke jumped straight up, mace held tight in both hands, and came down with a **[Power Strike]** primed and ready to go.

He misjudged the timing slightly, mostly in an effort to correct for the tusks shaking wildly back and forth. His landing on the pig's back wasn't as smooth as he'd hoped for, but the mace slammed into its neck, just behind the base of its skull, and Pigsly hit the ground with so much force that it tore a furrow twenty feet long and a foot deep through the dirt.

And yet, somehow, not dead. It got a wobbly hoof under it and pushed up so hard that Luke was nearly thrown off its back. He went up in the air a few feet, then came back down, his legs flexing to absorb the impact and shift with Pigsly's movement. Then he brought the mace around and up, triggered **[Power Strike]** again, and slammed it down a second time.

Pigsly's skull definitely broke with that hit. Luke could hear the sound of bone cracking. The pig took two drunken steps, more sideways than forward, then tipped over and crashed onto its side. Its flanks heaved up and down as it struggled to keep going, but the fight was over now. All that was left was to give it a quick death, to end its misery, and collect his XP.

When he circled around to the front to finish it off, Luke found himself surprised to see that the pig's beady black eyes were two blazing crimson pits now and that it actually seemed to be growing stronger, not weaker. It struggled ferociously to pull itself back upright and was hindered more by the many spikes it had driven into the ground with its fall than by the injuries Luke had laid on it.

"Oh shit," Luke said. Pigsly had some sort of berserker skill probably similar to his own **[Life Surge]**, and if he didn't end the fight soon, it was liable to get a whole lot harder.

He didn't really want to waste a third **[Power Strike]** on the same monster, but a quick fight followed by a break to catch his breath was way better than a long, drawn-out, knockdown, busted-face fight. Luke activated the skill one final time and brought it down directly on Pigsly's face.

Skin tore, bone chunks went flying, and brain matter splattered across the ground. A ding sounded in Luke's head, and he let out a heavy sigh of relief. "Whew, thought shit was about to go sideways on me there."

[You have slain Bonespike Boar (level 16). 263 XP awarded.]

"Not a bad start. Just need a minute here and we'll see what else is out here."

"Okay, you are really fucking creepy," Luke said.

The snake, which was flying circles around him on bat wings, three pairs of them spaced evenly along its body to be precise, hissed back. It was about eight or nine feet long and thick around as his thigh, black and green with frills around its head.

It was also, by his guess, level 20 or 21. Considering how fast the fucking thing was, he was willing to bet it specialized in agility. He'd missed every single swing he'd taken so far, and he wasn't eager to trade another round. The thing had fangs in its mouth three inches long, and he'd just bet they were venomous.

It snapped forward through the air, propelled in its weird up-and-down slithering-and-flapping motion that was so hard to track. Luke let **[Unarmed Martialist]** pull him to the side as it flashed by, and instead of trying to smack it with his mace, he snatched its ass end, about a foot or so before its tail ended in a hooked barb.

Then he swung it, hard. The snake smacked into a tree and whipped around it twice before it ran out of body length. Before it could free itself, Luke clobbered it with his mace. The first swing only caught its body, but the second one got it right across the jaw. A broken fang flew through the air, and the snake went limp. *Ding.*

"Sorry, Snakesly, but in my defense, you tried to kill me first. Also you're ugly AF."

[You have slain Chiroptic Viper (level 20). 415 XP awarded.]

"Nope! Nope! Nope, nope, nope, nope, nope, nopenopenope! Fuck this! Nope!"

Luke ran for his life while a swarm of mosquito monsters with needles longer than his forearm chased after him. There were at least a hundred of the fuckers, and every last one of them was level 10 or 12. The only bright side to things was that they were big enough that it was really easy to hit them out of the air, kind of like swinging a baseball bat at a soccer ball that wanted to murder him.

If they'd line up and come at him one at a time, he'd take his chances, but he was a lot less confident about them all coming in at once from every angle. He was sure he'd take down a few, maybe even twenty or thirty, and that whichever one of them got the killing blow would get a nice chunk of XP from him.

Two of the mosquito monsters caught up with him while he was jumping clear of a tangle of fallen trees, but even in the air and with both of them behind him, he clocked their approach with **[Peripheral Awareness]**. He twisted around, dodging one, and smacking the other one away. Its body disintegrated on contact, and what was probably two pounds of gore went splattering through the air to paint a nearby tree.

Ignoring the ding from a successful kill, Luke tumbled to the ground and whipped his legs around in a move that wouldn't have looked out of place in a break dancing competition to get back on his feet. The other mosquito monster was coming back at him from the front now, an easy shot, but before he could take it down, a dozen more caught up. Standing there and getting dive-bombed was a stupid decision, despite what **[Unarmed Martialist]** had to say about it.

He ran forward, killing the mosquito coming at him on the way, and threw himself into a forward roll when two of the other ones tried to stab him. He came out of it in a spin, his mace whipping out parallel to the ground and obliterating another one. That was three down, a hundred more to go.

They weren't as fast as him, but it was easier to fly over obstacles than to run around them, and Luke's escape attempt morphed into a running battle that saw him whittling them down one or two at a time while he desperately scrambled to not get caught by the main swarm. Eventually, he'd either killed enough or gotten far enough away from their territory that they left off attacking him.

While he was trying to catch his breath, Luke took a moment to check his messages. Despite the low level, he figured he'd killed enough that they were worth a good chunk of XP.

[You have slain 47 creatures between levels 9 and 14. 6016 XP awarded.]
[Congratulations! You have reached level 22. 22 AP awarded for use.]
[Congratulations! Peripheral Awareness has reached rank 2. 250 XP awarded.]

Luke took a second to consider the crazy amount of XP he'd just gained. It was easily more than he'd ever seen at one time, even more than the jumbo earth elemental had been worth by a wide margin. Bloodpike stirges, as the system called them, were very lucrative to hunt.

"Shit, I've been doing this all wrong. I should be looking for big groups of small creatures."

Before that though, he had decisions to make. 22 AP was enough to upgrade just about any of his skills once, but he kind of wanted to see if he could keep getting new ranks just from using them. Maybe he could earn back some of the AP he'd spent on things that weren't part of his build guide, plus it would be nice to get ahead on his stats.

They literally made him superhuman, able to jump fifteen feet straight up, break rocks with his bare hands, and run thirty or forty miles an hour for half the day. It was probably impossible to overestimate how important it was that he continue to grow in that way. The monsters certainly weren't going to get any easier to kill, even if he had freakishly high numbers by human standards.

Pigsly had taken three hits infused with **[Power Strike]** to put down, and it had only been level 16. Luke couldn't imagine a scenario where he ran into a level 50 monster and won if he didn't keep buffing his stats. As much as skills were a more immediate power upgrade, he could increase them in other ways. He was well past the point where some powerlifting or time on a treadmill was going to bump his stats up anymore.

Perception was what he needed most right now, both to help him find Zea and to help keep him from being ambushed again. He took a deep breath, scrunched his eyes closed, covered his ears, and dumped 10 points into the stat. The enhanced senses still just about knocked him on his ass, and he knew he'd be spending the next hour or two adjusting to them.

The remaining 12 AP got split into 4 agility and 8 stamina, which was much easier to acclimate to. Luke decided to head back to town after that and do a few more laps. Zea probably wasn't there yet, but it didn't hurt to check. Tomorrow, he'd resume grinding out XP, but no more mosquitos, not until he found a way to handle huge packs of monsters all at once.

Name	Luke Bennet
Level	22
XP	36695/39125
AP	0
Bloodline	SysAdmin
Strength	40
Agility	36
Stamina	34
Perception	39
Skills	Mace Mastery (2)
	Sword Mastery (1)
	Unarmed Martialist (2)
	Power Strike (1)
	Life Surge (1)
	Peripheral Awareness (2)
	Counter (2)
	Twitch Reflexes (2)
	Stealth (1)
	Survivalist (2)
	First Aid (1)
	Wood Carving (1)
	Leatherworking (2)
	Thalian (2)
	Disguise (2)
	Deception (1)

Skill	Rank	AP	Prerequisites	Effect
Peripheral Awareness	2	10	Rank 1	Calls attention to slight movements in peripheral vision

CHAPTER 68

A second day of hunting saw Luke rise up to level 23. He was frustrated though because he'd wasted a lot of his time discussing skill options with System. Trying to pry useful information out of it was always annoying, but not getting anywhere after hours of going around in circles had him ready to tear his hair out.

As far as Luke could tell, what he was trying to do just didn't work with a heavy mace. Never mind the fact that his strength was so high that he could probably hurl it at major league fastball speeds; there was no skill that was the agility equivalent of **[Power Strike]** that used a mace. He could do it with a sword or a dagger, even a whip or flail, but not a mace. It was complete bullshit.

He technically had **[Sword Mastery]**, but he'd just dumped almost all his money on a bitchin' mace that was supposed to be able to handle his strength no problem. He wasn't about to throw that away just because the stupid system didn't have a skill that did what he wanted.

Hitting multiple opponents at once was out, but that wasn't the point of Curt's build. He just hadn't bothered to leave any notes justifying his skill choices, and Luke didn't get it himself until he saw it all in action. The build was designed to keep Luke in the fight, keep him dodging attacks, and to let him overpower even the toughest opponents, but only one at a time. It excelled at close-range single-combat and endurance fights. The only reason his fights tended to end quickly was because of how liberally he relied on **[Life Surge]** to finish things, which he was starting to think wasn't a great idea.

Myla knew roughly what the skill did, even if she didn't actually know its name. She would plan for that when she took another swing at him, and that meant Luke needed to develop some new tricks before then, something she hadn't planned for. He'd thought an agility-based trump card would be the way to go, but that wasn't happening, not with his current weapon choice at least.

The closest skill he could find to something that would take advantage of his agility to keep him in the fight against multiple opponents was something called **[Tactical Foresight]**. It synergized with **[Unarmed Martialist]** to read the flow of battle or some shit like that. Luke didn't really understand what it meant, other than that it was supposed to make it easier to predict how enemies were going to move so he could defend against attacks and exploit openings in their defenses. For some reason, it hadn't been on Curt's build list.

It was 15 AP for the first rank of the skill, which felt kind of high, but Luke had learned by now that expensive skills were usually worth it. He would have bought it then and there except that, for the first time, he was considering a skill that had prerequisites, and he didn't meet them. He needed a 40 in agility, and he had the extra AP to push the stat up 4 points to meet that, but he also needed rank 4 **[Unarmed Martialist]**, and that was another 15 AP just to get to rank 3, plus however many he needed after that.

With 23 AP to spend, there was no way he could afford it now. **[Unarmed Martialist]** also wasn't his first pick for a skill to sink AP into, but it wasn't the worst possible decision. If he went after **[Tactical Foresight]**, it was going to be an ongoing project that he invested AP into for the next few levels while he acquired the needed prerequisites.

What it really came down to was how much time Luke had to get stronger before someone caught up with him. If he could gain four or five more levels, it would be fine. If Myla found him tomorrow, it could be a problem. So far, most of his choices had been driven by a need to be stronger right now, not in the future, but the one skill he'd saved up AP for, **[Life Surge]**, had easily become his most important skill.

It wasn't like **[Unarmed Martialist]** was a bad skill either, but if he was going to put 15 AP into something, he would have prioritized **[Mace Mastery]** instead. Luke had been hoping that either or both of those skills would gain a new rank on their own, but it hadn't happened yet. There was always the final option of just sitting on the AP until something changed and hoping he could make a better choice with more information, but Luke really wasn't a fan of that.

In the end, he decided to meet as many of the prereqs as he could with the AP he had. Agility got bumped up from 36 to 40, **[Unarmed Martialist]** went up to rank 3, which revealed a cost of 30 AP to reach rank 4, and the final 4 AP were split evenly between strength and stamina. He'd have to bank all his AP on his next level up, and then once he had two levels' worth in hand, he could upgrade **[Unarmed Martialist]** again and pick up **[Tactical Foresight]**.

It was already evening by the time he reached level 23, and though he killed a few more monsters, Luke wasn't going to make the push the rest of the way unless he found another swarm of mosquitos or something. He wasn't eager for another fight like that, especially since he'd utterly failed at acquiring a new skill to help him deal with swarms, so he resigned himself to a slow, but relatively safe, grind.

On the bright side, **[Unarmed Martialist]** was now very, very good at getting him into positions to dodge potential incoming attacks. It was so good, in fact, that **[Twitch Reflexes]** barely triggered at all anymore, and **[Counter]** was working overtime trying to point out all the different ways he could ruin some monster's day.

Luke returned to the outskirts of Landston and once again spent an hour or two surveying the town. It was his third time doing so that day, and though he wasn't expecting to see Zea, he was hoping she'd prove him wrong. Once it got fully dark, he even took the risk of sneaking around to where the inn was and trying to feel out if anyone inside was about the same level as her.

There were a few of them that were possibilities, but it didn't take long to get a glance through shutter slats or hear their voices and confirm they weren't who he was looking for. Luke wasn't interested in what they had going on, and besides, it seemed rude to just casually spy on them, so as soon as he confirmed Zea hadn't taken a room at the inn, he left.

That didn't mean he gave up his search though because there was also a strong possibility that she wouldn't go to the inn. Inns cost money, something she had little enough of on the best of days. There was every chance that she'd set up a forest camp much like his. The abrupt nature of their departure hadn't left them with a lot of time to make concrete plans, something that was extremely frustrating now that he was dealing with the aftermath.

The third day continued much like the second, with Luke venturing miles and miles into the forests to hunt for monsters that would push him up to level 24. Most of what he found was only around level 8 or 10, and he didn't go out of his way to attack anything that minded its own business. Animals that fled on contact were also left alone.

But frequently, something predatory would find him, and if it wasn't too low of a level, it would attempt to ambush him. Luke quickly found himself appreciating the 10 AP he'd put into perception, which made it much, much easier to detect and locate monsters with things other than his eyes. Considering how many monsters had coloring or skills that let them blend in and hide, being able to hear them or, in some cases, smell them made it much harder for them to pull off ambush tactics.

Luke was on his second lap around Landston that day when he spotted a short woman with long strawberry blonde hair walking down the street. His heart leaped in excitement and maybe just a bit of relief at the sight of her, but Luke restrained himself from rushing in. Zea was walking openly, without even the hood of her cloak pulled up. He was pleased to see that the clothes he'd bought had been put to good use as well.

Less pleasing was the man following about five hundred feet back. It took Luke a second to figure out why he seemed so familiar, but then it clicked. It was the guy who had been pretending to read a book when Myla had poisoned him. He appeared casual enough, like he was just out enjoying an afternoon stroll, but Luke wasn't fooled.

Five hundred feet was nothing with a high enough perception and could be closed in seconds with enough agility. The man was definitely keeping an eye on her too, which probably meant there were other church agents lurking around that he didn't recognize on sight. He wondered if Zea knew she was being followed.

Luke skulked around the edge of town, trying to make sure he kept out of sight of Zea's stalker, and waited for an opportunity to talk to her. He just needed her to go into a shop or turn a corner where he could meet her without the man seeing. He saw his chance when she passed through the town square and slipped onto a side street. If she kept heading the direction she was going, she'd pass an alleyway in a few hundred feet.

As long as Luke was in that alley, he could flag her down without the church spy seeing him. The angle of approach was good, he just needed to be quick. He sped toward town, **[Stealth]** activated, and slipped into the alley without being seen by anyone. If he had any sort of luck at all saved up, there wouldn't be anyone else from the church following Zea, or if there were, they wouldn't see him either. His skill didn't react as if he were about to be spotted, so he was hoping it worked.

"Zea," he hissed as she walked by. She looked over at him, eyes wide, and pivoted smoothly to walk into the alley.

"Get out of here," she said in a low, harsh voice. "I still haven't shaken these inquisitors."

"How many?"

"I don't know. At least three. Probably more. They've been handing me off for hours on the road."

"Damn. Okay, I'm going to set up a campsite outside of town on the west end. You find it tonight, and I'll take care of them."

The two of them moved while they talked, but he knew he didn't have much time left. Luke dashed off before she was halfway down the alley, hopefully well before the inquisitor turned the corner and noticed anything unusual. He would just have to hope Zea was able to lead them into the trap and that there weren't too many for him to handle.

It seemed like XP-suppressing skills were a standard part of the inquisitor tool kit, and Luke hadn't been able to get a good read on a single one of them yet. His best guess was that they were all at least low 20s in level, and he hoped none of them were up in the 30s. Otherwise it wasn't going to matter how well he prepared for the fight. They'd slaughter him.

There wasn't much time to prepare, and he had a lot to get done.

Name	Luke Bennet
Level	23
XP	41176/44653
AP	0
Bloodline	SysAdmin
Strength	42
Agility	40
Stamina	36
Perception	39
Skills	Mace Mastery (2)
	Sword Mastery (1)
	Unarmed Martialist (3)
	Power Strike (1)
	Life Surge (1)
	Peripheral Awareness (2)
	Counter (2)
	Twitch Reflexes (2)
	Stealth (1)
	Survivalist (2)
	First Aid (1)
	Wood Carving (1)
	Leatherworking (2)
	Thalian (2)
	Disguise (2)
	Deception (1)

Skill	Rank	AP	Prerequisites	Effect
Unarmed Martialist	3	15	Rank 2	Increases balance and flexibility and strengthens limbs to strike against armored opponents

CHAPTER 69

"Nice," Luke said as he looked at his handiwork.

[Survivalist] hadn't seen much use lately, but it was a general-purpose skill that was extremely flexible. It gave him the knowledge he needed to make basic traps, and using some of the ones the goblins had tried against him as templates, Luke had gotten to work.

He'd started by making thin ropes out of wood fibers. They were three times thicker than twine should have been, but that was as tight as he could weave it together. Having a sharp knife that never dulled helped immensely, as did 40 agility. His hands flew, practically machinelike, weaving the fibers into something useful.

With hundreds of feet of homemade rope manufactured in a matter of hours, Luke had then started constructing his traps. He looped the ropes into snares, collected claws and teeth from a few of the predatory animals he'd run across, and sharpened those to deadly points to be thrown forward with trip lines. He made small holes all over the ground, just big enough to catch a foot and roll an ankle, then covered them with screens of grass and leaves.

None of what he was capable of making was going to be lethal. Maybe if he'd had a bagful of poisons like Myla, he could have done some real damage, but lacking that, his only real goal was to trip his enemies up and slow them down. If he could draw them into traps that left them vulnerable and kept them from ganging up on him, he would consider his preparations to be time well spent.

There was only so much he could realistically accomplish with the tools and time he had, but Luke was satisfied with his efforts. He dug a small firepit in the center of the clearing to help set the scene and dropped his backpack nearby. Then he went back and forth toward town a few times to help break a trail through the underbrush and settled down to wait.

Evening fell, and Luke passed some time by carving a little palm-sized statue of Red out of a chunk of wood. He flicked the shavings into the center of the firepit to be used as tinder once it got cold enough, but most of his focus was on the forest around him. He went over every trap he'd set again and again and tried to think up scenarios where he led enemies into them.

There were a lot of variables to consider, and he doubted the actual fight would play out anything like he was envisioning, but if he could steer it the way he wanted even for a few seconds here and there, he thought he had a decent chance. Then, once he'd taken care of the inquisitors, they'd simply disappear before anyone else could find them.

He hoped it would be that easy. There were definitely a lot of assumptions about how things would go in that plan, but his biggest concern was that since the inquisitors were following Zea, she either wouldn't show up to lead them into an ambush because they'd already snatched her up, or she would show up but would end up getting caught up in the fighting.

Luke's hands paused for a second when he heard a soft rustle, then started moving again. He didn't feel any XP nearby, but something was definitely in the trees above and behind him. Whatever it was, it had stealth skills and probably a high agility stat to back them up. That could be any number of monsters, but the fact that it was also hiding its XP aura from his senses narrowed down the options considerably.

They had arrived. Luke closed his eyes and set all his senses to exploring the forest. There was a faint smell of metal and oil, not coming from him but somewhere in the brush to his right. Above him, he heard the creak of leather halfway up a tree. Straight down the trail, perhaps fifty feet away, a person was confidently walking forward. Their footsteps were soft, but they weren't actively trying to hide themselves. Luke could hear the slight clank of metal armor with each step the person took and feel their XP total coming closer. It was a small relief to see that it was similar to his own.

One to confront him and keep him occupied and two more to ambush him as soon as they had a chance. Luke's opening move would depend on who attacked first. If the one above him tried to get the drop on him, he would put his mace into the assassin's gut and throw them into the booby-trapped underbrush. If the one in armor charged first, he thought he'd lure them into his field of ankle-buster holes instead.

The upside was that Zea wasn't anywhere nearby. Hopefully that didn't mean something had gone wrong on her end, but if so, he'd worry about that later. Right now, he had three people approaching with what he was just going to assume was hostile intent.

Luke set down the little carving of Red, put his knife in its sheath on his belt, and stood up. His mace was in front of him, held across his body with both hands, and his feet were set wide apart. Then he waited to see what would happen first. His money was on the one approaching openly making first contact.

But then he thought about it and couldn't see any good reason to wait. That would just give them better odds when they ganged up on him. So he jumped straight up into the branches overhead and hauled himself up one-handed to land in front of the inquisitor who'd been crouched up there.

"Boo," Luke said. The man's eyes were wide, and he tried to throw himself backward while simultaneously flinging a handful of sharp-spiked metal balls into Luke's face. They all bounced off Luke's scalp when he ducked his head, drawing little pinpricks of blood and doing nothing at all to stop him from lunging forward to catch the man by the shirt.

Luke dragged the inquisitor forward and was pleased to find that he outmuscled his enemy by a considerable amount. If it weren't for the fact that they were balanced on tree branches, and that there were at least two other church agents nearby, he would have happily closed the fight to a grapple to abuse his obvious advantage.

Instead, he let himself roll backward off the branch and dragged the inquisitor with him. They twisted in the air, but Luke easily got the best of that and spun the man under him to slam into the ground first. Before the inquisitor could recover, Luke rolled to his feet and brought his mace down on the man's chest.

Bones snapped, and blood spurted into the air from torn skin and between the inquisitor's lips. He was still alive, but Luke didn't have the time to follow up and finish him. The inquisitor who'd been walking toward him entered the clearing and took the situation in at a glance. Roaring a challenge, he leaped forward fifteen feet. Luke ducked down to one knee, set his shoulder, and as the inquisitor tried to land on him, heaved upward.

Thanks to a twist in Luke's abdomen, he threw the inquisitor into the brush, directly into one of the snare traps he'd prepared. The loop pinched around the inquisitor's ankle, and the hook trigger slipped loose, allowing the branch the snare was tied to overhead to snap back into position and take the inquisitor along for the ride.

Luke figured he'd bought himself at most a few seconds before the man freed himself, but that was the point after all. He kicked the man whose chest he'd caved in with his mace out of the way, eliciting a ragged cry of pain, and approached the brush he'd smelled the last of his three assailants hiding in.

They were gone now, but even with whatever skills they were using to hide themselves, Luke wasn't fooled.

He should have buffed perception earlier. It was amazing how much of a difference it made in finding people that he couldn't see. The third inquisitor was completely silent, XP fully hidden from his senses and on the move, but Luke could smell them. He could track where they'd gone and where they were.

"That's handy," he muttered as he changed direction. Rather than move directly to them, he walked across the clearing and put another of his traps between himself and the last inquisitor. Conveniently, it also put his field of holes right in the way of the man who'd been caught in his ankle snare. That one had cut himself down with a hand ax and was now eyeing Luke warily from across the campsite.

"You got something to say, or should we just get back to it?" Luke called out to him.

"Die, you filthy fucking apostate," the inquisitor said as he approached Luke.

The holes weren't fooling the man. He slipped between them easily, his feet always finding solid ground. That was fine though. Keeping from turning an ankle in one once he was fighting for his life was going to be a lot harder, and Luke intended to abuse every single mistake.

The two clashed, the man with his axe and its twin that he pulled from his belt and Luke with his mace. The man was taller, but Luke's weapon was longer, and while they were close in strength, Luke had him beat in agility. His big disadvantage was his lack of armor, a fact the inquisitor took full advantage of. He was more than willing to take a hit if it meant he got to deliver one of his own.

But Luke kept him moving around, and twice the inquisitor stumbled, only to catch a **[Power Strike]** to his arm or hip. The first one robbed the inquisitor of one of his weapons when the armor crumpled and pinched his forearm. The second one stole much of his ability to keep his feet centered under him.

For his troubles, Luke took multiple gashes across his chest, one on his thigh that was worryingly close to his femoral artery and a nick just above his eyebrow. Blood leaked down the side of his face, and he had to blink it out of his eye.

It looked like Luke was winning, but he'd learned his lesson about fighting multiple opponents: never forget how many there were. So he wasn't surprised when the last of the inquisitors tried to ambush him with a dagger driven into his back. He'd been keeping track of their movements while he traded blows with the armored one, and the only really surprising part was how they managed to avoid being seen all the way up to the point of contact.

She seemed to appear out of thin air, but he'd tracked her progress by watching the grass flatten and listening to the sound of her heart beating as she drew closer. So when she was finally in position and ready to drive the blade home, Luke ruined her plans by bringing his mace around in a two-handed swing that arced a full 360 around him.

The armored inquisitor jumped back, easily dodging the attack, but the assassin was caught so off guard that the mace smashed into her side and sent her flying into a tree on the other side of the firepit. She stumbled to the ground, kicked a trip line, and then got a face full of quills that Luke had harvested from a giant porcupine earlier in the day.

He paid for that move when the armored inquisitor got right up into melee range and got a hand around Luke's throat. The man's face contorted into a vicious snarl, and he started squeezing, far harder than his strength stat should have allowed for. Everything started going black, and Luke dropped his mace to use both hands to pry at the fingers crushing his windpipe.

They were like steel wrapped around his neck, so tight that Luke thought the man might have had an easier time just ripping his head off his body. Desperate now, knowing he had at best seconds to think of a plan, Luke let his hand drop away from the inquisitor's fingers.

And then his knife flashed up through the air, severing the hand at the wrist. The man fell back with a scream and clutched at his stump. Luke sucked in a lungful of oxygen, coughed against the pain even breathing presented him, and picked his mace back up.

Name	Luke Bennet
Level	23
XP	41176/44653
AP	0
Bloodline	SysAdmin
Strength	42
Agility	40
Stamina	36
Perception	39
Skills	Mace Mastery (2)
	Sword Mastery (1)
	Unarmed Martialist (3)
	Power Strike (1)
	Life Surge (1)
	Peripheral Awareness (2)
	Counter (2)
	Twitch Reflexes (2)
	Stealth (1)
	Survivalist (2)
	First Aid (1)
	Wood Carving (1)
	Leatherworking (2)
	Thalian (2)
	Disguise (2)
	Deception (1)

CHAPTER 70

Abreak to catch his breath would have been fantastic right about then, but that third inquisitor, the woman who's been practically invisible, had disentangled herself from Luke's trap and was coming straight at him. He imagined there was probably a note of desperation there since both her companions were now wounded. Luke was surprised he hadn't gotten the kill notification from the one whose chest he'd caved in yet, but he planned on fixing that soon.

The armored inquisitor was out of the fight for at least a minute or two while he dealt with his new stump, but now that Luke was on level ground with the final inquisitor, he found it took all his attention to keep up with her. She was fast and accurate, not above throwing various bits of sharp metal with her left hand while her right worked a short sword in his general direction. Luke gave ground willingly when he couldn't parry or dodge her rapid-fire attacks.

He felt the heel of his foot smack up against the inquisitor he'd taken out early on in the fight and did his best not to stumble as he stepped backward over the man. The woman he was fighting was quick to take advantage of that, and Luke found himself twisting at the waist to try to avoid being gutted. He was partially successful, and a sharp line of fire drew itself across his abdomen.

He whipped his mace around in a wide horizontal arc to push her back, but it didn't have much power in it with his feet already tangled up trying not to trip over the man. The assassin inquisitor faded back a step to let it whoosh by, then rushed in before he could bring it back around, her sword already thrust forward and ready to sink into his chest.

There were no other options, at least not ones he could think of on the spot. **[Unarmed Martialist]** was screaming about his bad stance and all the ways he could have avoided being put in this situation if only he'd made different choices ten seconds ago, but it was **[Twitch Reflexes]** that actually saved him. He threw himself backward and straight down, a bad place to be in a fight but still better than getting skewered through the heart.

The assassin overshot her mark, perhaps too surprised that Luke had managed to get out of her way, and he used that opportunity to bring both legs up and kick straight out. Something snapped when his feet connected with her hips, and she cried out in pain. Luke scrambled to his feet, lined up his mace at the still-reeling woman, and swung as hard as he could. She stumbled backward, narrowly avoiding the attack, but he pressed her, and with the damage she'd taken from the kick, she couldn't keep away from him.

Blow after blow landed, and a few moments later, the ding of his first kill of the night sounded in his head. Luke glanced over to confirm it was from the woman and not the guy whose ribs he'd busted and organs he'd pulped. Somehow, that guy was still hanging on, probably from a high stamina stat. It wasn't getting him back into the fight though, so Luke left him where he was and turned his attention to the one-handed inquisitor.

"Don't suppose you'd just tell me where the woman your group was following is?" he asked. "After this, I'm going to have to go looking for her. You could make it easy on me."

"You think you're going to get out of here alive, apostate?" the inquisitor spat out.

Luke made a show of looking around. "Yeah, I think my chances are pretty good at this point."

"Even if you kill us, there will always be someone else ready to uphold the will of the Pantheon. We aren't going to let you tear this world down for your own selfish desires."

"Whoa there," Luke said. "You're making a lot of assumptions, buddy. I'm not trying to tear anything down. I'm just trying to get my family back so we can all go back to our own world."

The man just grunted and lifted one of his axes in his off hand. The stink of seared flesh and a bit of smoke wafted out of his stump, which was no longer bleeding. He moved in to attack again, but with only one hand and such a grievous injury distracting him, Luke had no problem deflecting the attacks and killing his opponent.

With a second kill notification up, there was only one more person to deal with. A strong part of Luke wanted to just walk away and leave the inquisitor there. He didn't particularly enjoy killing other people, had in fact lost more than a few hours of sleep over it. Plus it was always harder to look down at someone and make a deliberate decision to end a life than it was to take a lethal swing at someone doing their best to kill him.

On the other hand, this guy was unconscious and barely alive. Unless Luke carried him to town and found someone to help him, he was going to die anyway. Since it didn't look like the guy was going to wake back up, and Luke doubted he'd get much information from him, the only options were to kill the unconscious man immediately or let him die on his own. With a sigh, he dropped the mace directly down on the man's head and ended his life.

[You have slain Hestocian Human Inquisitor (level 24). 603 XP awarded.]

[You have slain Daranite Human Templar (level 22). 505 XP awarded.]

[You have slain Hestocian Human Inquisitor (level 23). 553 XP awarded.]

Luke took a few minutes to slice a long strip off one of their cloaks to tie around the cut going across his stomach, then cleaned himself up as best he could on what was left. After that, he looted the gold and silver out of their belt pouches, not that any of them were carrying all that much, then stripped the two that the system identified as inquisitors of a pair of gold rings with some weird script engraved on the inside.

He figured it was probably a religious thing, but worst-case scenario, they'd just melt the gold down and sell it as a nugget. Any bit of cash he could get now would make things that much easier once he found a place to cross the ocean. Unfortunately, none of their weapons appeared to be anything other than standard steel, and if there was anything else of value on the bodies, he missed it in his search. The armor was unfortunately the same distinctive style as his previous set, so he left it behind.

Luke stood in the middle of his campsite and debated what to do next. Zea was supposed to meet him here, but instead three church agents had shown up. Had they found him on their own and she was still on her way, or had they captured her and tortured the location out of her? Luke didn't want her to come into the camp while he was away and find a bunch of dead bodies and blood, and he especially didn't want her tripping any of the booby traps that were still set.

The risk that something had happened to her was too great for him to just stand in the camp and hope for the best, but rather than making a straight line for Landston, he swept back and forth through the woods. There were a lot of different angles someone could approach from, especially someone as small as Zea. He tried to limit himself to obvious trails though since he assumed she didn't have a lot of wilderness-traversal skills.

Luke didn't find Zea, but he did find two more inquisitors. They were searching for something in the woods, occasionally calling back and forth to each other to coordinate. He thought he recognized the voice of one as the man from the bakery but wouldn't swear by it without getting a look at the man's face.

Thankfully, he'd reached the point where the range of his senses outweighed the feeling his XP gave off, and by keeping himself far enough back, he was able to shadow the two inquisitors. Whatever they were looking for, they weren't having a lot of luck finding it. Luke started scanning ahead of them, both to see if he could spot whatever, or whomever, they were looking for and to find a good ambush spot. At this point, he was determined to leave as many inquisitor corpses behind him as he could. If the alternative was to have them harrying him every step of his journey, he'd save himself some grief and kill them all now.

Maybe if **[Survivalist]** was a higher rank, or if he'd spent some points on a more purpose-specific tracking skill, he could have followed whatever trail the inquisitors were working. That wasn't the case, and Luke navigated mostly by reacting to changes in direction from the two inquisitors he was shadowing. Keeping in front of them wasn't easy, but he was outclassing them in terms of pure stats, and he did have a single rank in **[Stealth]** to help.

Almost by accident, he stumbled across Zea crawling under some branches. She was covered in dirt and grime and had several new tears in her clothes from scrambling around in the underbrush, but it was definitely her. Luke circled around the brush and got in front of her about the same time she climbed back to her feet.

"Zea," he hissed quietly.

She flinched in surprise but didn't make any noise. Slowly, she exhaled a breath and shook her head. "There's four or five of them behind me. Come on, we have to keep moving."

"I killed three already. There's two more tracking you. I'll take care of them too. You wait here, and I'll come back when I'm done?"

"Wait," she said. "There are more in town, including that woman."

"Ah shit. Okay. Okay. Um, how many?"

"I don't know. Four? Maybe more. About half of them came after me when I escaped."

"They're going to know something's wrong when the three I took out don't come back. Best I can do is kill these other two, and we can make a run for it."

Zea hesitated, took in Luke's ragged and bloody appearance, then nodded. "Okay."

"I'll be back in a few minutes. Wait here if you can. Go north otherwise. I'll find you somehow."

He didn't know if he could, honestly, but he didn't want her in the middle of a life-and-death battle. Zea was all sorts of clever, much smarter than he was, but she just didn't have the levels to be fucking around with these guys.

Luke slipped back between the trees and tried to figure out how he was going to close in on two guys who'd sense him coming long before he was ready to strike and whether or not he'd be able to kill one before the other showed up to help. He didn't have a prepared battlefield this time, and while he was confident that he'd at least survive a one-on-one fight, he was also still tired from the last three people who'd tried to kill him.

He had **[Life Surge]** in the bank still and enough stamina for a **[Power Strike]** or three. If he was quick, maybe he could overpower the first inquisitor before his buddy could get there. The fight would have to end in seconds though; they really weren't moving that far apart, and most of those seconds would be spent getting to his target once they sensed his presence.

The trackers were getting closer to his position now, and Luke didn't want them noticing Zea behind him. It was time to move. Luke let his cloak fall to the ground so that it wouldn't hinder his rush, then picked the one with the least amount of brush in the way. Charging at full speed toward his victim, he used his hands to shove branches out of the way where he could. The ones he couldn't bend snatched at him and were snapped in half after scratching the shit out of his arms or snagging on his clothes.

Both inquisitors reacted to his sudden presence at the same time, but by then it was too late. Luke darted out from behind a tree and, mace raised, launched himself at his first target.

Name	Luke Bennet
Level	23
XP	42837/44653
AP	0
Bloodline	SysAdmin
Strength	42
Agility	40
Stamina	36
Perception	39
Skills	Mace Mastery (2)
	Sword Mastery (1)
	Unarmed Martialist (3)
	Power Strike (1)
	Life Surge (1)
	Peripheral Awareness (2)
	Counter (2)
	Twitch Reflexes (2)
	Stealth (1)
	Survivalist (2)
	First Aid (1)
	Wood Carving (1)
	Leatherworking (2)
	Thalian (2)
	Disguise (2)
	Deception (1)

CHAPTER 71

The inquisitor reacted quicker than Luke would have believed possible. It had to be some sort of skill, his own version of **[Twitch Reflexes]**. By the time the mace came whistling down through the space where the inquisitor had been standing, he'd already stepped smoothly to the side and unleashed a one-two combo of punches that hit Luke just below the ribs.

For all his speed, the inquisitor didn't have the strength to back it up, and Luke barely grunted at the impact. Instead of folding up in pain like his enemy no doubt expected, Luke lashed out and caught the man by the front of the leather jerkin he was wearing. He dragged the inquisitor down and threw him to the ground, then stomped down on the man's back, deliberately going out of his way to grind his heel into a kidney at the same time.

The man cried out, ensuring that his companion was also aware of Luke's attack, but that was a foregone conclusion anyway. The two had been careful not to get too far apart while they searched the woods. That just meant Luke had to deal with this one in the next two seconds, which he did with a pair of log-cutter-style swings to the back of the inquisitor's skull.

Ignoring the ding of the kill notification, Luke scanned the foliage for where the next one would come out and lined up his mace with his best guess. Despite how high his perception was, he couldn't literally track every step the man took, but considering the density of the underbrush, unless he was packing an extremely high strength stat, Luke figured he had a pretty good shot of being right.

If he wasn't . . . well, that's what all his avoidance skills were for.

Seconds passed with no sign of the inquisitor, and Luke started to worry that he was going to be dealing with another assassin type, except one good enough to beat his perception. It wasn't until he stopped to think about it that he realized what had happened. Aros wasn't a video game world; they weren't just going to rush in to die in waves. The last inquisitor either knew his friend was already dead or just didn't give a fuck.

Chasing down a runner would likely be impossible, especially if his agility was anything close to the that of the one Luke had just killed. Just letting him go wasn't a good option either. There were plenty of reinforcements not that far away, and they'd come out in force to catch him.

Luke was starting to suspect that the first three he'd encountered had been an accident, that they'd been looking for Zea after she'd given them the slip and had stumbled upon him first. Once they had proof that he was nearby, every inquisitor, templar, and whatever else the church could send would be out combing the woods to find him.

He could run, maybe even fast enough to get away if he went straight into the deep woods, but Zea would get left behind. She was only in this mess because of him, and he couldn't abandon her. That meant killing every inquisitor coming after him until they either gave up or there were none left. It would be easier to do that one at a time, and he definitely didn't want them coming anywhere near Zea.

The runner had a twenty-second lead, but Luke had 40 agility and had spent a lot of time over the last few days moving through this forest. He took off down the trail he'd blazed toward Landston at top speed, planning to reach the fields outside the town first and cut the inquisitor off as soon as he wasn't hidden in the forest.

It was a good plan, but he'd underestimated just how fast the man could move, and by the time Luke broke through the tree line, the inquisitor was already ahead of him. Heedless of any crops he might damage, Luke leaped forward with huge, bounding steps, accelerating to his top speed in moments. There wasn't any semblance of strategy of style in his attack, just pure mass times acceleration.

He hit the fleeing inquisitor hard enough to send the man flying more than ten feet. Luke tumbled right after him, but he got to his feet first and raced over to find the inquisitor groaning in the dirt with a broken arm and leg from the impact.

Before he could finish the man off, he started screaming for help. That only lasted a second, but the screams cut through the late-evening air, and the reaction from the town was immediate. Luke only waited long enough to confirm the kill ding, then he sprinted back toward the woods. It was too bad he couldn't take the time to loot the man, but the potential for a gold or two wasn't worth getting jumped by four or five of his buddies.

Luke hightailed it back into the woods but not fast enough to avoid being seen by some of the closest townsfolk. He left a lot of yelling behind him as he made his way back to his campsite. It was far enough away from where he'd left Zea, and he was making no effort to disguise his trail, so with any luck, the remaining inquisitors would follow him there, and he could use some of the remaining traps to even the odds.

He felt the XP rolling off something half a second before wood exploded and a massive humanoid body hurled itself at him. Easily eight feet tall with dark-purple skin, the monster burst out of nowhere at high speed and smacked into Luke without hesitation. The full body slam launched him sideways to crash into a tree.

Luke fell to the ground with a groan and blinked up at his attacker. It was man shaped but with overly large eyes and no nose. Quills bristled up in place of hair and spread down its back and shoulders like a mane. It regarded him with a snort, then took two wide steps, cocked its leg back, and kicked Luke in the stomach.

He rolled with the blow, or at least he tried to, but the tree was right behind him, and he ended up caught between the two. The creature leaned down to grab Luke under the arms and haul him to his feet, then slugged him in the face. Unlike that inquisitor, it actually had the strength to back the hits up.

Luke's nose broke on the first hit, and it wasn't until the third that he had the presence of mind to defend himself. **[Unarmed Martialist]** took over, and he snaked his arm around the monster's to give himself a bit of leverage, then lifted his body up to kick it in the stomach and groin.

The monster accepted the blows without flinching, apparently unimpressed with Luke's appropriation of Zammin's favorite tactic, then slammed him into the tree again. He couldn't break the damn thing's grip on his arm, and it was flinging him around like a rag doll when it wasn't pummeling him. As much as Luke wanted to save it, **[Life Surge]** seemed like the play to make. He triggered the skill and, flush with enhanced strength, slammed his elbow down into the arm holding him.

The creature still didn't let go, but the bones in the arm itself fractured, and Luke was able to pry the fingers off of him. He lashed out with a series of kicks, each one now much stronger than they were before, and quickly drove the monster back a step. That was all the room Luke needed to dart out of its range, scoop up his mace, and turn to pummeling the monster.

He broke it apart over the next twenty seconds, and then something weird happened. Instead of dying and giving him the kill notification, it started to dissolve into some sort of disgusting-smelling sludge that rolled across the ground until there was nothing left but a big, thick, goopy puddle.

"System, what the fuck was that?"

"It appears to be an artificial monster," System said, "It was likely created with a combination of spells for animating and controlling otherwise dead material such as clay or stone."

[Life Surge] gave out soon after, and Luke wobbled a bit before catching his balance. The aftereffects of the skill weren't so bad as long as he'd gotten a full meal in before, but he still didn't feel up to fighting anyone else, especially not if one of the inquisitors had a skill like that. If they could just wave a hand and casually create a monster that required that much power to put down, he didn't want to be anywhere near them.

It probably wasn't that simple, but since Luke had no idea how something like that was created, he was going to assume the worst. Actually, it was better to know. "Can whoever made it make another one?" he asked.

"It's possible, though time-consuming and expensive. If you look at its remains, you can see the core of the artificial monster. With that in hand, a new one could be made quickly and easily, provided you have the skills and spells to do so. Without it, it would take some time."

Now that System mentioned it, Luke realized he could see something in the muck. It was some sort of ball, though he couldn't make out any details without cleaning it off first. He leaned over, plucked the ball out of the puddle, and started to scrape off some of the gunk.

Once it was clean, he found it to be closer to a cube than a ball. It was a composite of a few different materials, all looped around one another like some sort of three-dimensional puzzle. "They can't find me with this, can they?" he asked.

"Possibly."

"Of course." Luke sighed and tossed the ball into a bush. It was probably valuable, might even be enough to pay for that boat ride they were going to need soon. If it led the church to them though . . . "Not worth it."

He knew he needed to get moving, but he was worn down. Not even including [Life Surge], he'd fought and killed five people already tonight. Adding the skill usage on top of that left him exhausted in a way he rarely felt anymore. At this point, it was all he could do to totter around between the trees, let alone walk in a straight line.

He felt four people with XP high enough to be noticed in a crowd, and all four quickly locked on him. "Shit," Luke snapped, and he forced himself into a run. It was a sad, limping motion that was barely faster than a jog back before he got stats.

The now-familiar sting of something small entering his back spurred him to move faster, and the notification he received after confirmed his fears. Myla had caught up with him.

[You have been afflicted by the following condition: Poison—Sour Gut Blight (14M37S).]

It wasn't immediately apparent what the poison did, but it was sure to be bad news with a name like that. Luke stumbled, not from the poison but just sheer exhaustion, and a second dart smacked into him.

[You have been afflicted by the following condition: Poison—Ramsridge Wyvern Venom (9M12S).]

That one he felt immediately. It was like his whole body was literally on fire from the inside, heat so strong that it would cook his bones and leave him a steaming corpse. He saw with some horror that there actually were little wisps of steam coming out of his pores. Then a third dart hit.

[You have been afflicted by the following condition: Poison—Essence of Manticore Blood (4H14M).]

"Oh, come on," Luke said. "Three darts is too much."

Then he collapsed face down in the dirt.

Name	Luke Bennet
Level	23
XP	43801/44653
AP	0
Bloodline	SysAdmin
Strength	42
Agility	40
Stamina	36
Perception	39
Skills	Mace Mastery (2)
	Sword Mastery (1)
	Unarmed Martialist (3)
	Power Strike (1)
	Life Surge (1)
	Peripheral Awareness (2)
	Counter (2)
	Twitch Reflexes (2)
	Stealth (1)
	Survivalist (2)
	First Aid (1)
	Wood Carving (1)
	Leatherworking (2)
	Thalian (2)
	Disguise (2)
	Deception (1)

CHAPTER 72

It might have been more merciful if the pain had knocked Luke out, but he wasn't that lucky. He got to see all four inquisitors approach him, or at least hear them and sense the XP that was infused into their bodies. He couldn't sense Myla at all, but she obviously had some sort of skill that let her adjust how many levels she put on display. Right now that number was 0.

"All three darts hit," one of the inquisitors reported.

"You doubted?" Myla said.

"No, ma'am."

"And the monster core?"

"Missing," another inquisitor said.

"Find it. It can't have gotten too far, and I'm not interested in listening to that old witch complain that we didn't bring it back. Hestoc knows we've already paid her a small fortune for her services."

Luke saw two of the inquisitors scouring the forest for the ball he'd thrown away and laughed silently. At least he'd been a casual inconvenience to them, if nothing else. He really didn't see himself getting away this time, not with so many poisons in him. Even if he could use another **[Life Surge]** right now, Myla had gone for overkill and made sure there was no way he'd escape.

Someone rolled him onto his back, and he found a pair of swords pointed down at his neck. "Quite dangerous, isn't he?" one of the inquisitors asked.

"Very much so," Myla replied. "The poisons should keep him tractable long enough for us to secure him, but I don't want to test that. He has repeatedly shrugged off powerful poisons that would defeat even level 30s who specialized in stamina."

Out came fetters and chains of all sorts and sizes, and in short order Luke found himself hobbled and bound. The part of his brain that still worked noted that they'd underestimated his strength if they thought regular steel would hold him, but the rest of him was screaming in agony and couldn't have broken free from the tie on a loaf of bread, let alone an actual restraint.

While they were doing that, the XP aura of one of the two that were searching for the ball disappeared. At first, Luke thought they'd just gotten far enough away that he'd lost track of them, but then he realized he could smell blood and that the person who'd disappeared was well inside the range of his perception. Something had killed an inquisitor.

The other inquisitors noticed a moment later and went on their guard. That wasn't enough to save them, and he felt the XP of a second one snuff out a moment later. "What the hell is that?" one of the still-living inquisitors whispered harshly.

"Knife wound to the throat," another one said.

"Impossible," Myla snapped. She took a deep breath and said in a much more even tone, "Take the apostate and retreat back to town. Whoever is out here must have an extremely powerful **[Stealth]** skill. We'll move as one and watch everything around us. If it can't sneak up on us, it will likely give up."

It didn't take much to connect the dots then. Luke wasn't sure exactly how she was doing it, but somehow Zea had followed him and was taking out people twice her level, all without being seen. He couldn't see a way that didn't end badly for her. The remaining three were on high alert now, and there'd be no more surprise attacks.

The two remaining inquisitors hauled Luke upright and started dragging his limp body back toward town. The fetters kept getting caught on things, but the inquisitors just tugged harder until whatever branch or vine or root he'd snagged on gave way. It was all just background pain for Luke, who was currently dealing with what felt like full-body cramps as his body tried to fold itself in half. His best guess was the first poison Myla had hit him with, Sour Gut Blight.

Between that and the wyvern venom laying the pain on him, they probably could have taken him without trouble. Adding the essence of manticore blood to the mix was just mean. It attacked both his muscles and his organs, making him feel limp and heavy while at the same time he struggled to breathe.

It all would have been much, much worse a few days ago before he'd put another 10 AP into stamina. Unfortunately for him, none of the poisons would wear off on their own before he got hauled back to town, and Myla had plenty of opportunity to dose him again if they needed more time. **[Life Surge]** might take care of the first two, but using it again so soon would have its own set of problems.

In short, he was completely fucked. Whatever they were going to do, he was powerless to resist it, and he was pretty sure the end result wasn't going to be him walking away. Hell, at this point he figured he'd be lucky if they skipped the torture and killed him quick. If that had been the plan, they'd probably have done it in the forest right after he'd killed that weird monster.

One of the inquisitors dragging him along cried out in pain and clutched at his gut, where blood was already seeping out through his fingers. While everyone was looking at him, something attacked Myla. She flinched away, practically leaping down the trail when a line of blood appeared on her leg. She whipped a pair of daggers around her in a full spin but hit nothing.

"Your invisibility won't save you," Myla called out. "I know how long such spells last, and you're surely running out."

Luke would have laughed if he was able. He knew how Zea was doing it, but he thought Myla was probably right. It wouldn't last much longer. If she was going to save him, she probably only had seconds left to do it. He needed to find some way to help, but the best he could do was to kind of flop around and groan.

But no, that wasn't all he could do. He had **[Power Strike]** and could easily channel that through a punch or a kick. The problem would be connecting with anything useful. If he could provide some sort of distraction, that might give Zea the opening she needed with what little time she had left to work.

Luke channeled the skill through his foot and twitched his leg up. His heel came down on the links of metal connecting his ankles together and snapped the metal with a loud, popping clang. Immediately, both inquisitors turned to look at him, but Luke barely noticed. It turned out diverting his stamina into another skill when it was hard at work keeping him from dying from a massive overdose of multiple poisons was not good for his health.

He turned his head to the side and hurled his guts out, with barely enough of a presence of mind to make sure he aimed at the inquisitor who was still holding him upright. Whether that was petty revenge or another attempt at distracting them wasn't something even Luke was sure of at that point. Either way, the next thing he knew, he was lying on his back, still bound and tied up.

"Got you!" Myla said.

"Get this, bitch."

And then there was an explosion of some sort. It rolled over him and pushed him down the trail until he collided headfirst with a tree trunk. New pain bloomed on top of the old familiar pain of the poisons, and Luke thought he might finally have had enough. Sweet oblivion was calling, and he rushed to meet her embrace.

* * *

"Come on," Zea said. "Open your eyes already."

"Wha?" Luke responded.

"Help a girl out here. You're too heavy to move."

He blearily realized that most of the straps binding him had been severed, leaving just a few of the metal chains remaining. More importantly, he was feeling significantly less like shit now. With a thought, he called up his status to check his condition.

[Condition: Poison—Essence of Manticore Blood (3H52M)]

"Oh, guhd," he mumbled. "Thoo don, wun tuh shoh."

"What's that? I can't understand you," Zea said.

"Bish posnd meh. Fuh ours."

"Yeah, I didn't get a word of that."

He tried to focus on Zea, but his vision was strangely blurry. It took him a second to realize the muscles controlling his eyes had also been affected by the poison. That also explained why he was having so much trouble talking; his words were basically falling out of the side of his mouth since he couldn't get his lips or tongue moving right.

Luke tried again, but it was just more of the same result. The only intelligent word he could get out was, "Shafe?"

"Safe? Not really," Zea said. "This thing's burned out now, and I don't think I can take another inquisitor in hand-to-hand combat."

She held up the feather he'd given her a few days ago and the little ball core thing he'd thrown out for him to see. "Oh, uh, I guess I should probably explain some stuff. Maybe later though? I need you to get up now."

Luke flopped over onto his side and managed to kind of drag himself to his feet. Everything felt all gummy, and he didn't see himself doing much walking. "Luut?" he slurred out, nodding his head at the bodies.

"Already took everything I could carry off them," Zea said with a smirk. Luke tried to smile back, but judging by her expression, he was guessing he just looked demented.

They managed to get Luke off the trail and kind of hidden in the trees, though anyone doing more than a casual inspection would find him. Until the poison weakened though, that was as far as he was getting. Zea spent her time patrolling the forest, the knife he'd gotten for her in her hand.

After a few hours, the poison symptoms started to alleviate, and it got a bit easier to move, but it was kind of like dragging himself out of bed when the flu was kicking his ass. He *could* do it, but he sure as hell didn't want to. It turned out that not chilling a hundred feet away from a bunch of corpses was a hell of a motivator though, so the next time Zea looped around to check on him, he stood up.

"Ready to go?" she asked.

"No, but do we have much choice? Seems like we're asking for trouble if we stay here any longer than we need to."

"Pretty much. Good news is we're eight gold richer."

"I picked up a few off the three I killed too. Call it ten gold."

The two of them went deeper into the woods, Luke slowly limping along and eating some food Zea had picked up and Zea herself shooting him the occasional worried glance when she thought he wasn't looking.

"You know you're going to need some new clothes," she said. "Yours are covered in blood."

"Not the first time," Luke said.

"You think they'll keep coming after you?"

"Probably. Only good thing that's happened to me since I got here was meeting you." Well, that wasn't quite true. He liked Red, and his bird person had been nice to Luke. Still, the amount of bad things outweighed the good by a lot.

Once the poison was fully out of his system, they picked up the pace. By the time the sun came up, they were twenty miles away, and Luke called for a break to rest for a few hours. They found a nice little mossy overhang to shelter under, and Zea gathered some firewood while Luke cleaned himself as best he could in a nearby stream. The clothes were probably a total loss, but for the moment, he didn't have anything better.

When he was clean, he settled down near the fire. Zea plopped down next to him and snuggled into his side. "I guess we should talk about some stuff," she said.

"Later. Sleep now."

She hesitated, then hugged him tighter. "Sleep is good."

Name	Luke Bennet
Level	23
XP	43801/44653
AP	0
Bloodline	SysAdmin
Strength	42
Agility	40
Stamina	36
Perception	39
Skills	Mace Mastery (2)
	Sword Mastery (1)
	Unarmed Martialist (3)
	Power Strike (1)
	Life Surge (1)
	Peripheral Awareness (2)
	Counter (2)
	Twitch Reflexes (2)
	Stealth (1)
	Survivalist (2)
	First Aid (1)
	Wood Carving (1)
	Leatherworking (2)
	Thalian (2)
	Disguise (2)
	Deception (1)

ABOUT THE AUTHOR

EmergencyComplaints grew up reading fantasy and tried his hand at writing his first novel on an old MS-DOS text editor program when he was seven years old. That story didn't pan out; maximum character limits were a thing back then. Undeterred, he kept writing on other platforms, reading full-time, devouring JRPGs, and playing *D&D*, and he is now the author of the God Machine and Ascendant series.